The Counts of Calvani

Sexy, Italian men…all looking for a wife!

**In this trilogy by bestselling,
award-winning author
Lucy Gordon
the pressure is mounting on the three
aristocratic Calvani brothers to marry and
produce heirs…**

D1471676

By Request™

In August 2006 Mills & Boon bring
back two of their classic collections,
each featuring three favourite
romances by our bestselling authors...

THE COUNTS OF CALVANI
The Venetian Playboy's Bride
The Italian Millionaire's Marriage
The Tuscan Tycoon's Wife
by
Lucy Gordon

THEIR SECRET CHILD
The Latin Lover's Secret Child
by Jane Porter
Her Baby Secret by Kim Lawrence
The Greek Tycoon's Secret Child
by Cathy Williams

The Counts
of Calvani

THE VENETIAN
PLAYBOY'S BRIDE

THE ITALIAN
MILLIONAIRE'S
MARRIAGE

THE TUSCAN
TYCOON'S WIFE

by

Lucy Gordon

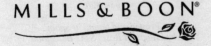

MILLS & BOON®

*MILLS & BOON and MILLS & BOON with the Rose Device
are registered trademarks of the publisher.
Harlequin Mills & Boon Limited,
Eton House, 18-24 Paradise Road, Richmond, Surrey, TW9 1SR*

THE COUNTS OF CALVANI
© by Harlequin Enterprises II B.V., 2006

The Venetian Playboy's Bride, The Italian Millionaire's Marriage
and *The Tuscan Tycoon's Wife* were first published in Great Britain
by Harlequin Mills & Boon Limited in separate, single volumes.

The Venetian Playboy's Bride © Lucy Gordon 2003
The Italian Millionaire's Marriage © Lucy Gordon 2003
The Tuscan Tycoon's Wife © Lucy Gordon 2003

ISBN-10: 0 263 84967 8
ISBN-13: 978 0 263 84967 7

05-0806

*Printed and bound in Spain
by Litografia Rosés S.A., Barcelona*

THE VENETIAN PLAYBOY'S BRIDE

by

Lucy Gordon

Lucy Gordon cut her writing teeth on magazine journalism, interviewing many of the world's most interesting men, including Warren Beatty, Richard Chamberlain, Sir Roger Moore, Sir Alec Guinness, and Sir John Gielgud. She also camped out with lions in Africa, and had many other unusual experiences which have often provided the background for her books. She is married to a Venetian, whom she met while on holiday in Venice. They got engaged within two days.

Two of her books have won the Romance Writers of America's prestigious RITA® award, SONG OF THE LORELEI in 1990, and HIS BROTHER'S CHILD in 1998 in the Best Traditional Romance category.

You can visit her website at www.lucy-gordon.com

Don't miss Lucy Gordon's exciting new novel
Married Under the Italian Sun
**out in September 2006 from
Mills & Boon® Romance.**

CHAPTER ONE

GUIDO CALVANI took another turn along the hospital corridor, trying not to think of his uncle, lying behind the closed door, desperately ill.

He was high up on the top floor. At one end of the corridor the window looked out over the heart of Venice, red roofs, canals, little bridges. At the other end was the Grand Canal. Guido stopped and regarded the flashing water, snaking its way through the heart of the little city to where it would reach the Palazzo Calvani, home of the Calvani counts for centuries. By tonight he might have inherited the title, and the thought appalled him.

His mercurial spirits weren't often depressed. He approached life with an optimism that was reflected in his appearance. His blue eyes might have been born gleaming, and a smile seemed to be his natural expression. At thirty-two, rich, handsome, free, he had no cares, save for the one that now threatened him.

Guido was a man of warm affections. He loved his uncle. But he also loved his freedom, and within a few hours he might have lost them both.

He turned swiftly as two young men appeared from the staircase below.

'Thank heavens!' he said, embracing his half-brother Leo, who clasped him back unselfconsciously. With his cousin Marco he merely clapped him on the shoulder. There was a proud reserve about Marco that even the open-hearted Guido had to respect.

5

'How bad is Uncle Francesco?' Marco demanded tersely.

'Very bad, I think. I called you last night because he'd started to have pains in his chest, but he wouldn't be sensible and see a doctor. Then early this morning he collapsed in agony, and I sent for an ambulance. We've been here ever since. They're still doing tests.'

'It surely can't be a heart attack,' Leo said. 'He's never had one before, and the life he's led—'

'Was enough to give any normal man a dozen heart attacks,' Marco supplied. 'Women, wine, fast cars—'

'Women!' Guido echoed.

'Three speedboats smashed up,' Leo recalled.

'Gambling!'

'Women!'

'Skiing!'

'Mountaineering!'

'*Women*!' They spoke with one voice.

A footstep on the stairs reduced them all to silence as Lizabetta, the count's housekeeper, appeared among them like doom. She was thin, sharp-faced, elderly, and they greeted her with more respect than they ever showed their uncle. This grim creature was the power in the Palazzo Calvani.

She acknowledged them with a nod that managed to combine respect for their aristocratic status with contempt for the male sex, sat down and took out her knitting.

'I'm afraid there's no news yet,' Guido told her gently.

He looked up as the ward door opened and the doctor emerged. He was an elderly man and had been the count's friend for years. His grave expression could mean only one thing, and their hearts sank.

The doctor pronounced. 'Get the silly old fool out of here and stop wasting my time.'

'But—his heart attack—?' Guido protested.

'Heart attack, my foot! Indigestion! Liza, you shouldn't let him eat prawns in butter.'

Liza glared. 'Much notice he takes of me,' she snapped.

'Can we see him now?' Guido asked.

A roar from within answered him. In his prime Count Francesco had been known as The Lion of Venice, and now that he was in his seventies nothing much had changed.

The three young men entered their uncle's room and stood regarding him wryly. He was sitting up in bed, his face framed by his white hair, his blue eyes gleaming.

'Gave you a fright, didn't I?' he bawled.

'Enough of a fright to bring me all the way from Rome and Leo from Tuscany,' Marco remarked. 'All because you've been stuffing yourself.'

'Don't talk to the head of the family like that,' Francesco growled. 'And blame Liza. Her cooking is irresistible.'

'So you have to gobble it like a greedy schoolboy,' Marco observed, not noticeably intimidated by addressing the head of the family. 'Uncle, when are you going to act your age?'

'I didn't get to be seventy-two by acting my age!' Francesco remarked with perfect truth. He pointed at Marco. 'When *you're* seventy-two you'll be a dried-up stick without a heart.'

Marco shrugged.

The old man indicated Leo. 'When *you're* seventy-two you'll be more of a country bumpkin than you are already.'

'That's cool,' Leo observed, unruffled.

'What will I be at seventy-two?' Guido asked.

'You won't. An outraged husband will have shot you long before then.'

Guido grinned. 'You should know all about outraged husbands, uncle. I heard that only last—'

'Clear off all of you. Liza will bring me home.'

As soon as they'd escaped the building they leaned against the honey-coloured stone wall and breathed out long sighs of relief.

'I need a drink,' Guido said, making a beeline for a small bar beside the water. The others followed him and seated themselves at a table in the sun.

Since Guido lived in Venice, Leo in Tuscany and Marco in Rome they saw each other only rarely, and the next few minutes were occupied by taking stock. Leo was the least altered. As his uncle had said, he was a countryman, lean, hard-bodied, with a candid face and clear eyes. He wasn't a subtle man. Life reached him directly, through his senses, and he read books only when necessary.

Marco was the same as always, but more so: a little more tense, a little more focused, a little more heedless of ordinary mortals. He existed in a rarefied world of high finance, and it seemed to his cousins that he was happiest there. He lived expensively, buying only the best, which he could well afford. But he did so, less because it gave him pleasure than because it would never have occurred to him to do otherwise.

Guido's mercurial nature had been born for a double life. Officially he resided at the palazzo, but he also had a discreet bachelor flat where he could come and go, free of critical eyes. He too had intensified, becoming more charming, and more elusive in his determination to remain his own man. He possessed a mulish stubbornness which he hid behind laughter and a sweet temper. His dark hair was a shade too long, curving over his collar with a slight shagginess that made him look younger than his thirty-two years.

Nobody spoke until they were on their second beer.

'I can't stand this,' Guido said at last. 'Being brought to the brink and then let off is going to finish me. And let off for how long?'

'What are you raving about?' Marco demanded.

'Ignore him,' Leo grinned. 'A man who's just been reprieved is bound to be light-headed.'

'That's right, mock me!' Guido said. 'By rights it should be you in this mess.'

Leo was his elder brother, but by a trick of fate it was Guido who was the heir. Bertrando, their father, had married a widow whose 'late' husband had subsequently turned up alive. By then she had already died giving birth to Leo, leaving him illegitimate. Two years later Bertrando had married again, and his second wife had presented him with Guido.

Nobody had worried about it then. It was a technicality that would cease to matter when Count Francesco married and had a son. But as the years passed with no sign of his marriage the anomaly began to glare. Although the younger son, Guido was legally the *only* son, and heir to the title.

He hated the prospect. It was a trap waiting to imprison his free spirit. He longed for a miracle to restore Leo's rights, but Leo didn't want them either. Only the earth interested him: growing wine, wheat and olives, breeding cattle and horses. He cared for the title no more than Guido.

The only discord between them had come when Guido tried to tempt his brother into legal action to legitimatise himself and stop 'shirking his duty'. Leo had bluntly replied that if Guido thought he was going to tie himself down to a load of pointless flapdoodle he was even more *cretino* than he looked. Guido had responded with equal robustness and it had taken Marco to stop an undignified brawl. As the son of Silvio, younger brother to Francesco and Bertrando, he had little chance of the title, and could afford to regard the shenanigans of the other two with lofty amusement.

'Of course it's bound to happen one day,' he mused now, maliciously. 'Count Guido, father of ten, a man of distinction, fat, sedate, middle-aged, with a wife to match.'

'That shirt looks like it's worth a thousand dollars,' Guido mused, fingering his half-full glass significantly.

'Only a joke,' Marco placated him.

'Not funny.' Guido took another swallow and sighed mournfully. 'Not funny at all.'

Roscoe Harrison's London home was no palace, but it had had as much money lavished on it as the Calvani abode. The difference was that he was a man without taste. He believed in display, and the crude power of cash, and it showed.

'I buy only the best,' he was saying now to the fair-haired young woman sitting in his office at the back of the house. 'That's why I'm buying you.'

'You aren't buying me, Mr Harrison,' Dulcie said coolly. 'You're hiring my skill as a private detective. There's a big difference.'

'Well your skill will do me just fine. Take a look at this.'

He thrust a photograph across the desk. It showed Roscoe's daughter, Jenny Harrison, her dark hair streaming over her shoulders in the Venetian sunlight, listening ardently to a young gondolier playing a mandolin, while another gondolier, with curly hair and a baby face, looked on.

'That's the character who thinks he's going to marry Jenny for her fortune,' Roscoe snapped, jabbing at the mandolin player with his finger. 'He's told her he isn't really a gondolier, but heir to a count—Calvani, or some such name—but I say it's a big, fat lie.

'I'm not an unreasonable man. If he really were a posh nob that would be different. His title, my money. Fair enough. But a posh nob rowing a gondola? I don't think so. I want you to go to Venice, find out what's going on. Then, when you've proved he's no aristo-crat—'

'Perhaps he is,' Dulcie murmured.

Roscoe snorted. 'Your job is to prove he isn't.'

Dulcie winced. 'I can't prove he isn't if he is,' she pointed out.

'Well, you'll be able to tell, 'cos you're top drawer yourself. You're *Lady* Dulcie Maddox, aren't you?'

'In my private life, yes. But when I'm working I'm simply, Dulcie Maddox, PI.'

She guessed that Roscoe didn't like that. He was impressed by her titled connections, and when she brushed them aside he felt cheated.

Last night he'd invited her to dinner in order to meet his daughter, Jenny. Dulcie had been charmed by the young girl's freshness and naïvety. It was easy to believe that she needed protection from a fortune hunter.

'I want you because you're the best,' Roscoe returned to his theme. 'You're posh. You act posh. You look posh—not your clothes because they're—'

'Cheap,' she supplied. The jeans and denim jacket had been the cheapest thing on the market stall. Luckily she had the kind of tall, slender figure that brought out the best in anything, and her mane of fair hair and strange green eyes drew admiration wherever she went.

'Inexpensive,' Roscoe said in one of his rare ventures into tact. 'But *you* look posh, in yourself. You can tell aristocrats because they're so tall and slim. Probably comes from eating proper food while the peasants had to make do with stodge.'

'Maybe with the others,' Dulcie said. 'But with me it came from not having enough to eat because all the family money was blown on the horses. That's why I'm working as a private investigator. I'm as poor as a church mouse.'

'Then you'll need a load of new gear to be convincing. I keep an account at Feltham's for Jenny. I'll call and tell them to do you proud at my expense. When you reach the Hotel Vittorio you've got to look the part.'

'The Vittorio?' She looked quickly out of the window, lest he guess that this particular hotel had a special meaning for her. It was only a few weeks ago that she had been planning her honeymoon in that very hotel, with a man who'd sworn eternal love.

But that was then. This was now. Love had vanished with brutal suddenness. She would have given anything to avoid the Vittorio, but there was no help for it.

'Most expensive hotel in Venice,' Roscoe said. 'So buy the clothes, then get out there fast. Fly first class. No cheap economy flights in case he checks up on you.'

'You mean he might employ a private detective too?'

'No knowing. Some people are devious enough for anything.'

Dulcie maintained a diplomatic silence.

'Here's a cheque for expenses. It's not enough to look rich. You've got to splash it around a bit.'

'Splash it around a bit,' Dulcie recited, glassy eyed at the size of the cheque.

'Find this gondolier, make him think you're rolling in money, so he'll make up to you. When you've got him hooked let me know. I'll send Jenny out there, and she'll see the kind of man he really is. She won't believe it, but the world is full of jerks on the look out for a rich girl.'

'Yes,' Dulcie murmured with feeling. 'It is.'

On the night of Count Francesco's return, supper at the palazzo was formal. The four men sat around an ornate table while a maid served dish after dish, under the eagle eyes of Liza. To the count this was normal, and Marco was comfortable with it. But the other two found it suffocating, and they were glad when the meal was over.

As they prepared for escape the count signalled for Guido to join him in his ornate study.

'We'll be at *Luigi's Bar*,' Marco called back from the front door.

'Couldn't this wait?' Guido pleaded, following his uncle into the study.

'No, it can't wait,' Francesco growled. 'There are things to be said. I won't bother to ask if the stories I've heard about you are true.'

'They probably are,' Guido agreed with a grin.

'It's time it stopped. After all the trouble I've taken, making sure you met every woman in society.'

'I'm nervous with society women. They're all after just one thing!'

'*What*!'

'My future title. Half of them never look at me properly. Their gaze is fixed on the Calvani honours.'

'If you mean that they're prepared to overlook your disgraceful way of life out of respect for your dignity—'

'Dignity be blowed. Besides, maybe I don't want a woman who'll overlook my "disgraceful" life. It might be more fun if she was ready to join in.'

'Marriage is not supposed to be fun!' Francesco thundered.

'I was afraid of that.'

'It's time you started acting like a man of distinction instead of spending your time with the Lucci family, fooling about in gondolas—'

'I like rowing a gondola.'

'The Luccis are fine hard-working people but their lives take one path and yours another—'

In a flash Guido's face lost its good humour and hardened. 'The Luccis are my friends, and you'll oblige me by remembering that.'

'You can be friends—but you can't live Fede's life. You've got to make your own way. Perhaps I shouldn't have allowed you to see so much of them.'

'You didn't allow me,' Guido said quietly. 'I didn't ask your permission. Nor would I. Ever. Uncle, I have the greatest respect for you, but I won't allow you to run my life.'

When Guido spoke in that tone the merry charmer vanished, and there was something in his eyes that made even the count wary. He saw it now and fell silent. Guido was instantly contrite.

'There's no harm in it,' he said gently. 'I just like to row. It keeps me fit after my other "excesses".'

'If it were just rowing,' Francesco snorted, recovering lost ground. 'But I've heard you even sing "O sole mio" for tourists.'

'They expect it. Especially the British. It's something to do with ice cream cornets.'

'And you pose with them for photographs.' The count took out a snapshot showing Guido in gondoliering costume, serenading a pretty, dark-haired girl, while another gondolier, with curly hair and a baby face, sat just behind them.

'My nephew,' he growled, 'the future Count Calvani, *poses in a straw hat.*'

'It's disgraceful,' Guido agreed. 'I'm a blot on the family name. You'll just have to marry quickly, have a son, and cut me out. Rumour says you're still as vigorous as ever, so it shouldn't be—'

'Get out of here if you know what's good for you!'

Guido fled with relief, leaving the building and slipping away down tiny, darkened streets. As he reached the Grand Canal he saw a collection of seven gondolas, moving side by side. It was a 'serenade', a show put on to please the tourists. In the central boat the baby-faced young man from the photograph stood singing in a sweet tenor that drifted across the water. As the song came to an end there was applause, and the boats drifted in to their moorings.

Guido waited until his friend, Federico Lucci, had assisted his last passenger to disembark before hailing him.

'Hey there, Fede! If the English *signorina* could hear

you sing like that she would follow you to the ends of the earth,' he said. 'What's the matter?' for Fede had groaned. 'Doesn't she love you any more?'

'Jenny loves me,' Fede declared. 'But her Poppa will kill me before he lets us marry. He thinks I'm only after her money, but it isn't true. I love her. That time you met, didn't you think she was wonderful?'

'Wonderful,' Guido said, diplomatically concealing his opinion that Jenny was a pretty doll who lacked spice in her character. His own taste was for a woman who could offer a challenge, lead him a merry dance and give as good as she got. But he was too kind a friend to say so.

'You know I'll help in any way I can,' he said warmly.

'You've already helped us so much,' Fede said, 'letting us meet in your apartment, covering for me on the gondola—'

'That's nothing. I enjoy it. Let me know when you want me to do it again.'

'My Jenny has returned to England. She says she will reason with her Poppa, but I'm afraid she may never return.'

'If it's true love, she'll come back,' Guido insisted.

Fede gave a shout of laughter and thumped him on the shoulder. 'What do you know about true love? With you it's here-today-and-gone-tomorrow. If they mention marriage you dive for cover.'

'Sssh!' Guido looked hunted. 'My uncle has ears everywhere. Now come on, let's join Leo and Marco at *Luigi's*, and we can all get drunk in peace.'

Two days later Dulcie flew to Venice, landing at Marco Polo Airport and waiting, with an air of aloof grandeur, while her luggage was loaded onto the Vittorio's private motor launch.

It was early June, and as the boatman started the trip across the lagoon the sun was high in the sky and the light glinted on the water. Surrounded by so much bright beauty Dulcie briefly forgot her sadness.

To her right she could see the causeway linking Venice to the mainland. A train was making its way across. On the other side the lagoon stretched far away to the horizon.

'There, *signorina*,' the boatman said, speaking with the pride all Venetians feel in their city.

What she saw at first were shining orbs, gradually resolving themselves into golden cupolas, gleaming in the sun. The city itself, delicate and perfect, came gradually into view, taking her breath away with its beauty. She stayed motionless, not wanting to miss anything, as the motor boat slowed down.

'We have to enter Venice gently,' the driver explained, 'so that we do not cause any large waves. This is the Cannaregio Canal, which will take us to the Grand Canal, and the Vittorio.'

Suddenly the brightness of the lagoon was blotted out and they were drifting in shadow between high buildings. Dulcie resumed her seat and leaned back, looking up to the narrow strip of sky overhead. After a few minutes they were in sunlight again, heading down the Grand Canal to a magnificent seventeenth-century palace. The Hotel Vittorio.

At the landing-stage hands reached down to help her up the steps and guide her into the hotel. She made a stately entrance, followed by porters bearing her luggage in procession.

'The Empress Suite,' declared a lofty individual on the desk.

'The Emp—?' she echoed, dismayed. 'Are you sure there hasn't been a mistake?'

But she was already being swept away to the third floor where gilded double doors opened before her and she walked into the palatial apartment. Everything about it was designed to look like the abode of an empress, including the eighteenth-century furniture. On one wall hung a portrait of the beautiful, young Empress Elisabeth of Austria, painted in the nineteenth century when Venice had been an Austrian province.

To one side was another pair of double doors, through which Dulcie found her bedroom, with a bed large enough to sleep four. She gasped, overwhelmed by such opulence. A maid appeared, ready to unpack her luggage. Just in time she remembered Roscoe's orders to 'splash it about a bit' and distributed tips large enough to get herself talked about even in this place.

When everyone had gone she sat in silence, trying to come to terms with the shock of being here, alone, when she should have been here as a blissful bride.

She forced herself to confront the memory of Simon, painful though it was. He'd assumed that *Lady* Dulcie Maddox, daughter of Lord Maddox, must have a potful of family money hidden somewhere. He'd courted her ardently, using practised words to sweep her away in a magic balloon, to a place where everything was love and gratification.

But the balloon had fallen to earth, with her in it.

Simon had lived lavishly—all on credit, as she'd later discovered. She hadn't cared about his money, only about his love. But the one was as illusory as the other.

He'd shown her the Hotel Vittorio's brochure one

evening when they were dining at the Ritz. 'I've already made our honeymoon booking,' he'd said, 'in the Empress Suite.'

'But darling, the cost—'

'So what? Money is for spending.'

She'd spoken with passionate tenderness. 'You don't have to spend a lot on me. Money isn't what it's about.'

His quizzical frown should have warned her. 'No, sweetie, but it helps.'

Then she'd said—and the memory tormented her still— 'You don't think I'm marrying you for your money do you? I love you, *you*. I wouldn't care if you were as poor as I am.'

She could still see the wary look that came into his eyes, and sense the chill that settled over him. 'This is a wind up, right? As poor as Lady Dulcie Maddox.'

'You can't eat a title. I haven't a penny.'

'I heard your grandfather blew twenty grand at the races in one day.'

'That's right. And my father was the same. That's *why* I haven't a penny.'

'But you lot have all got trust funds, everyone knows that.'

The truth had got through to her now, but she fought not to face it. 'Do I live like someone with a trust fund?'

'Go on, you're just slumming.'

She'd finally convinced him that she wasn't, and that was the last time she saw him. Her final memory was of him snatching a credit card statement from his pocket and tossing it at her with the bitter words, 'Do you know how much money I've spent on you? And for what? Well, no more.'

Then he stormed out of the Ritz, leaving her to pay for the meal.

And that had been that.

Sitting in the quiet of the Empress Suite Dulcie knew that it was time to pull herself together. Now there was another fortune hunter, but this time he was the prey and she the pursuer, seeking him out for retribution, the avenger of all women.

She showered in a gold and marble bathroom and chose something to wear for her first outing 'on duty'. She finally left the hotel arrayed in an orange silk dress, with a delicate pendant of pure gold. Gold earrings and dainty gilt sandals completed the ensemble. So much gold might be overdoing it, but she needed to make an impression, fast.

When she'd finished she took a final look at the picture, to make sure his face was imprinted on her mind. She dismissed the baby-faced boy at the back. There was the one she wanted, playing the mandolin, over-flowing with confidence, smiling at Jenny, no doubt ser-enading her with honeyed words. The rat!

Finding one gondolier among so many was a prob-lem, but she'd come prepared. Guidebooks had told her about the *vaporetto*, the great water buses that trans-ported passengers along the Grand Canal, so she headed for one of the landing stages, boarded the next boat, and took up a position in the front, armed with powerful binoculars.

For an hour the *vaporetto* moved along the canal, criss-crossing to landing stages on each side, while Dulcie searched for her quarry, without success. At the end of the line she turned back and started again. No luck this time either, and she was almost about to give up when suddenly she saw him.

It was only a glimpse, too brief to be sure, but there was the gondola gliding between two buildings while she frantically focused the binoculars, catching him clearly only at the last moment.

The *vaporetto* was about to cast off from a landing stage. Dulcie moved fast, jumping ashore just in time and looking desperately about her. The gondola had vanished. She plunged down an alley between tall buildings to a small canal at the far end. No sign of him there, but he must be somewhere to her left. She made for a tiny bridge, tore over it and into another dark alley.

At the far end was another small canal, another bridge. A gondola was heading towards her. But was it the same one? The gondolier's face was hidden by a straw hat. She placed herself on the bridge, watching intently as the long boat neared, the oarsman standing at the far end.

'Lift your head,' she agonised. 'Look *up!*'

He had almost reached the bridge. In a moment it would be too late. Driven by desperation she wrenched off one of her shoes and tossed it over the side. It struck his hat, knocking it off, before landing exactly at his feet.

Then he looked up, and there was the face she'd come to Venice seeking, the face of the mandolin player. Eyes of fierce, startling blue, set in a laughing face, seemed to seize her, hold her, almost hypnotise her, so that she found herself smiling back.

'*Buon giorno, bella signorina,*' said Guido Calvani.

CHAPTER TWO

NO SOONER were the words out of his mouth than he'd vanished under the bridge. Dulcie dashed to the other side as he emerged and began to negotiate his way to the shore. She took a quick look at the picture to make sure she had the right man. Yes, there he was, smiling at Jenny, playing the mandolin.

Thank goodness he didn't have a passenger, she thought as she hobbled off the bridge and along to where he'd pulled in.

'I'm so sorry,' she called. 'I just turned my foot and the shoe slid off and went right over the side of the bridge before I could grab it. And then it hit you on the head. I'll never forgive myself if you're hurt.'

He grinned, holding up the dainty gilt sandal with its absurdly high heel.

'But I am hurt, very badly. Not in my head but—' he bowed gallantly with his hand over his heart.

This was what she'd expected. Practised charm. Right! She was ready for him.

He'd pulled in by a short flight of steps that ran down into the water.

'If you will sit down, I'll return this to you in the proper fashion,' he said.

She sat on the top step and felt her ankle grasped in strong, warm fingers as he slid the shoe back onto her foot, adjusting it precisely.

'Thank you—Federico.'

He gave a little start. 'Fed—?'

22

'It's written there.' Dulcie pointed to a label stitched near his collar, bearing the name Federico.

'Oh, yes, of course,' Guido said hurriedly. He'd forgotten Fede's mother's habit of sewing nametapes on the gondolier shirts of her husband, two brothers and three sons. No matter. He would simply tell her his real name. But he became distracted by the feel of her dainty ankle in his palm, and when he looked up he found her watching him with a quizzical look that drove everything else out of his mind. What did names matter?

'And you are new to Venice?' he asked.

'I arrived only today.'

'Then you must accept my apologies for your rough introduction to my city. But let me say also that the stones of Venice will not be kind to those shoes.'

'It wasn't very bright of me to wear such high heels, was it?' she asked, looking shamefaced. 'But I didn't know, you see. Venice is so different to anywhere else in the world, and there's nobody to tell me anything.' She managed to sound a little forlorn.

'That's terrible,' he said sympathetically. 'For a beautiful young lady to be alone is always a shame, but to be alone in Venice is a crime against nature.'

He said it so delightfully, she thought. Lucky for her she was armed in advance.

'I'd better go back to my hotel and change into sensible shoes before I have another accident.' She became aware that his fingers were still clasped about her ankle. 'Would you mind?'

'Forgive me.' He snatched back his hand. 'May I take you to your hotel?'

'But I thought gondoliers didn't do that. Surely you only do round trips?'

'It's true that we don't act like taxis. But in your case

I would like to make an exception. Please—' He was holding out his hand. She placed her own hand in it and rose to her feet, then let him help her down the steps to the water.

'Steady,' he said, helping her into the well of the gondola, which rocked, forcing her to clutch him for safety.

'You sit here,' he said, settling into the rear-facing seats, an arrangement that would enable him to see her face. 'It's better if you don't face the front,' he hurriedly improvised. 'At this hour people get the setting sun in their eyes. And you might get seasick,' he added for good measure.

'I'll do just as you say,' she agreed demurely. She supposed she could be blinded by the setting sun from either direction, depending on which route he took, but she appreciated his strategy.

It suited her, too, to be able to lean back and stretch out her long, silk-clad legs before his gaze. True, she was supposed to be tempting him with the prospect of money, but there was no harm in using the weapons nature had bestowed.

He cast off, and for a while they went gently through narrow canals, where buildings rose sheer out of the water. They glided under a bridge and as it slid away she saw that it seemed to emerge direct from one building, over the water and straight into another. Dulcie watched in wonder, beginning to understand how this city was truly different from all others.

He was a clever man, she thought. He knew better than to spoil it by talking. Only the soft splash of his oar broke the silence, and gradually a languor came over her. Already Venice was casting its spell, bidding her forget everything but itself, and give herself up to floating through beauty.

'It's another world,' she murmured. 'Like something that fell to earth from a different planet.'

An arrested look came into his eyes. 'Yes,' he said. 'That's exactly it.'

They seemed to drift for ages, one beauty crowding on the last, too many impressions for her to sort them out. Vaguely she remembered that this wasn't why she was here. Her job was to work on the man standing there, guiding twenty-two feet of heavy, curved wood as though it was the easiest thing in the world.

She considered him, and found that she understood why a naïve, sheltered girl like Jenny found him irresistible. He was tall, not heavily built but with a wiry strength that she'd already felt when he'd helped her into the boat. Just a light gesture, but the steel had been there, unmistakable, exciting. He handled the heavy oar as though it weighed nothing, moving with it, lithe and graceful, as though they were dancing partners.

They passed into a wider canal, and suddenly the sun was on him. Dulcie looked up, shading her eyes against the glare, and at once he removed his straw boater and tossed it to her.

'You wear it,' he called. 'The sun is hot.'

She rammed it onto her head and leaned back, taking pleasure in the way the light illuminated his throat and the strong column of his neck, and touched off a hint of red in his hair. How intensely blue his eyes were, she thought, and how naturally they crinkled at the corners when he smiled. And he smiled easily. He was doing so now, his head on one side as though inviting her to share a joke, so that she couldn't help joining in with his laughter.

'Are we nearly there?' she asked.

'There?' he asked with beguiling innocence. 'Where?'

'At my hotel.'

'But you didn't tell me which hotel.'

'And you didn't ask me. So how do we know we're going in the right direction?'

His shrug was a masterpiece, asking if it really mattered. And it didn't.

Dulcie pulled herself together. She was supposed to toss the hotel name at him, advertising her 'wealth'. Instead she'd revelled in the magic of his company for—good heavens, *an hour*?

'The Hotel Vittorio,' she said firmly.

He didn't react, but of course, he wouldn't, she reasoned. A practised seducer would know better than to seem impressed.

'It's an excellent hotel, *signorina*,' he said. 'I hope you are enjoying it.'

'Well, the Empress Suite is a little overwhelming,' she said casually, just to drive the point home.

'And very sad, for a lady alone,' he pointed out. 'But perhaps you have friends who'll soon move into the second bedroom.'

'You know the Empress Suite?'

'I've seen the inside,' Guido said vaguely. It was true. His friends from America regularly stayed there, and he'd downed many a convivial glass in those luxurious surroundings.

I'll bet you've seen the inside, Dulcie thought, getting her cynicism back safely into place.

'When your friends arrive you'll feel better,' he said.

'There are no friends. I'm spending this vacation on my own.' They were pulling in to the Vittorio's landing stage, and he reached out to help her onto land. 'How much do I owe you?' she asked.

'Nothing.'

'But of course I must pay you. I've had an hour of your time.'

'Nothing,' he repeated, and she felt his hand tighten on her wrist. 'Please don't insult me with money.' His eyes were very blue, holding hers, commanding her to do what he wished.

'I didn't mean to insult you,' she said slowly. 'It's just that—'

'It's just that money pays for everything,' he finished. 'But only if it is for sale.' He spoke with sudden intensity. 'Don't be alone in Venice. That's bad.'

'I don't have a choice.'

'But you do. Let me show you my city.'

'Your city?'

'Mine because I love it and know its ways as no stranger can. I would like you to love it too.'

It was on the tip of her tongue to make one of the flirtatious replies she'd been practising for just this moment, but the words wouldn't come. She had a sense of being at the point of no return. To go on was risky and there would be no way back. But to withdraw was to spend a lifetime wondering 'what if?'

'I don't think—' she said slowly. 'I don't think I should.'

'I think you should,' he said urgently.

'But—'

His hand tightened on hers. 'You *must*. Don't you know that you must?'

The glow of his eyes was almost fierce in its intensity. She drew a sharp breath. She didn't come from a long line of gamblers for nothing.

'Yes,' she said. 'I must.'

'I'll meet you at seven o'clock at *Antonio's*. It's just around the corner. And wear walking shoes.'

She watched as he glided away, then hurried up to her suite, glad of the time alone to gather her thoughts.

It wasn't easy. In a few blazing moments he'd taken her ideas and tossed them into the air, so that they'd fallen about her in disorder. It took some stern concentration to reclaim her mind from his influence, but at last she felt she'd managed it.

Stage one completed successfully. Quarry identified, contact made. Ground laid for stage two. Professional detachment. Never forget that.

Guido got away from the hotel as fast as he could before he was spotted by someone who knew his true identity. In a few minutes he'd left the city centre behind and was heading for the little back 'streets' in the northern part of town, where the gondolier families lived, and their boatyards flourished.

At the Lucci house he found Federico at home watching a football match on television. Without a word he took a beer from the fridge and joined him, neither speaking until half time. Then, as he always did, Guido put the money he'd earned on the table, nearly doubling it with extra from his own pocket.

'I had a good day, didn't I?' Fede said appreciatively, pocketing the money with a yawn.

'Excellent. You're an example to us all.'

'At this rate I think I've earned a holiday.'

'I know *I* have.' Guido rubbed his arms, which were aching.

'Perhaps it's time you got back to the souvenir trade.'

Guido had established his independence of the

Calvani family by setting up his own business, catering to tourists. He owned two factories on the outlying island of Murano, one of which made glass, and the other trinkets and souvenirs.

'I suppose it is,' he said now, unenthusiastically. 'It's just that—Fede, have you ever found yourself doing something you never meant to do—just a word, a choice to be made in a split second? And suddenly your whole life has changed?'

'Sure. When I met my Jenny.'

'And you don't know how it's all going to end, but you do know that you have to go on and find out?'

Fede nodded. 'That's just how it is.'

'So what do I do?'

'My friend, you've already supplied the answer. I don't know what's happened, but I do know it's too late for you to turn back.'

An important decision demanded long, serious deliberation, so when Dulcie opened the palatial wardrobe to select something suitable for the coming evening she went through the multitude of dresses with great care.

'How did I ever buy all this?' she murmured.

She'd gone to Feltham's, as instructed, and found the staff already primed with Roscoe's demands. As these would have resulted in her looking like a Christmas tree Dulcie had waved them aside and insisted on her own kind of discreet elegance. After four outfits she tried to call a halt, but the superior person assigned to assist her was horrified.

'Mr Harrison said the bill must be at least twenty thousand,' she'd murmured.

'Twenty thou—? He can wear them then.'

'He'll be most displeased if we don't live up to his expectations. It could cost me my job.'

Put like that, it became a duty to spend money, and by the time she'd left the luxury store she was the owner of five cocktail dresses, two glamorous evening gowns, three pairs of designer jeans, any number of designer sweaters, a mountain of silk and satin underwear, and a collection of summer dresses. Some expensive make-up and perfume, plus several items of luggage completed the list.

She surveyed her booty now, hanging in the hotel's luxurious, air-conditioned closets, in a mood of ironic depression. This ought to have been a fun job, the chance to be Cinderella at the ball. If only it hadn't been Venice, and if only the high life she was to lead hadn't been so much like the life her Prince Charmless had expected of her.

Why had she accepted *this* assignment, in a place where every sight and sound would hurt her. Was she mad?

Then she set her chin. This was a chance to make a man pay for his crimes against women. She must never forget that.

She took so long making her choice that she was late when she finally hurried downstairs wearing a cocktail dress of pale-blue silk organza with silver filigree accessories. Her silver shoes had heels of only one inch, which was the nearest she could get to 'sensible'.

Antonio's was a tiny place with tables outside, sheltered by a leaf-hung trellis. It looked charming, but there was something missing. Him!

No matter, he'd be inside. She sauntered in, looking casual, but her air of indifference fell away as she saw no sign of him here either.

He'd stood her up!

It was the one thing she hadn't thought of.

Be reasonable, she thought. He's just a few minutes late—like you.

That's different, replied her awkward self. He's supposed to be trying to seduce me, and he can't even be bothered to do it properly.

Setting her jaw she marched out and collided with a man hurtling himself through the door in the other direction.

'*Mio dio!*' Guido exploded in passionate relief. 'I thought you'd stood me up.'

'*I*—?'

'When you didn't come I thought you'd changed your mind. I've been looking for you.'

'I was only ten minutes late,' she protested.

'Ten minutes, ten hours? It felt like forever. I suddenly realised that I don't know your name. You might have vanished and how could I have found you again? But I've found you now.' He took her hand. 'Come with me.'

He was walking away, drawing her behind him, before she could stop and think that once more he'd reversed their roles, so that he was now giving orders. But she followed him, eager to see where he would lead her, and curiously content in his company.

He'd changed out of his working clothes into jeans and a shirt of such snowy whiteness that it gave him an air of elegance, and made a contrast with his lightly tanned skin.

'You could have found me quite easily,' she pointed out as they strolled hand in hand. 'You know my hotel.'

'To be sure, I could go into the Vittorio and say the lady in their best suite has given me the elbow and would they please tell me her name? Then I think I should start running before they throw me out. They're used to dealing with dodgy characters.'

'Are you a dodgy character?' she asked with interest.

'They'd certainly think so if I told them that tale. Now where shall we go?'

'You're the one who knows Venice.'

'And from the depths of my expert knowledge I say that we should start with an ice cream.'

'Yes please,' she said at once. There was something about ice cream that made a child of her again. He picked up the echo and grinned boyishly.

'Come on.'

He led her into a maze, where streets and canals soon blurred into one. Flagstones underfoot, alleys so narrow that the old buildings almost seemed to touch each other overhead, tiny bridges where they lingered to watch the boats drift underneath.

'It's all so peaceful,' she said in wonder.

'That's because there are no cars.'

'Of course.' She looked around her. 'I hadn't even realised, but it's obvious.' She looked around her again. 'There's nowhere for cars to go.'

'Right,' he said with deep satisfaction. 'Nowhere at all. They can leave the mainland and come out over the causeway as far as the terminal. But then people have to get out and walk. If they don't want to walk they go by boat. But they don't bring their smelly, stinking cars into my city.'

'Your city? You keep saying that.'

'Every true Venetian speaks of Venice as his city. He pretends that he owns it, to hide the fact that it owns him. It's a possessive mother who won't release him. Wherever he goes in the world this perfect place goes with him, holding onto him, drawing him back.' He stopped himself with an awkward laugh. 'Now Venice thinks we should go and eat ice cream.'

He took her to a small café by a little canal so quiet that the world might have forgotten it. He summoned a waiter, talking to him in a language Dulcie didn't recognise, and making expansive gestures, while giving her a look of wicked mischief.

'Were you speaking Italian?' she asked when they were alone again.

'Venetian dialect.'

'It sounds like a different language to Italian.'

'In effect it is.'

'It's a bit hard on tourists who learn a bit of Italian for their vacation, and then find you speaking Venetian.'

'We speak Italian and English for the tourists, but amongst ourselves we speak our dialect because we are *Venetian*.'

'Like a another country,' she said thoughtfully.

'Of course. Venice was once an independent republic, not just a province of Italy, but a state in its own right. And that's still how we feel. That is our pride, to be Venetian first, before all other allegiances.'

As before, there was a glow on his face that told her he felt passionately about this subject. She began to watch him intently, eager to hear more, but suddenly the waiter appeared with their order, and he fell silent. She had a sense of let-down, and promised herself that she would draw him back to this subject later.

She understood her companion's mischievous expression when two huge dishes of vanilla and chocolate ice cream were brought to the table, plus two jugs, one containing chocolate sauce and one containing cream.

'I ordered chocolate because it's my favourite,' he explained.

'Suppose it isn't mine?'

'Don't worry, I'll finish it for you.'

She gave an involuntary choke of laughter, and bit it back, remembering the aloof role she was supposed to be playing. But she made the mistake of meeting his eyes, daring her not to laugh, so that she had to give in.

'Now tell me your name,' he insisted.

'It's—Dulcie.' She was mysteriously reluctant to say the rest.

'Only Dulcie?'

'Lady Dulcie Maddox.'

He raised his eyebrows. 'An aristocrat?'

'A very minor one.'

'But you have a title?'

'My father has the title. He's an earl. In Italy he would be a count.'

A strange look came over his face. 'A—count?' he echoed slowly. 'You are the daughter of a count?'

'Of an earl. Does it matter?'

She had the odd impression that he pulled himself together. 'Of course you didn't want to tell me that. I understand.'

'What do you understand?' she demanded, nettled.

He shrugged. 'Dulcie can do as she pleases, but *Lady* Dulcie can't let a gondolier think he picked her up.'

'You didn't pick me up,' she said, feeling uneasy, since she could hardly admit that she'd come here to pick *him* up. 'I don't care how we got to know each other. I'm just glad that we did.'

'So am I because—because I have many things I

want to say to you. But I can't say them now. It's too soon.'

'It's too soon for you to know you want to say them.'

He shook his head. 'Oh, no,' he said quietly, 'It's not too soon for that.'

CHAPTER THREE

'You must forgive me if I talk too much about Venice,' he said. 'I forget that everyone must feel the same about their own home town.'

'I don't know,' she said thoughtfully. 'I can't imagine feeling like that about London.'

'That's where you live?'

'It is now, but I was raised on my father's estate—'

'Ah yes, Poppa the earl. And he has huge ancestral acres, yes?'

'Huge,' she agreed, mentally editing out the mort-gages.

'So you were raised in the country?' he encouraged her.

'Yes, and I remember how peaceful it was there too. I used to sit by my bedroom window at dawn and watch the trees creeping out of the mist. I'd pretend they were friendly giants who could only visit me in the half-light, and I'd write stories in my head about the things they did—' she stopped and shrugged, embarrassed to have been lured into self-revelation.

But he was looking at her with interest. 'Go on,' he said.

She began to talk about her home, the childhood she'd spent there, and the imaginary friends she'd cre-ated, for her only sibling was a brother too much older than herself to be any fun. Soon she forgot all else ex-cept the pleasure of talking to someone who appeared absorbed in what she had to say. None of her family had the remotest sympathy with her 'dreaming', and at last she'd given it up in favour of good sense. Or so she'd told herself. Now she began to wonder if this side of herself had merely gone underground, to be brought back to life with the perfect listener on the perfect evening.

At some point he paid for the ice cream and took her arm to lead her out, murmuring about eating the next part of the meal elsewhere. But he did it without taking his attention from her, or interrupting the flow, and when she found herself crossing a bridge a few minutes later she wasn't quite sure how she'd arrived there.

He found another restaurant and ordered without asking her. That was how she discovered 'Venetian oysters', the shells stuffed with caviar with pepper and lemon juice, served on ice with brown bread and butter. It was ten times as good as the splendid meal served in Roscoe's house, prepared by his expensive chef. Her companion read her face, and grinned.

'We do the best cooking in the world,' he asserted without a trace of modesty.

'I believe you, I believe you,' she said fervently. 'This is pure heaven.'

'You don't mind my ordering for you?'

She shook her head. 'I wouldn't know what to ask for anyway.'

'Then you place yourself totally in my hands. *Bene*!'

'I didn't exactly say that,' she protested. 'I said you could choose the food.'

'Since we're eating, that's the same thing.'

'Well, I'm on my guard. I've heard about gondoliers,' she teased.

'And what exactly have you heard?' he was teasing her back.

'That you're a bunch of Romeos—'

'Not Romeos, Casanovas,' he corrected her seriously.

'Does it make a difference?' she asked, wondering if it was ever possible to disconcert this madman.

'Of course. This is Casanova's city. In the Piazza San Marco you can still see Florian's, the coffee-house where he used to go. Also he was imprisoned in Venice. So, you were saying—'

'You mean I can finish now?'

He placed a finger over his mouth. 'Not another word.'

'I don't believe you. Where was I?'

'We're all Casanovas—'

'Who count the girls as they come off the planes.'

'But of course we do,' he agreed shamelessly. 'Because we're always looking for the one perfect one.'

'Phooey! Who cares about perfection if it's only for a few days?'

'I always care about perfection. It matters.'

He wasn't joking any more and she was impelled to reply seriously. 'But everything can't be perfect. The world is full of imperfection.'

'Of course. That's why perfection matters. But you must know how to seek it in the little things as well as the great. Look out there.'

He pointed through the window to where the sun was setting exactly between two high buildings, looking like a stream of gold descending into the earth.

'Do you think the architect knew he was achieving exactly that perfect effect when he created those buildings?' he asked her. 'It seems fantastic, but I like to believe that he did. Perfection is where you find it.'

'Or where you think you've found it. Sometimes you must discover that you're wrong.'

'Yes,' he said after a moment. 'And then nothing looks quite the same again.' Then his laughter broke out again. 'Why are we being so serious? That comes later.'

'Oh, really? You've got our conversation all mapped out then?'

'I think we're travelling a well-worn path, you and I.'

'I'm not going to ask you which path. It might mean getting too serious again, and I'm here for fun.'

He regarded her quizzically. 'Are you saying that's why you came to Venice—looking for a holiday romance?'

'No, I—' Absurdly, the question caught her off-guard. 'No, that's not why.'

'What's the matter?' he asked at once. 'Have I said something to hurt you?'

'No, of course not.'

It was hard because this man was shrewder and subtler than she had allowed for. His eyes were warm and concerned, studying her anxiously, but she needed to evade them, lest they looked too deep.

'That was lovely,' she said, indicating her empty plate. 'What have you decided on now?'

'*Polastri Pini e Boni,*' he declared at once.

'And that is—?' She was searching the menu for enlightenment. 'I can't find it.'

'It's chicken, stuffed with herbs, cheese and almonds. You won't find it on the menu. They don't do it here.'

'Then—?'

'I'm going to take you to a place where they do serve it.'

'Are we going to have every course in a different place?' she asked, slightly giddy at the thought.

'Of course. It's the ideal way to eat. Come on.'

As soon as they were outside she became completely lost. Now they were far off the tourist track, plunging into narrow, flagstoned streets that she knew were called *calle*. High overhead the last of the daylight was almost blocked out by washing strung between buildings, across the street.

'I thought all the streets were water,' she observed as they strolled along, not hurrying.

'No, there are plenty of places where it's possible to walk, but sooner or later one always comes to water.'

'But why build it like this in the first place?'

'Many centuries ago, my ancestors were running from their enemies. They fled the mainland, out into the lagoon where there were a mass of tiny islands, and they settled there. They drove stakes deep into the water to create foundations, built bridges between the islands, and so created a unity that became a city.'

'You mean this canal beneath us—' they were crossing a small bridge '—was the seaway between two separate islands? It's only about twelve feet wide.'

'They were miracle workers. And a miracle is what they created.'

'But how? It just—just defies all the laws of architecture, of science, of common sense—'

'Oh, common sense—' he said dismissively.

'I believe in it,' she said defiantly.

'Then heaven help you! It means nothing. It creates nothing, it's the opposite of a miracle. Look about you. As you say, Venice defies common sense, and yet it exists.'

'I can't deny that.'

'So much for common sense! Never resort to it again. It's the root of all the troubles in the world.'

'I'm afraid I can't help it,' she confessed. 'I grew up sensible, reliable, practical—'

He put his hands over his ears. 'Stop, stop!' he begged. 'I can't bear any more of these dreadful words. I must feed you quickly and make you well again.'

He hustled her down some steps and into a door that was almost hidden in shadows. Behind it was a tiny restaurant which was almost full despite the fact that it seemed to be in hiding. One taste of the chicken was enough to explain this contradiction. If the last course had brought her to the gates of heaven, this one ushered her through.

Guido watched her with pleasure, intent on weaving a spell around her. He wanted her securely in his magic net before he was ready to reveal certain things about himself. He was an honest man, with a high regard for the truth, but he knew that truth wasn't always reached by sticking too rigidly to the facts.

Then, as if making his very thoughts tangible, a hand clapped him on the shoulder and a cheerful voice said, 'Hey, Guido! Fancy seeing you here!'

It was Alberto, a friend and employee, who managed his glass factory, more than slightly tipsy, full of good cheer, and about to blow his cover.

Guido tensed and his glance flew to Dulcie who was mercifully absorbed in feeding a kitten that had appeared under their table. She hadn't heard Alberto call him Guido but disaster was approaching fast. The one ray of hope was that Alberto was speaking in Venetian. Grabbing his friend's wrist Guido muttered in the same language.

'Hello, old friend. Do me a favour. Get lost.'

'That's not very friendly Gui—'

'I'm not feeling friendly. Now be a good fellow and take yourself off.'

Alberto stared, then he caught sight of Dulcie and his expression cleared. 'Aha! A beautiful lady. You devil. Let me make her acquaintance.'

'You'll make the acquaintance of the canal in a minute.' Guido's smile never wavered as he uttered this half-serious threat.

'Hey, all right!' Alberto became placating, backing off. 'If it's like that—'

'I'm warning you—another word—'

'Fine, I'm going.'

Guido watched him depart, feeling as if he'd aged ten years. He should have taken Dulcie to some place where nobody knew him, but where, in Venice, was he to find such a place?

Problems crowded in on him. Soon he must tell her of his innocent deception, but how to do it needed a lot of thought. Never mind. He would 'tap-dance' his way out of that problem when the time came. He was good at that because to a warm-hearted man with a tangled personal life tap-dancing was a necessary skill.

'If you've finished, let's walk again,' he said. 'Venice will have changed.'

She saw what he meant as they stepped outside. Night had created a different city. Little alleys that had led to mysterious corners now vanished into total darkness, and lights glittered like jewels reflected in the black water. He led her onto a small bridge and stood back, letting her drink in the beauty in her own way, in peace.

Already there were a thousand things he wanted to say to her, but he held back, fearful of breaking the spell by going too fast. He could wait, and let Venice do its work for him.

Dulcie watched and listened, entranced. Faintly, in the distance, she could hear the sound of mandolins, and occasionally a strange, soft, eerie yodel.

'Whatever is that sound?'

'It's the cry a gondolier gives as he approaches a corner,' he said. 'With twenty-two feet of boat in front of him he has to warn any traffic crossing his path, otherwise they'd be colliding all the time.'

As he spoke there was another yodel close by, and the prow of a gondola appeared around the corner, turning into the canal and heading for them. Dulcie leaned over the bridge, watching the boat with its young lovers clasped in an embrace. Slowly they drew apart, their faces illuminated by the lights from the bridge.

Dulcie felt a cold hand clutch her stomach. The man—it couldn't be—she was imagining things. As the gondola glided beneath she rushed to the other side of the bridge in a vain attempt to see better. But that was worse. There was only the back of his head. Perversely this only increased her conviction that she'd seen Simon.

A rich bride, a honeymoon in Venice, these were the things he'd wanted. But it was only four months since they'd parted. Could he have replaced one bride with another so fast? Suddenly she'd moved back in time to a turmoil of pain, disillusion, rejection, mistrust.

'Dulcie, what is it?'

She felt strong hands seize her, turn her. His face was dark.

'Tell me what's the matter.'

'Nothing.'

'That man—you knew him—'

'No—I thought I did, but it couldn't have been him, not so soon—not here of all places—I don't know, I don't want to talk about it.'

'I see,' he said slowly. 'It's like that.'

'You don't know what it's like,' she cried angrily. 'You don't know anything.'

'You loved him, and you thought you would be here with him. That much is obvious. And it wasn't so very long ago. So perhaps you love him still?'

'It wasn't him,' she said, trying to sound firm. 'Just someone else who looked a bit like him.'

'But you're avoiding my question. Do you still love him? Or don't you know?'

'Yes—no—I don't know. I don't know anything.'

'Were you coming to Venice for your honeymoon?'

'Yes,' she sighed.

'And now you come here alone—to think of what might have been?'

That did it.

'Rubbish!' she said trenchantly. 'Absolute codswallop! How dare you suggest that I'm some sort of—of— I don't know, some sort of forlorn maiden trailing in the shadow of a dead love. Of all the sentimental drivel I ever heard—I've a good mind to—'

How he laughed. '*Brava*! *Brava*! I knew you were stronger than that. Whatever he did to you, you won't be crushed. Don't get mad, get even! Shall we follow and tip him into the water?'

'Don't be idiotic,' she said, joining in his laughter unwillingly. 'I don't even know that it's him.'

'Let's tip him in the water anyway,' he suggested hopefully.

'You clown. Whatever for?'

'As a warning to all men to be careful how they treat women in future.'

'Let's forget him,' she said hastily. She didn't know what wicked imp had made him voice the very idea that had brought her here, but it was something she couldn't afford to think of just now.

'Yes, let's forget him and plan what we shall do tomorrow. There's so much I want to show you—'

'What about your gondola? It's your living.'

'Not tomorrow. Tomorrow I forget work and think only of you.'

'Oh, really,' she teased. 'Suppose I have other ideas?'

He looked crestfallen. 'There's another man you'd rather spend the day with?'

'No, I—' she bit back the rest, realising that she'd walked into a trap.

'You'd rather spend the day with me than any other man?' he said at once. '*Bene*! That's what I hoped.'

'You're twisting my words. Maybe I want to spend the day alone.'

'Do you?'

He wasn't teasing any more, and neither was she.

'No,' she said quietly.

'We could go to the seaside, if you like?'

'Does it have a really sandy beach?' she asked longingly.

'I promise you a really sandy beach. Venice doesn't just have the best cooking in the world, it also has the best beach in the world.'

'Anything else?'

'The best swimming, and the best company. Me.'

He was laughing again, playing the jester, inviting her to mock him. Then suddenly he drew her into his arms, holding her close, but not kissing her, content just to embrace. He drew back a little and touched her face with his hands, brushing back stray tendrils of hair, and studying her intently.

'Dulcie,' he whispered. 'There's so much—but not now—this isn't the right time.'

A tremor of alarm went through her. This was too sweet, too delightful. What was she thinking of?

'I can't,' she said. 'I can't see you tomorrow.'

'Then the next day—'

'No, I can't see you again,' she said desperately. 'I'm going home. I should never have come here. Please let me go.'

He made no attempt to hold onto her as she broke free and began to run down the nearest *calle*. She simply had to get away from what was happening here. It shocked and confused her. Nothing was going according to plan.

Her footsteps slowed, then halted. It looked the same in all directions, and she had no idea where she was. By the one lamp she groped in her bag for a map and tried to work out which way up it went. It was hopeless.

'Now I'm totally lost,' she groaned.

'Not while I'm here,' he said, appearing from nowhere. 'I'll take you to the hotel. It isn't very far.'

It seemed to her that they had come for miles, but when he'd led her through *calle* after *calle*, all looking the same, she found herself near the hotel, and realised that they'd only been walking for ten minutes.

'There it is, just ahead,' he told her. 'You don't need my help any more.' He was keeping back in the shadows.

'Then I'll say goodbye,' she said, holding out her hand. 'Thank you for a lovely evening. I'm sorry it all ended so abruptly—'

'Has it "all ended"?'

'Yes, it has to. Because you see—I can't seem to get my head straight.'

'Nor mine. But my response would be the opposite of yours.'

'I'm going home tomorrow,' she said quickly. 'I really must—I can't explain but I shouldn't have come here—goodbye.'

The last word came out in a rush. Then she walked away fast, and hurried into the hotel without looking back at him.

As she opened the door of the Empress Suite her mind was functioning like an investigator's again. Cool. Calm. Collected. She was a rational thinking machine.

And the sooner she was out of here the better.

The phone rang. She knew who it would be.

'Please don't leave,' came his voice.

'I—ought to.'

'You should never do what you ought. It's a big mistake.'

'Why?' she asked, knowing that she was crazy to ask.

'Because you really ought to be doing something else.'

'That's just clever words.'

'Now you're indulging in common sense,' he reproved her. 'You must stop that.'

'More clever words.'

'You're right. Actions are better. I'll be waiting for you at ten tomorrow morning, at the *vaporetto* landing stage near the hotel. Come prepared for swimming.'

'But—'

'Ten o'clock. Don't be late.'

He hung up.

She couldn't think what was happening here. She

should be in control, but suddenly everything was out of her hands. To help collect her thoughts she went out onto her balcony and looked down the Grand Canal. It was quiet now and just a few lamps glowed in the darkness. Now and then a gondola, empty but for the silent oarsman, drifted across the water like a ghost, gliding home.

She had called the evening magic, a word which troubled her practical mind. And staying practical was essential she thought, beginning to argue with him in her mind. Let him say what he liked. She wasn't to be tricked by pretty words.

But out here, in the shadows and the cool night air, the magic couldn't be denied. Awed, she watched as one by one the café lights went out, and the water lay at peace under the moon. Still she stayed, not wanting this night to be over.

The shrill of the telephone blasted her gentle dream. It was Roscoe.

'How are you doing?' he demanded without preamble. 'Have you got anywhere yet?'

'I only arrived today,' she protested.

'You mean you haven't managed to meet him?'

'Yes, I have—'

'Great! And he's a real creep, right?'

She answered cautiously. 'Mr Harrison, if this man was an obvious creep he'd never have impressed Jenny as he has. He's subtle, and clever.'

'You mean he's got to you?' Roscoe demanded.

'Certainly not!' she said quickly.

'Are you sure? Like you say, subtle and clever. Knows how to get any woman under his spell.'

'But I'm not any woman,' she told him crisply. 'I'm a woman who's seen through him before we started.

You can leave him to me. Tonight was stage one. Stage two will be my masterpiece.'

She hung up, feeling as though she'd been punched in the stomach. The call had brought her back to reality. What had she been thinking of to let this man weave fantasies about her when she knew the truth about him? It was simply—she searched for the worst word she knew—unprofessional.

But not any more, she assured herself. Tomorrow I'm going to be sensible.

Guido made his way through the streets by instinct and the fact that his feet knew the route by themselves. Lost in his blissful dream he didn't notice the two men approaching him until he collided with them.

'Apologies,' he murmured.

'Hey, it's us,' Marco said, grabbing his arm.

'So it is,' Guido agreed amiably.

'You weren't looking where you were going,' Leo accused him.

Guido considered. 'No, I don't think I was. Is this the way home?'

Any Venetian would have recognised this as an absurd question since, in that tiny city, all roads lead home. The other two looked at each other, then stationed themselves on either side of Guido like sentinels, and they finished the journey together.

The Palazzo Calvani had a garden that ran by the water. Marco signalled the butler to bring wine, and they all sat out under the stars.

'Don't talk, drink,' Marco ordered. 'There are few troubles that good wine can't cure.'

'I'm not in trouble,' Guido told him.

'What's got into you?' Marco demanded. 'Are you crazy?'

'I'm in love.'

'Ah!' Leo nodded wisely. 'That kind of crazy.'

'The perfect woman,' Guido said blissfully.

'What's her name?' Marco asked.

But Guido's sense of self-preservation was in good working order. 'Get lost,' he said amiably.

'When did you meet her?' Leo wanted to know.

'This afternoon. It happened in the first moment.'

'You always say they're after the title,' Leo reminded him.

'She doesn't know about the title, that's the best thing of all. She thinks I'm a gondolier, scratching a living, so I can be sure her smiles are for me. The one honest woman in the world.'

'Honest woman?' Marco echoed scathingly. 'That's asking a lot.'

'We're not all cynics like you,' Guido told him. 'Sometimes a man must trust his instincts, and my instincts tell me that she's everything that is good. Her heart is true, she's incapable of deception. When she loves me, it will be for myself alone.'

Leo raised his eyebrows. 'You mean she doesn't love you already? You're losing your touch.'

'She's thinking about it,' Guido insisted. 'She's going to love me—almost as much as I love her.'

'And you've known her how long?' Leo asked.

'A few hours and all my life.'

'Listen to yourself,' Marco snorted. 'You've taken leave of your senses.'

Guido held up a hand. 'Peace, you ignorant men!' he said sternly. 'You know nothing.'

He wandered away under the trees, leaving the other two regarding each other uneasily.

When he was out of their sight Guido stopped and looked up at the moon.

'At last,' he said ecstatically. 'She came to me. And she's perfect.'

CHAPTER FOUR

'I SHOULD be getting home soon,' Leo said next morning. 'I only came to see Uncle, and he's fine now.'

'Don't leave just yet,' Guido hastened to say. 'He sees you so seldom, and who knows how long he'll be around?'

They were having breakfast on the open-air terrace overlooking the water, relishing in the warm breeze and Liza's excellent coffee in equal measure.

'Uncle will outlive us all,' Leo insisted. 'I'm a farmer, and it's the busy time of year.'

'It's always the busy time of year, according to you.'

'Well, I don't like cities,' Leo growled. 'Hellish places!'

'Don't talk about Venice like that,' Guido said quickly.

'For pity's sake!' Leo said, exasperated. 'You're no more Venetian than I am.'

'I was born here.'

'We were both born here because Uncle made Poppa bring his wives to Venice for the births of their children. Same with Marco's mother. Calvani offspring must be born in the Palazzo Calvani.' Leo's tone showed what he thought of this idea. 'But we were both taken home to Tuscany when we were a few weeks old, and it's where we belong.'

'Not me,' Guido said. 'I've always loved Venice.'

As a child he'd been brought to stay with his uncle during school vacations, and when he was twelve

52

Francesco had made a complete takeover bid, demanding that he reside permanently in Venice so that he could grow up with the inheritance that would be his. Guido had only the vaguest idea about the inheritance but the city on the water entranced him, and he was glad of the move.

He had loved his father but was never entirely at ease with him. Bertrando was a countryman at heart, and he and Leo had formed a charmed duo from which Guido felt excluded. Bertrando had wept and wailed at the 'kidnap' of his son, but a large donation from Francesco to ease the effects of a bad harvest had reconciled him.

In due course Guido had come to feel his destiny as a poisoned chalice, but nothing could abate his love for the exquisite city. The fact that he'd made an independent fortune from catering to its tourists was, he would have said, an irrelevance.

Marco joined them a moment later, just finishing a call on his mobile phone. As he sat down he said, 'It's time I was going home.'

Guido went into overdrive. 'Not you as well. Uncle loves you being here. He's an old man and he doesn't see enough of you.'

'I'm neglecting business.'

'Banks run themselves,' Guido declared loftily.

This was flagrant provocation since he knew, and the others knew he knew, that Marco was far more than a simple banker. He was a deity of the higher finance, whose instinct for buying and selling had made many men rich and saved many others from disaster. Guido himself had profited by his advice to expand his business, but couldn't resist the chance to rib him now and then.

Marco bore up well under the treatment, ignoring

Guido's teasing, or perhaps he managed not to hear it. Although his father had been a Calvani his mother was Roman, and he lived in that city from choice. Austerely handsome, proud, coolly aristocratic, unemotional and loftily indifferent to all he considered beneath him, he was Roman to his fingertips. Anyone meeting him for a few minutes would have known that he came from the city that had ruled an empire.

Just once he'd shown signs of living on the same plane as other men. He'd fallen in love, become engaged and set the date for the wedding. His cousins had been fascinated by the change in him, the warmth that would flare from his eyes at the sight of his beloved.

And then it was all over. There was no explanation. One day they were an acknowledged happy couple. The next day the engagement was broken 'by mutual consent'. The wedding was cancelled, the presents sent back.

That had been four years ago, and to this day Marco's sole comment had been, 'These things happen. We were unsuited.'

'Unsuited?' Guido had echoed when Marco was safely out of earshot. 'I saw his face soon after. Like a dead man's. His heart was broken.'

'You'll never get him to admit it,' Leo had prophesied wisely. And he'd been right.

Marco had never discussed the cancellation of his wedding, and the others would have known nothing if Guido hadn't happened to bump into the lady two years later.

'He was too possessive,' she explained. 'He wanted all of me.'

'Marco? Possessive?' Leo echoed when Guido related the conversation to him. 'But he's an iceberg.'

'Evidently not always,' Guido had observed.

It was doubtful if Marco would have confessed to the possession of a heart, broken or not. But these days he was never seen without a beautiful, elegant woman on his arm, although no relationship lasted for very long. In this respect his life might be said to resemble Guido's, but Guido's affairs sprang from the impetuous warmth of his nature, and Marco's from the calculating coolness of his.

He seated himself at the breakfast table now, ignoring Guido's attempts to rile him, and reached for the coffee. Instantly Lizabetta appeared with a fresh pot which she contrived to set down, remove the old one and clear away used dishes without speaking a word or appearing to notice their presence.

'She terrifies me,' Guido said when she'd gone. 'She reminds me of the women who knitted at the foot of the guillotine in the French revolution. When we're loaded into tumbrels and hauled off for execution Liza will be there, knitting the Calvani crest into a shroud.'

Leo grinned. 'They won't bother with me. I'm a hard-working son of the soil, and that's what I ought to be doing this minute.'

'Just a few more days,' Guido begged. 'It'll mean so much to Uncle.'

'To you, you mean,' Leo said. 'You just want us to occupy his attention while you get up to no good.'

'You're wrong,' Guido said, grinning. 'What I'm getting up to is very, very good.'

He was ahead of Dulcie getting to the landing stage, and for a horrid moment he was sure she wasn't coming. He knew he'd somehow put a foot wrong the previous night, but he could recover himself if he saw her again.

But she wasn't coming. She'd left the hotel, left Venice. He might never see her again...

There she was!

'Quickly,' he said, seizing her hand, 'the *vaporetto* is just coming.'

As the boat drew up he hurried her on board as though fearful that she might change her mind. He found her a seat at the side, near the prow, and sat silently, content to watch her as she beheld marvels unfold.

Dulcie could hardly believe that she was here. As she'd packed the black satin bikini she'd told herself that this was pointless because she wasn't really going to spend today with him. She'd stressed this again as she'd donned the scarlet sun dress, but then her feet had walked themselves out of the Empress Suite and into the lift.

And now here she was, sitting beside him as the *vaporetto* left the Grand Canal behind and settled in for the half-hour journey to the Lido, the strip of land that marked the boundary of the lagoon. The warm wind whistled past her, making her hair stream out, catching all her troubles and whirling them away across the blue water.

From the landing stage to the beach was just a short walk across the narrow island, and then she was gazing at an expanse of blue sea and golden sand that did her heart good.

He hired cubicles for them, and a huge umbrella which he ground into the sand. When she emerged from the cubicle wearing the bikini and a floating gauze top he'd already spread the towels on the sand and was waiting for her. His eyes never left her as she approached and slipped off the top, revealing a body that

was slender, elegant and beautiful. She held her breath
for his reaction.

'Where is your sun cream?' he demanded.

'My what?'

'With that fair skin you need it.'

'But I never catch the sun,' she protested.

'Nobody catches the sun in England because you
don't have any. Not what I call sun. Here you need sun
cream. Come, we'll go to the shop.'

Great, she thought, exasperated, as he steered her
along the sand to the beach shop. That was all the reaction she was going to get.

In the shop he bought cream and a large straw hat.
She protested until he settled the matter by ramming the
hat onto her head, so that it covered her eyes and he
had to lead her out, threatening dire retribution if she
touched it. Only when they were back under the umbrella did he let her remove the hat and the top so that
she could apply the cream.

'All over,' he instructed.

'Aren't you going to help me?'

'Sure. Turn around and I'll do your back and shoulders.'

He did exactly what he'd said without taking advantage. Her back and shoulders. Then he sat waiting while
she covered every other inch of her. He didn't even
offer to do her legs. Obviously, she thought, Jenny was
very lucky and he was faithful to her.

So what were they doing here?

Perhaps he just wanted English female company, to
remind him of the woman he really missed. It was a
depressing thought. Except for Jenny, of course.

'Now we can have a swim,' he said, 'just a short one
at first while you get used to the sun gradually.'

'It's like being taken out by my father,' she said indignantly.

'Was it really like this when he took you out?'

'No,' she admitted wryly. 'He never took me to the beach, it was always the races, and then he—well, he had other things to think about.'

'But didn't he ever just want to give you a treat?'

'No,' she said after a moment. There had been 'treats' for her brother, who'd been a chip off the old block, but, 'He said it was no fun taking me out because I didn't know how to enjoy myself.'

'Your father said *that*?' He sounded scandalised, and she had the same feeling as the night before, of having found her first sympathetic listener.

'He's just a big kid himself, really. He likes to have fun.'

'Well, today, *you* are going to have fun,' he declared. 'I am going to be the Poppa, and treat you to everything you want. We go swimming, we throw a beach ball, we eat ice lollies, we do everything.'

'Oh, yes,' she breathed. 'Yes, *please*.'

Grabbing her hand he began to race down the beach until they were in the shallows, where he danced about, splashing water onto her. She splashed back, thinking that nothing could have looked less like a 'Poppa'. He was lean and hard, with a smooth chest, a neat behind and long, muscular thighs.

Afterwards they strolled hand in hand along the edge of the water, for which he made her wear the sun hat again, although she felt no more than pleasantly warm in the brisk wind that swept along the shore. They stopped to rest by a little rock pool, and Dulcie let her toes dangle in the water, breathing in the salty air, and wondering how she'd lived without doing this.

'Watch out for crabs,' he said casually.

'*Aaargh!*' Her yell split the air as she snatched her toes away, while he laughed and laughed until she thought he would never stop. '*You rotten so and so—*' She was thumping him while he tried to fend her off, but not very effectively because he was weak from laughter. Somewhere in the tussle her hat vanished, whisked away by the wind and deposited out to sea.

'Are there really any crabs?' she asked, peering down into the water.

'Of course not, or I wouldn't have let you put your foot in there.'

'Well, you wait. I'll make you sorry, see if I don't,' she said, taking his hand for the return journey.

He led her to the beach restaurant and settled her at an outside table, under an awning, while he went inside, glancing hurriedly around. To his relief he saw only one person who knew his real identity. Nico was the son of one of the count's gardeners, earning extra in his college vacation. Guido grinned at him and murmured a few words in Venetian. Some notes changed hands.

After this, no more dodges, he promised himself as he walked out. *From now on I shall be as open and virtuous as she is herself. She has reformed me.*

The thought made him stop and consider. A reformed character.

A better man.

It'll be pipe and slippers next. You've always run a mile from them.

But who cares, as long as she's there?

He was grinning as he joined her at the table.

'What's so funny?' she asked.

'It's not funny exactly, it's just—have you ever suddenly looked around and found that life was a completely different shape to what you'd thought?'

'Well—'

But he didn't really want an answer. He was driven by the need to express the thoughts that overwhelmed him. 'Suddenly all the things you thought you'd never want became the objects of your desire—'

'How much did you drink while you were in there?'

'Why does everyone think I'm drunk? But I am!' he cried up to the sky. 'After all, there's drunk and drunk.'

'What are you talking about?' she chuckled.

'I don't know. I only know that—that—'

'Buon giorno, signore!'

It was Nico, being the perfect waiter. Guido ground his teeth. Surely there were other waiters? He gave the order and Nico departed, returning a moment later with pasta. He would have hovered further, enjoying the joke, but a look from Guido sent him scuttling off.

The food was delicious and Dulcie tucked in.

I shouldn't be enjoying this so much, she thought. *I'm here to work. But—just a few more hours, and then I'll be good.*

He was the perfect companion, telling her funny stories, refilling her glass with sparkling mineral water with as much of a flourish as if it were the finest wine. Afterwards he made her lie down in the shade for an hour before he would allow her to go into the sea.

But once in the water she was overcome with the longing to strike out. She was a strong swimmer and in a moment she was heading out to sea, ignoring his cry of protest, making him chase after her. By the time he caught up they were in deep water, and she was feeling good.

Laughing, she turned to face him, treading water, and found him wild-eyed.

'You crazy woman,' he said. 'To do such a thing in strange waters! You don't know what the currents are like.'

'You could always swim to my rescue,' she teased.

'And suppose I couldn't swim?'

'Oh, sure! A Venetian who can't swim! Even I know better than that!'

'I'm a lot feebler than I look,' he protested.

'Oh, yeah!'

'I've got a bad back,' he clowned. 'And a bad everything.'

'You look fine to me,' she said, surveying his smooth brown chest and muscular arms with pleasure.

'It's an illusion. Beneath this young exterior is the frame of a creaking old man, I swear it. In fact I— *Aaargh*!'

With a theatrical yell and a waving of arms he vanished beneath the water. Dulcie watched, amused, calculating when he would have to come up.

'Right,' she murmured. 'I said I'd get my own back. Watch this.'

She saw his shape reappearing below the surface from whatever depths he'd sunk to, and in the split second before his head broke the surface she slipped underwater, staying just close enough to hear his cry of, 'Dulcie! *Dulcie*! *Dio mio*! *Dulcie*!'

'Fooled you,' she said, coming up just behind him.

'You—*you*—!'

'Come on, it's only what you did to me.'

'You knew I was playing. I thought you'd drowned, you just vanished and—and—the whole ocean to search— *Come here*!'

'No way,' she said, seeing in his face that she'd pushed him just a little too far. Turning tail she began to swim back as fast as she could, managing to stay ahead, but only just. As soon as she reached the sand she began to run and covered several hundred yards before he caught up, seizing her arm.

'Ouch!' she said, for suddenly her skin stung where he touched it.

He released her at once. '*Basta*!' he said. Enough. 'You've been too long in the sun.'

He curved his arm near her shoulders, not touching, but insisting that she turn back to their umbrella. She found it was a relief. An ache was starting in the back of her head and she felt she'd had enough fun for one day.

'Sorry if I worried you,' she said.

'*Worried me*? Do you know—? No matter. I'll postpone my revenge.'

She lay down under the umbrella while he brought her a cold drink. It refreshed her a little, but the pleasure had gone out of the day, and when he suggested that they drift home she agreed. She was beginning to feel sleepy, and that made her annoyed with herself, because there was so much of the day left that she might have enjoyed.

On the journey back across the lagoon she stared out over the water, and must have dozed because suddenly it was time to disembark. Her nap hadn't made her feel any better, although she tried to seem brighter than she felt. The headache had now taken over completely. Her whole body felt hot and uncomfortable and the spell of the day was rapidly dissolving in a very prosaic feeling of being poorly.

'I've been thinking,' Guido began to say, but stopped as he looked at her. 'What's the matter with you?'

She tried to laugh. 'Just a bit of a headache.'

'Let me look at you.' He took gentle hold of her shoulders and turned her to face him. 'My poor girl!'

'What is it?' she asked, feeling more ill by the moment.

'Despite our precautions you've caught the sun badly. That fair skin of yours can't cope with this heat. I should have bought a stronger cream. Are you feeling bad?'

'Yes,' she said wretchedly. 'My head aches terribly.'

'Right, we're going home. Stay here.'

He settled her on a low stone wall and disappeared. She had no choice but to do as he'd said and stay there. The whole world seemed to be thundering inside her brain. She was only vaguely aware of him returning, saying, 'I've got us a taxi. Hold onto me.'

He half carried her down the steps to the boat, then sat in the back, holding her close, her head on his shoulder. She felt the vibration as the motor boat started up, the swift movement over the water, and the inexpressible comfort of his arms about her. The pain in her head was dreadful, yet she had a confused feeling that she could go on like this forever, if only he would hold her as he was doing now. Once she was vaguely aware of him making a call on his mobile phone, then everything went hazy again.

Then they were stopping and she was groping her way out, her eyes half closed, guided by him.

'Nearly there,' he said. 'You'll find the rest of the way more comfortable like this.' And he was lifting her in his arms.

She was too weak to protest, although she could

guess what a figure she must cut, being carried through the foyer of the Vittorio. How they would all be staring at her! She heard doors opening and closing behind them, then there was the blessed relief of being out of the sun.

'Thank you,' she murmured. 'What must they think of us?'

'Who?'

'The people in the hotel.'

'We're not in the hotel. I've brought you to my home.'

She managed to open her eyes and realised that she didn't recognise anything in her surroundings. Gone was the high, painted ceiling of the Empress Suite. There was no elaborate furniture or gilded decor, only a small, austerely furnished room, with wooden beams overhead. She was still in his arms and he was moving towards a door that he managed to pull open. With her eyes half closed she waited for him to lie her down. Instead she was set on her feet, and the next moment she was drenched in cold water.

She yelled with shock and made a feeble attempt to struggle, but he was holding her firmly to stop her falling.

'I'm sorry,' he yelled over the water, 'but getting under the shower is the quickest way to cool you off.'

'It's freezing,' she gasped.

'All the better. Lift your head. Let it pour over your face and neck. Please, you'll feel better.'

She did as he said. It felt good, insofar as anything could feel good at this moment. At last he turned the tap off and they stood there together, drenched and gasping.

'Here's the bath towel,' he said. 'I'll leave you alone

to get undressed.' But as he loosened his grip she nearly fell again. 'I'll have to do it for you,' he said.

'Will you?' she asked faintly.

He gritted his teeth. 'I'll force myself.'

He was very brave about it, loosening her buttons and slipping her dress off, then her sodden slip. Only her bra and panties were left.

'You've got to remove those too or you'll get pneumonia,' he said, working on them. At last she was naked, and he towelled her down until she was almost dry, then wrapped her in the vast towel like a parcel, and sat her on the stool while he ripped off his own soaking shirt.

'There's no point in me making you wet again,' he grunted, lifting her up.

This time he carried her into the bedroom and put her to bed, not unwrapping her until the last moment, then tucking the duvet up to her chin with his eyes averted.

'Don't worry about anything,' he said gently. 'It's quiet here and you can recover in peace.'

The next moment his front doorbell buzzed. When he returned he was accompanied by a plump middle-aged woman.

'This is Dr Valletti,' he explained. 'I called her on the way back. I want to be sure it isn't serious.'

He left the room at once. Dr Valletti regarded her with something akin to exasperation.

'You English! When will any of you learn to be sensible about the sun?'

'We don't have sunshine like this in England,' she said weakly. 'I did have a hat, but it blew away.'

'So I understand. And water magnifies the sun's rays. People with your fair colouring should stay covered up.'

She felt Dulcie's forehead, took her temperature and asked a few questions before pronouncing, 'You're lucky he got you under that cold shower fast. Now a day's rest in the cool will see off the worst. After that you take it easy for a while. You can go out, but only for a short time, and you cover up. Understand?'

'Yes, but I can't—'

'I'll leave these pills for your head. In summer I keep a supply on me, especially for the English. Goodbye now. Just do everything Gui—your friend tells you to. He's very worried.'

Through the throbbing in her head Dulcie heard only 'your friend' and 'very worried'. She lay back as the doctor departed, and vaguely sensed them talking behind the closed door. A few minutes later he entered the room, bearing a cup.

'Tea,' he announced, setting it down beside her. 'To take your pills. Let me help you up.'

His arm was firm beneath her back, raising her gently and holding her against his shoulder while she sipped the tea, which was perfectly made.

'You'll be nice and cool now, because I've turned the air-conditioning on,' he said as he laid her down again. 'When I've gone, try to get some sleep. Nobody will bother you, I promise.'

He went to the window and closed the shutters, making the room almost dark. Then he was gone. Dulcie lay still, willing the pills to take effect, and at last they began to do so. Gradually her consciousness slipped away.

She didn't know how much time had passed when she awoke. The light was dim because of the shutters. Her head was better but she still felt weak. His words, 'Nobody will bother you, I promise,' were there in her mind. He'd spoken them like a knight laying his sword on the bed between himself and his lady, a chivalrous vow of chastity.

It was a strange thought. This was the man she'd come here to expose as a liar and a cheap seducer. Yet he'd averted his eyes, as much as a man could avert his eyes from a woman he was undressing, and whatever her head might say, her heart instinctively trusted him.

She dozed, half awoke, dozed again, in the grip of a dream that seemed always to be with her, waking or sleeping. She was gliding, as if on an endless canal, but then suddenly she was falling endlessly. She reached out and felt her hand clasped by another which held her tightly, keeping her safe. With their fingers entwined she sensed all trouble fall away. Then she was gliding on again, and all about her was the sound of water and music, and happiness.

CHAPTER FIVE

SHE opened her eyes on total darkness. Her headache was gone and she felt light. Easing her way out of bed she discovered that she hadn't yet recovered. It took all her strength to walk to the window and undo the shutters.

Outside was a world of calm shadows. It was dark, the only light coming from the moon seeking to penetrate the narrow canals below. This little apartment seemed to be in a backwater, with a narrow canal, or *rio* running beneath. She couldn't tell where she was, except that this wasn't the glamorous part of the city. It was the homely part, where the Venetians lived. A young couple wandered along the opposite bank, dressed almost alike in jeans and sweaters. They looked up, saw her watching them and vanished into the shadows.

Switching on the bedside light she saw that the bathrobe was now lying on the bed, although it hadn't been there when she'd fallen asleep. When had he done that? She had no idea, but there was no doubt he'd entered the room and left it without disturbing her.

She realised that she was still more overheated than she'd thought, because the fire that had consumed her body earlier hadn't quite died down. Either that or it was the knowledge that he'd looked at her while she was oblivious.

She slipped the cotton robe on and quietly opened the bedroom door. It led straight into a large living room, also in darkness except for moonlight. By its light she managed to identify the bathroom, and crept in, closing the door silently behind her.

The first thing she saw was her sodden clothes hanging over the bath, perfectly arranged, as if by an artist.

The sight of herself in the mirror was a shock. Her normal pale colour had given way to a pink that she didn't find becoming. Under the bathrobe her shoulders felt tender, and a glimpse beneath it showed her the worst. The sun had burned her wherever it had touched.

'So much for the temptress,' she thought wryly. 'Turning into a lobster wasn't part of the plan.'

She splashed cold water on her face, but it didn't do much for her. She'd used up a lot of strength just getting this far, and the journey back looked like a marathon.

Emerging from the bathroom she had a clear view of someone sleeping on the sofa. Since he was a tall man and it was a short sofa his discomfort was evident, even under the duvet that half covered him. Her face softened as she viewed him, wondering how long he'd been there, and what state he would be in when he awoke.

She began to make her way back to the bedroom, but it was hard because her remaining strength was seeping away fast. After a few steps she stopped, clinging onto a chair, breathing hard, her forehead damp. The next chair was three feet away. She began to plan how she would make it, short steps, sliding her feet along an inch at a time, then a quick dash.

She managed the first bit all right, but she miscalculated the dash, fell short by several inches and collided hard with the sofa, making its occupant slide to the floor and awaken, tangled in the duvet and cursing vividly.

'I'm sorry,' she gasped, clinging onto the back of the sofa.

He was on his feet in a moment, a lithe, smooth-chested figure in shorts and nothing else. 'It's all right,' he said quickly. 'Here. Hold onto me.'

She did so, thankfully. 'I thought I was better,' she murmured, 'but when I got up—I just don't know—'

'You don't get over this sort of thing in five minutes. It'll take a day or two. How's your headache?'

'It had gone, but it's coming back.'

'Let's get you into bed then, and I'll make you some tea and you can have two more of those pills. The doctor left me complete instructions.'

They had reached the bed but he put her into a chair and held up a finger to tell her to stay there. Then he descended on the bed in a whirl of activity, finding fresh pillowcases, smoothing the undersheet and shaking the duvet out until it was fluffy.

'You're very domesticated,' she said admiringly.

'My father taught me. He said you should never depend on women for these things because they weren't reliable.' He spoke with a straight face, but his eyes twinkled. 'Back to bed.'

She made a move as if to undo the robe, but then remembered that she had nothing on underneath. He pointed to some drawers. 'You'll find some vests in there.' He left.

She chose one of his vests and had slipped back into bed by the time he returned with tea. She drank it thankfully and took more pills for the headache which had returned with a vengeance.

'There's a little bell by the bed,' he said, removing the cup and settling her. 'Ring it if you need me.'

'You're a wonderful nurse,' she murmured, sliding down contentedly.

'Go to sleep.'

This time she slept long and awoke feeling refreshed. Throwing open the shutters she found a brilliant morning and took some long, deep breaths. Her head was better, although she still felt wobbly.

Donning the robe, she peered around the bedroom door, but found no sign of her host. In a small, single-floor apartment, with all rooms leading off the main one, it took no time to ascertain that he'd gone out.

It was a peaceful, pleasant place, with white walls, a cool terrazzo floor, and furniture that was sparse and functional. The only sign of flamboyance was the profusion of masks that hung on the walls. Some were simple, some fantastic with long noses and sinister slits for the eyes. They seemed to cover every wall, and Dulcie surveyed them with interest.

Looking at the tiny sofa she winced with sympathy for him. It seemed so unfair for him to sleep in that cramped place while she had his whole double bed at her disposal.

But of one thing there was no further possible doubt. This was a man who had very little money.

An inspection of her dress in the bathroom showed that it was unwearable after its drenching. An inspection of herself showed that the pink of her skin had faded, but still wasn't a colour she'd have chosen. She was considering how matters stood when she heard the front door open, and went out to see him enter, loaded down with shopping. She hastened to rescue some bags that were slipping from his fingers.

'Dump them in the kitchen,' he said. 'No, just these. I'll take those.' He whisked a couple of items away from her, dropped them on the sofa and guided her into the kitchen. 'You're looking better.'

'I feel it. I just wish I looked it.'

'Good healthy colour.'

'T'isn't! It just tells the world I'm an idiot.'

'I'm not answering that. Let me sit down. I've been staggering under this lot for too long.'

'Shall I make you some coffee?'

'No thank you,' he said with more speed than gallantry.

'Why not?'

'Because you're English,' he said, not mincing matters.

'Meaning we don't know how to make coffee?'

He just grinned and rose to his feet. 'I'll make the coffee for both of us, then I'll get your breakfast. Something light I think. Soup, and then—yes, that would be it.'

He refused to say any more, watching her with a glint of mischief as she helped him unpack the food. He seemed to have shopped for an army.

'I've been having a look at my dress,' she said.

'Did the shower leave it in a state? Sorry about that. I suppose I should have ripped it off you first.'

'No, you shouldn't,' she said firmly. 'I'm not complaining, you did the right thing. It's just that I'm having visions of me going back to the Vittorio looking a fright.'

'You don't have to do that. Go and have a look at the bags in the other room.'

Puzzled, she did so, and her eyes widened at the contents.

'I knew you'd be needing some fresh clothes,' he said, standing in the kitchen doorway and watching her.

'It's just cheap stuff from market stalls, and not what you're used to.'

That made her feel bad because it was exactly what she was used to. He'd bought her a pair of white jeans and two coloured tops to go with them. And he'd assessed her size perfectly, as she realised when she considered the other items.

'You had the cheek to buy me—?'

'You need underwear,' he said defensively. 'Excuse me, the coffee's perking.'

He vanished into the kitchen and closed the door, leaving Dulcie examining the bras and panties that he'd chosen for her. They were lacy, delicate confections, designed to be seen. A woman would choose such things if she planned to undress in front of a man. And a man would choose them if he wanted to see them on a woman, or wanted to see the woman remove them, or wanted to think about her wearing and/or removing them.

Dulcie hastily silenced her thoughts. But what she couldn't shut out was the way he'd hurried away and put a door between them. It was almost as though he was shy as well as shameless.

Further investigation revealed a nightgown. Unlike the underwear it was fiercely sexless, unadorned cotton, with a front that buttoned up to the neck. She sat for a while, contemplating the prosaic nightgown on the one hand and the sexy underwear on the other. There was no understanding him. Which was strange, considering how simple she'd expected him to be.

She glanced up as the kitchen door opened again, and one eye appeared. It looked nervous.

'Oh, come on,' she said, chuckling.

The other eye appeared. 'The coffee's ready. Am I forgiven?'

'I'm not sure,' she said, joining him in the kitchen, where he set coffee before her. 'You had a cheek buying me panties that look like that.'

'But I like them,' he said innocently.

'And you had an even bigger cheek buying me a nightie that my grandmother could wear.'

His hint of mischief disappeared. 'I think I was right,' he said simply. 'While you are ill it's better that you look…' he hesitated '…like a grandmother. At least, not a grandmother exactly because you could never look like that but—safe. You must feel safe.' He tore his hair. 'I'm not saying this very well—but perhaps you understand—'

'Yes,' she said, touched. 'I do understand you. It's very kind of you to think of my safety.'

'Somebody has to think of it. You're shut up here alone with a man of bad character, enfeebled by illness, nobody to protect you if you shout for help.'

'Perhaps he isn't a man of bad character.'

'But he is. Definitely. You should dress in sensible clothes to prevent him indulging in disgraceful thoughts about—' he caught her enquiring eyes on him '—about what you would look like if you weren't wearing sensible clothes, or even if you weren't wearing—I'll start the soup,' he finished hurriedly.

Dulcie's lips twitched. She wasn't fooled by this apparent boyish confusion, but she appreciated the way he'd paid her a compliment without getting heavy about it.

'But I shan't be here long,' she said. 'I can go back to the hotel when I've eaten.'

'I don't think so. You're not well yet, and the doctor

is coming for you again today. You feel strong now, but it won't last.'

In fact her strength was already fading, and when he set soup before her she took it gladly. This was followed by a bowl of rice and peas, cooked to perfection. A few more hours' rest would set her up, she told herself as she headed back to bed, to find that it had been freshly made. She slipped on the 'grannie' nightgown and got thankfully back under the duvet.

This time, when she awoke, it was to find Dr Valletti just entering the room.

'Yes, you seem better,' she agreed when she'd checked Dulcie over. 'But take it easy for another day. Tomorrow you can go out, but only for short periods, and keep covered up against the sun.'

'I'm really well enough to go back to the hotel,' she said guiltily when the doctor had departed.

'No,' he said at once. 'You must stay here where I can look after you. In the hotel there are only servants. What do they care for you?'

She made a face. 'If I tip them well enough, they'll care.'

'Oh, yes. Is that kind of caring enough?'

She shook her head.

'Besides,' he added, 'I don't trust you.'

'I beg your pardon!'

'You'll do something stupid if I'm not there. So you stay here where I can watch over you. And I don't want a tip.'

'Well, maybe I'll leave it for now. I'll go tomorrow.'

'You'll go when I say.'

'Yes *sir*! Is it all right if I get up now and take a shower?'

While he cooked supper she showered and donned

some of the lacy underwear, thinking it was a pity that her complexion wasn't more becoming. She selected the pale-yellow top to go with the white jeans. Now her appearance was simple and elegant, and much more to her own taste than the elaborate confections she had hanging up in the hotel.

'What are you cooking?' she asked, sauntering into the kitchen and standing where he could see her.

'To start with, mushroom risotto.' He paused from chopping parsley and stood back to regard her. '*Bene*! Very nice!'

'You think so?'

'Yes, I got the size exactly right. I was wondering about that. Can you hand me that onion?'

She nearly threw it at him.

At his instruction she laid the little table for two by the open window. It was evening and a soft, bluey light lay over the scene outside. Lamps were coming on, reflected in the water, and from somewhere in the distance came the echoing warnings of the gondoliers, sounding like melancholy music.

He opened a bottle of *prosecco*, a sparkling white wine.

'It's very light,' he explained, 'so it won't upset your stomach.'

They chinked glasses.

'In fact, I've arranged the whole meal to be light,' he explained. 'The next course is pasta and beans, then a shrimp omelette. And to finish—fried cream.'

'Fried—? You're kidding me.'

'No, I promise. You shall watch.'

And she did watch as he blended flour, sugar, eggs and milk into a thick cream, that he proceeded to fry. It was delicious.

Afterwards he washed while she dried, wondering at a certain embarrassment in his manner.

'Is something the matter?' she asked.

'Well—Dulcie would you mind if—when we've finished this?—only if you want to, of course—'

'What is it?' she asked with a little pang of dismay. Here it came, the amorous advance that would make him cheap in her eyes. It was what she'd come here for, and suddenly she would have given anything to put him off.

But duty came first, so she merely looked at him expectantly while her heart beat with apprehension.

He took a deep breath and went on with the air of a man plunging off the deep end. 'There's a really important soccer match on television tonight—'

'A soccer match?'

'It's Juventus playing Lazio, or I wouldn't ask,' he pleaded. 'You don't mind?'

'No,' she said, dazed. 'I don't mind.'

They spent the rest of the evening sitting side by side on the sofa, holding hands, until he declared that it was time for her to go to bed. But he had to say it twice because she'd fallen asleep against his shoulder.

Next morning he let her sleep late, and she awoke knowing that the last of her illness had gone. While dressing she noticed with delight that she was no longer red. The colour had softened into a light tan that looked marvellous against her fair hair and green eyes, and even better against the soft-pink top that she matched with the white jeans.

'Who won the match?' she asked, appearing in the kitchen.

'I forget. You look great. How do you feel?'

It was on the tip of her tongue to say she felt splendid, but she amended it to, 'Better than I did, but not quite my normal self.'

That was true, she told her conscience. She would never feel like her normal self again.

'Then we'll take it easy today. A light breakfast, then a gentle walk.'

His solicitude made Dulcie feel a little guilty because she'd allowed him to think her more frail than she actually was. But, to someone who'd lived such a practical life, there was a sweet pleasure in being cosseted, and she reminded herself that her mission was to discover the truth about him. If the truth turned out to be that he was a marvellous man, kind, gentle, affectionate, considerate and chivalrous, then she would report this truth and be happy for Jenny.

Over rolls and coffee he said, 'I have to buy food this morning, so we can take a stroll.'

'You mean I've eaten you out of house and home?'

'You've hardly touched anything.'

She was about to mention the clothes he'd bought her, then hesitated, remembering the first night, the intensity in his voice as he'd said, 'Please don't insult me with money.'

Suddenly inspired she said, 'Let me cook something for you today. An English meal.'

He regarded her quizzically. 'Her Ladyship can cook?'

'Her Ladyship spent lots of time with the cook because she was the most interesting person in the house,' Dulcie said truthfully. 'And the kindest. She was almost a mother to me after my own died. And she made me learn everything she knew. She thought it might come in handy one day.'

'You mean when the revolution happened and the tumbrels came for you?' he teased.

'Well—' she considered, also teasing '—if I was being carried off to the guillotine I'm not sure that cooking would help me much, but you've got the general idea. I'm sure Sarah pictured little old ladies sitting at the foot of the guillotine, knitting the Maddox family crest into a shroud. What's the matter?' she asked quickly, for he'd dropped a dish on the floor, where it shattered.

'Nothing,' he said hastily, dropping down to clear the pieces.

'You jumped. Was it something I said?'

'Just a feeling of having been here before. Let's go out and get food.'

He took her to the market by the Rialto Bridge where the food stalls stretched in profusion, and he pointed out fruit, vegetables, meat and fish. But he kept himself at a slight distance, and then slid out of sight while she did the buying, which puzzled her even while she appreciated that it gave her the chance to pay for the food without upsetting him.

Afterwards he took the bags from her, refusing to let her carry even one, and they strolled hand in hand.

'This isn't the way we came,' she said, looking around. 'At least, I don't think so, but the streets all look the same.'

'No, we're going a different way. I thought we'd take a detour through St Mark's Square. You haven't seen it yet.'

In St Mark's he took her to an outside table at one of the many cafés and they sat drinking coffee and listening to the music from a four-piece orchestra. Dulcie crumbled up a small cake and fed it to some of the thousands of pigeons that thronged the visitors. The sun hadn't reached its height, making it no more than pleasantly warm, and she leaned back, eyes closed, over-whelmed by a blissful content that she could never re-member feeling before.

She opened her eyes at last, turning to him, smiling, and caught an unguarded expression on his face. His feelings were there, open and defenceless. It was a look not merely of love but almost of adoration, with nothing held back, and it took her breath away. Beneath his smiles and jokes there was *this*?

Then a sound disturbed the pigeons and they rose up with a wild beating of wings, thousands of them, dark-ening the sky, making the air swirl. Her head spun, though whether it was the pigeons or what she had just seen Dulcie was too confused to know.

And when the flight was over and she could see him again she found that he was rising, gathering bags and saying things about leaving. She managed to take a bag in the teeth of his protests, and they wandered away along the waterfront until it was time to turn inland where some of the *calles* were so narrow that she had to walk behind him, but still with her hand clasped in his.

In her mind she could still see his face, transported with joy yet with a strange look of peace, like a man who'd come home and found it a blissful place. She wanted to close her eyes against that look, and she wanted to see it all her life.

'What is it?' he asked, looking back at her. 'You're lagging behind. Are you tired?'

'No, I'm fine.'

'I've kept you out too long.' He slipped an arm about her shoulders. The smile he gave her was almost like those she'd seen before, just friendly. But behind it she could see the shadow of the other look. She slipped an arm about his waist and let him guide her home through streets of gold.

CHAPTER SIX

HE ORDERED her to rest in front of the television while he unpacked the food in his tiny kitchen, and made her a cup of tea. Remembering his strictures about English coffee she was half looking forward to returning the compliment, but the tea was excellent.

She spent the afternoon at work in the kitchen while he helped with the 'menial tasks', fetched and carried and generally did as he was told, but with an air of meekness that belied the wicked glint in his eyes.

Several times she glanced at him, wondering if she would catch the intense look that had seemed to suggest so much, but he had himself under command now. Except that often she sensed him watching her too.

But he had his timetable, she knew that now. While she was officially an invalid he would act like her brother. And after that she would be gone, she remembered with a little ache.

In the early evening they sat down to eat and her meal was a triumph. He approached it cautiously, as if to say that he'd heard about English cooking but was prepared to be kind. He ended up scraping the plate and asking for more.

Afterwards he settled her on the sofa with a glass of *prosecco*, while he prepared the coffee. When he returned she was reclining peacefully on the sofa, admiring the masks on his wall.

'Ah, you're looking at my *zanni*,' he said, setting the cups on a low table.

'*Zanni*?'

'It means clowns. In English you would say they are "zany". Most of the masks there are clowns, Harlequin, Columbine, Pierrot, Pierrette, but there are others too because masks have always been so important in Venice, right back to the thirteenth century. Ladies of the night would offer themselves in a variety of "faces", aristocrats who wanted to indulge themselves anonymously. And sometimes the "ladies of pleasure" and the "great ladies" were the same. There were couples who grew very amorous—then removed the masks and discovered they'd been married for years.'

'All very disreputable,' she said.

'A lot of it was, which was why at different times in Venice's history masks have been banned. They concealed a little too much.'

'You make it sound as though masks were Venice's exclusive preserve, but surely every civilisation has appreciated them.'

He shrugged. 'Certainly, you'll find them in other countries, but it was the Venetians who turned them into an art form.'

'But why? Why you and not the others?' she asked, genuinely interested.

'Perhaps it's something to do with the Venetian character, a certain fluidity.'

'What exactly do you mean, fluidity?'

He grinned. 'Unkind people have called it unscrupulous. We are not a solid, respectable race. How can we be?' He indicated the canal beneath the window. 'We don't live on solid foundations. We travel through streets that move beneath us. Our city is sinking into the lagoon, and it has changed hands so often through the centuries that life itself isn't solid. We live on our wits, and we've learned a certain—let's say—adaptability. And the best way to be adaptable, is to keep a variety of masks available.'

'A variety?'

'One is never enough. Over the centuries we've played so many roles. We've conquered the surrounding areas, and in our turn we've been conquered. Venetians have been both masters and servants, and we know that each is just a role to be played, with its proper mask. Come and look more closely.'

She did so, wondering at the variety of expressions that could be encompassed by a little painted cardboard.

'There are so many. It's incredible.'

'There are as many as there are expressions on the human face, or types of the human heart.'

'Then how is anyone to know who you really are?'

'Because sooner or later each person dons the mask that reveals the truth.'

'But which truth?' she asked quickly, 'when the truth itself is always shifting?'

He made a sudden alert movement. 'You understand. Something told me that you would. Of course, you're right. I can only say that when people's faces are hidden they are free to become their true selves.'

'Then their selves shift also, and they become another self,' she pressed him. It was somehow important.

'Of course they do,' he countered. 'Because people turn into different people all the time. Are you the same person you were last year, last week, the day before you came to Venice?'

'No,' she said slowly. 'Not at all.'

He took down a mask with a very long nose and held it before his face. 'Pantalone, the merchant, greedy for profit.' He changed the mask for one with a shorter nose, but ugly. 'Pulcinella, he's a bit of a thug. In England you call him Mr Punch.' Another change to a broad, plump mask. 'The doctor, spouts yards of pseudo science.'

He whisked another mask off the wall and held it up so that his eyes looked through the slits. It was uncannily like his own face.

'Harlequin,' he said. 'His name derives from Hellecchino, which means "little devil". He's like a rubber ball, always bouncing back: cunning and inventive, but not as clever as he thinks he is, and his mistakes always bring him to the edge of disaster. He wears a multi-coloured costume because his kind friends have given him their old cast-offs to sew together.'

'Poor fellow,' she said laughing. 'And are you like him?'

'What makes you say that?' he asked quickly.

'You say more about him than the others.'

'True. Yes, I suppose I do. I hadn't realised. But that's my point. A man may be Harlequin today and Pantalone tomorrow.'

'You, the greedy merchant?'

'Well, a merchant anyway.' Almost to himself, he added, 'With a pipe and slippers.'

He saw her puzzled look and hastened to change the subject. 'Anyway, it's good to see you laugh. You don't laugh enough.'

'I laugh a lot with you.'

'But not at other times. I wonder why.'

'You don't know what I'm like at other times.'

'I think I do. Something tells me that you're a too-serious person.' He touched her arm lightly. 'You let yourself get burned because you're not used to spending time in the sun. That's not just true of your body. Your mind and spirit aren't used to the sunshine.'

She was about to tell him that this was nonsense, when she was overwhelmed by the sense of its truth. Watching her, he saw the dawning of comprehension in her face.

'Why?' he said. 'It's not just because of the man who broke your heart.'

'No, it's not,' she said slowly.

Her mind was ranging back over a sea of memories. How old had she been when she'd sensed that her family lived on a knife-edge? When had she started doing the sums for her father? He'd never been able to add, perhaps because the truth was too frightening to know.

She'd been fifteen when she'd cried— 'Dad, you can't afford it. You're in so much debt already.'

'Then a little more can't hurt, can it? C'mon sweetie, don't pull a long face.'

A charmer, her father. But a selfish charmer who'd taught her the meaning of fear without ever knowing it. She'd built her own defences, working hard at school, promising herself a brilliant career. But it hadn't happened. She'd ended up without a single exam pass, because a run of ill luck had convinced her father of the need for a long stay abroad. When they returned a year later her chance had passed. So she'd found a job where she could live on her wits, because in the end, they were all she had.

'Tell me,' he begged, his eyes on her face.

'No,' she said quickly. This tale of poverty wasn't for him. 'You're right, I've been too serious.'

'Maybe it's time to put on another mask. Perhaps you

should be Columbine. She's a sensible person, but she's also sharp and witty, and can see life's funny side.'

'Which one is she?'

The mask he took down was painted silver, adorned with sequins and tiny coloured feathers. He fitted it gently over her face and tied the satin ribbons behind.

'What do you think?' she asked, regarding herself in the mirror. Almost all her face was covered, with only her mouth showing.

To her surprise he shook his head. 'No, I don't think so.'

'Why? I like it. Shall I try another?'

'No. Somehow I don't think masks are right for you. Not you. Well, not this one. She's charming, but she's also a deceiver, and you could never be that. Look at the sequins, how they flash and catch a different light every time. That's Columbine, but it's not you.'

She looked at him, wondering if she'd understood his meaning, and feeling uneasy.

The telephone shrilled.

It took her a moment to realise that it was her own mobile phone, ringing from her bag on the floor. She'd been too poorly to think of switching it off. Frantically she dived for it.

'Why haven't you called me?' Roscoe's voice rasped.

'It's been difficult the last few days,' she said in a low, hurried voice. 'I can't talk now.'

'Why not? Are you with him?'

'Yes.'

'Going great then?'

'Yes. Fine. Wonderful. I'll call you later. Goodbye.'

She hung up and switched the phone off. Her heart was beating hard. Roscoe was a terrible intrusion from the outside world, one she would have given anything to avoid. But it was too late now.

'Is everything all right?' he asked.

'Of course. Everything's fine,' she said brightly.

But it wasn't. Nothing was fine.

She realised that she was still wearing the mask and hastily pulled it off.

'Must you really go so soon?' he begged her the next morning. 'Stay another day.'

'No,' Dulcie said hurriedly. 'I can't take up any more of your time. After all, that gondola is your living, and you've already lost several days' work because of me.'

He hesitated, then plunged on. 'Actually, I don't rely on the gondola to live. There's something about myself I have to tell you—'

Suddenly she was filled with dread. It was coming, the pretence of being a Calvani. And only now did she understand how much she'd relied on him not making any such claims. Without that she could still see him as an honest man, and if she lost that belief it would hurt almost as much as saying goodbye to him.

'Dulcie—'

'Not now,' she said quickly. 'I have to get back. I have things to do—' She knew she wasn't making sense but she was desperate to stop him.

'You're right,' he said. 'This isn't the moment. Will you meet me tonight?'

'All right.'

He went down to the water with her and hailed a motor taxi. She kept her eyes on him as it drew away, feeling heavy hearted. Whatever happened tonight the magic that had encompassed her for the last few days was over. If he started spinning tales about being a

Calvani he would confirm her worst fears. If not, he was an honest man, and belonged to Jenny.

Casting her mind back over the last few days she was unable to recall anything that could be read as the behaviour of a lover. Even that searing moment in the square might have been her imagination, although her heart told her it wasn't. Apart from that there had been the odd semi-flirtatious remark. If she hadn't become ill and dumped herself on him, it would all have been over after the day on the beach.

And if her own heart had somehow become entangled she could only blame herself for being unprofessional, and sort it out as best she could. Alone. Away from here. One way or another, tonight would mark the end.

As she entered the Empress Suite her phone was already ringing.

'It took me time enough to get through to you,' Roscoe grumbled.

'I'm sorry, Mr Harrison, I've been very occupied.'

'With this Fede character?'

'Yes.'

'Has he given you his Calvani story?'

'Not exactly—'

'Aha! You mean he's laying the ground. That's how he dazzled Jenny. Now, you check that out. This Calvani character must have an heir. Find him. See what he looks like. Call me back when you've done that.'

He hung up.

Dulcie glared at the dead phone, at the world in general. 'So how am I going to—'

And then she heard a voice speaking far off in her memory.

'Such a handsome man, my dear. We were all madly in love with him, and he loved all of us.'

Lady Harriet Maddox, her grandfather's sister, and a dazzling beauty in her day. She'd scorched her way around Europe, flirting outrageously and leaving a trail of broken hearts, before marrying a man with no title but a large bank balance, which she'd proceeded to gamble away.

She was always discreet about her indiscreet past, but there was one man whose memory could bring a warm light to her eyes—if only Dulcie could recall his name. Harriet had travelled in Italy and probably met Count Calvani among many others, but was he the one she'd called 'the latter-day Casanova'?

'He could have been,' Dulcie mused, 'And that's all I need. Right. To work.'

It took three hours to get her appearance exactly right, but when she left the hotel she was satisfied. Her attire was costly and elegant without being over-the-top, and she looked every inch *Lady* Dulcie.

A water taxi took her to the Palazzo Calvani, and a steward came to meet her.

'Is Count Calvani at home?' she asked.

'I am not quite sure, *signorina*,' the man replied. 'If I could have your name—?'

'I am Lady—' she stopped, suddenly swept by the wild gambling instinct that bedevilled her family '—please tell him that Lady Harriet Maddox is here.'

He bowed and retired, leaving Dulcie wondering if she'd gone quite mad.

She didn't have to wait long to find out. There was a hasty step on the marble floor, a voice calling, '*Carissima*,' and she turned to see an elderly man standing there, his look of pleasure dissolving into bafflement. Even through his lines and white hair she could see the remains of remarkable good looks.

'Forgive me,' she said quickly, advancing with her hands outstretched. 'I gave you the name of my great-aunt in the hope that you would remember it as well as she remembered you.'

He stretched out his own hands and clasped hers warmly. '*Bellisima Harriet*,' he said. 'How well I remember her! And how kind of you to visit me.'

He kissed her on both cheeks and looked warmly into her eyes. Although he must have been at least seventy, his charm was still dazzling and Dulcie felt its full effect. But she was unable to detect the slightest resemblance to the man with whom she'd spent the last few days.

'So you are not Lady Harriet?' he asked. 'You are—?''

'I am Lady Dulcie.'

The count commanded refreshment to be served on the terrace, and led her out there with her hand tucked in his arm, and his own other hand holding it. He handed her to a seat with an air of old-world gallantry, only releasing her hand at the very last moment.

'I'm an old man,' he said sadly, 'and it's so rare for me to have the pleasure of a beautiful woman on my arm. You'll forgive me if I make the most of it?'

He was a shameless fraud, she thought, entertained by his slightly theatrical air. But it was easy to imagine him as 'the latter-day Casanova'.

Over coffee and cakes he demanded to know all about her family in England.

'Dear Harriet told me about Maddox Court where she grew up,' he recalled, 'and about her brother William—'

'My grandfather.'

'Still alive I hope?'

'No, he died fifteen years ago.'

'Then it is your father who is now the earl?'

'Yes. But tell me about your family, your wife and children.'

'Alas,' he said mournfully, 'I'm just a lonely old bachelor, with no wife or children to comfort my old age.'

And I'm the Queen of the May, she thought, amused. *You're just like my Uncle Joe who was fighting paternity suits in his sixties.*

Aloud she said, 'You mean you live in this great place, all alone?'

'Well, there are servants,' he said with a sigh. 'But what are servants when a man is lonely? I have a nephew who will one day be the count. He's a good boy, but not a comfort to me as a son would be.'

'A nephew?' she echoed, speaking lightly as though this was a matter of total indifference to her.

'Three actually. The other two live in different parts of the country, but they're visiting me now, and I should so like it if you would come to dinner with us this evening, and meet all three of them.'

'That would be lovely.'

'And please bring whoever is in Venice with you. Your husband perhaps?'

'I have no husband, and I'm here alone.'

'You must seek a husband in Venice,' he said at once. 'We make the best husbands.'

'But how do you know?' she teased him, 'if you've never tried being one.'

He laughed heartily. '*Bravissima*. A lady of wit. Now I look forward to this evening even more. My boat will call for you at eight o'clock.' He rose and took her hand again, leading her out to the landing stage where the gleaming white Calvani boat was waiting to take her back to the hotel.

He stood watching until the boat was out of sight. Then he returned to the terrace to finish the wine. Leo and Marco found him there, looking pleased with himself.

'What mischief are you up to?' Leo demanded at once.

'Merely protecting my family line,' Francesco said with relish. 'I've introduced suitable women to Guido until I've grown exhausted doing it. But never let it be said I've shirked my duty. I thought there was nobody else left, but she'll do very well.'

'She? Who?' they both wanted to know.

'A lady of birth and breeding, and moreover, related to an old flame of my own.'

Leo began to protest, 'But half the women in Europe are related to your—'

'Silence. Show some respect. She's coming to dinner tonight, and he'll meet her.'

'But he won't be here,' Marco observed. 'He called to say he won't be home tonight.'

'Whatever engagement he has, he will break it.'

'Uncle, there's something you should—'

'Enough. I expect you all to present yourself for dinner, properly attired out of respect for our guest. Now I shall take a nap, as I wish to be at my best tonight.'

Never had paperwork seemed more boring than the mountain of it that confronted Guido when he returned to work after playing hookey to be with Dulcie. He ploughed through it grimly, comforting himself with the thought of the evening ahead, when he would see her again.

He would take her out to a restaurant a safe distance from Venice where he could pass unrecognised, although soon that would cease to matter, because he would tell her the truth about himself.

He wondered if she would blame him for his innocent deception. Surely not, when once he'd poured out his heart to her? While she was ill and dependent on him he'd restrained himself, carefully editing out all passion, and even love. He could recall a few moments when his resolution had frayed, but he'd pulled himself back into line. No words had been spoken, but he knew they had understood each other perfectly. She *must* love him as he loved her. It was impossible that he should be mistaken about her.

Lost in his happy dream he didn't at first hear the ring of his mobile phone and had to snatch it up hastily.

'Where the devil are you?' his uncle barked.

'In my office, working hard,' Guido said with a conscious attempt to sound virtuous.

It was wasted. 'You've got time for all those knick-knacks you call a business, and time to fool around, but no time for your old uncle.'

'That's not fair—'

'I've hardly seen you this last week.'

'You've had Leo and Marco, you didn't need me.'

'Well, I need you tonight. We're having a dinner party for a very special guest.'

'Uncle please, not tonight, I've made plans—'

'Nonsense, of course you haven't. It's all arranged. A beautiful lady is coming to dinner, and she's looking forward to meeting you.'

Guido groaned. Another prospective wife. Would his uncle never learn? And how could he sit through this evening knowing that his heart had already chosen his future wife.

'Uncle, let me explain—'

Francesco's voice grew mournful. 'There's no need to explain. I'm an old man and I ask for very little. If even that little is too much, well, I suppose I understand.'

Guido ground his teeth as he always did when Francesco went into 'forlorn mode', because he knew he was going to give in. He was fond of his uncle and couldn't bear to hurt him. His blissful evening began to recede.

'All right, I'll try to make it,' he said.

'You're a good boy. I don't want to be a trouble. Of course when a man gets to my age he always *is* a trouble—'

'Uncle will you cut it out?' Guido yelled. 'I'll be there, I swear it.'

'All evening?'

'All evening.'

'In a dinner jacket?'

'In a dinner jacket.'

'I knew you wouldn't let me down. Don't be late.' He hung up.

Guido drew a long breath. Why did life have to be so complicated? And how was he going to explain to Dulcie that he was standing her up to meet a woman his uncle wanted him to marry. No, he hastily decided against that. Whatever excuse he found, the truth was out of the question. Another mask, he thought despondently. Never mind. Soon all that would be over.

CHAPTER SEVEN

THE evening dress Dulcie chose was a stunning, ice-blue floral Jacquard that left her arms and shoulders bare. Dainty diamond studs winked in her ears and a diamond pendant hung about her throat. Now that she'd become an attractive pale-biscuit colour the effect was delightful.

She felt guilty, decking herself for an evening's entertainment when she should be calling Fede to say she must break their date that evening. But she kept putting it off, not sure what the right words might be. How could she possibly explain to him that she was standing him up to go to dinner with the Calvanis to see if he was one of them? No, whatever excuse she found, the truth was out of the question.

There was no putting it off any longer. She reached for the phone, but it rang before she could touch it.

'*Dulcie, cara.*'

'Hello,' she said, flooded with delight before she could get her defensive caution into position.

'I've been trying to find the courage to call you. You're going to be annoyed with me. I can't make it tonight, but it really isn't my fault.'

'You can't make it?' she echoed. She felt ridiculously disappointed, almost as though she hadn't been about to do the same thing herself.

'Something's come up. I can't get out of it.'

'Can't you tell me what it is?'

In the brief silence she sensed his unease. 'It's—complicated,' he said at last. 'I don't want to talk about it over the phone. You're not cross with me, are you?'

'Of course not,' she said, not entirely truthfully. 'It's just that I was looking forward to seeing you.'

'And I you. I'll call you tomorrow. *Ciao*.'

So that was that, she thought as she hung up. He'd made it easy for her. She should be glad. And she would be glad, just as soon as she'd silenced the little voice that said something was wrong. He couldn't tell her the real reason for his defection, and he hadn't worked out a convincing excuse.

Or perhaps he didn't think her worth a convincing excuse. He wouldn't call her tomorrow after all. This was the brush-off.

Stop being absurd, she told herself. He only did what you were planning to do. What's the difference?

But there was a difference, and a small dark shadow hovered over the evening ahead.

It should have been unalloyed pleasure. She was collected by a motor boat bearing the Calvani arms, and driven slowly along the Grand Canal just as the sun was sliding down the sky and turning the water to red. All around her Venice was settling in for the evening. Lights came on along the waterfront, bars and cafés buzzed with life, some gondoliers drifted home after a hard day while others emerged to start work on the late shift.

And then they were passing under the Rialto Bridge and there was the Palazzo Calvani, the whole great building ablaze with light. For a moment Dulcie had a glimpse of how it must have looked in its glory days, when Venice ruled the Adriatic, and palaces were alive with powerful men and glamorous women. It was a dream, of course. Reality had never been like that. But, looking at the gorgeous building, she could almost believe it.

And there was the count, resplendent in dinner jacket and snowy white shirt, looking as though he'd stepped out of that other age. Now she was glad that she'd dressed up in her gladdest of glad rags, and wouldn't feel out of place.

As the boat drew up at the landing stage he was there to assist her out, bowing low over her hand and declaring, 'You honour my house.'

Behind him were two fine-looking young men, both apparently in their early thirties. Neither looked remotely like the man she was investigating.

'My nephews, Marco and Leo.' Both young men greeted her with a flourish. 'You are very fortunate to find them here. Leo lives in Tuscany and Marco in Rome, but they came to see me when I became ill. My other nephew, Guido, lives with me all the time. He'll be here soon.'

So Guido was the one she needed to see, Dulcie thought. Alive to every nuance, she hadn't missed the way Leo and Marco had studied her without seeming to, and exchanged glances. They were gallantry itself, but the count outdid them both, brushing them aside to lead her out onto the terrace where he had ordered drinks.

From here the view was dazzling, not just the Grand Canal but the Rialto Bridge, bathed in floodlight. Dulcie looked a long time, awestruck by so much beauty.

'I see you understand my city,' the count said, smiling. 'You pay it the compliment of silence.'

She nodded. 'Words would only spoil it.'

'I linger here every night. It is best enjoyed alone

or—' he bowed '—with charming company. But I neglect your comfort. What will you drink?'

She accepted a wine that he recommended and returned to studying the view. Although the balcony looked out over the water she could see grounds to either side of it, ending in trees and shadows.

Then it seemed that one of the shadows moved, but the impression vanished in an instant.

'Is something the matter?' Francesco asked.

'No, I just thought I saw someone move down there. I must have been mistaken.'

They looked down into the gardens, but all was still and silent.

A last-minute phone call from an important customer meant that Guido was later reaching the palace than he'd meant to be, and arrived in jeans and sweater. Knowing this would incur his uncle's censure he slipped into the garden by a small gate to which only the initiated had the key, and moved quietly through the growing shadows. With luck he could reach his own room and change quickly into what Francesco called 'the proper attire' and what he called 'stuffed shirt.'

Through the trees he could discern the terrace overlooking the water, where the count would be entertaining their guest to pre-dinner drinks. Yes, he could see him now, also Leo and Marco, but the lady was still obscure. He could just make out that she was wearing an ice-blue dress, but not her face. It would be useful to discover more of her and know the worst that awaited him this evening. As he emerged from the trees he hugged the wall, flattening himself against it as he edged nearer the terrace.

There was a flash of pale blue as she turned to look outwards, and suddenly he saw her face clearly.

For a split second he froze with shock. Then he moved fast. It was too late to return to the trees. The only concealment lay directly under the terrace. A swift dash, and he just made it.

'Is something the matter?' he heard his uncle ask over his head.

Then Dulcie's voice. 'No, I just thought I saw someone move down there. I must have been mistaken.'

Guido's brow was damp. This couldn't be happening to him! What had become of his famous luck that had protected him through a thousand scrapes? Creditors— he'd paid them all eventually, but his early days in business had involved much tap-dancing—ladies with marriage in their eyes, husbands with shotguns, he'd side-stepped them all with wit and charm.

But where was his guardian angel now? Absent without leave, that was where. Another few minutes and he'd have walked in on Dulcie and his family, to be introduced in his true identity. It was no use saying that he'd meant to tell her soon anyway. He hadn't meant it like this.

Muffled noises from above, Leo and Marco voices, then his uncle's, irritated. 'What's happened to the fellow? My apologies for my nephew's tardiness. Call him one of you and ask when he'll be here.'

Guido moved fast to switch off his mobile before it could ring and reveal his location. He mopped his brow.

Marco spoke. 'His phone is off.'

'No matter,' Francesco declared. 'He'll be here at any moment.'

Not on your life! Guido thought desperately.

'I do hope so.' That was Dulcie. 'Because I'm really looking forward to meeting your third nephew, count…'

Their voices faded.

With calamity staring him in the face, Guido thought fast. Nobody had seen him. He could still get away. His mind was racing. Slip out the way he'd come in, call his uncle to apologise for the unexpected crisis that would prevent him having the pleasure of joining them tonight. Then tap-dance like mad.

He was about to begin his journey back through the garden when a truly appalling thought turned his bones to jelly.

He knew his uncle's routine with new guests. It never varied. Dinner, then a tour of the palace, finishing in his study. There he would produce his photo albums and display family pictures in which Guido would feature prominently.

He groaned aloud, wondering what he'd ever done to deserve this. But the list was too long to contemplate. At all costs Dulcie mustn't be allowed to see those pictures.

Backing against the wall he encountered a small door that he knew was never used. If he could get through he would be in a passage that led past the kitchen to the rear of the house and from there it was just a step to his uncle's study.

As he'd expected, the door was locked, but the wood was so old that a thump from a stone splintered it easily. The passage was pitch-black and he had to grope his way along, stumbling on the uneven floor, and once actually falling. He picked himself up, sensing that he was covered in dirt, but he had no time to worry about that. There was a light up ahead. The kitchen would be busy tonight and he must get past the door without being seen.

It took five minutes anxiously waiting for the right chance to present itself, and then he had to take a flying leap. Then he was in a narrow corridor, at the end of which was a secret door. By pressing the right knob he could make a section of the wall revolve, and bring himself into the study. The device had been installed in the seventeenth century by a count who feared assassination. Guido felt assassination might be a merciful end compared with what faced him if he couldn't get those photo albums.

His luck held. The study was empty and dark. The less light the better, so he put on just one small lamp and went to the desk drawer where his uncle kept the key to the glass-covered bookcase where the albums were kept. Moving quietly he knelt down and began to turn the key in the lock.

'Freeze!'

The voice came from behind him. He took a deep breath, hoping against hope that the cold metal he could feel against his ear wasn't what he thought it was.

'Stand up and turn around slowly with your hands up.'

He did so and found his worst fears realised as he stared down the length of a double-barrelled shotgun.

As the minutes ticked past with no sign of the missing heir the count's smile became glassy, until at last he announced that dinner could wait no longer. The four of them entered the vast, ornate dining room where Dulcie was escorted to the place of honour.

Francesco reminisced about Lady Harriet, with many anecdotes which Dulcie was sure he'd either invented or transposed from other ladies. Now and then he reverted to the bachelor theme.

'I keep hoping my nephews will marry and comfort me in my old age,' he mourned. 'But they're all stubborn and selfish.'

'Very selfish,' Leo agreed with a grin. 'We have this funny idea of marrying to suit ourselves rather than "serving the blood line".'

'I'm afraid we're all lonely bachelors in this family,' Francesco sighed.

'And your nephew Guido,' Dulcie asked. 'Is he a lonely bachelor?'

'Well, he's certainly a bachelor,' Marco observed.

His uncle gave him a look that would have cowed an easily frightened man.

'I must apologise to our guest for Guido's tardiness,' Francesco announced. 'But I have no doubt he will be here very soon.'

He raised his voice on the last words, as if sending a message to the delinquent to remind him of his duty. But no erring nephew materialised, and the three Calvanis exchanged glances, wondering where he could possibly be.

'Liza, please put that thing away,' Guido begged nervously. 'Here, let me take it.' He relieved the housekeeper of the shotgun and assisted her to a chair.

'It's not loaded,' she said faintly. 'I thought you were a burglar. *Maria vergine*! I might have killed you.'

'Not with an unloaded gun,' he pointed out. 'Although you nearly gave me a heart attack. And if I'd been a burglar what were you thinking of to tackle me like that? You've been watching too many gangster movies.'

'Yes,' she said with a sigh. 'I just thought a little excitement would be nice.'

'A little ex—? You need a restorative. Where does my uncle keep his best brandy? Here you are.' He handed her a glass, saying kindly, 'This will make you feel better. And if you want excitement, you can help me out of a spot I'm in. I need to get rid of these,' he indicated the albums. 'Just for a few hours.'

'But he always shows them to his guests,' Liza declared.

'I know, that's why I've got to make them vanish. I can't explain but a lot depends on it. In fact, everything depends on it. Liza, my whole future life is in your hands, my marriage, my children, my children's children, the whole Calvani blood line for the next hundred years. If you don't help me it's all finished. You wouldn't want that on your conscience, would you?'

'You're up to something.'

'Have you ever known me when I wasn't?'

'No. But you won't manage it this way. If he finds them missing he'll call the police.'

Guido tore his hair. 'Then what can I do?'

'Leave it to me, *signore*.'

Count Francesco was at his best when talking about the past glories of Venice, and although Dulcie recognised that it was a performance she still fell under its spell.

'Everyone came here for carnival,' he said expansively. 'It was a time for pleasure. You know, of course, why it's called carnival?'

'I'm afraid I don't,' she said. This was clearly the reply expected.

'It comes from *carne*, meaning flesh. Knowing that it would soon be Lent, a time of austerity, people rev-

elled in the pleasures of the flesh, preferably from behind the safety of a mask. The orgies continued right
up until Shrove Tuesday and stopped on the stroke of
midnight.'

'So that's why Carnival is in February,' Dulcie said.

'The February carnival is a modern revival, designed
to attract tourists during the winter. But who can make
merry in the cold? I mark carnival in my own way, with
a masked ball in summer. This year's ball will take
place next Wednesday, and I hope you will honour me
by attending.'

'Well, I'm not quite certain if I'll still be here next
week,' she murmured.

'Oh, but you must,' he said earnestly, 'if only to spare
my blushes about tonight. I don't know how to apologise for Guido's reprehensible behaviour in not turning
up. I shall inform him of my displeasure.'

'But you've already done that,' Dulcie smiled, 'when
he telephoned to apologise, half an hour ago. I'm disappointed not to have met him, but since this was a
last-minute arrangement it must have been difficult for
him.'

'You are most gracious to say so. But next week he
will make his apologies in person.'

There was no turning him from this idea, so Dulcie
murmured something vague and polite, and gave herself
up to the enjoyment of the palazzo. When the guided
tour was at an end they all drank brandy and coffee,
and then the three men accompanied her to the landing
stage where the boat was waiting. Leo and Marco would
have taken her hand but the Count waved them away
with an imperious gesture.

'To assist a beautiful lady is *my* privilege,' he said
with old-world courtesy. '*Buona notte, signorina*. I'm

sorry the evening wasn't more satisfactory. I'd hoped to show you my photo albums. I can't understand how my housekeeper came to lose the key. It's not like her to make such a mistake.'

'I shall look forward to seeing them another time,' Dulcie said.

'Yes, when you come to the masked ball. Next Wednesday. Don't forget. And Guido will be there.'

'I'm really looking forward to meeting him.'

The boatman settled her comfortably, and a moment later they were on their way down the Grand Canal. The Calvanis waved until she was out of sight.

'She's perfect,' the count said.

'Just the same uncle, you're barking up the wrong tree,' Leo observed.

'What do you mean?'

'Guido's romancing a new woman,' Marco said. 'It's the talk of Venice that he's spent all this last week with her, even taking days off work. When does Guido ever neglect his business? I tell you uncle, it's serious.'

'Why the devil didn't you tell me this before?'

'It seemed safer to get the evening over first,' Leo said.

'Is anything known about this woman?' Francesco demanded, in alarm.

'Only that he met her while he was rowing.'

Francesco snorted. 'A tourist, looking for a holiday romance, ready to disport herself with the first gondolier she meets. Lady Dulcie is a woman of *class*, and he neglects her for a floozie! Is he crazy?'

'He's a Calvani,' Leo observed.

The moon was high in the sky as Dulcie sat watching the Grand Canal drift by her. Venice was gently closing down for the night. The little waterside bars were emptying, and lights were going off. Now and then she could see a couple wandering by the water, arms entwined, then vanish into a *calle*, swallowed up by darkness the moment before their lips touched. A few gondolas were still drifting past, seeming to move from shadow to shadow. Every one of them seemed to contain lovers embracing, oblivious to the gondolier who grinned and looked over their heads. He'd seen so many lovers before.

But as far as Dulcie could see none of them was the man she was seeking, and she sighed, wondering what he was doing right now, what had kept him from her tonight, and how soon must she say goodbye to him? Perhaps he would call to say how much he'd missed her, and must see her. There might even be a message for her in the hotel.

She controlled her impatience, hurrying to the suite and fumbling with the key in her eagerness. But when she called the desk there were no messages. Dispiritedly she sat and stared at the telephone.

Suddenly she realised that she wasn't alone. There was a noise from the second bedroom, and the next moment the door opened.

'Jenny!' Dulcie exclaimed.

'Hello!' The young girl threw her arms about Dulcie in an eager greeting. 'It's so lovely to see you.'

'But what are you—I mean, I didn't know you were coming.'

'Dad said he thought we might enjoy a little vacation together. That's why he booked this suite, so that there'd be room for both of us.'

'Did he say why I was here?'

'Only that you were doing some market research for him. I know he's always expanding his business.'

It didn't seem to occur to Jenny to be suspicious, but then, Dulcie realised, she knew nothing about her work, and so there was no reason for her to think the worst. Yet Dulcie had a terrible feeling that things were going badly wrong.

'You look gorgeous,' Jenny said, surveying the evening dress. 'Oh, Dulcie, is it a man?'

'I've had dinner with three men, and none of them the one I wanted,' she said distractedly. 'Now I don't know whether I'm coming or going.'

'Three is too many,' Jenny said wisely. 'One is better, if it's the one you want. Oh, Dulcie, I'm so blissfully, blissfully happy. It was wonderful to see him again.'

Dulcie tensed. 'What was that?'

'When I arrived I called Fede straight away, from the airport, and he came to collect me, and we kissed and kissed. He said he'd missed me so much and then—'

'Wait a minute,' Dulcie said, trying to ignore the cold hand that clutched at her stomach. 'You've been with Fede this evening?'

'But of course. Who else? He didn't think he could make it at first—'

'But no doubt he changed his arrangements,' Dulcie said, her eyes kindling.

'I suppose so. I didn't ask. What does anything matter beside the fact that we're together?'

So that was where he'd been tonight, Dulcie seethed inwardly. He was playing fast and loose with the pair of them. And to think she'd been trying to see the best in him!

'Where are you going?' Jenny called as Dulcie strode to the door.

'Anywhere!' she flung over her shoulder.

As soon as she was out of the hotel she plunged into the maze of little dark streets. She didn't look where she was going. She didn't care. Jenny's innocent words had ripped the lid off the pretence that had sustained her for days. She'd read herself lectures about being on her guard, being professional, never quite trusting him. And all the time she'd been slipping under the oldest spell in the world.

It was dark in the *calles*. With only one light halfway along each one it was easy to stay out of sight, so she flattened herself against a wall, and stayed there as couples drifted past in the gloom, heard rather than seen, their voices low and full of emotion, fading into silence.

The city of lovers…

And she'd tumbled into its trap like a green girl who knew no better. Forewarned, forearmed, she'd still tumbled giddily into love while kidding herself that she was safe. Fool! Fool!

Serve me right, she thought defiantly. I'll know better next time.

But there couldn't be a next time, not quite like this. There might be other relationships, but never again would she feel the happiness and safety that had been like a blessing while he tended her. All an illusion. That was what hurt the most.

She moved further into the shadows, wondering if she would ever see a way out.

From his vantage point at a little bar across the Grand Canal Guido was able to watch Dulcie's departure. He leaned his arms on a rail as she went past in the boat, thinking how tragic it was to be so near and yet so far.

He allowed half an hour for safety before returning

home, even managing to whistle as he entered, only slightly out of tune.

So far, so good, but had his cover been blown? Liza had promised to 'lose' the key to the cabinet where the albums were housed, but suppose his uncle had a spare and had managed to take out the family snaps? There would be his face for Dulcie to recognise. Then she would have said—and Uncle Francesco would have replied—and there would have been a row—Leo and Marco would have roared with laughter—and now here he was heading for another row.

He considered emigrating. A snake-infested swamp might be nice. Or anywhere that was a long way away.

'There you are, you villain!'

The voice echoed down the long marble hall, followed by Francesco with a face like thunder, then Leo and Marco, determined not to miss the fun.

'Uncle, I can explain—' That was safely vague when you weren't quite sure what you were supposed to be explaining.

'Certainly you should explain, not to me but to that charming young lady. The way you've treated her is abominable.'

'That—depends on how you look at it,' Guido said, carefully feeling his way.

'That any nephew of mine—' Francesco broke off, fulminating, leaving Guido as much in the dark as ever. 'Get yourself in here.' He indicated his study which struck Guido as ominous.

The study was unrevealing. Wine glasses stood about, suggesting that everyone had spent some time in here, but the count took up his position in front of the cabinet, hiding the contents.

'She's a *lady*, do you realise that?' the count boomed.

'And you've behaved as though she were no more than—well, I don't know what to say!'

I wish you'd say a lot more, Guido thought. *Then I might get a clue.*

'She was charming about it,' Francesco went on. 'Oh, yes! Breeding tells, although she probably wants to hang you from the highest lamppost after what happened tonight.'

'What—exactly—happened tonight?' Guido asked.

'You ask me that?'

'Yes, I did actually. And you two—' Guido whirled on Leo and Marco '—can stop grinning or I'll have your hides.'

Had she seen the pictures or hadn't she? If he didn't find out soon he'd have a nervous breakdown.

'*Scusi signori.*' Liza had glided in like a ghost and began gathering wine glasses. Moving directly in front of Guido she gave him a brief thumbs up sign. He relaxed, but only a little.

'I'm sorry about tonight but something came up,' he said. 'And if, as you say, she was charming about it—'

'Lady Dulcie,' Francesco said with awful dignity, 'was naturally very disappointed not to have met you. She particularly asked me to tell you that.'

'Did she?'

'I also assured her that you would be at the masked ball, and she said how much she looked forward to meeting you there. She stressed that this meeting meant a great deal to her.'

In his eagerness to bring Dulcie and Guido together the count was gilding the lily, giving Dulcie's polite words a meaning they were never meant to bear. To Guido, his nerves already jangling, they sounded ominous. Clearly Dulcie had discovered the truth, but in-

stead of denouncing him she was keeping her wrath for
their next meeting. This was her message to announce
the approach of doom.

'Er—I think perhaps—excuse me, Uncle, something
else has come up.'

He got out as fast as he could.

CHAPTER EIGHT

It was a mile to the Vittorio if you knew the backstreets well. Guido dodged and dived, taking a short cut that led through the house of a friend called Enrico, pilfered a glass of Enrico's wine and a kiss from Enrico's wife, before vanishing, calling his thanks over his shoulder.

A few minutes short of the hotel he found himself beside a small canal. Hurrying along, he nearly collided with a woman coming the other way.

'I'm so sorry—*Dulcie*! I—'

But her face told him the worst, and her words confirmed it.

'You are the lowest of the low,' she flung at him.

'If I could just explain—'

'What is there to explain? Only that you're a devious rat, and that I know already.'

'*Dio mio*! You did see them.'

'See what?'

He tore his hair. 'I wouldn't have had this happen for the world—'

'Then why do it? Oh, of course, you meant being found out. I suppose you thought I'd never discover the truth about you—'

'I was going to tell you myself, I swear I was.'

'And that was going to make it all right?'

'Of course not but—if I could make you understand how it came about. It was an accident. I know I should have told you everything from the start, but does it really matter so much. Just one tiny little deception—'

'*One tiny little*—? I don't believe you said that. I should have known when you stood me up tonight, giving a very fishy excuse, in fact no excuse at all. Something came up! Surely you could have managed something better than that?'

'I couldn't think of anything,' he admitted. 'But now you know, can't we start again?'

'Am I hearing things? Even you couldn't be so devious and unscrupulous—'

'*Cara*, please, I know I don't measure up to your high standards, but I will. I swear I will. Did I really do something so terrible?'

'If you have to ask that you wouldn't understand the answer. There's no point in talking any more. Goodnight, and goodbye.'

'You mustn't leave now. Stay and listen to me.' In his eagerness he took hold of her shoulders.

'I don't want to stay, and please let go of me.'

'I can't just let you go.'

'You can't do anything else. Take your hands off me.'

'Just another few minutes,' he begged.

'What kind of fool do you take me for? Let go.'

She tried to thrust her way past him, but he dropped his hands to her waist and drew her close.

'I'll let go,' he said firmly, 'when I've explained *this*.'

She tried to escape. This kind of 'explanation' was too dangerous. But his lips were unexpectedly fierce on hers. He was kissing her like a man whose life depended on it, as if he feared he might never get the chance again, and there was a forcefulness in his lips and his arms that thrilled her even while she fought to stay aloof.

She could feel the treacherous excitement creeping

through her. Her heart and sensations cared nothing for the warnings of her head. They wanted him, wanted what was happening now, wanted it to continue…

'Let me go,' she gasped, managing to free her mouth.

'I can't do that,' he said, also gasping. 'I daren't in case I never find you again. I won't risk that.'

'You've already lost me. I was never yours in the first place—'

He silenced her in the only way possible. It wasn't fair, she thought wildly. She'd fought this temptation since the moment she'd met him, and now he was forcing her to feel it when he'd just come from Jenny.

The thought of Jenny gave her the courage she craved. Putting out all her strength she managed to free herself. He took a step back, fighting to keep his balance while she fended him off. Neither of them realised they were standing so close to the water until he toppled in with a yell and an almighty splash.

Venetians live in and out of the water from their earliest years, and for one of them to fall into a canal is no big deal, except for the pollution. Guido kept his mouth firmly closed until he broke the surface, then rubbed his eyes and looked around for steps. But there were none in sight, and since it was low tide the stone bank was too high for him to climb out.

He reached up his hand, calling, 'Help me out, *cara*.'

Dulcie had dropped to one knee and was regarding him anxiously. 'Are you hurt?'

'No, but I'm wet. Help me out.'

'Why? You can swim!'

'Sure, I'm a great swimmer—'

'Good. Then swim home.'

She rose to her feet and turned away.

'*Cara*!'

Before his horrified eyes she vanished into the darkness, leaving him bobbing in the water.

It took another hour's walking before Dulcie had talked herself back into a sensible frame of mind. So he was a treacherous creep. She'd always known that. It was what she'd come here to prove. Now she'd done so, earned her fee, and she was very happy. The feel of his lips was still on hers, telling her she was lying to herself, but she would be strong-minded about it.

In this mood she returned to the Empress Suite, having made up her mind to warn Jenny about him. She'd waited too long already. Firmly she knocked on Jenny's bedroom door.

'I need to talk to you,' she called.

Jenny's voice came from inside. 'Can't it wait until morning?'

'No, it's important.'

Strange muffled sounds reached her, and a grunt that had a masculine tone. Full of foreboding, Dulcie opened the door.

The room was in darkness, but in the silver light from the window she could see the huge double bed. On one side of it was Jenny, hastily clutching the sheet to her. On the other side was a suspicious bump.

Dulcie stared at that bump, disbelief warring with anger and misery. He'd not only played her false, but he'd rushed straight back here after their encounter by the canal.

'This really isn't a good time,' Jenny protested.

'I think it's a great time to expose a man as a cheat and a liar,' Dulcie said firmly, making for the far side of the bed and grabbing the sheet.

A pair of hands grabbed it back. She yanked. He

yanked. But she yanked harder, wrenching the bed-clothes right back to reveal the naked man beneath.

She had never seen him before in her life.

'This is Fede,' Jenny said in a small voice.

'*This*?' Dulcie stared. 'He's not Fede.'

'Yes I am,' the young man declared, trying to haul the sheet back and cover his embarrassment. Having succeeded, he politely offered her his hand. 'I am Federico Lucci. How do you do?'

'Very badly,' Dulcie said in a dazed voice. 'In fact I think I'm going slightly crazy. If you're Fede, who did I just throw into the canal?'

They both stared at her.

Dulcie turned away suddenly and went to stand in the window, looking out. She was beyond thought, and almost beyond feeling. Buried deep in her turmoil was something that might yet turn out to be happiness. It was too soon to say.

The other two seized the chance to get out of bed and put some clothes on. When she looked back Fede had switched on the light, and now things began to be clearer—and more confused.

In the picture Roscoe had shown her there had been two men, one playing the mandolin and singing to Jenny. Naturally she'd assumed this was Fede. The other man, sitting just behind them, was little more than a baby-faced boy. It had never occurred to her—or to Roscoe, she was sure—that he might be Fede.

Yet it seemed that he was.

Then who—?

It was Jenny who recovered her composure first. 'What do you mean?' she asked. 'Why have you been going about throwing people into canals?'

'Because he asked for it,' Dulcie said wildly. 'Because he—oh, no, he couldn't have.'

'Perhaps you have been too much in the sun?' Fede suggested kindly.

'Yes I was,' Dulcie admitted. 'I was very poorly and he looked after me. But I thought he was you—he was wearing your shirt—at least, it had your name on it—and rowing a gondola—'

'It sounds like Guido,' he said.

The name stunned her. She'd been hearing about Guido all evening. 'Guido who?'

'Guido Calvani. He's been my friend since we were at school. One day he'll be a count, but what he really likes best is rowing my gondola. So I let him borrow it, but he has to pretend to be me because he doesn't have a licence.'

Dulcie forced her limbs to unfreeze long enough to go to her purse and take out the photograph.

'Is that him? The one playing the mandolin?'

'That's Guido,' Jenny said. 'He's been a good friend to Fede and me. When I first came to Venice he used to do Fede's stints on the gondola so that we could be together.'

'We knew we were being followed,' Fede put in, 'so sometimes we'd all go out together, to confuse her Poppa.'

'You confused him all right,' Dulcie said, sitting down suddenly.

Jenny gave Dulcie a puzzled look. 'But how do you come to have this picture?'

'Your father gave it to me,' Dulcie said reluctantly. 'As you suspected, he had you followed when you were last here. He thought Fede was—well—'

'A fortune hunter,' Fede supplied wryly.

'I'm afraid so, but it's worse. He seems to have got you totally muddled with Guido, and thinks you claimed to be heir to a title.'

'That's what Guido was telling me when that picture was taken,' Jenny remembered.

'Your father's spy must have been near enough to hear that,' Dulcie said, 'but not near enough to get the story straight. He obviously just overheard bits. Did he take this picture?'

'No, it was taken by one of the street photographers to sell to tourists,' Fede said. 'I know because I bought a copy off him, and one seems to have reached the count, Guido's uncle, and he's been giving him a hard time about it ever since. Signor Harrison's spy must have bought one too, and carried back a garbled version of what he'd overheard.'

Jenny was looking at Dulcie curiously. 'But why did Dad give this picture to you?'

'Can't you guess?' Dulcie said bitterly. 'I was sent here to find Fede and set him up.'

'How?'

'Pretend to be rich, divert his attention from you. Find out if he really was an aristocrat, as he's supposed to have claimed.'

'But I'm not,' Fede said blankly. 'I've never pretended to be. That's Guido.'

'I know that now. I was supposed to make a play for Guido—Fede—flaunt my money—Roscoe's money—then show you that he wasn't faithful, that he'd follow the cash. I'm a private detective, Jenny.'

'You're a *what*?'

'Your father hired me to ''open your eyes''. It seems that he's the one who's blind. Oh, Jenny, I'm so sorry.

I thought I was saving you from a deceiver. But I got it all wrong.'

She braced herself for the shock and disillusion in Jenny's eyes. But after the first moment Jenny relaxed and shrugged. As she looked at Fede a smile came over her face, and the next moment they were in each other's arms.

Dulcie understood. Jenny had the love of the man she loved, and nothing else mattered.

'You mean you've been sweet-talking the wrong man all this week?' she asked from the shelter of Fede's embrace.

'Something like that,' Dulcie said stiffly.

Jenny gave a choke of laughter, and Fede joined her. After a moment Dulcie too managed a weak smile.

'It's not funny,' she said. 'He's been deceiving me.'

'Well, you were deceiving him too.'

'Only in a good cause,' Dulcie said firmly. 'But I don't understand about this title. I've been to his home. It's in a backwater. It's not—'

'Not what you'd expect from a future count,' Fede supplied. 'That's why Guido likes it. Actually he's a very rich man in his own right. He started a business making souvenirs. He owns two factories, one making glass, and one making all sorts of tourist knick-knacks, fancy dress, pictures, videos—'

'Masks?' Dulcie asked in a strange voice.

'Oh, yes, masks. They're his speciality. He even designs some of them himself, but mostly he's a very sharp businessman. His official home is in the Palazzo Calvani, but he keeps that little apartment as a refuge, and of course it's a good place to take the kind of ladies he doesn't want his uncle to know ab—' he stopped as Jenny kicked him.

'Thank you,' Dulcie said blankly. 'I get the picture.'

'It's a pity you didn't hit on the right man,' Jenny mused.

'Pardon?' Fede was startled. 'You *want* other women chasing me?'

'Only because I know you'd have been faithful, my darling,' she told him fondly. 'Then Dulcie could have straightened the whole thing out with Dad.'

'I'm not sure I could,' Dulcie said. 'He wants you to marry a rich man, or a title, preferably both.'

'And all I want is Fede,' Jenny said. 'I don't care if I never see a penny of Dad's money. I'm of age. I don't have to do what he says. It's just that I wanted to avoid a split with him. You see, he's terribly stubborn. Once he's "cast me off" he'll feel he has to stick to it forever. And I'm all he's got. If we have a break he'll never see his grandchildren and he'll have a miserable, grumpy old age.'

'He's very set on having his own way about this,' Dulcie said.

'So am I.' For a moment Jenny's face looked astonishingly like Roscoe's. 'So we just have to think of something.' She yawned. 'But let's do it in the morning.'

'It *is* the morning,' Dulcie said. 'It's five o'clock.'

'There's plenty of night left,' Jenny said firmly. 'Goodnight, Dulcie. You should go and get some rest.'

Dulcie could only go to her own room and strip off, trying to come to terms with her turbulent thoughts. Part of her was furious with Guido. This was all his fault for pretending to be Fede when he must have known he wasn't, she thought illogically.

But part of her was gloriously happy because he wasn't a heartless schemer after all. All the best of him was true, the gentle consideration he'd shown her in his apartment, the chivalrous way he'd kept his distance while delicately hinting that he wanted something very different. It wasn't the calculation of a man pursuing a woman's fortune. It was the honest behaviour of a man who didn't need her fortune.

Her heart sank a little when she considered her own actions. But they had fooled each other, and surely they could put that behind them?

She'd been holding back her feelings, but now there was nothing to stop her admitting her love, and the world was bright again. At last she fell into a deep sleep which lasted until nine the next morning. She rubbed her eyes, wondering what the day would bring.

She showered and dressed hurriedly. As she left the bedroom she saw that breakfast had been served on the terrace. Jenny and Fede were sitting there drinking coffee, and they hailed her with smiles.

'Isn't it a wonderful morning?' Jenny said blissfully. 'I'm so happy I could die.'

'Then I will die with you,' Fede said gallantly.

'We'll all die if Roscoe gets wind of this,' Dulcie said, but she too was happy. Guido was a free man. The delicate emotion that had built up between them over the last few days was love after all, and she was free to give her feelings full rein. If only she could see him soon.

There was a knock on the door.

'I ordered more coffee for you,' Jenny said.

'Thanks, I'll answer it,' Dulcie said, rising and making her way to the outer door, where someone outside was knocking again, impatiently.

She pulled it open and saw Guido.

Mingled with her first leap of joy was amusement at

his expression. He looked definitely sheepish, and entered cautiously, as though expecting boiling oil to fall on him. Remembering their last meeting Dulcie wondered if she herself should be looking for boiling oil.

'You're not still mad at me?' he asked, studying her smiling face.

'Should I be?' she fenced.

'Well, you were pretty mad last night. I should remember because you threw me into the water.'

'I didn't throw you, you tripped.'

'You didn't help me out.'

'You can swim.'

'And I had to. In the end I got picked up by a barge carrying garbage and I got home smelling so bad even the alley cats fled from me. It's not funny,' he added as her lips twitched.

'Yes, it is.'

'Yes, I guess it is,' he conceded wryly. 'When I awoke today I knew I had to see you and explain, try to make you understand how it happened—but now—all that really matters is—' he became absorbed in watching her face '—all that matters—kiss me, my darling, *kiss me!*'

He pulled her against him in the same moment that she opened her arms to him. She knew now how badly she'd longed for the feel of his lips on hers. She'd pretended it wasn't true, but secretly she'd ached for him to kiss her.

'I've wanted to do this so often,' he murmured between kisses. 'I knew from the first moment that it was you, and you knew it too, didn't you, *cara*?'

'I don't know what I knew,' she whispered, dazed.

'You did, you must have done.' He kissed her again

and again. 'So many kisses to make up,' he said against her mouth. 'And all our lives for more kisses.'

'All our—?' She could hardly believe what she was hearing. Everything was going too fast.

'Of course. Years and years to spend kissing you and loving you in every possible way. Years to have beautiful children with you.' He pulled back, taking her head gently between his hands, and she never afterwards forgot the sight of his face, gloriously happy, blazing with triumphant love. It lived in her mind as a terrible contrast to what followed.

'Tell me, darling,' he said crazily, 'do you believe in Fate?'

'Well, I—'

'Because it was Fate, wasn't it, that brought us together, Fate that made your sandal fall off straight into my boat?'

'Not exactly,' she said, beginning to see danger.

'It wasn't an accident?' he asked, eyes wide. Suddenly he burst into joyful laughter. 'You saw me from the bridge, and you said to yourself, "I must have this handsome fellow", so you tossed your shoe to get my attention. Oh, *cara*, say that it's true. Think what it will do for my ego.'

'Your ego is quite big enough without help,' she countered, playing for time. '"This handsome fellow" indeed!'

'Last night when you were angry I thought my life was over.' Abruptly his tone changed and he spoke in a moved voice that startled her. 'Because that's what you are to me. My life.'

'But you don't know me—'

'I knew you from the first moment. I know you have a kind heart and will forgive my innocent deception, because you know it didn't spring from malice. But tell me, how did you find out? I was going to ask you last night, but you were too busy throwing me into the canal.' With his mercurial nature he'd gone from serious to clowning in a split second. Dulcie could barely keep up with him.

'I don't blame you for ducking me,' he hastened to add. 'When you found out I wasn't whom you thought—how did you find out by the way?'

'I didn't, not until later.'

'But—then why were you mad at me? I'm not an unreasonable man, *cara*, but when someone throws me into the canal I like to know why.'

'Does it matter?' she asked, finding his fun irresistible, even at this fraught moment. 'I should think Venice is full of people who'd like to throw you into canals.'

'Sure to be. But they usually control it.'

What a life it would be with this enchanting madman, she thought. If only she could navigate the shoals ahead first.

'Listen,' she said urgently, 'I've got something to tell you—'

'Tell me that you love me,' he broke in. 'Tell me that first and last and what do I care for anything else? You do love me, don't you?'

'Yes, yes, I do. But listen to me, it's important—'

'Nothing is important except that we've found each other. Kiss me, now and always—'

She was in his arms again, her troubled words silenced by his lips, and this time it was different, as though her confession of love had invigorated him. Before, his embrace had been troubled, cautious, asking her response. Now he was a man who knew himself

loved and it was there in the possessiveness of his
mouth and his arms. She would tell him everything in
a moment, she promised herself, but just a moment—
and another moment—

'Is that the coffee?' came a call from the next room.

'A curse on anyone who interrupts us,' Guido sighed.
'We shall have to go and be polite *carissima*, but soon
we must be alone together, and then—'

There was another shout from inside and Guido reluctantly let her go.

'Later,' he whispered, then raised his voice to call,
'Fede,' and went in search of the voice. 'What the devil
are you doing here? And Jenny! How wonderful to see
you again!'

Dulcie followed him into the main room to find him
laughingly embracing Jenny.

'You two know each other?' he said, looking from
Jenny to Dulcie.

'Only slightly,' Dulcie said quickly.

'Guido my friend, I was going to call you and beg
your help,' Fede said quickly.

'You two don't look as if you need my help. I never
saw two lovers so happy.'

'But Jenny's Poppa still wants to break us up. He
even put a private detective on our trail to discredit me.'

Guido made a sound of disgust. 'A private detective?
What kind of miserable apology for a human being deliberately chooses such a sneaky, underhand job? Still,
what harm can he do you?'

There was an awkward silence. Dulcie took a deep
breath.

'It's not a he,' she said. 'It's me.'

Slowly Guido turned to look at her.

CHAPTER NINE

'WHAT did you say?' Guido asked quietly.

It took all her courage to say, 'I'm the private detective.'

'You?' he sounded as though he didn't know what the words meant.

'But Dulcie is on our side now,' Fede said eagerly, 'so it's all right. She's going to help us.'

'I don't know if Roscoe will listen to me,' Dulcie said, 'but I'll do everything I can.'

Guido was gazing at her curiously, but his manner was still calm. He hadn't quite understood yet. Or maybe he didn't want to.

'You're—a private detective?' he repeated slowly, still in that strange way, as though he was trying to decipher meaningless sounds.

'Yes.'

'And you came here to—?'

'Roscoe's worried about Jenny. He got the wrong end of the stick. He thought Fede was claiming to be you.'

'Can you imagine that?' Fede chuckled. 'Me, related to a count! So he sent Dulcie to find me and tempt me away from my Jenny. As though anyone could do that. Only—here's the joke—she thought you were me!'

'And so she targeted me instead,' Guido said lightly. 'Yes, it's an excellent joke.' A light had gone out of him, not just from his eyes but from his whole being. 'So that's what it was all about.'

Jenny made a slight restless movement at an intonation she heard in Guido's voice. Fede, an innocent, was merely trying to put Guido in the picture without realising the implications. Jenny tried to attract his attention but he was in full flight.

'There aren't many who fool you, Guido,' he observed cheekily.

'Until today I'd have said none at all,' Guido responded at once. He raised Dulcie's hand to his lips. 'My congratulations, *signorina*. A wonderful masquerade, played out to the finish with utter conviction.'

'You got the better of him, Dulcie,' Fede said. 'Someone should give you a medal.'

'That will be my privilege,' Guido said quietly.

There was no anger or condemnation in his eyes. Just a puzzled look, as though he were wondering how the world could have changed in a moment. Dulcie ground her nails into her palm. If only she could have told him in her own words. Now he'd heard in the worst possible way.

'Perhaps,' she said carefully, 'you should wait until you know the whole story. There's so much you don't know—that I must explain—'

'A man never knows the whole of it,' he agreed. 'But enough to matter. Enough to cast a strange light over what he thought was true, and show it in very ugly colours.'

It was hard for her to answer, but before she could even try he'd given Jenny a friendly, reassuring smile, saying, 'So we have a problem. We have to solve it. That's all. At least you can tell your Poppa that Fede has made no false claims. That should please him.'

'You don't know my father,' Jenny said. 'When he takes ''agin'' someone, that's it.'

'And it's my poverty that really offends him,' Fede

said gloomily. 'When he knows the truth he'll want Jenny to marry you, and be a countess.'

'Don't worry,' Guido said lightly. 'I shall tell him I'm going to become a monk. Love is too complicated for me.' He turned to Dulcie. 'So you were sent here to delude us. Are you going to tell us your real name?'

'I've been using my real name,' she said, adding softly, 'unlike some people.'

He had the grace to redden, but recovered himself. 'But what's in a name?' he asked her. 'That isn't always where the truth lies.'

'Yes, there's also the work people do, and pretending to live one kind of life while actually living another.'

His eyebrows rose. 'You talk to me about a "pretend" life?'

That silenced her.

'Have you thought of anything yet?' Fede asked anxiously.

'Patience,' Guido adjured him. 'I've only just discovered how things really stand.' A tremor went through him, although his face still smiled. 'Even a genius like me can only think so fast.'

'It's hopeless,' Fede said, immediately plunged into gloom. 'Nothing can be done.'

'Why don't we ask Dulcie?' Guido suggested. 'After all, intrigue is her profession, and she does it surpassingly well.'

'No,' she said hastily. 'This is a Venetian intrigue, and my talents don't stretch to it.'

'You do yourself an injustice, *signorina*,' Guido assured her quietly. 'You have the Venetian gift for dodging around corners, looking at one fact, seeing another, and believing a third. It's a great skill and most outsiders never acquire it. You, I believe were born with it.'

'On the contrary, *signore*,' she said, meeting his eyes defiantly. She'd found her second wind now, and if this was the game he wanted to play, then he would find she could give as good as she got. 'You forget that I've recently been taking lessons from a master.'

'And I,' he murmured so softly that only she could hear, 'I, who thought I had nothing left to learn, have found differently.'

'Life is full of unexpected lessons,' she murmured back. 'People may be more innocent than they seem.'

'People may certainly be very different to how they seem,' he said, subtly twisting her words.

She nodded. 'For instance, you shouldn't trust someone who plays games.'

He shrugged. 'You could say that about everyone.'

'No, some of us have a living to earn.'

'Ah, yes,' he seemed much struck. 'When it's done for money it's so much more virtuous, is it not?'

Her eyes met his and found in them something unexpected. He was angry but he was also hurt and confused. This situation had caught him off balance, and he wasn't coping as smoothly as he tried to make out.

A moment later he rose, kissed Jenny's cheek, shook Fede's hand and said with a flourish, 'Bless you. I'm happy for you. And don't worry, I'll think of something. And you, *signorina*—' he turned to Dulcie '—it was a pleasure talking to you but now I must be going. I've been unaccountably neglecting my work recently and now there's a mountain of it awaiting me, that will occupy me for some time.'

He was gone without waiting for a reply, but she had none to make. What could she say to a man who so clearly wanted to get away from her?

* * *

At Guido's souvenir factory on the island of Murano his employees were becoming concerned. For several days their employer had been absent without warning. Once a day he'd called them, but then switched his phone off and was impossible to contact.

His return caused general relief, which soon turned to surprise. Guido had always run an efficient business, but he'd done so with good humour, teasing, and the occasional semi-flirtatious coaxing. No more. His orders were still given with courtesy, but coolly, crisply, like a man with no time to spare. When someone cracked a joke in his presence he looked blank, as though wondering what a joke was.

It took Dulcie a day to track him down, and as she walked into the factory she had a horrible suspicion that everyone there knew who she was and why she was here. But the young man in the entrance directed her upstairs without fuss.

On the top floor she found Guido's office, and through the windows that formed the walls she could see him there at his desk, talking to a middle-aged man. The man saw her and nudged Guido, making him look up.

His face startled her. It was tired and worn, as if he hadn't slept for an age and had forgotten how to smile. He glanced in her direction, then away, and for a dreadful moment she thought he would refuse to see her. But then he nodded and indicated for her to be shown in.

The inside of his office reminded her how little she really knew him. The computer, the multiple phone lines, the stacks of files, the walls covered in plans and diagrams, all these told her that this was a man who took his business seriously.

'Is this the real you?' she asked lightly.

'One of me,' he answered briefly. 'I'm surprised to find you still in Venice. I thought you'd have gone yesterday.'

'You know I didn't because you heard me knocking on your door last night.' She added quietly, 'I knocked for a long time before I went away.'

'It wasn't a good moment,' he said. 'I wouldn't have known what to say, especially in that place.' His eyes challenged her with memories of the few happy days they'd spent in the little apartment. Then he looked away and began to pace his office, never getting too close to her. 'But I'm glad you came to see me.'

'You are?' she asked hopefully.

'Yes, it's right that we should say goodbye properly.'

His coolly dismissive tone annoyed her. 'I'll say goodbye when I'm good'n ready, not when you tell me to. There's a lot more to be said first.' In a softer tone she added, 'I listened to you when you were making your excuses yesterday.' She added, 'And that's not all I listened to you saying.'

She regretted the words at once. If his face wasn't closed against her before it was now. She'd reminded him of what he didn't want to remember.

'It wasn't kind of you to bring that up,' he said. 'You should have laughed over your victory in private, not to my face.'

'Laugh over—? What are you saying? I'm not laughing. I never meant any of this to happen.'

'You never *meant*? Excuse me, I understood that you came to Venice deliberately, for a purpose.'

'But it had nothing to do with you,' she cried.

'Ah, yes, I'd forgotten. You came to deceive and ruin my friend, not me, which of course makes everything all right.'

'I came to protect Jenny from a fortune hunter.'

'And how could you be so sure he was a fortune hunter? Your information was hardly brilliant since you confused him with me.'

'The information was lousy,' she admitted. 'It came from Roscoe. But the idea was to find out if he was right.'

'He'd made up his mind before you started.'

'He had, I hadn't.'

He stopped pacing and spoke angrily, 'For pity's sake, what kind of woman does this? Is it how you get your kicks?'

'No, I do it to eat. I've got nothing. Roscoe paid for everything.'

He regarded her with what might almost have been a smile. 'Like a theatrical performance, really. Set and costumes courtesy of Roscoe Harrison, and script by— who? Did you cook it up between you?'

'It wasn't like that—'

'*Answer me,*' he said sternly. There was no trace in him now of the light-hearted young man who'd enchanted her. There was something grim in his manner that she wouldn't have believed without seeing it. 'Answer me,' he commanded again. 'How much of what happened between us was planned?'

'I came to seek out Federico. I thought it was you because of the picture.' She showed him the snapshot. 'Yes, I was looking for your face, but when I found you, you were wearing his shirt, with his name on it—'

'And how did you happen to find me?'

'I was searching for you,' she admitted.

He raised his eyebrows sardonically. 'So our very meeting wasn't the accident I thought. And that touching moment when your sandal fell at my feet in the gondola?'

The moment he'd called Fate, with shining eyes, full of love.

'I threw it,' she admitted in despair. 'I stood on the bridge hoping you'd look up, and when you didn't I tossed my sandal.'

She flinched, watching him. She no longer knew how this man would react to anything.

For the moment there was no reaction at all. Then abruptly he broke into laughter, that filled her with relief, until she heard the disturbing edge to the sound, not like real amusement at all.

'That's hilarious,' he said at last. 'You calculated the whole thing, down to the last detail, and the poor sap fell for it, hook, line and sinker. He even burbled something stupid about it being Fate. Or did he? Remind me. No, on second thoughts, don't remind me. There are some mistakes a man should be able to forget in peace.'

'But it wasn't just me, was it?' she said indignantly. 'When I saw the name on your shirt you could have said, "I'm not Fede, just a rich playboy, fooling about in a boat". Why didn't you?'

'I forget,' he said stonily.

'I don't think that's a truthful answer. You could have stopped everything right there and then. Why didn't you?'

'I've forgotten,' he repeated. 'All right, maybe I've only forgotten because I want to. Believe what you like, but most of all believe that it's best if you go away from here and never come back.'

'I'm not ready to give up and go yet.'

'That's a pity because I don't think Venice is big enough to hold both of us.'

The door was thrown open abruptly by a middle-aged woman, full of excitement, who gabbled something Dulcie didn't understand. Guido gave her a brief smile and replied tersely. The next moment she surged into the room, followed by two young girls, their arms filled with masks.

'No,' Guido started to say, but his protest was lost in the hubbub. He shrugged and gave up. 'Our new line,' he said to Dulcie, sounding harassed. 'We've been waiting for them, but this isn't the moment—oh, be damned to it!'

The masks were magnificent, not merely painted cardboard like the ones on his walls, but covered in satin and sequins, many with gorgeous feathers.

Guido admired them and spoke kindly to his employees, but managed to shoo them out of the room fairly quickly.

'Harlequin,' Dulcie said, holding up a creation in scarlet satin with multi-coloured feathers on top. 'And this one—' she lifted a long-nosed mask in purple satin, 'Pantalone, the merchant. I remember what you told me.'

'But there were other things I didn't have time to tell you,' Guido mused. 'About Columbine, for instance.'

'You said she was sensible, but sharp and witty, and could see the funny side of life.'

'I also said she's a deceiver. She teases and beguiles Harlequin, leads him into her traps, while all the while laughing up her sleeve because he's fool enough to believe in her. He, poor clown, ends up wondering what's hit him.'

He spoke lightly but she had a sensation of his pain that was almost tangible. She guessed that he wasn't used to unhappiness, his life had contained so little of it. Now he was floundering. She longed to reach out to him, but didn't dare.

'You told me I wasn't like Columbine,' she reminded him.

He smiled sadly. 'I was wrong. You think I'm unfair because we both deceived each other, but your deception was planned before you ever came here. That's what I can't get past. Mine was an impulse that I yielded to—stupidly perhaps, but on the spur of the moment because—well, no matter.'

'Tell me,' she begged. It was suddenly terribly important.

But he shook his head. 'It doesn't make any difference now. I wish it did. Go away, Dulcie. There's nothing so dead as a dead love.' His face contracted suddenly. 'For pity's sake, go,' he said harshly.

If she could have thought of any way of moving him she would have tried, even then, but there was about him a kind of wintry stubbornness that she couldn't fight. He'd grown older since yesterday.

His phone shrilled and he made a grab for it with a mutter of impatience. Dulcie turned to go, wondering if the end could really come like this. But she turned as Guido barked, '*Fede*!'

'What is it?' she asked with a feeling of foreboding.

He was talking in Venetian. Dulcie caught the word 'Jenny,' then Fede's name repeated several times as though Guido was trying to calm him down. Dulcie could just make out the tinny sound of a voice from the phone, and it sounded as though Fede was in a rare panic.

'What is it?' she said as Guido hung up.

He was snatching his jacket down from a hook.

'Come on,' he said, grasping her arm. 'We've got to hurry.'

They were out of the factory and by the waterside before she had breath enough to ask, 'What's happened?'

A motor boat was waiting with a man at the wheel. Guido helped her down into it and then they were roaring away across the lagoon, feeling the spray in their faces. He had to shout above the noise of the engine.

'Your employer has arrived.'

'My—you mean Roscoe?'

'Right. Jenny's Poppa. She managed to call Fede and he called me. We have to do something fast to stop him taking her back to England.'

'You promised Fede you'd think up a plan.'

'I'm thinking of one now. First we have to walk into the hotel together.'

'And say what?'

'I'm trying to work that out,' he said tensely. 'We must put this man straight about the facts, and for that I need you there.'

'So sometimes Harlequin needs Columbine's help?'

'Sometimes he can't do without her, even if he doesn't like it. It's time to make up your mind whose side you're on.'

'I'm on Jenny's side. You heard me tell them I'll help.'

Instead of answering he yelled something to the boatman, and their speed increased, so that further talk became impossible. Soon they'd reached the Grand Canal, and had to slow down dramatically.

'Can't we go any faster?' Dulcie asked.

'No, it's the law. There's the hotel.' As he handed

her out of the boat he said, 'We're going to have to put on a rare performance.'

'But what's the script?' she asked frantically.

'Play it by ear.' He was sweeping her through the lobby to the lift.

'But suppose we're using different ears?' she demanded as they reached the top floor.

'You're the one that's good at this.'

'Don't give me that. I'm an amateur. You could give me lessons.'

'All right, how's this? You know this man and I don't. You lead, I'll follow. Do it for Jenny. Do it for Fede whose life you tried to ruin.'

There was no time to answer. The lift door was opening. Ahead were the double doors of the suite, and from behind them came the sound of voices, Jenny's distraught, Fede's frantic.

Guido was looking at her expectantly.

'Here we go,' she said, throwing open the doors.

As entrances went, it was splendid. The three inside stared at them. Then Jenny rushed to her in appeal, Fede rushed to shake Guido's hand, babbling in Venetian. Dulcie fixed her eyes on Roscoe, who was red-faced and shouting, 'I don't know who this man is—' jabbing a finger at Fede.

'It's Fede,' Jenny protested.

'The hell he is!' Roscoe snapped.

'The hell he isn't!' This, from Guido.

'You—' Roscoe swung around to him '—you're the one who's caused all this trouble.'

For the first minute Dulcie's mind had been a blank, but now suddenly the clouds parted. She pulled herself together and spoke with apparent confidence.

'Mr Harrison,' she said, 'allow me to introduce

Signor Guido Calvani, nephew of Count Calvani, a family that I've now discovered was once well acquainted with my own.'

The mention of Dulcie's family made Roscoe pause, as she'd hoped. It gave her time to rush on, 'It was only after I arrived here that I realised the significance of the name Calvani. It turns out that my great-aunt, *Lady* Harriet, knew Guido's uncle very well, if you know what I mean,' she managed a coy simper, 'and *the count* welcomed me most warmly when I visited his *palazzo* yesterday.'

She was laying it on with a trowel, stressing the words that would send signals to Roscoe's snobbery, and every one of them was hitting the bull's eye, she was glad to see.

True to his promise to follow her lead Guido wrung Roscoe's hand and said all the right things at length. Then he said them again at even greater length. Roscoe managed a reasonably civilised reply, but then became himself again.

'But you're in that picture making up to my daughter.'

'But only under the eye of her true love,' Guido said quickly, drawing Fede forward. 'I gather you've already met my friend, Federico Lucci, who's been fortunate enough to win Jenny's affection.'

'Now wait,' Roscoe blustered, 'what were you doing in that outfit? That's why I thought you were Fede—'

'He's Fede,' Guido said. 'I'm Guido.'

'*Count* Guido?'

'Not while my uncle lives, which hopefully will be many years yet.'

'But you—' Roscoe looked from Guido to Fede and from Fede to Dulcie '—you—no, wait—'

Then inspiration came to Dulcie in a blinding flash.

'Mr Harrison, pretty soon you and I need to discuss this fiasco,' she said, sounding slightly truculent. 'How am I supposed to do a decent job of work when your briefing to me was so inaccurate?'

He gaped. 'I—'

'Look at this picture.' She produced the snapshot. 'You assured me that the man with the mandolin was Federico Lucci. On that basis I allocated you a portion of my time which, let me remind you, doesn't come cheap. And after a week when I've given you my best efforts, I discover that ''Fede'' was really the other man, and I've been on a wild-goose chase.'

'But you said you knew him,' Roscoe hollered.

'I said no such thing. I said my family knew his, way back. He could have been anybody for all I knew. I've been glad to make contact with the count, who once knew Lady Harriet, but apart from that the whole thing has been a waste of time, for which I hold you entirely to blame.'

'OK, OK, maybe I got it a bit wrong,' Roscoe said in a placating voice, 'but it hasn't been a *total* waste of time. We've established that *he*—' indicating Fede '—is no aristo.'

'Since he never claimed to be, that's hardly surprising,' Dulcie said briskly. 'Can we drop this nonsense now? I've established that the man your daughter loves isn't trying to beguile her with false claims, which is surely what really matters.'

Roscoe was uncharacteristically hesitant. His slow-moving wits had taken in that Guido was a real 'aristo' and therefore to be cultivated, and that Fede was his friend. To have repeated his suspicions of Fede without offending Guido would have taken social skills Roscoe didn't possess. He fell silent, fuming. Guido divined what was going through his mind, and stepped into the breach, all charm.

'I know that my uncle would be anxious to extend to you his hospitality,' he said smoothly. 'He's giving a fancy-dress masked ball next week, and your presence, with your daughter, would make it complete.'

Roscoe's snobbery warred with his desire to hasten Jenny back to England. Snobbery won.

'That's generous of you,' he bawled. 'We'd like that, wouldn't we, pet? That's very—well, I must say—'

Under cover of his noisy pleasure, Guido murmured to Dulcie, '*Brava!* Columbine has worked her magic. You knew just how to deal with him.'

'He was getting on my wick,' Dulcie said crisply.

Roscoe had recovered himself and was wringing Guido's hand. 'Tell your uncle I'll come to see him right away. Men of substance should stick together—'

'My uncle is away just now,' Guido improvised hastily, 'but he will have the pleasure of your acquaintance at the ball.' He turned swiftly to Dulcie before Roscoe could think of any more tortures for him. 'I understand that you will be there, *signorina*. It will be delightful to see you. Fede, let us leave.'

'But I—' the hapless Fede started to say.

'Not now,' Guido said through gritted teeth, urging him out with more vigour than gentleness. 'For pity's sake, my friend, quit while you're ahead.'

CHAPTER TEN

GUIDO had prevented Roscoe taking Jenny away, thus buying the lovers some time, but the strain of the ensuing days nearly turned Dulcie's hair white.

He moved into the suite, taking over the second bedroom so that Jenny and Dulcie had to share the first. He spent his time exploring the city, dragging his daughter along, and proud to bursting point of having Lady Dulcie as his guide.

He demanded a full account of her dinner at the *palazzo*, with diversions regarding the social niceties to be observed at a count's residence.

'Just because I'm a self-made man it doesn't follow that I'm an ignoramus,' he declared belligerently. 'And I don't want any mistakes in that direction.'

Dulcie assured him that nobody could possibly make any mistakes.

Guido telephoned her once, explaining coolly that the best masquerade outfits were to be found at a shop in the Calle Morento. She should take Jenny there and make sure she chose a Columbine costume.

'Shouldn't that be me?' she asked wryly.

'On no account. They have a wide choice and I'm sure you'll find something suitable, but definitely not Columbine. But please tell Jenny that if all goes well she'll be with Fede from then on.'

'You're planning for them to run away that night?'

'I'm planning a little more than that, but everything has to be done just right.'

141

'Do I have any part to play?'

'Yes, and I'm sure you'll play it superbly when the time comes.'

But you don't trust me enough to tell me now, she thought.

'A lot depends on your following my instructions exactly,' Guido continued. 'Put yourself in the assistant's hands, she knows your requirements.'

'I suppose you have a connection with the shop?'

'I own it,' he said with some surprise.

'Of course.'

That was her only contact with him. There wasn't another word, and she was too proud to seek him out again. Although he wanted her to stay, he hadn't relented. She would be useful in his plan to help Jenny and Fede. That was all.

It was hard to believe that the magical web that had been spun between them during those few precious days could have been wrecked so easily: harder still to realise that the gentle jester who'd nursed and protected her was also the austere man who judged her harshly.

And unreasonably, she reminded herself. Her deception might have been greater than his, but he could have sorted it all out in a moment. Instead he'd let her mistake pass because—because of what? Something he couldn't bear to tell her. She might guess, but it was better not to, because then the ache of 'might-have-been' started all over again.

She'd thought that Simon had left her unhappy, but now she could see that misery in proportion. He'd been a skunk all the time and she was well rid of him. She'd known that even while she suffered. But Guido was different. She'd fallen deeply in love with him during those few precious days alone, and now that he'd changed towards her she couldn't dismiss it as a lucky escape. He was the one. Unlikely as it seemed there had been truth between them, concealed, perhaps, by masks, but he himself had said, 'when people's faces are hidden they are free to become their true selves.'

If only things had been different, how they could have enjoyed discovering their own and each other's true selves. It could have been the work of a lifetime.

Now there was nothing, and a fearful blank facing her. She couldn't persuade this man because she didn't know him. And the new Guido, curt, withdrawn, unreachable, was an alarming man.

As he wanted she took Jenny to the hire shop. Roscoe insisted on accompanying them, and chose a lavishly bejewelled Henry VIII costume for himself. Dulcie beat off his efforts to dress her as Anne Boleyn, but then he insisted on Cleopatra, which she felt was almost as bad.

Jenny went through this in a dream, following Guido's instructions as relayed by Dulcie, but without conviction. With her father's arrival her confidence seemed to have drained away. Despite her brave words about being of age and pleasing herself she reacted to Roscoe like a rabbit trapped in headlamps. Sometimes she managed to telephone Fede, but the conversations were always hurried affairs and she usually had to hang up quickly.

'Stand up to your father,' Dulcie insisted one evening. 'Tell him you're going to marry Fede and that's it. Or just walk out.'

'You make it sound so easy,' Jenny sighed.

'It is easy.'

'It would be for you. You're not afraid of anyone or anything.'

I'm afraid of my future, Dulcie thought. It's looking bleak and lonely right now.

'Dulcie, what am I going to do? You say Guido's going to make everything right, but how? If it doesn't work, Dad's going to haul me off home. I can't see Fede, I can only call him for a minute at a time. Dad watches me like a hawk.'

'Write Fede a letter,' Dulcie said at once. 'I'll take it to him.'

'You'd do that for me? Oh, thank you.'

'Write it now. Will Fede be rowing tonight?'

'I don't know,' Jenny said, scribbling hurriedly. 'But I'll give you his family's address.'

In a couple of minutes the letter was being sealed in an envelope, and Dulcie was hurrying out, hoping to avoid Roscoe, but failing.

'Where are you going?' he boomed. 'It's time to go out to dinner.'

'I'll join you later. I've got something to do first.'

'Don't be late.'

She had to consult a map to find the tiny Calle Marcello, well away from the tourist haunts. Darkness was falling, lights blazed from the grocery shops that were still open, and from the rooms overhead.

She found the little alley and almost walked past no: 36. The door was dark and easy to miss. She hesitated before knocking, suddenly shy. From inside she could hear sounds of movement, cheerful voices, laughter. She knocked.

The door was opened by Guido.

For a moment they stared at each other. Dulcie found no softening in his face, only a dismay as great as her own.

'I came to see Fede,' she said at last. 'Is he here?'

'Sure,' he said briefly, and stood aside for her to pass.

'Who's that?' came a hearty female voice from deep in the house.

The next moment its owner came into view. She was large, middle-aged and had a ruddy, smiling face, flushed from cooking.

'*Ciao*!' she boomed.

'This lady is English, Maria,' Guido said. 'She wants to see Fede.'

'Aha! You know my son?'

'A little,' Dulcie said hastily. 'I have a letter for him, from Jenny.'

Maria screamed with delight. 'You are a good friend. I am Maria Lucci.'

'I'm Dulcie,' she gasped, swallowed up in the woman's embrace.

'*Si*. I know. Lady Dulcie.'

'No,' she said hastily. 'Just Dulcie.'

Maria bawled, '*Fede*!' and urged Dulcie towards an inner door. 'You go through there. We just start eating. You eat with us.'

'Oh, no, I don't want to intrude,' she said hastily. It was unnerving to have Guido standing there in silence. 'I'll just give him the letter and go.'

'No, no, you eat with us,' Maria insisted. She stomped away, bawling something in dialect that Dulcie guessed was a demand for an extra chair.

'You have to stay,' Guido said quietly. 'When a Venetian family asks you into their home it's an honour. We're not like the English who just go through the forms.'

'But you don't want me to stay, do you?' she challenged.

'That means nothing. This isn't my home.'

'No, you never honoured me with an invitation to your home.'

'But I did. I took you to my real home, the home of my heart. There I thought I began to know your heart, which only proves what a fool I am.'

Dulcie was in despair. Where was the man she'd found so easy to love? Vanished, replaced by someone with a steely core. But he must always have been there, beneath the bright surface. It had taken herself to bring him out.

Fede appeared in a rush. 'Mama says you have a message for me.'

Dulcie gave it to him. He read it in a blaze of joy, and kissed the paper. Then he kissed Dulcie.

'*Grazie, grazie, carissima Dulcie.*' He glanced quickly at Guido, 'I kiss her like a brother—you don't mind—'

'Not a bit,' Guido said with a grin that would have fooled anyone but Dulcie. Now she was alive to his every nuance, and knew that his charming manners were one of the masks with which he protected himself.

'Come and eat,' Maria yelled from down the passage.

'I can't,' Dulcie protested.

'Maria will be hurt if you don't,' he said.

'But Mr Harrison wants me back—'

It was the wrong thing to say. Guido's mouth twisted in a mirthless grin.

'The man with money snaps his fingers and you go running. Yes sir, no sir, shall I break another life for you today, sir?'

'I haven't broken any lives.'

'*How would you know?*' he flashed in a voice that startled her with its bitterness, and for a moment she caught a glimpse of real pain beneath his anger. She gazed at him in the dim light, shocked to realise just how much she had hurt him. A broken life? This rich playboy who pleased himself? What could possibly touch him?

'Guido—'

She reached out her hand and in another moment she would have touched him, but then Maria yelled from the garden and he called back, 'She's just coming.'

His hand was on Dulcie's arm, gentle but insistent, and again she had the sensation of steel. He wasn't asking her, he was telling her.

The way out led to a small garden with two long tables in the centre, decorated with flowers. It was dusk, and small glasses containing candles were laid along the tables, so that on each side the faces of the Lucci clan glowed. Dulcie tried to keep up as she was introduced to Poppa, his two brothers, his three elder sons, his daughter, her husband, and various children. By that time she'd lost track.

To her embarrassment she was greeted as a heroine by everyone: Fede's friend, doing all she could to bring him together with Jenny. Since there was no way of explaining what had really happened she was forced to endure it in silence.

Fede was sitting at the end of the table. Eagerly he grasped Dulcie's hand and took her to a seat at right angles to his own. Guido seated himself facing her.

'Tell me how Jenny is,' Fede begged. 'Does she miss me? Is she as unhappy apart as I am?'

She told him as much as she could, stressing how much Jenny loved him.

'*Grazie*,' he said fervently. 'While we have friends like you and Guido I know there is still hope.'

'Be careful, Fede,' Guido said sharply. 'Have you forgotten that Dulcie came here to ruin you?'

'It wasn't like that—' she protested.

'Of course it wasn't,' Fede said at once. 'You were deluded by the Poppa, and you are our friend now, that's all that matters.' He clapped Guido on the shoulders. 'Forget it.'

'Not everyone is as generous and forgiving as you, Fede,' Dulcie said impulsively. 'Jenny's very lucky to have such an understanding man.'

'No, no, it's I who am lucky.' Suddenly he clasped her hands. 'Dulcie, you don't believe that I'm a fortune hunter, do you?'

'Of course I don't,' she said warmly, clasping his hands back and smiling into his face with as much reassurance as she could. 'I know everything's going to work out for you, because when two people really love each other, it has to. It can't just end. It can't.'

She wondered if Guido was listening, and hearing the message she was trying to send him. Glancing up, she saw him watching her from across the table, but the glow from the candles masked his eyes.

There seemed an endless line of dishes; pasta, followed by fish, followed by veal, followed by sweet cakes. Dulcie ate heartily, which won the approval of everyone there, even Guido.

'Will you tell Jenny that I shall be waiting for her tomorrow night?' Fede begged.

'Are you going to be at the ball?' she asked.

'Not officially,' Guido said. 'But he'll be there.'

'Guido has promised to make all well, with your help,' Fede said. 'By this time tomorrow all our problems will be over.'

He bounced up out of his seat and went to help his mother at the far end.

'What mad promises have you made?' Dulcie said to Guido across the table.

He slid round into Fede's seat. 'Not mad promises at all. What I say I do, I'll do.'

'You've filled those two up with false hopes, but remember, Harlequin isn't as clever as he thinks. He'll overreach himself and fall flat on his face.'

'Not with Columbine's help. She always picks him up and remembers the things he's forgotten.'

'Don't count on Jenny.'

'I didn't mean Jenny.'

'But I'm going to be Cleopatra, didn't your shop assistant tell you?'

'Yes. A good choice. Very eye catching. Roscoe will never know that it isn't you in the costume any more.'

'And what will I be doing?'

'I'd have thought you could have worked it out by now. You slip away and change into another Columbine costume.'

'It's mad,' she breathed.

'Just mad enough to work.'

He'd put his head close to hers so that his breath whispered against her face. His eyes glinted. He wasn't reconciled to her, but her nearness affected him, as his did her. The others at the table had drawn away, smiling at these two lost in their own world.

Guido took her hand in his and looked down at it, while she felt him tremble and sensed the indecision that wracked him. Her heart ached. In a few hours she would have lost him forever unless she could find a way past the barrier he'd put up against her. And something told her that she was no nearer to her goal. He was having a moment of weakness, but he was a stronger and more stubborn man than she would ever have believed.

More of a challenge, she thought, as the gambler's instinct flared in her. But when he was gone from her life, the desolation would be the greater. She wouldn't think of that now. There was everything to play for.

Gathering all her courage she leaned forward and laid her mouth on his, feeling his shock, and his fleeting determination to resist her. Another moment and she knew that the gamble had paid off. His mind was telling him to draw back, but he couldn't do it. She'd taken him by surprise and won the first trick.

'Stop this,' he murmured against her lips.

'You stop it,' she told him. 'Tell me you don't love me.'

'I don't—'

'Liar,' she said silencing him.

After a long, intense moment she drew back a little, but not far because his hand was behind her head. His eyes, close to hers, were burning with resentment at how easily she could play on him, but still he held her face close to his. Far off she could hear applause as the family enjoyed what was happening. But the two at the end of the table weren't lovers as everyone thought. There was a deadly duel going on, with no quarter asked or given.

'Don't do this, Dulcie.'

'I will. I don't think you'll push me away in front of everyone.'

'Don't gamble on that.'

'You forget I come from gambling stock. I know more about odds than you do.'

'The odds are all in my favour. You can't win.'

'If you love me one tenth as much as you said you did, I can't lose.'

'I don't love you.'

'I say you do,' she countered.

'Is this how it has to be with you? Complete surrender? But you've already had that once. Remember that morning I came to the Vittorio and said you were my life, begged you to forgive me for concealing my identity? And all the time you knew the truth, yet you let me burble on.'

'Because I loved what you were saying,' she said passionately. 'Because I loved *you*. I remember the other things you said, too, about the years we'd spend together. It sounded wonderful.'

'Sure, it meant you'd done your job well. What satisfaction it must have given you to have me at your feet! Be satisfied with that, without trying to get me there again. Leave your victim a little dignity.'

'The hell with dignity. Look how I'm risking mine. What am I supposed to do after tomorrow night, Guido? Walk off into the sunset and spend my life in memories of a man too stupid and stubborn to see when a woman's in love with him? I told you once before, I'm not like that.'

'What are you like? How am I ever supposed to know?'

'Why don't you find out?'

'And be made a fool of again?'

The words were barely out when his lips were on hers. He wanted to quarrel with her and he wanted to make love to her, and he didn't know which one he wanted more. Then she would show him, she thought, moving in a little closer, and sensing her victory.

For a moment she thought he would fight her, but he

couldn't make himself do it. He was shaking as he slipped an arm about her shoulders, drawing her close, increasing the pressure of his mouth on hers, kissing the breath out of her. He was furious and bitter and it was all there in the way his lips moved over hers. Yet she sensed that he wasn't only angry with her, but also with himself for being unable to resist her.

Cries of appreciation went up around them but neither heard. Dulcie's heart was beating strongly, with love tinged with victory. He was still hers whether he wanted to admit it or not.

Her phone rang.

She said a very unladylike word.

Guido drew back as if shot, breathing hard and looking at her with burning eyes. Dulcie switched the phone off without answering but it was too late, the moment was gone.

'You shouldn't do that,' Guido said. 'Your employer will be angry.'

'To blazes with my employer. After tomorrow I'll enjoy never seeing him again.'

'Don't be hard on him. He did me a favour.'

Dulcie was shaking with suppressed passion and frustration at how everything had been snatched away at the last moment. Tears filled her eyes but she forced them back, determined to show no sign of weakness in front of him.

'I'd better be going,' she said.

She went round the family, saying her goodbyes and promising Fede that she would tell Jenny how much he loved her. Maria escorted her to the door, and there, to her surprise, she found Guido.

'I'll come part of the way with you,' he said.

CHAPTER ELEVEN

SHE half expected Guido to make an excuse to leave her as soon as they were out of the door, but he walked along with her for a while. He'd recovered himself now, and was on his guard.

'That was a terrible thing to say,' Dulcie said at last. 'That Roscoe did you a favour.'

'I'm sorry, I didn't mean to be rude.'

'Much I care about that!' she cried. 'That's not what this is about! We could still have it all.'

'If only that was possible!' he said at last. 'You know how much you tempt me. But it's no use.'

'Why are you so determined to hold out against me?' she asked passionately.

'Yes, I'm making a fuss about nothing, aren't I? Why should a man care if he meets his ideal and she turns out to be deceiving him for money?'

'Ideal?' she whispered, not certain that she'd heard right.

'It's a laugh, isn't it? I thought I was so street smart. Alive to every trick. Boy, was I kidding myself!'

'And that's why you hate me?'

'I don't hate you. Hating is a waste of time. It's just that you don't look the same any more, and I wish you did. The trouble with Fool's Paradise is that it's so beautiful, especially after you've been shut out. You long to find a way back in, to convince yourself that you don't know what you *do* know. Believe me, I've spent the last few days trying to get back into Paradise,

153

even if it's only the Fool's kind. Because it's the sweetest thing that's ever happened to me, or ever will.'

'To me too,' she said wistfully. 'Is there really no way back?'

'Do you think I wouldn't have found it by now?'

'It could all have been so different, if we'd met another way.'

'The truth is,' he said wryly, 'that you have the soul of a Venetian. Tricky as they come. All the time we've known each other you've been wearing a mask.'

'Not all the time,' she urged. 'Only at the beginning.'

'All the time,' he repeated. 'When you seemed to be removing the mask you were merely changing to another. Why, you have a whole armoury of them. And who should understand that better than me?'

'I'm not the only one. You could have told me who you were from the beginning.'

'And I should have done, but I was looking at you, falling in love with you on the spot. What did names matter? I thought you were the most dazzling girl I'd ever seen and nothing else registered. Then it was too late. Besides, I get tired of my uncle matchmaking, introducing me to women who look past me to the title. You were looking at *me*, or at least I thought you were, and I couldn't resist making it last, just while we got to know each other.' He gave a crack of laughter. 'It's nauseating isn't it, like some idiot character in a fairy tale. There was me, delighted that *you* weren't a fortune hunter, and all the time you thought that *I* was.'

'You made it easy for me to think the worst. When I told you I was Lady Dulcie you went strange, as though it was important.'

'It was. I couldn't believe my luck in meeting someone that I could love and marry without my uncle giving me grief about it. I thought you were wonderful, the one honest woman in a world of schemers.' He sighed. 'Well, perhaps I should apologise for being unfair to you. It was unfair to put you on a pedestal, because if I hadn't done that I'd probably have coped better when you fell off.'

Her anger began to stir. 'Then it's as well I fell off now, because sooner or later I'd have disillusioned you. Your dreams weren't real Guido. I'm an ordinary woman struggling my way through the world as best I can. I make compromises, I don't always behave well, but mostly I just do what I have to, whether I like it or not. I'm hemmed in by circumstances, like everyone else. Except you perhaps. You've got more freedom than anyone I know. Two lives, and you hop back and forth between them to please yourself, so you can't have any sympathy with ordinary mortals.'

'You don't expect me to believe that Lord Maddox's daughter really has to do this for a living?'

'Yes, I do damned well expect you to believe it,' she flashed. 'Every penny my father had went on the "gee-gees" as he calls them, or on the tables at Monte Carlo. The estates are mortgaged up to the hilt and the bank is getting restive about the size of the overdraft. Marry me? You'd have had to be out of your mind. Dad would have touched you for a loan in the first five minutes, and if you'd been mad enough to say yes he'd have been back for more. You're better off without me. So we do agree on something. In fact I reckon I've done you a favour.'

She walked on without waiting for his reply, and he had to run to catch her up and they walked awhile in silence. Overhead the laundry hung from lines strung between buildings. Above it the moon seemed to float behind the shirts and vests. Dulcie turned aside into a dark *calle*, finding her way more readily now. He'd called her a Venetian and perhaps she was becoming one, sure-footed when faced with confusion. At any rate she moved under the single lamp, and then away from it into the gloom.

'But in the end, it's not really about money at all,' she said, her voice sounding mysterious as it whispered to him from the darkness. 'I really took this job because I wanted to punish all men for Simon. I told you about him the first evening.'

'The man you loved and thought you saw? That was real?'

'Yes, that was real. I didn't make him up. I told you we were going to come to Venice for our honeymoon, but what I didn't tell you was that it was going to be the Vittorio, the Empress Suite. He had it all planned, with me paying the bills. He thought I was an heiress. When he discovered the truth he vanished.'

Guido murmured something that sounded like a Venetian curse. 'And you came here, to that hotel?'

'Roscoe was set on it, and I thought, "What the hell?" What does anything matter?'

'He was here with you?' Guido asked sharply. 'In your mind, in your heart—?'

'All the way across the lagoon from the airport,' she agreed. 'All the way down the Grand Canal and right into the suite. He was there when he shouldn't have been, reminding me that he *should* have been there, and he wasn't. Always his ghost, whispering in my ear that the whole world was nothing but a great con trick, and no man was anything but a deceiver. Turning Venice into a huge, bitter joke, when it should have been so lovely—' She broke off, overwhelmed with anguish at the thought of how lovely this man had made Venice for her, how lovely he could have made the whole world.

But she had lost him, and now she was tossing her last chance away with her own hands. It was suddenly impossible to do anything else.

Guido sensed rather than saw her emotion and took an involuntary step towards her, but she backed away, fending him off. She needed all her strength to force herself to do what was best for both of them. He stood helplessly, listening to her choked breathing in the dim light.

'He was a pig,' he said at last. 'You're well rid of him.'

She gave a high, hysterical laugh. 'That's just what I thought, but here's the joke. I'll *never* be rid of him. He changed me. Men don't look the same now. I keep trying to see behind their eyes to discover what lies they're telling. When Roscoe told me what he wanted me to do I was glad. There! You want the truth, and that's it! Ugly, isn't it? Like me, deep inside.'

'I never said—'

'*I* know what I'm really like. You're only just finding out the worst. I was *glad* of the chance to hunt down and punish a man like Simon, a man who deceived a woman for her money and abandoned her when she had none.'

'And you were sure I was like this, on Roscoe's say so?'

'I saw you through the distorting lights that Simon put there. I can't get rid of those lights, and they make all men look suspicious. I guess they always will now. I am as I am. It's done. I can't change back.'

'And these were your thoughts all the time we were together,' he whispered in horror.

'No,' she whispered. 'Not all the time. When you were looking after me everything became very confused.'

'And you couldn't tell me then?'

'How could I? I thought you were Fede, and I began to think Jenny was lucky. And then I learned the truth and it was too late. I'd ruined everything, hadn't I? *Hadn't I?*'

He couldn't answer.

She was shaking with anguish as she forced the truth out. 'I've turned into someone you can't love. I guess I can't blame you for that. You loved an illusion. The real me isn't really very loveable. She's hard and cynical—'

He became angry. 'Don't say that about yourself.'

'Why not? It's what you've been saying to yourself about me these last few days. I couldn't make you happy, I see that now.' She gave a harsh, self-condemning laugh that fell painfully on his ears. 'I hated Simon so much, but it was for the wrong reasons. The real injury he did me—isn't it funny?—is to make me just like him. Do you know the saying, "Never trust a mistrustful man—or woman"? I can't trust, and so I can't *be* trusted.'

'Dulcie,' perversely, now that she'd turned on herself, he felt the urge to defend her. But she warded him off, driven by the need to put her thoughts into words.

'We can't alter anything now, and why should we try?' she asked passionately. 'It wouldn't work. You'd never really feel you knew me, or could trust me, and how could we love each other like that?'

'You tell me,' he said, almost pleading with her. 'Columbine is the one with all the answers.'

'She doesn't know the answer to this riddle. I don't think there is one. Maybe, in the end, *I'm* better off without *you*. I'm sorry if I hurt you, Guido, but I also think you're suffering from damaged pride.'

'You really think it's my pride that's been speaking?' he asked, his voice growing angry again.

'A lot of the time. Underneath all those smiles you don't forgive easily. You believe that masks are only for you. When someone else uses them your world falls in. Pride. Well, I have pride too. It's finished. Tomorrow night belongs to Jenny and Fede, so we'll say our goodbyes now.'

'Oh, will we? Maybe I have something to say about that.'

'You've already said all I'm prepared to listen to. You win some and you lose some. I lost but there are other games to play.'

She saw his eyes gleam. 'Lining up your next victim, Dulcie?'

She was about to say that there could be nobody after him, but checked the impulse. That was weakness.

'Maybe,' she said defiantly. 'Once I've left Venice it won't matter to you what I do. But I'll say *this* before I go.'

She pulled his head down to her with a swift movement that took him by surprise. She took full advantage of that surprise, putting her arms about him, drawing his body close to hers. After a moment his arms went about her, but it was still her kiss. She was the one who took it deeper, teasing him with subtle movements against his mouth, reminding him of everything he'd thrown away.

'*Dulcie…*'

'It's over,' she murmured against his mouth. 'We might have had something wonderful but we lost our chance. I've seen myself clearly now, and I'm not the one for you.'

'Does a woman kiss a man like this when it's over?' he asked hoarsely.

'Yes, if she wants him to remember her. And I do want you to remember me.' She drew back a fraction. In the darkness Guido couldn't see her, but he could feel the whisper of her warm breath against his face.

'Remember me, Guido, but only when I'm gone. Columbine always gets away—'

'Unless Harlequin makes her stay.'

She laughed softly and it made his blood race. 'Harlequin never managed to make her do anything. He isn't clever enough.'

'That's right.' He tried to see her face, searching for something he didn't know how to find. 'Whatever he thinks, the poor sap is always dancing on the end of *her* string, isn't he?' he growled. 'Who are you? *Who are you?*'

'That's the problem, isn't it, my darling?' she asked, speaking huskily through her tears. 'You'd never really know, and it would always come between us. It's just lucky that we found out in time.'

She kissed him again, gently this time, a kiss of farewell, and slipped out of his arms. He heard her footsteps on the flagstones and at the end of the *calle* he saw her again as she reached the lights of a small canal. When she walked out of sight he waited, sure that she would return to him. But nothing happened and he began to run until he reached the canal. There was a small bridge, and on the other side he could just make out three ways she could have taken.

He tore over the bridge and stood straining his ears, hoping for some sound that would direct him. But she'd vanished into the night, and there was only the soft lapping of tiny waves against the stones. He touched his face. It was wet. But whether with her tears or his own, he couldn't have said.

Next morning the Palazzo Calvani buzzed with life like a hive of bees. Every servant in the place was on duty to make that evening's ball a success. Costumes for the family had arrived from Guido's shop and been laid out in their rooms, in readiness.

Liza was in her element, bustling everywhere, giving directions. At last she allowed herself to sit down for five minutes in the waterfront garden, and it was here that Guido found her.

'I want you to have this in thanks for what you did for me the other night,' he said. 'I should have given it to you before, but it wasn't finished until this morning.'

It was an exquisite little diamond brooch, inscribed with her name on the back. She turned it over and over, her thin face flushed with pleasure.

'*Grazie, signore*, but there was no need for any special thanks. I'm here to serve the family.'

'This was above and beyond the call of duty. Did my uncle get mad at you for losing the key?'

'He is never angry with me. Besides, I convinced him that he'd lost it himself, and he apologised to me.'

Guido's face was a study. 'I should have guessed.'

'But did it help you?'

He sighed. 'It's a long story.'

'Why don't you tell me?'

He told her as honestly as possible, not skipping his own deception, but finally coming to the point he found most painful.

'All that time, I was in love, but—I don't think she was.'

'How do you know?'

'She was pursuing me for a purpose.'

'No, she was pursuing Fede for a purpose and you confused her. And however it started, why couldn't she honestly have come to love you? You're a well-set-up young fellow, not bad looking in a poor light—'

'Thank you.'

'A bit crazy in the head, but women overlook that. In fact they sometimes prefer it. It doesn't do for a man to be too intelligent. Luckily that doesn't happen often.'

Guido's lips twitched. 'You think she might have found something tolerable in my unimpressive self?'

'Well, if, as you say, you were dancing attendance on her for days, she'd be a very strange woman if she didn't fall for that.'

He stared. 'For that?'

'Yes, that. Not your pretty face and your tom-fool jokes, or your money because she didn't know you had any, but because you were kind to her. There's something about a man's kindness that gets women in a spin. You didn't know that, did you, Signor Casanova?'

'No—I mean—of course I know that they like to be treated nicely, and I do—'

'I'm not talking about kissing their hands and buying them flowers. That's easy. I'm talking about what you did, day after day.'

'But she was vulnerable, she needed looking after.'

'The hotel would have done that, and most men would have dumped her there.'

'Leave her to strangers? No way. I wanted to know she was being cared for properly. Taking her home with me just seemed the natural thing.'

'And undressing her and putting her in your bed.'

'If you're suggesting that I—Liza, don't you dare even think—it's monstrous!'

'So you didn't?'

'No, I didn't,' he said firmly. 'I didn't even kiss her.'

'Oh, well, *that* did it.'

'Pardon?'

Liza smiled, almost to herself. 'There are times when *not* being kissed is the most romantic thing in the world. Unless, of course, you didn't want to?'

Guido groaned at the memory. 'More than I've ever wanted anything in my life. But she trusted me. Sometimes she was unconscious. On the first night she was feverish and she put her hand out and held mine, like a child. I couldn't have abused her trust.'

'According to you, she abused yours.'

'It's not the same.'

'Maybe she wasn't really unconscious at all. That was just part of the pretence.'

He shook his head. 'No,' he said quietly. 'That was real.'

'*Signore*, you don't understand being poor, like her,' Liza said firmly. 'When have you been poor as a church mouse? When it's a struggle to survive you do things you don't want to do. So she did.'

'It wasn't just that,' Guido admitted. 'There was a man who treated her badly—thought she had money and dumped her when he found otherwise.'

'*Fio di trojana!*' Liza spat.

Guido stared, for the Venetian words meant 'Son of a prostitute'. But most Venetians, himself included, would have said, '*Fio di putana*,' which meant the same, but was slightly less vulgar. Liza had expressed her contempt in no uncertain manner.

'Yes,' he agreed. 'That's what he was. It left her bitter and unhappy.' Then a burst of inspiration made him take a long breath and he said quickly, 'Her mind was clouded by misery when she first came here. She didn't mean to deceive me. She didn't really know what she was doing.'

He had it at last, the thing he'd been seeking through wretched days and sleepless nights: an explanation that would put Dulcie back on her pedestal.

'That must be it. But it's a bit late in the day to say it. My guess is that you've been hard on her. She's been judged by a man who understood nothing. And that came as a shock to her, because he'd deceived her into thinking he was kind and gentle. How could she know it was just a delusion and he wasn't really like that at all?'

'It wasn't a—OK, OK, I get the point.'

'So you thought she was perfect! Are you perfect? But like all men, you say one thing and do another.'

'When do I do that?'

'I've heard you talk about women when you thought I wasn't listening. No milksops for you, you said. You wanted a woman who'd be a challenge, you said. One who would keep you guessing, you *said*!'

There was a silence.

'I didn't exactly live up to that, did I?' he asked wryly.

'The first time you met a real woman with guts enough to play you at your own game you took fright.' Liza addressed the heavens in exasperation. 'And these are our lords and masters!'

If Guido had been less bemused he might have noticed that Liza was speaking to him with far less than her usual respect. It wouldn't have bothered him, but he would have wondered about it. Now his attention was fully occupied trying to keep up with her.

'She's too good for you,' Liza went on. 'And she was quite right to leave you. Such a pity that she'll come back.'

'You think so?' Guido asked hopefully.

'You two are fated to get married. And serve you right.'

'*What*?'

'Oh, she'll lead you a merry dance,' Liza said with relish. 'You won't know whether it's today or tomorrow.'

Guido gave her a strange look. 'I won't, will I?'

'It'll never be peaceful.'

'It'll never be dull,' he murmured.

'Whatever you expect her to do, she'll do the opposite.'

'She'll keep me guessing.'

'And you'll come by your just deserts.'

'Yes,' he breathed. 'I will.' The next moment he'd leapt up, planted a huge kiss on her cheek and headed out of the garden at a run.

'*Signore*, where are you going?'

'To get my just deserts,' he yelled over his shoulder. 'Thanks, Liza.'

He tore down to the landing stage, yelling for the boatman, who came running. Marco and Leo were in the garden. Seeing Guido speed past they exchanged puzzled glances and immediately went after him, catching up by the water.

'Where's the fire?' Marco demanded.

'No time to explain. Claudio—' this to the boatman '—the Hotel Vittorio.'

He got in and the other two joined him.

'You're not leaving our sight,' Marco said. 'You've dragged us into this stunt you're pulling tonight, and you're not vanishing, leaving us holding the baby.'

As the engine roared into life they took up position each side of him like a pair of guard dogs.

Guido slapped his back pocket. 'I've left my phone behind!'

'Use mine,' said Marco, who was never careless about these things.

Guido hurriedly dialled the hotel and was put through to the suite, but it was Jenny who answered.

'I need to speak to Dulcie urgently,' he said.

'But, Guido, she's gone.'

'Gone how? Where?'

'Left Venice. Just packed her bags and went. At least, she didn't pack all her bags because she said that stuff didn't really belong to her.'

'Didn't she leave any word for me?'

'No, she said you wouldn't want to hear anything from her.'

'The silly woman!' he yelled. 'Of course I want to hear from her. I love her.'

'Well, don't blame me. I'm not the one who's been pig-headed.'

'No, I have. But Jenny, help me put it right. What flight is she getting?'

'She's not. The flights were all booked so she's going by train. Twelve o'clock.'

'But that's only five minutes away.' He clapped Claudio on the shoulder. 'The railway station, *fast*.'

Soon the broad steps came into sight. The boat was

still a foot away when Guido leapt out. The platform for the noon train was straight ahead and he ran as though his life depended on it. He could see the train still there. Another few feet…

It began to move.

In despair he urged his legs faster and just made it onto the platform, but he couldn't catch up.

'*Dulcie*!' he roared. It was a wonder that his lungs still had any breath, but he managed to send the sound echoing down the length of the moving train.

Somewhere in the distance a head appeared through a window of one of the carriages. He couldn't see clearly but he would have known her at any distance.

'*I love you,*' he yelled. '*Don't leave me.*'

But then the head withdrew. The train was gathering speed. She was going away, and he couldn't tell if she'd heard him. Then the last carriage clattered out of sight and he was left alone on the platform, gasping and in despair.

'Let her go,' Marco advised, catching up with him and putting a hand on his shoulder.

'No way,' Guido said at once. 'I've got to get her back.'

'Phone her,' Leo said.

'Great idea.'

He called Dulcie's mobile. The train's first stop was just a few minutes away in Mestre, on the other side of the causeway. She could be back with him in half an hour.

The next moment there came the click of an answer.

'*Carissima*,' he said urgently, 'I love you. I can't live without you. I've been a pig-headed idiot but don't hold that against me. Let me spend my life making it up to you. Get off the train in Mestre, and take the next one back to Venice. I'll be waiting right here on the platform. Just say that you forgive me and come back. Please, *please* darling, come back. *Ti prego mia dolcissima Dulcie.*'

There was a silence.

'Hello?' said Jenny's voice.

'What?' Guido whispered, in shock. 'Jenny?'

'Yes. Dulcie forgot her phone. I found it under a cushion.'

Guido managed a polite thank you, and hung up. 'She's gone,' he groaned. 'I've lost her. There's got to be a flight, if not from here then from Milan—'

'No!' Leo and Marco spoke as one man.

'Think of Fede and Jenny, depending on you,' Leo pointed out.

'Besides,' Marco added practically, 'the train to England takes twenty-four hours. You can do what you have to at the ball tonight, catch the first flight tomorrow, and still get there ahead of her. You can even meet her at the station.'

'That's right,' Guido said, calming down. Then he clutched his head in despair. 'But how am I going to get through the next few hours?'

'Because we're going to be there to make sure you do,' Leo said firmly.

CHAPTER TWELVE

As always Count Calvani made sure nobody outshone him at his own ball. His long flowing robes glittered with gold thread, and on his head he wore the distinctive cap, plain at the front, raised at the rear, that said he was a Doge, one of the great men who had ruled Venice in the old days. His mask was an elaborate creation in scarlet satin, sporting tiny red and gold feathers.

He made a grand entrance into Guido's room, where his three nephews had congregated, and stood, tall and splendid, for them to admire him. When they had done so to his satisfaction he gave his opinion of their attire.

'Why are you all Harlequins?' he complained. 'The place will be crawling with Harlequins. Do you want to be mistaken for other men?'

They presented a handsome sight in their identical skin-tight costumes of coloured diamond shapes, alternating with white. Only a young man with a flat stomach and taut muscles could risk the revealing garb, and while Marco might be a fraction taller, and Leo slightly heavier, what would really distinguish them from other Harlequins was their ability to dress like this without looking ridiculous.

The costume was topped off by a small white ruff around the neck. On his head each wore a black tricorne hat, and beneath it the mask, the eyebrows raised to give a quizzical look. Francesco snorted.

'I suppose you're planning something disgraceful, like making inroads among the female guests and leaving them wondering which one of you it was.' He then spoiled his righteous indignation by adding, 'That's what we did in my day.'

'I don't think our chaste ears are ready to hear about your youth, Uncle,' Leo said, grinning.

'You'd get a few surprises,' Francesco agreed. 'But now I'm a reformed character. Guido, you'll be glad to hear that I'm going to do what you've always wanted.'

'Get married?' Guido gasped.

Marco coughed. 'But Uncle, isn't it a little late for you to be thinking—I mean—'

'I'm in my prime,' the count declared firmly.

'Of course he is,' Guido said. 'The nursery will be full in no time.' An agreeable vista of freedom was opening before him. 'Will we meet her tonight, Uncle?'

'No, she won't be at the ball.'

'But surely—?'

'Any more than Lady Dulcie will be at the ball,' Francesco said, glaring at him. By now he knew that they'd met, but Guido hadn't burdened him with too many precise details. 'I won't ask what you've done to offend her, but I'm sure it's something unforgivable.'

'She seems to think so,' Guido grunted. 'I aim to put it right soon, but now that my marriage will no longer matter to the family line, since you're marrying yourself, I'd rather discuss it no further.'

When Guido spoke in that firm tone nobody argued with him. A few minutes later they were all on their way downstairs to meet the torchlit procession that was coming along the Grand Canal. Gondola after gondola approached the landing stage to be greeted by their hosts, and a stream of masked figures passed into the glittering palazzo.

Music was already playing. Lights shone from every

door and window. A line of footmen stood bearing trays on which stood glasses of the finest crystal, filled with the best champagne.

'If only they'd show a little originality,' Francesco growled as he stood waiting, a smile fixed on his face. 'So many Columbines, Pantelones, Pulcinellas.'

'They can't all be the Doge of Venice,' Guido muttered. 'Not many men could carry it off.'

'That's true,' Francesco agreed, mollified.

'And if you want something unusual,' Leo said, 'how about Henry VIII?'

The Vittorio motor launch was just drawing up, with Roscoe standing in the rear.

'Roscoe Harrison,' Guido said. 'You are delighted to see him.'

'Am I?'

'For my sake, yes. The Columbine in the back is his daughter Jenny.'

'Another Columbine! How many is that?'

Guido need not have feared. The count gloried in his skills as a host, and the next few minutes went smoothly. Francesco bowed low over Jenny's hand murmuring, 'How charming!' and he and Roscoe eyed each other's attire with respect.

Guido took charge of the new arrivals, feeling Jenny cling nervously to his arm, and led them into the house. He would have been glad to skip this evening which was going to be so different from his hopes. Dulcie should have been around, helping him out, and then, while they were working together—here his invention failed, but surely something would have happened. He scowled. When Harlequin ran out of ideas Columbine was supposed to come to his rescue.

He'd managed to get a seat on an early flight next

morning. In the meantime he had work to do. He studied Jenny, noting with approval that she'd dressed to his instructions, with a black silk cap concealing her hair, a small black tricorne hat and a crimson satin mask, so heavily trimmed with lace that it covered most of the lower part of her face as well.

Her dress was a mass of white tulle, with a tight waist, puff sleeves and a huge ballerina skirt that ended just below the knee. She looked delicate and enchanting.

'Fede won't be able to resist you,' he said when he'd swept her away into the dance.

'Oh, Guido, is he really here? I'm so nervous.'

'He's outside in the boathouse. We'll wait until it's a bit more crowded and your Poppa can't see you so well, and then my brother Leo will ask you to dance. Your father will think it's me, but I'll be dancing with another Columbine and so we'll keep him confused.' His gaze fell on a detail that troubled him. 'I wish you weren't wearing that diamond necklace. It looks like it cost a fortune.'

'Ten thousand,' she said with a sigh. 'Dad insisted on giving it to me just before we came out. He said it was to "console me" for losing Fede.'

'That figures. But you can bet he'll keep his eyes on it, and it'll complicate the switch over to the other Columbine. I've persuaded one of the maids to help out.'

'It was supposed to be Dulcie, wasn't it? She's really gone then?'

'Yes, but I'm going to get her back. Jenny, I simply must talk to you about her.'

'We will, I promise. But I see Dad waving to me. I'll be back later.'

She slipped away and Guido lost her in the crowd. He spent the next half hour on hot coals, doing duty dances, watching the time pass, wondering how soon he could get away to England.

Roscoe was enjoying himself. He and the count had squared up to each other, and he hadn't backed down. And those diamonds of Jenny's! Anyone could see that they'd cost a pretty penny. It never hurt to show people you had money, and Roscoe had big plans for his daughter.

He looked around and frowned when he couldn't see her. She'd been there just a moment ago, dancing with Guido. Then she'd vanished in the crush.

No, there she was again, a pretty Columbine, threading her way through the crowd, her diamonds sparkling magnificently.

'They look wonderful on you, darling,' he growled.

But Columbine didn't seem happy. She made a gesture as if to remove the diamonds, but he stopped her.

'You keep them on. Guido was looking at them. Keep working on him, and you'll be a countess yet.'

Columbine sighed and began to thread her way back through the crowd to where Harlequin was looking around him.

'There you are,' he said with relief.

'You wanted to talk about Dulcie.'

'I'm going to follow her to England.'

Columbine put her head on one side, teasing him. 'And when you see her, what will you say?'

He groaned. 'I don't know. Just ask her to forgive me for being a pompous jerk, I suppose. Who knows what she's thinking now? I don't even know if she heard me calling to her down the platform. She didn't telephone you?'

'I haven't spoken to Dulcie,' Columbine said truthfully. 'And even if I had, I doubt she'd tell me much. Once she's made up her mind, that's it!'

Through his mask Guido's eyes widened with alarm. 'You don't mean that she'd never forgive me? I don't believe that.'

'Dulcie's stubborn. When she's decided against somebody—' she gave an eloquent shrug.

'But you don't really know her well.'

'Neither do you after just a few days—'

'A few days is enough when you've met your ideal. Or a few minutes. I knew at once, when she tossed that sandal down into my gondola—'

'But you didn't know she threw it,' Columbine reminded him. 'You thought it was fate but actually it was her. I think she was dreadful, deceiving you like that.'

'But she didn't deceive me,' Guido said earnestly. 'Not if you look at it the right way. Dulcie and I were always destined to be together, so when she threw that sandal she was only doing what fate demanded. And when I let her think I was Fede, that was fate too, because that way she saw *me*. Not a Calvani with a palace and a title at his back, but just a man falling in love with her.'

He wondered if Columbine would speak, but she danced in his arms, gazing intently at him, as if she were waiting for something. He was several inches taller, and from this angle he could see little of her lower face, because the lace of the mask blocked his vision. But he could see her green eyes, and a strange feeling began to creep over him.

'I'll make her listen to me,' he said. 'I'll remind her what it was like during those days we spent together, because that's when we were most truly ourselves. She was so—' he hunted for the word, not easy for him, a man not used to analysing '—so surprised. As though nobody had ever taken care of her before.'

'That's very clever of you,' Columbine said thoughtfully. 'I don't think anyone ever really has. The rest of her family were so irresponsible that she couldn't afford to be. She had to grow up too fast and she's been lonely all her life, but people don't see it.'

'I once told her that masks could make people free to be their real selves,' Guido said. 'Now I think maybe your real self can come as a surprise. I'm not who I thought I was.'

'Who are you, Guido?' Columbine asked earnestly. 'Do you know now? And do you know who she is?'

'I'm the man who loves her, come what may,' he said.

'But is she the woman who loves you? Suppose she doesn't?'

'She must, even if I have to spend the rest of my life convincing her.'

Columbine smiled as though she'd discovered a secret treasure. But instead of answering him directly she said, 'Someone's trying to attract your attention.'

Guido saw two Harlequin figures beckoning him from the window that led into the garden. He murmured something to Columbine and followed to where Leo and Marco were waiting for him.

'It all went like clockwork,' Leo said from behind his mask. 'We delivered Jenny to the church, Fede was waiting for her with his family, and they're probably married by now.'

'But Jenny's still here,' Guido said thoughtfully. The

strange, haunted feeling was back. 'I was just dancing with her.'

'Jenny was with us.'

'Then who—?' He remembered now. Jenny's eyes were blue.

Dazed, he returned to the ballroom, looking this way and that, searching for Columbine. But, like an elusive ghost, she'd vanished.

Suddenly there seemed to be a thousand Columbines, and none of them was the right one.

What he was thinking couldn't be true, he told himself. It was a mental aberration. But while his head might be muddled his heart had never been more clear. He knew everything now. Or at least, Harlequin knew what Columbine thought it was good for him to know.

He spotted her at last, drinking champagne and talking to Leo, who'd removed his mask. Suddenly inspired, he made sure his own mask was in place, and bore down on them.

'You'd better keep out of Guido's way,' he said, clapping his brother on the shoulder. 'That little revelation has put him on the warpath.'

'So I saw,' Leo said, studying him cautiously. 'Marco?'

'Sure, I'm Marco, and I'm about to ask this lady to dance.' He slipped his arm firmly around Columbine's waist, and glided with her onto the floor. Her eyes were on his face, laughing, not fooled one little bit.

'So Guido's annoyed?' she asked provocatively. 'Serve him right!'

'Don't be so hard on him,' Guido said. 'He's not a bad fellow.'

'He's a clown and someone should take him in hand and reform him.'

'You can do that when you're married.'

'Me? Marry him?' Columbine sounded shocked. 'Never!'

'You've got to marry him,' Harlequin said urgently. 'You can't leave him running amok the way he is. Think of the family reputation. Besides, he's madly in love with you. I know he hasn't been clever about it, but you can be clever for both of you. After all, you're really in love with him too, aren't you? Otherwise you wouldn't abuse him so much.'

'Never mind about Guido,' Columbine said, looking at her partner's mouth and thinking how badly she wanted to kiss it. 'After all, he isn't very interesting.'

'You don't think so?'

'I've never thought so,' she said with a fair assumption of indifference. 'But I played along to keep him happy.'

Their eyes met through the slits in their masks, each understanding the other perfectly.

'You—' he breathed, 'you—I've a good mind to—'

'To do what?' she asked with interest.

'To do *this*!'

Swiftly he removed his mask, then hers, and pulled her into his arms for a long, breathless kiss, while the crowd cheered and applauded.

'It was you all the time,' he said when he could speak.

'I fooled you for a while, didn't I?' Dulcie teased.

'Only a very short while,' he growled, interrupting himself with another kiss. 'How did you get here?' he asked breathlessly after a while. 'You were leaving.'

'I left the train at Mestre and caught the next one back. Not just because you came after me. I was going to do it anyway. I stormed off because I was furious, but I wouldn't really have let Jenny and Fede down.'

'I see. You only came back for them?'

She chuckled. 'Of course not. There was another reason.'

He held her tightly. 'Tell me.'

'I had to retrieve my mobile phone,' she teased.

'*Cara*, you'll drive me too far—' he broke off. She was laughing at him and it was like music.

'I would always have come back,' she said, 'because I wasn't going to give up on us just like that.'

He kissed her again and again, while the music played and they swayed in its rhythm.

'So,' she resumed as he whirled her about the floor, 'at Mestre I telephoned Jenny, and she told me about your calls, and the very interesting things you'd said.'

'But why not call me?' he demanded. 'You knew I loved you. I should think the whole world knew after I shouted it the length of the platform.'

'I did call you, but Marco answered. You'd all just got back from chasing me to the station. Leo was there too, and they told me one or two things—'

'Like that I was going out of my mind. Just tell me how big a fool you've all made of me.'

'I came back, Leo met me at the station and brought me here. Then I just slipped into the role you'd always meant me to play, wearing the costume you supplied. Roscoe complicated things by giving Jenny that necklace, but in a way it actually made things easier. Jenny gave it to me just before she left, and while I wore it nobody doubted that I was her.'

'And you made the switch—when? When Jenny saw Roscoe waving to her. She left me—'

'Slipped into a side room, where Leo and Marco were

waiting, gave me the necklace, and told me you wanted
to speak to her about me. They left. I went out to speak
to Roscoe—'

'And he didn't know his own daughter?'

'He knew his diamonds, which were all he was looking at. I came back to you and took up the cue she'd
given me, about you wanting to talk about Dulcie.'

'But why couldn't you simply have told me?'

She chuckled, and the sound went through him pleas-
urably. 'I wouldn't have missed the last hour for anything. I've discovered things I couldn't have learned any
other way.'

'And of course you've enjoyed setting me up.'

She tilted her head. 'That's Columbine's nature, I'm
afraid. Harlequin will just have to learn to cope with
her.'

'Will she always be with him?'

'Always in his hair,' she assured him.

'Always in his life, in his heart?'

'Wherever he wants me.'

He kissed her again. When she opened her eyes they
were dancing past Roscoe, whose eyes were popping at
the sight of her. It would soon be time for explanations,
but just now she wanted to talk to nobody but Guido.

'When did you know?' she asked.

'It was your green eyes. Jenny's are blue. And then
Marco and Leo told me Jenny had left, so I couldn't
have been dancing with her.'

'Did the plan work?'

'Like a dream apparently. They took her to a little
church where a priest was waiting. By the time Roscoe
sees them again they'll be married. And talking of marriage, I have a confession. I can't make you a countess.

Uncle Francesco is going to get married and have a son, to cut me out. He's promised.'

'Don't be silly! As though I cared about being a countess.'

'Then there's nothing standing in the way of our marriage.'

'I didn't say—'

'You have to marry me, after all those things you said to Marco.'

'I haven't spoken to Marco since the ball started.'

'You started this dance with him.'

'Yes, but that was you.' She eyed him with suspicion. 'And what am I supposed to have said?'

'You said you couldn't live without me, and you'd die if I didn't propose.'

'In your dreams!' she said wrathfully.

'But you already fill my dreams, *carissima*, and you always will. What's a poor fool to do?'

She couldn't help laughing at his serpentine way with the facts. She was dealing with a master of deception. But not all deceptions were bad.

'Don't worry,' he said. 'I'm quite prepared to marry you to save you from going into a decline. *Don't do that!* I'm ticklish!'

'That'll teach you to get funny with me,' she murmured into his ear, so that the soft whisper of her breath sent him into a whirl.

'Darling,' he said ecstatically, 'am I going to be a hen-pecked husband?'

'Definitely.'

'You'll teach me how to say, "Yes, dear", "No, dear"?'

'Can't start too soon. And if you're out late I'll be waiting for you with a rolling pin.'

'I *adore* you!'

'I hate to break up the happy dream,' Marco said, appearing beside them, 'but Signor Harrison is getting agitated.'

He and Leo stationed themselves protectively as Roscoe approached. Dulcie removed the diamond necklace and handed it to him.

'I promised Jenny I'd see this safely returned,' she said. 'She didn't feel she could accept it since she was doing something that you wouldn't like.'

'And just what does that mean? Where the devil is she?'

'Signora Lucci is just leaving for her honeymoon with Fede,' Guido announced. 'The bride and groom are very happy.'

Roscoe's eyes narrowed. 'What are you talking about? Where's my Jenny? If she thinks she can defy me—'

'She's already done it,' Dulcie said. 'She's married the man she loves. Please Roscoe, try to be happy for her.'

'Happy? You did this. I trusted you, and I ran up bills to keep you here. Well, you can pay for all those posh clothes *Lady* Dulcie, and see how you like that!'

Guido stepped forward. 'As Dulcie's future husband let me say that I'll be glad to refund you every penny you spent on her clothes—and then dump the lot in the lagoon. And if you dare speak to her like that again, you'll follow them. Do I make myself plain?'

Roscoe squared up to him, but there was something about Guido at the moment that made his courage fail. He took a step back, covering his retreat with sharp fire.

'I'm done with the lot of you. And you can tell that

precious pair that they'll never get a penny of my money. Not a penny.'

'Good,' Guido said. 'Stick to that. They'll be a lot happier.'

Roscoe gaped. He just didn't understand.

'He won't stick to it,' Dulcie said when Roscoe had stormed off. 'Like she said, he doesn't have anyone else.'

'*My boy!*'

Francesco bore down on them in grandeur. He kissed Dulcie, wrung Guido's hand and flung his arms out as if to say that he'd brought the whole thing about.

After that there were toasts and then more toasts, and the ball went on into the early hours. A light was already appearing on the water as the gondola procession wended its way back, and the family was left alone. Francesco embraced Dulcie again.

'I knew as soon as I met you that you were the only woman who could keep him in order,' he declared.

'And what about you, Uncle?' Leo demanded with a grin. 'Guido says you're making plans too. One wedding begets another.'

The count raised his hand for silence.

'This is true. I have finally managed to persuade the only woman I have ever truly loved to become my wife.'

While his nephews looked at each other in bafflement he went to the door, opened it, and reached out to somebody outside. In a gentler voice than they had ever heard him use, he said, 'Come, my darling.'

There was a tension-filled pause, then Count Calvani's future bride appeared, and everybody stared with astonishment.

'*Liza!*' Guido gasped.

'I have loved her for years,' Francesco said simply. 'Many times I've begged her to marry me, but she always refused. She said I would be marrying beneath me, which is nonsense, for she is the greatest lady in the world.'

Liza smiled at him, and for a moment they could all see her as Francesco did, as the sweet-faced girl who'd come to work there nearly fifty years ago, and won the young count's heart on the first day. She was arthritic, elderly, and she was the greatest lady in the world. For a moment Dulcie's eyes misted over.

Guido was the first to embrace Liza and call her 'Aunt'. Marco and Leo followed.

'There's no escape for you after all,' Marco told Guido with a touch of malicious relish. 'You'll have to put up with being the count.'

'Get lost,' Guido growled.

'Do you mind very much?' Dulcie asked gently.

'Are you still going to marry me?'

'Of course I am.'

'Then I don't mind anything else.' He took her hand possessively, drawing her away from the others and leading her out to the peace of the garden.

There they faced each other with truth between them at last.

'No masks now,' she whispered.

'No, masks, *carissima*. Never again. Not between us.'

He took her face between his hands, searching it, as if for the first time; seeing there everything he wanted in life, wondering how he could ever have been so blind.

'Say my name,' he begged. 'Mine, not Fede's.'

'Guido,' she said softly.

In response he spoke her own name, over and over, making it music.

'How could I have misunderstood you?' he asked. 'I knew from the start that there was only truth and honour in you. The rest was an illusion.'

'Darling, it wasn't,' she began to protest.

'Yes it was,' he said quickly. 'I saw it clearly today. You were so unhappy that you weren't yourself. It coloured everything you did, as though someone else was doing it. Now the real you has come back, the woman I couldn't help loving.'

'You're saying dangerous things,' she said, swiftly laying her fingertips across his mouth. 'I can't live on a pedestal. I'm human. I'll disappoint you and fall off.'

'Ah, but you can't,' he said eagerly. 'Because I'm going to make sure you're never, ever unhappy again. So that solves the problem, don't you see? It's easy.'

She made one last effort. 'Don't think me better than I am.'

'I shall think of you what I please,' he said, smiling and stubborn.

He was incorrigible, she thought. And he always would be.

She had told him that she was as she was, but the same was true of him. It was buried deep in his nature, this need, not merely to love but to idolise. He'd tried being angry with her, and hated the feeling so much that in future, if disillusion threatened, he would tap-dance his way around awkward facts, so that his precious image of her would remain undisturbed. And so, throughout all their years together, she would be incapable of doing wrong in his eyes.

It was wonderful, but it was an awesome responsibility. For a moment she almost quailed under it, but his eyes were upon her, full of warmth and passionate adoration. He'd laid a heavy burden of trust on her, but his love would always be there to bear her up.

He drew her close and kissed her. It was nothing like the tormenting kisses they'd given each other last night, after the dinner with the Luccis: nor the exuberant embrace of the ballroom. This one was quiet and full of many promises. One journey had brought them safely home into each other's arms. Another journey was about to begin.

'Now you're mine,' he said quietly. 'And I shall never, never let you go.'

Three months later there were two weddings at St Mark's Basilica. It wasn't a double wedding because Liza dreaded being the centre of a large crowd and Francesco, after loving her so long, would do anything she wanted.

So they married quietly in a small chapel, with only the Calvani family present, and as soon as the wedding was over the new countess insisted on busying herself with the final preparations for the second wedding next day, to which most of Italian and English society had been invited.

At the reception and dance afterwards the two bridal couples took the floor, amid applause. And there was another couple, drawing curious eyes as they danced in each other's arms.

'Marco and his fiancée seem very happy,' Guido observed as they paused for champagne.

'You sound surprised,' Dulcie said. 'I thought you liked Harriet when we went to their party in Rome a few weeks ago.'

'I did. I do. It's just that there's something about that engagement that I don't understand.'

'Well, it certainly came about very suddenly,' Dulcie agreed. 'Harriet just appeared out of nowhere, and suddenly they were engaged.'

'Are they in love, do you think?'

Dulcie regarded Marco and his fiancée, Harriet d'Estino, gliding gracefully by. 'I don't know,' she said thoughtfully. 'But you've got to admit that what happened at that engagement party was very strange.'

'Strangest thing I ever saw,' Leo observed over her shoulder. 'Marco was a lot more upset than he allowed to appear. You know how he keeps his feelings to himself. And he wouldn't tell the world he was in love, either.'

'More fool Marco,' Guido said, his loving eyes on his bride.

The wedding was a lavish extravaganza, which neither of them had wanted, but also which neither of them noticed. Today they were the centre of a performance, wearing the glamorous masks that the world expected, playing their parts to perfection. Tonight all masks would fall away, and so now they could be patient, waiting for their moment.

Nobody knew the honeymoon destination. Several were mentioned—New York, the Bahamas, the south of France—but never confirmed. Only Liza knew that when, late in the evening, they slipped away from the reception, they headed, not to the airport, but to the landing stage where a gondola awaited, with a familiar gondolier keeping it safe.

'Fede!' Guido shook his friend's hand warmly, and Dulcie kissed him.

'Here it is,' Fede said, indicating his gondola. 'Jenny

asked me to say sorry she left the reception early. She was feeling a bit queasy, and Roscoe got rather over-protective.'

'How is the future grandfather?' Dulcie asked.

'Trying to take over, but we're resisting. He's almost as hard-going now as when he was hostile, but Jenny's happy, and that's all that matters.'

He helped to settle Dulcie in the boat, handed the oar to Guido, and retreated, waving.

Dulcie sat facing Guido, her bridal veil billowing around her. 'Let's go home,' she said. 'Our real home.'

He began to ply the oar. 'You're sure you want to have our honeymoon there? We could still fly away if you like. Anywhere in the world.'

'But we have the world waiting for us,' she said softly.

He headed out into the Grand Canal, then turned the gondola into the small canals for the short journey home.

The palace and its turmoil slid away from them. The glitter faded into the distance. Music floated faintly across the water. Under the stars Harlequin and Columbine drifted in an endless dream.

asked me to see Larry the lift the reception early. She was feeling a bit queasy, and Roscoe got rather overprotective.

How is the future grandmother? Guido asked.

'Dying to make over, but we're resisting. He's almost — but time enough when we've inside the drawing — lamp and light, all time entered.' ... ...

He helped the old man to ... the boys, kissed the white ... to Guido, and returned, waving ... ...

Below sat facing Guido, her broad veil folding the around her. 'Let's go back,' she said, 'I'm not happy.'

He began to pull the oars. 'Are you sure you want to have our honeymoon there? We could still try away, if you like. Anywhere in the world.'

'But we have the right, staying here too,' she said softly.

He pulled out into the Grand Canal, then turned the gondola into the small canals for the short journey home.

The palace and its turmoil slid away from them. The gates fade into the distance. White flashed from across the water. Under the stars, Haleyon and Columbine drifted in an endless dream.

THE ITALIAN MILLIONAIRE'S MARRIAGE

by

Lucy Gordon

PROLOGUE

'I DO not need a husband, do you understand that? I do *not* need a husband. And I certainly don't want one.' These last words were said with a mild shudder that shocked Harriet d'Estino's listener.

'Harriet, calm down,' she begged.

'A *husband?* Good grief! I've lived twenty-seven years without troubling myself with a creature so bothersome and unnecessary—'

'Will you just listen?'

'—and when I find my own sister matchmaking for me— Stars above! You've got a nerve, Olympia.'

'I wasn't matchmaking,' Olympia said placatingly. 'I just thought you might find Marco useful.'

Harriet made a sound that would have been a snort if she hadn't been a lady.

'No man is ever useful,' she said firmly. 'The breed isn't made that way.'

'All right, I won't argue.'

They were half-sisters, one English, one Italian. Only their rich auburn hair linked them to their common parent, and each other. But in Olympia, the younger, the glorious tresses were teased into a glamorous creation. In Harriet, the same colour hung, straight and austere on either side of an earnest face.

Their clothes too revealed their opposing characters. Olympia was dressed in the height of Italian fashion. Harriet looked as though she'd put on whatever was comfortable and handy. Olympia's figure was slender and se-

5

ductive. Harriet was certainly slender. It was hard to be sure about anything else.

Olympia looked around her at the exquisite shop in the heart of London's West End. It was filled with fine art and antiques, several of which caught her interest.

'He's splendid,' she exclaimed, noticing a bronze bust of a young man.

'First-century Roman,' Harriet said, glancing up. 'Emperor Caesar Augustus.'

'Really dishy,' Olympia purred, studying the face close up. 'That fine nose, that aristocratic head on the long, muscular neck, and that mouth—all stern discipline masking incredible sensuality. I'll bet he was a tiger with the women.'

'You spend too much time thinking about sex,' Harriet said severely.

'And you don't spend enough time thinking about it. It's disgraceful.'

Harriet shrugged. 'There are more interesting things in life.'

'Nonsense, of course there aren't,' Olympia said with conviction. 'I just wish you were as interested in living men as dead ones.'

'Listen to you!' Harriet riposted. 'You've just been mooning over a man who's been dead for two thousand years. Anyway, dead ones are better. They don't tell lies, get legless or chat up your friends. And you can talk to them without being interrupted.'

'So cynical. Mind you, Marco's pretty cynical, too. Otherwise he'd have married long ago.'

'Aha! He's a grey-beard!'

'Marco Calvani is thirty-five, loaded, and extremely good-looking,' Olympia said emphatically.

'So why aren't you marrying him? You said he asked you first.'

'Only because his mother's an old friend of Pappa's mother, and she's got this sentimental idea of uniting the two families.'

'And he does what she tells him? He's a wimp!'

'Far from it,' Olympia said with a little chuckle. 'Marco is a man who likes his own way all the time. He's doing this for his own reasons.'

'He's a nutter!'

'He's a banker who devotes his life to serious business. He reckons it's time to make a serious marriage and he isn't into courting.'

'He's gay!'

'Not according to my friends. In fact, his reputation is of a ladykiller, with the emphasis on killer. You might say he "loves 'em and leaves 'em" except that he doesn't love 'em. No emotional involvement just a quick fling and goodbye before things get too intense.'

'You make him sound irresistible, you know that?'

'It's only fair to tell you the downs as well as the ups. Marco doesn't go for moonlight and roses, so you can see why he'd be doing this. It would be more of a merger than a marriage, and I thought that since you were serious, too—'

'I'd be happy to take on one of your rejects. Gosh, thanks Olympia.'

'Will you stop being so prickly? I took all this trouble to warn you that he might turn up here next week—'

'And I'm grateful. I've been planning a vacation on the other side of the world. Next week will suit me just fine.'

'*Dio mio!*' Olympia threw up her hands in sisterly exasperation. 'It's impossible to help some people. You'll end up an old maid.'

Harriet gave a cheeky grin that transformed her face delightfully.

'With any luck,' she said.

CHAPTER ONE

'My dear boy, have you really thought this through?'

Signora Lucia Calvani's face was full of concern as she watched her son lock the suitcase. He gave her a brief smile, warmer for her than for anyone else, but he didn't pause.

'What is there to think through, Mamma? In any case, I'm doing what you required of me.'

'Nonsense! You never do anything except to suit yourself,' she retorted with motherly scepticism.

'True, but it suits me to please you,' Marco replied smoothly. 'You wanted a union between myself and the granddaughter of your old friend, and I consider it suitable.'

'If you mean that you like the idea, kindly say so, and don't address your mother like a board meeting,' Lucia said severely.

'I'm sorry.' He kissed her cheek with a touch of genuine contrition. 'But since I'm doing as you wished I don't understand your concern.'

'When I said I'd like to see you marry Etta's granddaughter I was thinking of Olympia, as you well know. She's elegant, sophisticated, knows all the right people in Rome, and would have been an admirable wife.'

'I disagree. She's frivolous and immature. Her sister is older and, I gather, has a serious mind.'

'She's been raised English. She may not even speak Italian.'

'Olympia assures me that she does. Her pursuits are

9

intellectual, and she sounds as if she might well suit my requirements.'

'Suit your requirements?' his mother echoed, aghast. 'This is a woman you're discussing, not a block of shares.'

'It's just a way of talking,' Marco said with a shrug. 'Have I forgotten to pack anything?'

He looked around his home which was at its best in the brilliant morning sun that came in through the balcony window. He stepped out for a moment to breathe in the fresh air and enjoy the view along the Via Veneto. From this apartment on the fifth floor of an elegant block he could just make out St Peter's in the distance, and the curve of the River Tiber. In the clear air he caught the sound of bells floating across the city, and he paused a moment to listen and watch the light glinting on the water. He did this every morning, no matter how rushed he might be, and it would have surprised many people who thought of him as a calculating machine and nothing else.

The inside of his home, however, would have reinforced their prejudices. It was costly but spartan, without any softening touch, the home of a man who was enough unto himself. The cool marble of the floors gleamed. The furnishings were largely modern, adorned with one or two valuable old vases and pictures.

It was typical of Marco that he had chosen to live in the centre of Rome, for his heart and mind, his whole presence were Roman. Height, bearing, and the unconsciously arrogant set of his head all spoke of a man descended from a race of emperors.

Nor was it far-fetched to see him as one, for were not international bankers the new emperors? At thirty-five he lorded it over his contemporaries in the financial world. Buying, selling, merging, making deals, these were the breath of life to him, and it was no accident that he spoke of his prospective marriage in a businesslike way that scandalised his mother.

Now he gave her his most charming smile. 'Mamma, I wonder that you dare to reprove me when you yourself proposed the merger.'

'Well, somebody has to arrange proper marriages for this family. When I think of that old fool in Venice, getting engaged to his housekeeper—'

'By "old fool" I take it you mean my Uncle Francesco, Count Calvani, the head of our family,' Marco said wryly.

'Being a count doesn't stop him being an old fool,' Lucia said robustly. 'And being his heir doesn't stop Guido being a young fool, planning to marry an English woman—'

'But Dulcie comes from a titled family, which is very proper,' Marco murmured. He was teasing his mother in his dry way.

'A titled family who've blown every penny on gambling. I've heard the most dreadful stories about Lord Maddox, and I don't suppose his daughter's much better. Bad blood will tell.'

'Don't let either of them hear you criticising their ladies,' Marco warned her. 'They're both in a state of positively imbecile devotion, and will resent it.'

'I've no intention of being rude. But the truth is the truth. Someone has to make a good marriage, and there's no knowing what that bumpkin in Tuscany will do.'

Marco shrugged, recognising his cousin in this description. 'Leo probably won't marry at all. There's no shortage of willing females in the area. I gather he's very much in demand for brief physical relationships on account of—'

'There's no need to be coarse,' Lucia interrupted him

firmly. 'If he won't do his duty, all the more reason for you to do yours.'

'Well, I'm off to England to do it. If she suits me, I'll marry her.'

'And if *you* suit *her*. She may not fall at your feet.'

'Then I shall return to you and report failure.'

He didn't sound troubled by the prospect. Marco had found few women who were unimpressed by him. Olympia, of course, had turned him down, but they'd known each other since childhood, and were too much like brother and sister.

'I worry about you,' Lucia said, studying his face and trying to discern what he was really thinking. 'I want to see you with a happy home, instead of always wasting yourself on affairs that don't mean anything. If only you and Alessandra had married, as you should have done. You could have had three children by now.'

'We were unsuited. Let's leave it there.' His voice was gentle but the hint of warning was unmistakable.

'Of course,' Lucia said at once. When Marco's barriers went up even she knew better than to persist.

'It's time I was leaving,' he said. 'Don't worry, Mamma. I'm simply going to meet Harriet d'Estino and form an impression. If I don't like her I won't mention the idea. She won't know anything about it.'

As he boarded the plane for London Marco reflected that he was behaving unlike himself. He believed in thinking things through, but he was committing an impulsive action.

An *apparently* impulsive action, he corrected the thought. He was an orderly man who lived an orderly life, because success flourished from good order. That meant stability, the correct action performed at the correct time.

He'd intended to marry at thirty, and would have done so if Alessandra hadn't changed her mind.

That thought no sooner lived than he killed it. Everything concerning his aborted engagement, including the emotional fool he'd made of himself, was past and done. A wise man learned from experience, and he would never open himself up like that again.

His mother's suggestion of a sensible marriage had been a godsend. To found a family, without involving his heart suited him exactly.

He arrived in London in the late afternoon, taking a suite at the Ritz and spending the rest of the day online, checking various deals that needed his personal attention. The five-hour time difference between America and Europe was too useful to be missed, and it was past midnight before he was through. By that time the Tokyo Stock Exchange was open and he worked until three in the morning. Then he went to bed and slept for precisely five hours, efficiently, as he did everything.

This was how he spent the night before meeting the woman he was planning to make his wife.

He breakfasted on fruit and coffee before setting out to walk the short distance to the Gallery d'Estino. He judged his time precisely, arriving at a quarter to nine, before it was open. This would give him a chance to form an impression of the place before meeting the owner.

What he saw, he approved. The shop was exquisite, and although he could discern little of the merchandise through the protective grilles over the windows, what he could make out seemed well chosen. His mental picture of Harriet d'Estino became clearer: a woman of elegance, *mental* elegance, as well as intellect. He began to warm to her.

The warmth faded a little as nine o'clock passed with no sign of the shop opening. Inefficiency. The unforgivable sin. He turned and collided with someone who yelled, 'Ouch!'

'My apologies,' he murmured to the flustered young woman who was hopping about on the pavement, clutching one foot.

'It's all right,' she said, wincing and nearly losing her balance until Marco took hold of her.

'Thanks. Did you want to go in?'

'Well it is past opening time,' he pointed out.

'Oh, gosh yes, it is, isn't it. Hang on, I've got the key.'

While she scrabbled through a large collection of keys he studied her and found nothing to approve. She wore jeans and a sweater that looked as though they'd been chosen for utility, and a blue woollen hat that covered her hair completely. She might have been young. She might even have been attractive. It was hard to tell since she looked like a worker on a building site. Harriet d'Estino must be desperate for staff to have employed someone so gauche and clumsy.

After what seemed like an age she let him in.

'Just give me a moment,' she said, dumping her packages and starting work on the grilles. 'Then you can have all my attention.'

'Actually I was hoping to see the owner.'

'Won't I do?'

'I'm afraid not.'

The young woman grew suddenly still. Then she shot him a nervous glance and her whole manner changed.

'Of course, I should have realised. How stupid of me. It's just that I'd hoped for a little more time—that is, *she* hoped for a little more time—I'm afraid Miss d'Estino isn't here just now.'

'Can you tell me when she will be here?' Marco asked patiently.

'Not for ages. But I could give her a message.'

'Could you tell her that Marco Calvani called to see her?'

Her eyes assumed the blankness of someone who was playing 'possum'.

'Who?'

'Marco Calvani. She doesn't know me but—'

'You mean you're not a bailiff?'

'No,' Marco said tersely, with an instinctive glance at his Armani suit. 'I'm not a bailiff.'

'You're sure?'

'I think I'd know if I was a bailiff.'

'Yes,' she said distractedly. 'Of course you would. And you're Italian, aren't you? I can hear your accent now. It's not much of an accent, so I missed it at first.'

'I pride myself on speaking other languages as correctly as possible,' he said, enunciating slowly. 'Would you mind telling me who you are?'

'Me? Oh, I'm Harriet d'Estino.'

'You?' He couldn't keep the unflattering inflection out of his voice.

'Yes. Why not?'

'Because you just told me you weren't here.'

'Did I?' she said vaguely. 'Oh—well—I must have got that wrong.'

Marco stared, wondering if she was mad, bad or merely half-witted. She pulled off the woolly cap, letting her long hair fall about her shoulders, and then he realised that she was speaking the truth, for it was the same rich auburn shade as Olympia's hair. This was the woman he'd been considering as a wife. He took a deep cautious breath.

Harriet was watching him, frowning slightly. 'Have we met before?' she asked.

'I don't believe so.'

'It's just that your face is familiar.'

'We've never met,' he assured her, thinking that he would certainly have remembered.

'I'll make us some coffee.'

Harriet went into the back of the shop and put on the coffee, annoyed with herself for having made a mess of everything after Olympia's warning. But she'd half convinced herself that Marco wouldn't bother coming to see her, and her mind had been so taken up with worries about her creditors that she'd had little time to think of other things.

As an expert in antiquities Harriet had no rival. Her taste was impeccable, her instincts flawless, and many an imposing institution accepted her opinion as final. But somehow she couldn't translate this skill into a commercial profit, and the bills were piling up.

The coffee perked and she brought herself back to reality. She would have given anything not to have betrayed her money worries to this man, but perhaps he hadn't noticed. Then he appeared beside her and she became distracted by the resemblance. Just where had she seen him before?

She'd promised Olympia not to let Marco suspect that she'd been forewarned, so it might be safest to play dumb for a while. It was a melancholy fact, she'd discovered, that if you pretended to be really stupid people always believed you.

'Why did you want to see me, Signor—Calvani, was it?'

'My name means nothing to you?'

'I'm sorry, should it?'

'I'm a friend of your sister Olympia. I thought she might have mentioned me.'

'We're only half-sisters. We grew up far apart and don't see each other often.' She added casually, 'How is she these days?'

'Still the beautiful social butterfly. I told her I'd look you up while I was in London. If it's agreeable to you we might spend this evening together, perhaps go to a show and have dinner afterwards.'

'That would be nice.'

'What kind of show do you like?'

'I've been trying to get into *Dancing On Line*, but the seats are like gold-dust and tonight's the last performance.'

'I think I might manage it, just the same.'

She was conscience stricken. 'If you're thinking of the black market, the tickets are going for thousands. I shouldn't have said anything.'

'I shan't need to resort to the black market,' he said, smiling.

She regarded him with something approaching awe. 'You can get seats for this show, at a moment's notice?'

'I can't afford to fail now, can I?' he remarked, somewhat wryly. 'Leave it to me. I'll collect you here at seven.'

'Fine. And we can always go to a different show. I really don't mind.'

'We shall go to this show and no other,' he said firmly. 'Until tonight.'

'Until tonight,' she said, a trifle dazed.

He turned to the door, but stopped as though something had just occurred to him.

'By the way, I believe in mixing business with pleasure. Perhaps you would look at this and value it for me.'

From his bag he drew a package which he unwrapped before her eager eyes, revealing a fabulously beautiful ornate necklace in sold gold. She took it gently and carried it to a desk, switching on a brilliant light.

'I have a friend in Rome who specialises in these things,' Marco said smoothly. 'He thinks this is one of the best Greek pieces he's ever seen.'

'Greek?' she said, not raising her eyes. 'Oh, no, Etruscan.'

She'd passed the first test, but he concealed his pleasure and pressed her further.

'Are you sure? My friend is a real expert.'

'Well it can be difficult to tell them apart,' she conceded. 'Etruscan goldsmiths of the archaic and classical periods...'

She was away and there was no stopping her, he recognised. Words poured out. 'Their jewellery of the third to first centuries BC often closely resembles Greek works but—Celtic influence—'

He listened with growing satisfaction. She might be a little strange but here was the educated lady he'd hoped for. This fabulous piece had been in his family's possession for two centuries. It was pure Etruscan. And she'd spotted it.

Then she blew his satisfaction out of the water by saying regretfully, 'If only it were real.'

He stared. 'Of course it's real.'

'No, I'm afraid not. It's a very good copy, one of the best I've ever seen. I can understand why it fooled your friend—'

'But not you,' he said, feeling illogically annoyed at her slander of his non-existent 'friend'.

'I've always taken a special interest in artefacts from Etruria,' she said, naming the province that had later become Rome and its surrounding countryside. 'I visited a dig there a couple of years back and it was the most fascinating—'

'And this qualifies you to pronounce on this piece?' Marco interrupted, his annoyance overcoming his good manners.

'Look, I know what I'm talking about, and frankly this "expert" of yours doesn't, since he can't tell Greek from Etruscan.'

'But according to you it's a fake which means it can't be either,' he pointed out.

'It's a copy, and whoever did it was copying an Etruscan piece, not a Greek one,' she said firmly.

The transformation in her was astonishing, he thought. Gone was the awkward young woman who'd collided with him at the door. In her place was an authority, steely, assured, implacable in her own opinion. He would have found it admirable if she wasn't trying to wipe a million dollars off his fortune.

'Are you saying that this is worthless?' he demanded.

'Oh, not entirely worthless. The gold must be worth something.'

She spoke in the manner of an adult placating a disappointed child, and he ground his teeth.

'Would you like to explain your opinion?' he said frostily.

'All my instincts tell me that this isn't the real thing.'

'You mean feminine intuition?'

'Certainly not,' she said crisply. 'There's no such thing. Funny, I'd have expected a man to know that. My instincts are based on knowledge and experience.'

'Which sounds like another name for female intuition to me. Why not be honest and admit it?'

Her eyes flashed, magnificently. 'Signor Whatever-

Your-Name-Is—if you just came in here to be offensive you're wasting your time. The weight of this necklace is wrong. A genuine Etruscan necklace would have weighed just a little more. Did you know that scientific tests have proved that Etruscan gold was always the same precise weight, and—?'

She was away again, facts and figures tumbling out of her mouth at speed, totally assured and in command of her subject. Except that she was completely wrong, he thought grimly. If this was the level of her expertise it was no wonder her business was failing.

'Fine, fine,' he said trying to placate her. 'I'm sure you're right.'

'Please don't patronise me!'

He was about to respond in kind when he checked himself, wondering where his wits were wandering. When he'd considered this encounter his plans hadn't included letting her needle him to the point of losing his temper. Coolness was everything. That was how victories were won, deals were made, life was organised to advantage. And she'd blown it away in five minutes.

'Forgive me,' he said with an effort. 'I didn't mean to be impolite.'

'Well, I suppose it's understandable, considering how much poorer I've just left you.'

'I don't accept that you have left me poorer, since I don't accept your valuation.'

'I can understand that you wouldn't,' she said in a kindly voice that took him to the limit of exasperation. She handed him back the necklace. 'When you return to Rome why don't you ask your friend to take another look at this? Only don't believe a word he says because he doesn't know the difference between Greek and Etruscan.'

'I'll collect you here at seven o'clock,' Marco said, from behind a tight smile.

CHAPTER TWO

SEVEN o'clock found Harriet peering out of her shop window into a storm. She'd been home, dressed for an evening out and returned in a hurry, not wishing to keep him waiting.

But it seemed he had no such qualms about her. Five past seven came and went, then ten, and there was no sign of him. At seven-fifteen she muttered something unladylike and prepared to leave in a huff.

She'd just locked the door and was staring crossly at the downpour when a cab came to a sharp halt at the kerb, a door opened and a hand reached out from the gloom within. She took it, and was seized in a powerful grip, then drawn swiftly inside.

'My apologies for being late,' Marco said. 'I took a cab because of the rain and found myself trapped. Luckily the show doesn't start until eight, so even at this crawl we should make it in time.'

'You don't mean to say that you managed it?' Harriet asked incredulously.

'Certainly I managed it. Why should you doubt me?'

'Who did you blackmail?'

Marco grinned. 'It was a little more subtle than that. Not much, but a little.'

'I'm impressed.'

She grew even more impressed when she discovered that he'd secured the best box in the house. No doubt about it. This was a man with good contacts.

Marco offered her the chair nearer the stage so that he

was a little to the rear and could glance at her as well as
the show. She wasn't beautiful, he decided. Her slender-
ness went, perhaps, a little too far: not thin he assured
himself hastily, but as lean as a model. Elegant. Or, at
least, she would be if she worked on her appearance,
which she clearly didn't.

Her chiffon evening gown was all right, no more. It
descended almost to her shapely ankles, and clung
slightly, revealing the grace of her movements. The deep
red was a magnificent shade, but it was exactly wrong
with her auburn hair, which she wore loose and flowing.
She should have put it up, he thought, revealing her face
and emphasising her long neck. Was there nobody to tell
her these things?

Her few pieces of jewellery were poorly chosen and
didn't really go well together. She should wear gold, he
decided. Not delicate pieces, but powerful, to go with her
aura of quiet strength. He would enjoy draping her with
gold.

The thought reminded him of the necklace, but he was
in a good humour now, and bore her no ill will. If anything, their spat had been useful in breaking the ice.

Dancing On Line was a very modern musical, a satire
about the internet, dry, witty, with good tunes and sharp
dancers. They both enjoyed it, and left the theatre in a
charity with one another. The rain had stopped, and the
cab he'd ordered was waiting.

'I know a small restaurant where they do the best food
in London,' he said.

He took her to a place that she, a Londoner, had never
heard of. Slightly to her surprise it was French, not Italian,
but then she realised that surprise was the name of the
game. If he really was planning an outrageous suggestion
then it made sense for him to confuse her a little first.

'Perhaps I should have asked if you like French food,' he said when they had seated themselves at a quiet corner table.

'I like it almost as much as Italian,' she said, speaking in French. It might be showing off but she felt that flying all her flags would be a good idea.

'Of course you're a cosmopolitan,' he said. 'In your line of work you'd have to be. Spanish?'

'Uh-uh! Plus Greek and Latin.'

'Modern Greek or classical?'

'Both of course,' she said, contriving to sound faintly shocked.

'Of course.' He smiled faintly and inclined his head in respect.

The food really was the best. Harriet notched up a mark to him. He was an excellent host, consulting her wishes while making suggestions that didn't pressure her. She let him pick the wine, and his choice exactly suited her.

The light was dim in their corner, with two small wall lamps and two candles in glass bowls on the table, making shadows dance and flicker. Even so she managed to study his face and had to give him ten out of ten for looks. His dinner jacket was impeccable, and his white, embroidered evening shirt made a background for his lightly tanned skin. He was a handsome man. She conceded that. His lips, perhaps, were slightly on the thin side, but in a way that emphasised his infrequent smiles, giving them a quirky irony that pleased her.

His eyes drew her attention, being very dark brown, almost black. She would have called them beautiful if the rest of his face hadn't been so unmistakably masculine. They were deep set and slightly shadowed by a high fore-head and heavy eyebrows. That gave his face a hint of mystery, because she couldn't always see whether his eyes had the same expression as his mouth. And she suspected that they often didn't.

So far, so intriguing. It was lucky Olympia had warned her what was afoot, or she might have been completely taken in; might actually have found him seriously attractive. As it was, she held the advantage. She decided to disconcert him a little, just for fun.

'What brings you to London?' she asked innocently. 'Business?'

If the question threw him he gave no sign of it. 'A little. And I must pay my respects to Lady Dulcie Maddox, who became engaged to my cousin Guido a few weeks ago.'

Harriet savoured the name. 'Lord Maddox's daughter?'

'Yes, do you know her?'

'She's been in the shop a couple of times.'

'Buying or selling?'

'Selling.' Harriet fell silent, sensing a minefield.

'Probably pieces from the Maddox ancestral home, to pay her father's debts,' Marco supplied. 'I gather he's a notorious gambler.'

'Yes,' she said, relaxing. 'I didn't want to tell tales if you didn't know.'

'It's common knowledge. Dulcie has to earn her living, and she was working as a private enquiry agent when she came to Venice and met Guido. What did you think of her?'

'Beautiful,' Harriet said enviously. 'All that long fair hair—if she still has it?'

'She had when I said goodbye to her a few weeks back. As you say, she's beautiful, and she'll keep Guido in order.'

She laughed. 'Does he need keeping in order?'

'Definitely. A firecracker, with no sense of responsibility. That's my Uncle Francesco talking, by the way. Count

Calvani. He's been desperate for Guido to marry and produce an heir to the title.'

'Hasn't he done that himself?'

'No, the title will go to one of his nephews. It should have been Leo, Guido's older half-brother. Their father married twice. His first wife, Leo's mother, was supposedly a widow, but her first husband turned up alive, making the marriage invalid and Leo illegitimate, and unable to inherit the title.'

'That's dreadful!'

'Leo doesn't think so. He doesn't want to be a count. The trouble is, neither does Guido, but that's going to be his fate. So uncle tried to find him a suitable wife, and was giving up in despair when Guido fell for Dulcie.

'My uncle is also, finally, going to get married. Apparently he's been in love with his housekeeper for years and has finally persuaded her to marry him. He's in his seventies, she's in her sixties, and they're like a pair of turtle-doves.'

'That's charming!' Harriet exclaimed.

'Yes, it is, although not everyone thinks so. My mother is scandalised that he's marrying "a servant" as she calls her.'

'Does anyone care about that kind of thing these days?'

'Some people,' Marco said carefully. 'My mother's heart is kind but her views about what is "proper" come from another age.'

'What about you?'

'I don't always embrace modern ways,' he said. 'I make my decisions after a lot of careful thought.'

'A banker would have to, of course.'

'Not always. Among my banking colleagues I have the reputation of sometimes getting carried away.'

'You?' she asked with an involuntary emphasis.

'I have been known to thrown caution to the winds,' he said gravely.

'Profitably, of course.'

'Of course.'

She studied his face, trying to see if he was joking or not, unable to decide. He guessed what she was doing and regarded her wryly, eyebrows raised as if to ask whether she'd worked it out yet. The moment stretched on and he grew uncomfortably aware of something transfixed in her manner.

'Would you like some more wine?' he asked, to bring her back to earth.

'I'm sorry, what was that?'

'Wine.'

'Oh, no—no, thank you. You know your face really is familiar. I wish I could remember—'

'Perhaps I remind you of a boyfriend,' he suggested delicately. 'Past or present?'

'Oh, no, I haven't had a boyfriend for ages,' she murmured, still regarding him.

What was the matter with her he wondered? Sophisticated one minute, gauche the next. Still, it told him what he needed to know.

As they were eating he asked, 'How do you and Olympia come to have different nationalities?'

'We don't,' Harriet said quickly. 'We're both Italian.'

'Well, yes, in a sense—'

'In every sense,' she interrupted with a touch of defiance. 'I was born in Italy, my father is Italian and my name is Italian.'

'I'm sorry,' Marco said, seeing the glint of anger in her large eyes and thinking how well it suited her. 'I didn't mean to offend you.'

'Hasn't Olympia told you the story?'

'Only vaguely. I know your father married twice, but naturally Olympia knows very little about his first wife.'

'My mother loved him terribly and he just dumped her. I remember when I was five years old, finding her crying her eyes out. She told me he was throwing us out of the house.'

'Your mother told you that?' he echoed, genuinely shocked. 'A child?'

'She was distraught. I simply didn't believe it. I adored my father and he acted as though he adored me. He used to call my name first when he came home. I thought it would always be like that.'

'Go on,' he said gently, when she paused.

'Well, his girlfriend was pregnant and he wanted a quick divorce so that he could marry her before the child was born. We were out. Mum said he even forced her to go back to England by threatening to be mean about money if she didn't.'

Marco thought of Guiseppe d'Estino, a fleshy, self-indulgent man of great superficial charm but cold eyes, as he now realised. He could well believe this story.

'It must have been a sad life for you after that,' he said sympathetically.

'I kept thinking he'd invite me for a visit, but he never did. I couldn't understand what I'd done to turn him against me. My mother never recovered. She grieved every day of her life. She only lived another twelve years, then she had heart trouble and just faded away. I thought he'd send for me then, but he didn't. I was about to go to college and he said he didn't want to interrupt my education.'

Marco murmured something that might have been a swear word.

'Yes,' Harriet said wryly. 'I suppose I was beginning

to get the picture then, very belatedly. I was rather stupid about it really.'

'The one thing nobody could ever call you is stupid,' Marco said, regarding her with new interest. 'I know that much about you.'

'Oh, *things,*' she said dismissively. 'Anyone can learn about things. I'm stupid about people. I don't really know much about them.'

'Or maybe you know too much about the wrong sort of people,' he said, thinking of the father who'd selfishly cast her off, and the mother who'd made the child bear the burden of her grief. 'Did your father totally reject you?'

'No, he kept up a reasonable pretence when he couldn't help it. I studied in Rome for a year. I chose that on purpose because I knew he'd have to take some notice of me. I even thought he might invite me to stay.'

'But he didn't?'

'I was asked to dinner several times. His second wife sat and glared at me the whole time, but Olympia was always nice. We got quite friendly. After that my father sent me a cheque from time to time.'

'Did he help you buy the shop?'

'No, that was money I inherited from my mother's father. I was able to buy the lease and some stock.'

'Your father could have afforded to help you. He ought to have stood up to that woman.'

'You mean his wife? Do you know her?'

'And detest her. As do most people. Of course she was determined to keep you out. My poor girl. You never stood a chance.'

'I guess I know that now. But at the time I thought I could win him over by doing well, learning languages, passing exams, being as Italian as possible.'

Marco was growing interested in her strange upbringing. He suspected it had moulded her into an unusual person.

'Did you really think I was a bailiff?' he asked curiously.

'For a moment.' She gave a gruff little laugh. 'You'd think I'd know how to recognise them by now. I keep thinking things will get better—well, they do. But then they get bad again.'

'But why? That shop should be a gold-mine. Your stock is first-rate. It's true, you made a mistake about the necklace, but—'

'I did *not* make—never mind. Sometimes I get on top of the figures, but then I see this really beautiful piece that I just have to have, and bang go all my calculations.'

'Why not just sell up?'

'Sell my shop? Never. It's my life.'

He ran up a flag. 'There's more to life than antiques.'

She shot it down. 'No, there isn't.'

'You seem very sure of that.'

'It's not just antiques, it's—it's the other worlds they open up. Vast horizons were you can see for thousands of years—'

She was away again. Recognising that it would be impossible to halt the flow until she was ready Marco settled for listening with the top part of his brain, while the rest considered her.

He'd grown more agreeably impressed as the evening wore on. She was an intriguing companion, intelligent, educated, even witty. It was a shame that she wasn't beautiful—at least, he thought she probably wasn't. It was hard to be sure when her hair shielded so much of her face. But her green eyes flashed fire when she spoke of the 'other worlds' that she loved, and in them was a kind of beauty.

Her lapses into gaucheness were hardly her fault. She'd been denied the chance to grow up in sophisticated society. A few trips to the discreetly luxurious shops on the Via dei Condotti would greatly improve her. He felt he had the basis for a deal that would be beneficial on both sides.

Harriet was bringing her passionate arguments to a conclusion. 'You don't think I'm crazy, do you?' she asked anxiously.

'You care passionately about your subject,' he said. 'That isn't being crazy. It's being lucky. So saving your shop means more to you than anything in the world, and perhaps I can help. How much would it take to extricate you from your difficulties?'

She named a large sum with the air of someone plunging into the deep end.

'It's a lot,' Marco said wryly, 'but not too much. I think we're in a position to help each other. I can make you an interest-free loan that will solve your problems.'

'But why should you?'

'Because I want something in return.'

'Naturally. But what?'

He hesitated. 'You may find this suggestion a little unusual, but I've considered it carefully, and I assure you it makes sense for both of us. I want you to come to Rome with me, and be my mother's guest for a while.'

'Are you sure she'll want that?'

'She'll be delighted. Your paternal grandmother was her dearest friend, and her hope is that our families can become united. In short, she's trying to arrange my marriage.'

'Who with?' Harriet asked, not wanting to seem to understand too much too soon.

'With you.'

She'd known that this moment was coming, but without warning she was embarrassed. Watching him sitting there in the corner, the candlelight on his face, he was suddenly too much; too forceful, too attractive, too like an irresistible gale storming through her life, flattening all before it. Too *much*.

'Hey, hold on,' she said, playing for time. 'Things aren't done like that these days.'

'In some societies marriages are still arranged—or at least, half arranged. Suitable people are introduced and the benefits of an alliance considered. My parents' marriage was created like this, and it was very happy. They were compatible, but not blinded by emotions too intense to last.'

'And you're asking me—?'

'To think about it. The final decision can be taken later, when we know each other better. In the meantime I'll sort out your financial problems. Should we make a match I'll wipe the loan out. If not we'll part friends, and you can repay me on easy terms.'

'Whoa there! You're going too fast. I can't take this in.' It was true. She'd thought herself well prepared, but everything was so different to her imaginings that it was taking her breath away.

'You can't lose. At the worst you get an interest-free loan that will save your shop.'

'But what's in it for you?' she demanded bluntly. 'You can't get married just to please your mother.'

It seemed to her that he hesitated a fraction, then answered with a little constraint. 'I can *if that is what I wish*.

It's time for me to have a settled life, with a family, and it suits me to arrange it in this way.'

'It will give us both time to think,' he went on. 'You return with me, try out life in my country—*your* country, and consider whether you'd enjoy it permanently. If you and my mother get on well, we'll discuss marriage.'

'What about you and me getting on well?'

'I hope we may, since we could hardly have a successful marriage otherwise. I'm sure you'll be an excellent mother to our children, and after that you won't find me unreasonable.'

'Unreasonable about what?' she asked, beginning to get glassy eyed.

'Come, we're not adolescents. We needn't interfere with each other's freedom as long as we're discreet.'

She tried to study his face, but it was hard because his eyes were in shadow.

'Don't you mind doing it this way?' she asked at last. 'Don't you have any feelings about it?'

'There's no need for us to discuss feelings,' he said, suddenly distant.

'But you've got everything planned like a business deal.'

'Sometimes that can achieve optimum results.'

The cool precision of his tone sent a frisson of alarm through her. For the first time she understood the extent to which he'd banished human warmth from this plan, and it gave her a sense of unreality. Only a man who'd built fences around himself could act like this. She wondered how high the fences were, and why he needed them.

And what about your own fences? murmured an inner voice. You know they're there. Brains are safe. Your head can't hurt you like your heart can. Maybe you're two of a kind, and he sensed it?

She quickly rejected the idea, but it lingered, troubling her, refusing to be totally dismissed.

Playing for time, she said, 'If we married you'd expect me to come to live with you, right?'

He looked slightly startled. 'That is the usual arrangement.'

'But if I move to Rome I'll lose the shop that I'm trying to save.'

'You can leave your establishment here and have it run by a manager, or move it to Rome. You might even find it helpful to be there. I'm sure there's a great deal you haven't explored yet.'

He'd touched a nerve. Not meeting his eyes Harriet said, 'I suppose you know everybody.'

'Not quite everybody. But I know a lot of people who could be useful to you.'

He would know Baron Orazio Manelli, she thought. He'd probably been in the Palazzo Manelli, with its vast store of hidden treasures. Harriet had been writing to the Baron for two years now, seeking permission to study that Aladdin's cave. And for two years he had barred her entry. But as Marco's fiancée…

She bid the tempter be silent, but he whispered to her of bronze and gold, of ancient jewellery and historic sculptures.

'A visit,' she said. 'With neither of us committed.'

'That's understood.'

'We might simply decide it wouldn't work.'

'And part friends. But in the meantime my mother would have the pleasure of your company.'

Torn between conscience and temptation she stared at his face as though hoping to find the answer there. And then, against all odds, she did.

'That's it!' she breathed. 'Now I know where I've seen your face.'

'I'm glad,' he said, amused. 'Who do I remind you of?'

'Emperor Caesar Augustus.'

'I beg your pardon!'

'I've got him in the shop—his bust in bronze. It's your face.'

'Nonsense. That's pure fancy.'

'No it's not. Come on, I'll show you.'

'What?'

'Let's go and see. We've finished eating, haven't we?'

He'd planned a leisurely liqueur or two, but he could tell it would be simpler to yield. 'Yes, we've finished,' he agreed.

He was a man who led while others followed, but he found himself swept along by her urgent enthusiasm until they were back in her shop, and she'd turned the lights on the bust.

'Now is that you or isn't it?' she demanded triumphantly.

'No,' he said, astounded. 'There's no resemblance at all. You brought me all the way back here to look at that?'

'I'm not imagining it. That's you. Look again. Look.'

He didn't look. Instead he gave a soft laugh, as though something had mysteriously delighted him, and came to stand in front of her, putting one hand on her shoulder. With the other he lifted her chin so that he could look into her eyes. She could feel his warm breath against her skin, whispering across her mouth so that a tiny shiver went through her. But although their faces were so close, he didn't lower his head, only gave her a small, intriguing smile.

'A sensible man would run for his life at this point,' he said wryly.

'And you're a very sensible man, aren't you?'

He brushed back a stray wisp of hair. 'Maybe I'm not as sensible as I thought I was. I know you're not a sensible woman. You're completely crazy.'

'I suppose I am. A woman who wasn't crazy wouldn't even consider your idea.'

'True. Then I must be grateful.' He looked down into her face, still smiling, still meeting her eyes.

Then something happened that shocked her. His smile faded. He released her and stepped back. 'Can you be ready to leave in two days?' he asked with cool courtesy.

She was too stunned to speak. One moment her body had been vibrating from the intimacy of his closeness, his hands, his breath. The next, it was all over, and by his choice, that was clear. He'd deliberately slammed the door shut on whatever might have happened between them next.

She pulled herself together and replied in a voice that matched his own. 'Speaking as a businesswoman, will I have the money by then?'

'You will have it by midday tomorrow.'

'But you haven't seen my books,' she said, suddenly conscience stricken.

'Do I need to? I'm sure they're terrible.'

'Suppose you can't afford me?'

'I assure you that I can.'

She gave a sharp little laugh, half-tension, half-anger. 'Then perhaps I should marry you for your money.'

'I thought that was what we'd been discussing.'

She surveyed him defiantly, arms folded. 'I can't put one over on you, can I?'

'I try to ensure that nobody can. It's the best way to achieve—'

'*Optimum results.*' She said the words with him, and he gave her a nod of respect.

'Let me take you home,' he said.

'No thank you.' Anger had faded as she realised that the threat to the thing she loved most in the world had gone. With a sudden beatific smile that startled him she said, 'I want to be alone here for a while. Now that it's safe.'

'I'll wait for you outside,' he said firmly. 'It's midnight, and I won't leave you alone with these valuables, a target for robbers and worse. Your untimely death wouldn't suit me at all.'

'No, you'd have to rethink the whole plan,' she agreed affably.

He took her hand. 'It's a pleasure to do business with someone who understands what matters. I'll be outside.'

He held her hand for a moment, then raised it and brushed his lips against the back before walking out.

Left alone, Harriet looked down at her hand, where she could still feel the light imprint of his mouth. She was shaken and her heart was beating either with pleasure or apprehension, she wasn't sure. She could only do this if she felt in control, and he'd threatened that control. Furiously she rubbed the back of her hand until the feeling had gone.

Then she looked around her and her eyes shone. Safe. At least for a while.

The tempter was there again, whispering that the 'engagement' could last just long enough for her to investigate the Palazzo Manelli, and no longer. And why not? The plan would be heartless if Marco's feelings had been involved, but he'd been at pains to emphasise that they weren't. He'd looked her over as a piece of merchandise that he could make use of, so why shouldn't she do the same with him?

She knew another brief flare of resentment at the way he'd drawn close to her then backed off. A man who was so much in control of himself wouldn't be easy to deal with. If she let him, he would call all the shots. But she wouldn't let him.

His face came into her mind and her eyes fell on the bronze face of Augustus, the two so exactly alike—whatever Marco thought. She remembered Olympia's words, 'Really dishy. That fine nose, and that mouth—all stern discipline masking incredible sensuality.'

It was true, Harriet realised. The wonder was that she alone had seen it in the living man.

CHAPTER THREE

DURING the next couple of days the whirl of arrangements was so intense that she had no time to think. Marco inspected the shop's books, groaned at her business practices—'pure Alice in Wonderland'—but advanced a money order that cleared her debts. It also left her something over to pay extra to Mrs Gilchrist, her excellent manager, who was to take sole charge.

There was one tense moment when Harriet brought a customer to the verge of buying a very expensive piece, only to start talking it down until he lost interest and left the shop empty handed.

'There was nothing the matter with it,' declared Marco, who had watched, aghast.

'I didn't like him.'

'What?'

'He wouldn't have given it a good home,' she tried to explain. 'You don't understand do you?'

'Not a word!' he said grimly.

'These aren't just things I buy and sell. I love them. Would you sell a puppy to a man you thought wouldn't be kind to it?'

'Harriet, puppies are alive. These things are not.'

'Yes they are, in their own way. I won't sell something to a person I don't trust.'

'You madwoman. You've got windmills in your head. Let's leave this place while I can still stand it.'

They left next day on the midday flight to Rome.

38

Signora Lucia Calvani was waiting for them, and the moment she saw Harriet her face lit up.

'Etta,' she cried, advancing with her arms open. 'My dear, dear Etta.'

Enveloped in a scented embrace Harriet felt a lump come to her throat at this unexpected welcome.

'You know why I call you Etta, don't you?' Lucia asked, taking her shoulders and standing back a little.

'My father used to call me that, when I was a little girl,' Harriet said eagerly. 'He said it was because of his mother—'

'Yes, her name was Enrichetta, but people called her Etta. I did, when we were girls together. Oh, you're so like her.' She hugged Harriet again.

Her greeting to her son was restrained but her eyes left no doubt that he was the centre of her life. Then she immediately turned her attention back to her guest, drawing Harriet's arm through her own and leading her towards the chauffeur-driven Rolls-Royce.

Their route lay out in the countryside, giving Rome a wide sweep until they were south of the city and hit the Via Appia Antica, the ancient road alongside which stood the ruins of tombs of aristocratic Roman families, going back a thousand years. Here too were the mansions of their modern counterparts. They stood well back from the road, hidden behind high walls and elaborate metal gates, housing families who quietly ran the world. A Calvani could live nowhere else.

Signora Calvani was a beautiful, exquisite woman with white hair, dressed in the height of Roman fashion. Harriet guessed her to be about seventy, but with her tall, slender figure and elastic walk she could have been younger. Her voice and gestures were those of someone who'd always been surrounded by money.

'I was so delighted when Marco said you were to pay us a visit,' she said as the car glided through the countryside. 'The house seems very empty sometimes.'

They had passed the wrought-iron gates of the villa and were gliding between trees until the Villa Calvani came into view suddenly. It was a huge white house with flower-hung balconies and broad steps rising to the double front door, and Harriet could understand how it must seem empty to someone who lived there alone.

An unseen servant opened the front door and Lucia led her graciously into the hall, and from there into a large salon. A maid appeared to take Harriet's coat. Another maid wheeled in a tea trolley.

'English tea,' Lucia declared. 'Especially for you.'

As well as tea there were sweet biscuits and savouries, sandwiches, cakes. Whatever her taste it was catered for. For a while they exchanged standard pleasantries, but behind the questions Harriet sensed that Lucia's real attention was elsewhere. She was studying her guest, and was evidently delighted with what she found. It was a welcome such as Harriet had never received in her life. Marco was looking pleased as the extent of his mother's warmth became clear.

'Now I'll show you your room,' Lucia said, rising.

Her room was even more overwhelming, with floor-length windows that looked out onto the magnificent Roman countryside. Harriet could see a river and pine trees stretching into the distance, all glowing in the afternoon sun.

The bed was big enough for three, an elaborate confection of carved walnut with a tapestry cover. The floor was polished wood, and the furniture was old-fashioned with the walnut theme repeated. The ornaments were traditional pieces, carved heads, pictures, some of them valuable Harriet automatically noted with a professional eye.

But she didn't want to think about work just now. She was basking in the feeling of being wanted, so unfamiliar to her.

'Do you think you'll be comfortable here?' Lucia asked kindly. 'Would you like anything changed?'

'It's all beautiful,' Harriet said huskily. 'I've never—' To her dismay a sudden rush of tears choked her and she had to turn away.

'But whatever is the matter?' Lucia asked in alarm. 'Marco, have you been unkind to her?'

'Certainly not,' he said at once.

'Nobody's been unkind,' Harriet said huskily. 'On the contrary, you've all—I've never—'

'It's time I was getting back to my work,' Marco said, looking uncomfortable. 'I've neglected it too long—'

'What do you mean "too long"?' his mother demanded, scandalised.

'I beg your pardon, and Harriet's. I didn't mean to be impolite. But I really must return to my office, and then to my own apartment for a few days.'

'You aren't coming to supper tonight?' Lucia demanded. 'It's Etta's first evening with us.'

'Regretfully I must decline that pleasure. I'll call soon and let you know when to expect me.'

He kissed his mother and, after a moment's hesitation, kissed Harriet's cheek. Then he departed hastily.

'Such manners!' Lucia exclaimed.

'Well, I've already gathered that he's a workaholic,' Harriet admitted. 'And I suppose he must have lost a lot of time.'

'You and I will spend the next few days getting to

know each other.' Lucia seized Harriet's hands. 'I am *so* happy.'

Harriet's feeling of having landed unexpectedly in heaven showed no sign of abating. Lucia had ordered various English dishes to please her and proudly put them on display when they dined together that evening.

'For of course I realise that you are *partly* English,' she explained, with the air of someone making a generous concession. 'But Italian in your heart, *si*?'

'*Si*,' Harriet agreed, wondering just how much Marco had told her. Lucia's eyes were full of understanding.

From then on she switched to the Italian language, and in no time they were the best of friends.

'Why not call your father to let him know that you're here?' Lucia asked.

Harriet felt a strange reluctance, as though there was something to be feared, but she went to the telephone and called her father's number. She was answered by an unfamiliar voice, a man, who explained that Signor d'Estino and his family were away for several days. Nor would he divulge their destination, even when Harriet explained that she was his daughter. It was clear that he had never heard of her. She left a message, asking her father to call, and hung up, refusing to let herself feel pain.

The next morning Harriet arose refreshed, to find that Lucia had planned their day. 'We'll have lunch in town,' she said, 'and just look around.'

It was a joy to Harriet to renew her acquaintance with Rome, the great city that lived in her dreams. Once it had been the centre of the known world. Now it was a place of traffic jams and tourists, yet still dominated by glorious ancient monuments. After lunch they strolled along the luxurious Via Veneto, and Lucia pointed out Marco's apartment, high up on the fifth floor. Harriet looked up at the windows, but they were closed and shuttered. Like the man himself, she thought.

She spent the next day alone as Lucia was on several charity committees and had meetings to attend. Now she could reclaim Rome in her own way. Happily she wandered its cobbled streets, exploring narrow alleys, and finally coming across a shop that specialised in Greek items. The next moment she was inside, inspecting, bargaining, and finally securing. When she left the shop her debt had grown substantially.

She was looking forward to showing her bargains to Marco, but so far there was no word from him, and that evening the two women dined alone. Later, as they sat together over coffee, Lucia suddenly said, 'Perhaps we should speak of what is on our minds. My dear, does it seem very terrible to you that I'm seeking a suitable wife for my son?'

'A little odd perhaps. Doesn't Marco mind the idea of marrying a stranger?'

'That's the worst of it, he doesn't mind at all. He was engaged once but it came to an end. Since then he's acted as though emotion was nothing but a stage in life that he'd put behind him and was relieved to have done so.'

'Did he love her?'

'I believe so, but he's never spoken about it. He slammed a door on the subject and nobody is allowed past, even me. Perhaps I'm a sentimental fool, but I loved Etta so much, and she died far too young. If I could see our families united in marriage and then in children, that's all I could ask for.'

'I wish you'd tell me about her.'

'I was friends with one of her sisters, who took me home to meet the family. Etta was ten years older than me, but she took me under her wing, for my mother was dead. I was a bridesmaid at her wedding, and one of the first people to see your father when he was born.

'We wanted our sons to grow up together, but I married late, and then it was years before Marco was born, so it didn't happen. And then my darling Etta died, and I still miss her so much. She was the only person I could confide in. Men aren't the same.'

'Am I really like her?'

For answer Lucia opened a cupboard and pulled out a photo album.

'There!' she said, opening it at an early page. 'That's Etta when she was your age.'

The young woman in the picture was dressed in the fashion of fifty years earlier, and her face was the one Harriet saw in her own mirror.

'I really am her granddaughter,' Harriet said, in a slow, wondering voice.

'Much more than Olympia,' Lucia confirmed. 'She would have been quite unsuitable. A sweet girl but an airhead, although, of course, I thought of her first because I'd known her for years. I wish I'd known you better. If only your mother hadn't kept you from us!'

'If only—*what?*'

'Your father said she wanted nothing to do with any of us after the split. She insisted on going home to England and raising you to be English.' She was looking at Harriet's face. 'Isn't that true?'

'No,' Harriet seethed, 'it most certainly isn't. He forced her to go back to England and just shut us out.'

'That woman!' Lucia said at once. 'He's always been in thrall to her. I never liked your father. He's a spineless weakling and quite unworthy of his mother. Now I'm totally disgusted with him.'

'So am I,' Harriet fumed. 'He denied me my Italian heritage.'

'Well, now you can claim it back again,' Lucia said warmly.

'Yes,' Harriet mused. 'I can.'

'Would it be tactless of me to suggest that you start by dressing in our country's fashion?'

'You mean my clothes look as if I bought them second-hand?' Harriet asked bluntly.

'Of course not. But among the many English talents *haute couture* is not perhaps—' she left the sentence delicately unfinished.

'No, it's not,' Harriet said decisively. 'You're right. It's time I started being who I am.' Then her confidence wavered. 'Whoever that is,' she added uncertainly.

'Never say such a thing again,' Lucia commanded. 'From this moment, you start life again.'

Next morning they went to the Via dei Condotti, the most exclusive shop in Rome. There Lucia cast a critical eye over the parade of garments, loftily dismissing this one, ordering that one set aside.

Slowly the pile of clothes grew, some to be taken as they were, some to be altered. The total wipe out of her wardrobe gave Harriet the feeling of being another person. It was strange, but she liked it.

Then she was introduced to Signora Talli, an ultra-fashionable modiste who spent a whole afternoon studying her face and redesigning it. Harriet had barely bothered with make-up. A touch of lipstick, a hint of eye shadow, and who needed more? That was her philosophy. She was soon shown the error of her ways.

Her eyes—such a magnificent shade of green, they must be highlighted, made larger—'How?' she asked nervously. The colour of the lipstick must be balanced with the colour of the eyes. Apparently any shade other than the one she normally wore would be preferable. She relapsed into cowed silence, convinced that she'd stumbled onto a branch of the higher science.

At last everything was in place. The woman who looked back at her from the mirror was a stranger with enormous, shadowy eyes and a mouth whose width had been cleverly emphasised. She herself had always tried to minimise that width.

Then Signora Talli took up a pair of scissors.

'Not my hair,' Harriet said, alarmed.

'Your face needs to be seen,' Lucia explained. 'You can't hide it behind that curtain.'

But Harriet, so pliable until then, became suddenly stubborn, inexplicably dismayed by the thought of losing her mane. The other two finally yielded, but insisted that she wear it up. In a few moments her long hair was piled high, altering the whole shape of her head, and revealing an exquisitely long, slender neck that she'd almost forgotten that she had. She surveyed herself, torn between dismay and a tingle of excitement. Unbidden the thought came into her mind that she would enjoy Marco's surprise when he saw her.

They finally selected six garments, five to be altered and delivered by the following day, and one, an olive-green trouser suit and satin shirt, that they took home with them. Harriet could see that it suited her perfectly, and when she sat down to supper with Lucia she felt good. Marco too, she thought, would approve if he happened to walk in now.

But the evening passed with no sign of him, and no word. Lucia called his mobile phone and growled with displeasure at finding herself talking to a machine.

'No, I will not leave a message,' she snapped.

'He's very busy,' Harriet placated her, although in truth she too felt like snapping.

'It's been several days. So he's busy. He can't spare some time for his—his—?'

'But I'm not his anything,' Harriet said quickly. 'I'm only here so that Marco and I can get to know each other.'

Lucia gave her a speaking glance. 'Well, you're certainly getting to know my son. Selfish, blinkered, indifferent.'

It seemed to be true. Was this really Marco's idea of courtship, to leave her here to win his mother's good will, as though that was the only thing that mattered?

By the time they went to bed neither woman was in a good mood.

The rest of the clothes arrived next day at the end of the afternoon, and Lucia made her parade in them while she surveyed her critically.

'I'm not sure about this evening dress,' Harriet said. 'It's tight.'

'And why not? You have the figure for it. It shows off your curves admirably.'

Harriet twisted before the mirror. 'I don't have cur—goodness, yes I do.'

She turned around, trying to see as much of the saffron satin as possible, without being too alarmed at the way it revealed her figure.

'Hmm!' she said, beginning to feel good.

'You should have bought yourself decent clothes before, instead of wasting your time on ancient history. Dead men are all very well in their way, but they don't wolf whistle.'

'Maybe I don't want to be wolf whistled.'

'Are you a woman or not? You have a splendid bust. You should show it off.'

'I am showing it off,' she said, tugging at the bosom in a vain attempt to get it higher. 'Lots of it. Oh, dear! This satin is so tight that you can tell I'm not wearing anything underneath.'

'Good. Excellent. *Marco, my dear boy!*'

Startled, Harriet swung around to see that Marco had come quietly into the room and was watching them with pleasure. Lucia rose and gave him an embrace which he returned affectionately before dropping a kiss onto Harriet's cheek. His aftershave reached her faintly, tangy, sharp, intensely masculine.

She wondered if he'd heard what she said about being naked under the dress. Or did he just know anyway? She wished she could stop being so conscious of her own body with only the thin satin to protect it. She resisted the temptation to tug again at the material over her bosom. She had the sensation that Marco was looking at the swell of her breasts; which was nonsense, because he wasn't even facing in her direction.

'Don't you think Harriet is improved?' Lucia demanded robustly.

'I think she's very beautiful,' Marco agreed. 'But her hair should be up.'

'I agree,' Lucia said. 'Etta, why haven't you put it up today? It looked so nice.' She seized a handful of hair and swept it up onto Harriet's head.

Startled, Harriet said, 'No,' sharply, and pulled it down again. It covered her exposed bosom a little, but there was another reason, that she couldn't understand.

She began to turn away but Marco's hands were on her shoulders, bringing her around to face him. Then she felt his fingers on her neck, twining in her hair, drawing it up and back.

'Why do you want to hide your face?' he asked.

'That's not what I—'

'I think it is.' He looked at her for a moment before saying gently, 'I also think your father has a lot to answer for.'

'I don't know what you—' The words died on her lips. Hearing it put into words she knew exactly what he meant.

'Just because your face didn't please him, you think it won't please any man,' Marco said. 'And you're wrong.'

She was stunned at the sudden revelation. That early rejection that she'd believed she could cope with, had marked her to this day. And this cool, unemotional man had been the one to see the truth in her heart.

She met his eyes. Then she drew in a sharp breath and became still as she saw something in them—or had she? It was gone so fast that it might have been an illusion.

'Put it up,' he said abruptly. 'Long hair is all wrong with that dress.'

The prosaic reason brought her back down to earth. She hurried away to her room to find the woman Lucia had deputed to act as her maid, and who swirled her hair into the exquisite creation of the previous day.

When she went down Marco put a glass of wine in her hand. He didn't mention her appearance but he smiled and gave a brief nod of pleasure. Lucia had recovered from her joy at the sight of her son and remembered that she was displeased with him.

'I suppose we should feel grateful that you've deigned to remember us at last,' she said caustically. 'Do we get five minutes of your precious time, or ten?'

'Don't be angry with me, Mamma,' he said, laughing. 'I've come to make amends by taking Harriet out tonight.'

CHAPTER FOUR

BELLA FIGURA was a nightclub on the Via Veneto, a few yards along from Marco's apartment. It was hidden away in the depths of the building, and as soon as they arrived Harriet could sense the atmosphere; sophisticated, knowing, and above all discreet. She wondered how many women Marco had brought here, and how many notes had changed hands with close-mouthed doormen.

He led her to a table near the stage, yet sufficiently to one side to afford some privacy. The floorshow had not started waiters hurried to and fro, taking orders. Marco summoned one of them with a look, which annoyed several customers who'd been waiting longer. He seemed not to notice.

As before he was an excellent host and she relaxed, even beginning to feel easier about the revealing dress.

'I'm sorry to have been so remiss,' he said. 'My mother is very annoyed with me. Are you?'

'No,' she said, not entirely truthfully. 'You must have been deluged with work after being away, although I daresay you travel with a laptop, and don't miss very much.'

He nodded. 'I have a good assistant, but I prefer to keep my own finger on the pulse. I'm grateful that you understand. I'm afraid my mother doesn't. She thinks you'll be offended and rush back to England.'

'No way,' she said cheerfully. 'I'm having a wonderful time. Your mother and I get on splendidly.'

'So I gather from her. By the way, did I imagine that I saw you in the Via Veneto yesterday?'

'No, I picked up a cab there after I'd done some shopping. I found a shop a couple of streets away—'

It all came tumbling out, her visit, the treasures she'd discovered, the difficulty of deciding which to buy, the moment of half-guilty indulgence, the thrill of possession. Marco listened to her, at first with a smile, then with growing alarm.

'What in heaven's name did you buy?'

She rattled of the list.

'And they cost *how much?*'

'They're bargains,' she defensively. 'They'll look wonderful in the shop.'

'The shop that's already up to its ears in debt. Good grief woman, have you no sense of the value of money?'

'Look, I know money's important, I'm not saying it isn't.'

'Now there's a concession!' he said scathingly.

'But it isn't necessarily first on my list of priorities—'

'I'd be interested to know just where it does come on your list of priorities.'

She was annoyed into frankness. 'Pretty low when I'm negotiating for an object of beauty.'

'Beauty costs money,' he said bluntly.

'Oh, really!'

'All right, tell me I'm wrong.'

She couldn't. An antique dealer knew better than anyone how much beauty cost, and having to concede the point exasperated her more than anything.

'I've seen your accounts remember,' Marco said, 'and a more soul-destroying experience I don't recall. I think you see good business practice as a sort of optional extra.'

'Rubbish!'

'What did you say?'

'All right, I admit I tend to leave that kind of thing to take care of itself.'

He stared at her glassy eyed. *'You leave business to take care of itself?'*

'Well, you knew I was like that.'

'I didn't know you were going to be "like that" in Rome.'

'I'm like that everywhere,' she said defiantly.

'So I'm beginning to understand. Maybe I should have spelled it out that a condition of my loan was that you don't make your financial situation worse.'

'I haven't made it worse. That stuff will sell at a profit.'

'Always assuming that you can find "kind" homes for it? Of all the—look, you're a dealer. Don't you know better than to walk into another dealer's shop and buy at full price?'

'Of course I do, but I couldn't help myself.'

'Maria vergine! You couldn't help yourself. If I bought stock in Novamente instead of Kalmati I should like to see my clients' faces when Novamente collapsed and I explained that it wasn't my fault because I couldn't help myself.'

'That's different,' she said frostily.

'I don't see why. Let's all live on emotional impulse with no sense of responsibility. If you, why not me?'

'Because you wouldn't know how to live on emotional impulse.'

'Thank heavens!' he said fervently.

'I am *not* irresponsible. I know all this stuff—'

'It's not enough to know it. You have to live by it.'

'When I saw those pieces I fell in love with them. You don't understand that, do you?'

'Only too well. You fell in love and abandoned all common sense, all perspective, all objectivity. Never, never make a decision when you're in love, whether it's with an object or—' he checked himself. He was breathing rapidly.

The appearance of a waiter was a diversion, one that he was glad of, she thought. He didn't look at her as the plates from the first course were cleared away and the second course served, and when they were alone again he smiled as though the moment had never happened.

'I didn't bring you out to criticise you,' he said. 'Perhaps I went a little too far.'

'Just a little,' she agreed. 'I suppose to someone who operates in higher finance I must seem raving mad.'

'Don't let's start on that again,' he begged. 'But let me look at the paperwork. I can tell you how to—that is, I may be able to suggest things you might find useful.'

'Thank you,' she said meekly.

He seemed about to reply, then caught the gleam in her eyes and thought better of it.

'What exactly do you do?' she asked.

'I work for the Banco Orese Nationale. It's a merchant bank, and I deal in stocks and shares, advising clients, research into market trends.'

'Go on.'

He settled into an explanation that lasted well into the second course and Harriet listened with genuine interest.

'Control is the answer,' he said once. 'If you're not in control, somebody else is. So you must always be the one in control. If I'm trying to beat someone down on the price of stock I always make sure I have one piece of information more than he does. Then I'm in control. He may think he is but I know that I am.

'You lost control of your shop, and now I'm in control—no, don't get mad. I'm not getting at you. I'm just helping you to avoid predators like me in future.'

'It's OK, go on,' she said, too fascinated to take up the cudgels again. She lacked the killer instinct to put really tough business practises into action, but she could follow complicated financial arguments.

When Marco checked himself and said, 'Let me put that another way,' she answered indignantly.

'You don't have to talk down to me. I understand every word.'

'Well it's a damned sight more than your sister can,' he growled. 'What is it?'

She had burst out laughing. Now she choked and said, 'It was just the thought of you talking like this to Olympia, and her trying to look interested.'

He grinned. 'Her eyes were glazed. Come to think of it, most women's eyes glaze after the first minute.'

'I should think so, too. If you take someone out on a date she doesn't want to be lectured about market trends.'

'You didn't mind.'

'That's different. We're business partners.'

'So we are,' he said after a moment. 'And this is a board meeting.'

'To consider the project so far, and work out *modus operandi* for the next stage.'

'Well, as a start, can we agree that you'll curb your purchasing instinct for a while? I'd like some input in future.'

'You meant you want to stop me spending money?'

'I was trying to put it politely. The blunt version is that from now on I hold the purse-strings.'

She'd been feeling more kindly towards him but that vanished abruptly. 'What did you say?' she asked with a sweetness that should have warned him.

'No more buying. *Basta!* Enough.'

'Because you say so?'

'Because I say so. I'm doing a complete overhaul of your financial arrangements and you do nothing more until I've got them on a sensible footing.'

'Well, well! What happened to tact?'

'To hell with tact. Tact will bankrupt you.'

'Bankrupt *you*, you mean?'

'Nonsense,' he said impatiently. 'It isn't in your power to bankrupt me.'

'How interesting! I really must marry you for your money. Let's announce the engagement at once.'

'What a proposition. Irresistible!'

'Well, let's face it, you haven't anything else to offer. You're rude, overbearing, dictatorial, arrogant—'

'Is that supposed to floor me? Think again. There's nothing wrong with arrogance if you're sure of your ground.'

'And I'll bet you're always sure of your ground.'

'Too right. It stops me being wrong-footed by people who don't know what they're talking about.'

'Meaning me?'

'Meaning anyone.'

'Meaning the entire rest of the world, as far as you're concerned. So now you'll have exactly the wife you need, someone who's seen the worst of you and will put up with it for the sake of your money.'

He grunted. 'You think you've seen the worst of me?'

'Well, I hope the rest isn't even more unpleasant.'

'It can be,' he said, his eyes glinting. 'It can be a lot more unpleasant. Think hard before taking me on.'

'Fine! It's all off. Here endeth the shortest engagement in history. The protagonists couldn't stand each other.'

She dropped her voice on the last words, aware that she was attracting attention. Marco also looked around, before lowering his voice and leaning closer to her.

'You're being melodramatic,' he said coldly. 'There's no need for all this emotionalism.'

She too leaned closer. 'I'm not being emotional, I'm being coldly realistic. Why not? It works for you.'

'You know nothing about me,' he snapped. 'All this because I want to organise your finances—'

'You don't want to "organise" my finances, you want to control them, and me. Where would it stop if I let you?'

'*Let* me? Do you think I'm asking permission?'

'I think you'd better be.'

'Harriet, I'm telling you, no more buying.'

'And I'm telling you that you've made me a loan, not bought me body and soul. The shop is mine.'

'For how long if I decided to turn really nasty?'

'You? Nasty? Surely not! Listen to me, Marco, I own that shop, I run it, and I alone decide what it needs. If I see stock I want, I won't ask you first, I'll buy it and tell them to bill me.'

'And if I insist on returning it?'

'That'll be hard because I'll be back in England.'

'Having smuggled an Etruscan necklace or two under your jacket, I suppose?' he said with heavy irony.

'It was a fake and I'll do whatever is necessary,' she said through gritted teeth.

'*Marco, my boy!*'

They both looked up quickly to see a large, middle-aged man who'd approached their table while they were preoccupied. Marco rose to shake his hand, introducing him to Harriet as Alfredo Orese.

Orese, she thought. And he worked for the Banca Orese Nationale.

'Unforgivable of me to interrupt two lovebirds,' Alfredo said jovially, purloining a chair from another table and joining them. 'Nice to see a young couple absorbed in each other, head to head, oblivious to the world, know what I mean?'

That must be how they had looked, Harriet realised, smiling noncommittally.

'Not a word, Alfredo,' Marco said amiably. 'Let us keep our secrets.'

Alfredo put his finger over his lips and winked. He was somewhat the worse for wear, and seemed less like a banker than a man who liked a good time. He ordered a bottle of the best champagne, toasted them noisily, kissed Harriet's cheek and finally, to their relief, took himself off.

'I'm sorry about that,' Marco said, letting out his breath. 'He's a good fellow, means no harm.'

'And likes playing at being a banker,' she said wryly.

'How did you know?'

'The name. But I reckon the name is the only reason he's there.'

He grinned. 'Yes, but to his credit he understands that and doesn't interfere. You ought to marry him. He's got ten times what I have and he'd let you blow the lot without protest.'

'Ah, but he wouldn't give me a good fight like you do.'

'You can count on me for those.'

'All right, I'll grant you that my financial management leaves something to be desired—'

'I wouldn't myself have dignified your carry-on with the name of financial management—'

'Do you want to fight again?' she asked sweetly.

'No, it's too soon after the last time. Let's space them and get our breath back.'

'Will you be quiet while I make a sort of concession?'

He looked at her attentively.

'I admit I've made some mistakes—did you say something?'

'Not a word.'

'I've made a few mistakes, and I shall be *interested* to hear your advice.'

His lips twitched. 'Interested?'

'Interested.'

'To the point of taking it?'

'Let's see what the future holds.'

He grinned. Humour altered his face as though a light had come on inside him. He could be charming, she thought, when he allowed himself to relax. She was beginning to understand his habit of describing everything in business terms. They were the words he understood most easily, but they covered something else deep inside him, and she was beginning to be intrigued by what that 'something else' might be.

'Enough for tonight,' he said. 'It's a draw.'

She laughed and let it go.

As the coffee was being served the lights were lowered. Members of the band took their place on the low stage. A young woman came to the microphone and began to sing in a breathy voice. It was a song about loss and physical longing, the persistence of desire when all hope had gone.

'I feel you touching me—though we're apart—your hands, your lips are everywhere…'

She was a skilful artist, managing to squeeze the last ounce of sensuality from every word, every cunningly placed pause. A new atmosphere, romantic, delicate, subtly erotic, began to pervade the club.

By slow degrees Harriet felt herself come alive with the consciousness that she was sitting close to an attractive man, with only a thin layer of material between him and her nakedness. Suddenly the dress felt alarmingly low.

She stole a look at Marco to see if he was equally aware of her, but he was watching the stage. Her eyes were drawn to his hands, which were long and fine, but with a hint of power.

'*Your hands touch me everywhere—*' crooned the singer.

It was absurd to feel her body responding merely to a thought, but she couldn't control the warmth that was stealing over her. How would those hands touch a woman? How would it feel to be touched intimately by them? It was as though she already knew. She took a deep, shuddering breath and fixed her eyes on the floor.

For his part, Marco was directing his eyes to anywhere but her. He'd gone to his mother's villa tonight prepared only to stay for supper and depart, his duty done. One look at Harriet had changed his mind. Here was the sensual, flamboyant creature who'd hidden beneath her dowdy disguise, tantalising him with her elusiveness from the very first night.

His decision to take her out had been spur of the moment, something which shocked him but did not deter him. He kept a room at the villa and a set of evening clothes, so a change of plan presented no problems. As he drove her into Rome he'd wondered how the evening would go, what they would talk about. It hadn't occurred to him that they would fight, but now he thought perhaps it should have done.

Finally he stole a glance at her, and saw that her face was averted from the stage, slightly towards him, but not looking directly at him. He realised that she wasn't seeing anything external, but was lost in an inner world where he wasn't invited. It was absurd to feel jealous, but he wished she would notice him. She didn't.

The blue light from the stage drained all other colour from her, and sharply emphasised the shadows. For a moment she didn't look like a living woman but like the statue of some ancient queen, perhaps Nefertiti or Cleopatra: some great lady, statuesque, imperious, magnificent.

But he knew that this was only part of her. The next moment she could come alive with the mischievous laughter of a child, or glare at him with the fierceness of an adversary. There was no knowing.

He saw that Alfredo was attracting his attention from a few yards away and forced himself to smile. Alfredo was a good fellow, not the brightest, but amiable, and he would be useful in gaining a partnership. He was indicating Harriet, winking, making 'ho ho' gestures implying that they were both men of the world. Suddenly Marco wanted to knock him down.

The singer departed, amid applause and the band struck up for dancing.

'Would you care to take the floor?' Marco asked politely.

She took his hand and he led her onto the dance floor, which rapidly became too crowded to do more than shuffle. He held her firmly, close but not too close, and she found that her step fell in with his easily. The effect of the sultry song was still on her, driving out all thoughts except that she was enjoying this moment and anticipating the next one. She smiled.

'What is it?' he asked at once.

'I'm just having a good time.'

'That smile meant something.'

'It meant I'm having a good time.'

'No, more than that. Tell me.'

His insistence disturbed her. She met his eyes and saw in them something that was too intense for the trivial question. Then somebody collided with her and she felt Marco's hands tighten, steadying her. She was pressed against him, his face close to hers. Her senses swam and she closed her eyes to hide whatever they might have revealed to him.

'Look at me,' he murmured.

She did so and found him watching her intently. She could feel the movement of his thighs against hers, and the warmth of his hand in the small of her back, seeming to move with the flexing of her body, as though the material between had vanished. She was possessed by thoughts and sensations that shocked her with their frankness and urgency, and a little gasp broke from her.

'What is it?' he wanted to know.

'I—nothing—nothing—' she struggled to make sense. 'Just the heat.'

'Yes, the atmosphere is getting a little too much,' Marco agreed. 'My apartment is close by. Let me give you a coffee there.'

It was half past two when they emerged, and the stars were bright in the sky. Except for a few wanderers like themselves the street was deserted. Marco drew her hand through his arm and they strolled the short distance to the apartment block where he lived.

To Harriet's relief the walk and the night air calmed her down. By the time they'd taken the lift to the fifth floor she felt in control of herself again.

She was curious to see the place Marco called home. She'd tried to imagine it and been unable to. He was so impenetrable that it was impossible to conjure up anything that he hadn't chosen to reveal. Now she saw the truth, and at first it took her by surprise. Then she realised that it was exactly what she had subconsciously expected.

No home was ever more austere and unrevealing. The marble floors were honey-coloured, the walls white. The greatest splash of colour came from a dark red leather sofa. The lighting was concealed. Some modern pictures hung on the wall, and a few decorative pieces stood on the shelves. To Harriet's cursory glance they seemed excellent.

It was the home of a man who hid himself away, perhaps even from himself, she thought. There was a photograph of Lucia, but nothing else personally revealing. Through the open door to his bedroom Harriet could see a computer, a fax machine that was inching out paper at that moment, a range of telephones, and two television screens. This man took his work to bed.

Into her mind came Olympia saying, 'A lady-killer…you might say he "loves 'em and leaves 'em" except that he doesn't love 'em.'

Whatever happened in Marco's personal life, it happened there, in that large unadorned bed, in front of the technology that brought the world's stock markets to him at all hours.

'I'll make some coffee,' he called from the kitchen.

The kitchen was also austere, but beautiful, its white relieved by copper and blue. He moved about it easily, like a man used to doing his own cooking, which figured, she thought. Even a small prosaic action, like making coffee, he performed perfectly.

'Delicious,' she said, sipping with relish. 'You have a beautiful home.'

'Thank you. Not everyone likes it.'

'It's peaceful, I like that a lot. And you know how to show off your art pieces to advantage. The plain background does a lot for them, and the way you've arranged the lighting.'

'Thank you. Praise from you is praise indeed. Would you like to give me your opinion of my collection?'

She finished her coffee before approaching a vase on its own plinth. It was oddly flamboyant against the austere background, and she correctly assessed it as French fifteenth century. 'And it's genuine.'

'Everything in my collection is real,' he said firmly.

She smiled, replacing the vase on its plinth and moving away. 'Let's not argue about that.'

'I agree,' he said, standing before her. 'Arguing is a waste of time.'

Very deliberately he leaned forward, placed one hand behind her head, and drew her towards him. His lips touched hers lightly, cautiously, feeling his way before taking the next step. He evidently decided that the signs were favourable for he increased the pressure of his mouth on hers.

The sensation was pleasant, and Harriet let herself go with it, enjoying the cool ease with which he took possession. He acted as though there was all the time in the world for them to explore each other, and she found this relaxing. When his arm curved about her waist she moved in easily, slipping her own arms about him, letting her hands enjoy the sensation of whipcord strength that came through his elegant evening clothes.

He felt good, not bulky and muscular, but lean and hard, with a concealed strength that pleased her. But everything about Marco was just right, most of all his embrace. He was as smooth and expert at this as at every other social skill. He would know just the moment to deepen the kiss and increase their mutual excitement. She waited, but the pressure on her lips eased and she had a sudden view of his face and it troubled her.

Harriet stirred, feeling strangely disturbed. Her body was responding but her mind was growing tense. Something about this wasn't right. She put up her hands to push Marco away but he resisted, moving his mouth slowly over hers in a way that bid her leave everything to him. There was nothing for her to do but be acquiescent.

Like blazes!

She tightened her hands on his shoulders in a way that he couldn't mistake. 'That's enough,' she said firmly and stepped away, freeing herself. 'You've got a nerve, you really have!'

'For pity's sake!' he said, exasperated. 'This is the twenty-first century, not the nineteenth. You couldn't have thought I was just going to hold your hand. We've spent a delightful evening together, we've danced and held each other close, and you say you didn't expect me to kiss you?'

'You weren't kissing me,' she said in a shaking voice. 'You were damned well inspecting the property.'

'What?'

'You know what I mean. That wasn't a kiss, it was a survey to see if a takeover would be in your interests.'

'Now you're being foolish.'

'I could hear your mind ticking away,' she said furiously. 'Test the ground, so far and no further. You wouldn't want me to get any ideas before you've made your own mind up in case I was a nuisance afterwards, you cold, calculating—'

'Don't say any more,' he snapped. 'I get the picture. I just wish I knew what it is you want.'

'It's very simple. If you're going to kiss me, do it properly, not—'

She never got to say the last words. Her mouth was silenced by another mouth descending fiercely onto it. She didn't recall how she came to be in his arms, but there they were about her, holding her still while his lips worked over hers with skill and determination. She tried to protest about the way he was using her, but he muttered, 'Shut up! You said this was what you wanted, and it's what you're going to have.'

She didn't try to argue further. This was a very angry man, giving a very angry kiss, and how could she complain when she'd brought it on herself? But she found she didn't want to complain. An excitement she'd never known before was running through her like wildfire. It wasn't the soft, sensual thrumming that had pervaded her in the club, but a heady, intoxicating thrill that caught her unaware. She couldn't think, she could only feel, and yearn, and reach for him.

His hands were beginning to wander over her, feeling her small waist, flaring out to discover the smooth satin curve of her behind. There they lingered as though relishing the discovery, before reaching the zip at the centre and inching upwards to the hook at the top. A few more movements and the zip would come down, leaving her nearly naked in his arms. How long would it take him then to have the dress off her, and what would she do? She knew she must decide quickly but it was hard because her body was tense with delight, driving everything out of her head.

She could sense that he was drawing her to the bedroom, past the point of no return. It mustn't happen like this, when they were half hostile, but she couldn't think how else it might happen. The undercurrent of hostility was often there, she realised, giving spice and surprise to their relationship. Her urgency increased.

The buzz was so faint that she almost didn't hear it. She tried to blot it out, but Marco was already disengaging himself from her. He made a sound of annoyance at the interruption, but he disengaged himself nonetheless.

Dreamily she watched as he snatched up the phone and she waited for him to put the caller off. Instead he tensed, alert.

'Yes,' he barked into the phone. 'This is Marco Calvani—go on—'

Harriet stared, stunned by how quickly he'd switched his attention, as though he hadn't really been involved at all. But she couldn't believe that, not while she could still feel the heat from his nearness and the driving force of his mouth.

At last Marco took the phone from his ear, but he didn't hang up.

'I'm sorry, but this is important,' he told her. 'I won't be able to drive you home, but there's an excellent cab firm—the number's in that book.'

'Wh-what?' she asked, dazed.

'Just there on the table beside you—hello!' He'd turned back to the phone. 'Yes, I'm still here. Let's talk.'

'And you know what really made me mad,' she told an outraged Lucia later that night. *'He even left me to call my own cab.'*

CHAPTER FIVE

THE following day a delicate bouquet was delivered to the villa, with a beautifully worded note from Marco, regretting that their delightful evening had been 'so unfortunately cut short'. Harriet passed it to Lucia, who expressed her own opinion with a sound of disgust, but mercifully didn't ask Harriet any questions. Her manner was that of a woman biding her time.

After two days Marco telephoned, inviting them both to lunch at the bank. The Orese Nationale had a private restaurant where the top levels of the hierarchy dined in exclusive grandeur, and where they entertained their most important guests. The two women were treated like queens, by Marco and some of his colleagues.

Lucia had been here three times before, but she was the only woman Marco had ever invited, until now. Harriet understood the implication, that none of his passing relationships had been so honoured. She'd meant to protest about his unchivalrous behaviour after the night-club, but it was impossible in these circumstances. Lucia too was silenced, which might, she thought cynically, have been Marco's idea.

Alfredo Orese couldn't keep a secret, and the news was soon all over Rome that Marco had been seen at the night-club with a new woman. But this one was different. She was staying with his mother, and she had dined at the bank. After that speculation raged, and came to more or less the right conclusion.

'So now your engagement isn't a secret,' Lucia said

with satisfaction some days later. They were sitting at breakfast, Marco having arrived late the night before, and slept over.

Harriet looked at her quickly. 'It isn't precisely an engagement,' she said.

'Then what is it, precisely?'

She looked at Marco but he gave her no help, and she floundered, 'It's sort of—unofficial.'

'I have no patience with all this shilly-shallying. Anyone can see that you're right for each other, and now the world knows you're engaged.'

'You wouldn't have given them that impression by any chance?' Marco demanded ironically.

'I didn't need to. Everyone saw you lost in each other at *Bella Figura*.'

Since they could hardly explain that they'd been fighting at the time neither of them answered, and Lucia took this for confirmation.

'And taking us to the bank was practically an announcement,' Lucia added. 'So now we must have a party. Everyone will expect it. They'll also expect a ring. See to it.' She bustled away before they could answer.

'What are we going to do?' Harriet demanded.

'A party's actually a good idea,' Marco said. 'It's time you met some family friends.'

'But an engagement party—a ring—'

'It changes nothing. We get engaged, we change our minds, we get unengaged. And my mother's right about the ring.' He scribbled an address and gave it to her. 'That's the best jeweller in Rome. I'll tell them to expect you.'

'You're not coming with me?'

'I have urgent business to attend to,' he said, not meeting her eye. 'They'll have a fine selection ready for you. Pick the best.'

She attended the jeweller later that day. He treated Signor Calvani's fiancée with awed respect, and showed her a selection of diamond rings, all of which looked lavish and frighteningly expensive. There was one that pleased her, a band of tiny diamonds set in white gold, crowned with one large diamond of marvellous quality. But she knew too much about jewellery not to guess its fabulous price, and there was no way she could accept it.

'Don't you have something a little—smaller,' she asked, feeling that 'cheaper' might be tactless.

'These are the ones Signor Calvani selected,' the jeweller said.

So he'd been to the shop. But not with her. Worse, he was trying to control her choice, and up with that she would not put.

'I'd like to see something else,' she said firmly.

He was aghast. 'But Signor Calvani—'

'Will not be wearing this ring. I will.'

'But—'

'Of course, if it's too much trouble, I can go elsewhere.'

Defeated, the little man produced a tray of less extravagant rings. Then he mopped his brow.

She finally chose a charming solitaire, resisting his attempts to direct her back to the luxury rings, and went away with it on her finger.

Marco arrived at the villa that evening, bearing a large black jeweller's box.

Harriet hadn't expected him to give in easily, and reckoned she didn't have to be clairvoyant to guess that the box contained the rings she'd rejected.

So it was war then! She was ready for him.

Marco greeted his mother pleasantly before taking Harriet aside.

'Thank you for my lovely ring,' she said, holding up her hand.

He took her hand between his and firmly removed the solitaire without even looking at it.

'Hey, what are you doing?'

'There was a mistake. He must have shown you the wrong tray.'

'There was no mistake. This was the one I liked.'

'My fiancée does not wear cheap rings,' Marco said firmly.

'Cheap? It must be worth ten thousand euros.'

'Exactly,' he said in a clipped voice. It was clear that he was keeping his annoyance under control.

'I see. If "your fiancée" was seen flaunting a mere ten grand your clients would start checking the value of their stocks and shares, to see if you were losing your financial touch.'

'Since you obviously understand I don't see why we're having this discussion.'

'Please give me back that ring.'

'No.'

'It's the one I want.'

There was a silence in which he raised his clenched hands to his head in a gesture that was an odd combination of frustration, obstinacy and helplessness. Their eyes met, determination on both sides. Marco opened the box.

'I would prefer you to select one of these,' he said, speaking carefully.

'And I would prefer the one I chose.'

Through gritted teeth he demanded, 'Why must everything be an argument?'

'Because you try to control me at every turn, and I won't have it.'

'Nonsense. I'm merely asking you to do what's proper to our situation. Good grief, Harriet, just the other day you spent more than this without turning a hair. Money I hadn't authorised, let me remind you.'

'Are we going to start that again?'

'I just think it odd that you'll plunder my pockets with the ruthlessness of a corporate raider when it's a question of an old carved stone, but over this you suddenly get delicate about the price. Where's the logic?'

'Who says there has to be logic?'

'It helps sometimes,' he said savagely.

'Then how's this for logic? It's not the price. It's you directing me here and there like a train running on rails. This train is coming off the rails and going her own way.'

'And never mind how it affects me?'

'Your clients will get over it.'

But he was cleverer than she had allowed for, and the next moment he come up with the one thing she wasn't prepared for. The anger died out of his face, and he looked at her with a rueful smile.

'Harriet, for a brilliant woman you can be remarkably stupid.'

'What does that mean?' she asked cautiously, divining a trap but unable to see where it lay.

'It's not my clients I'm afraid of. It's my mother.'

'Oh, really! If you're trying to persuade me that you're afraid of your mother—!'

'Terrified. What do think she's going to say to me if she thinks I've treated you shabbily over the ring?'

He was smiling at her in a way she found disturbing.

'I'll explain to her that this way my choice—'

'It's no good,' he sighed. 'She'll say I should have asserted myself. She doesn't know how hard that is with you. If you won't help me out I'll—well, I just don't know what I'll do.'

'Now you stop that,' she said severely, trying not to respond to his smile. 'I see right through you, d'you hear?'

'I'm sure you do.'

'And you don't care a rap, do you, as long as you get your own way?'

'You understand me perfectly.'

'Well, of all the admissions—! You ought to be ashamed of yourself.'

'Why? Nothing wrong in getting your own way. Don't you like to do that?'

'Of course, but I have some scruples how I go about it.'

'Scruples are a waste of time,' he said seriously. 'If it works for you, go for it.'

'No matter who else—?'

'No matter anything.'

'But that's dreadful.'

'No, it makes sense and it gets things done. Now, why don't you just try this on?'

As he spoke he was slipping onto her finger the white gold ring that had drawn her attention in the shop. And he knew, of course. The jeweller had told him that this one had made her waver. At every turn he was there before her, and she must fight him.

But indignation faded in the beauty of the diamond band with its crown of one perfect jewel. She stretched out her hand to watch the light winking off the great stone, awed by its sheer extravagant glory.

'I can't take it,' she said desperately. 'I just can't.' But she didn't lower her hand.

'Mamma!' Marco hailed his mother, hovering eagerly in the doorway. 'Come and congratulate us on our engagement.'

As he spoke he held up Harriet's hand and Lucia gave a cry of admiration. 'Oh, *cara*, what a beautiful ring!'

'Yes, isn't it?' she said, regarding her betrothed with cynical eyes. There was no turning back now.

'How they'll all gasp when they see it!' Lucia exclaimed. 'Now we can really settle down to enjoy planning the party.'

'I shall have to be out of town for a few days,' Marco said instantly.

'Go away then,' his mother told him. 'We'll do much better without you.'

She departed, humming.

'I won't say anything about your total lack of scruples,' Harriet said, 'because we've already covered that. But I want it clearly understood that if I don't go through with this—and right now that seems very unlikely—you will take this ring back.'

'Naturally,' he said, shocked. 'You don't think I'd have let you keep it? I'd need it for next time.'

His eyes were teasing her, and suddenly she didn't mind very much after all. He was overbearing and impossible, but there was nothing to be done about that. And he had a certain sly charm that could sneak in under her radar.

But there was something else, that she hardly dared admit to herself. Sensible Harriet was retreating into the shadows, banished by another Harriet who wanted to take risks and live life to the full: as long as it was with him.

The realisation shook her. She needed time to think about it.

By the end of supper Lucia and Marco had agreed a

guest list. Looking over it Harriet saw a name that made her eyes light up. 'Baron Orazio Manelli,' she said excitedly.

'Do you know him?' Marco asked.

'No, but I want to. I've been trying to get past his front door for ages.'

'I suppose he has some antique that you want?'

'A thousand antiques, and from what I hear a lot of them have never been properly catalogued. He won't let anyone near them. But it'll be different now.' Her voice became casual. 'Do you know him well?'

'Well enough to get you past his front door. I gather that's what I'm expected to do?'

'It's not a problem is it?'

'Would it make any difference if it was?'

'Well—'

'Don't bother being polite. I'm glad to be of use.'

That was one hurdle cleared, she thought, glad that Marco seemed merely amused. A happy vista of unexplored treasures was opening up to her.

Marco was away for a week. Harriet and Lucia spent the time in a flurry of activity. Every one of the villa's army of servants was engaged in spring cleaning the place and bringing it to new life. A stream of invitations went out, including one to Harriet's father, but since there was no reply it seemed that he was still away.

Within a day a stream of acceptances started to come in. All society was agog to see the woman who had 'conquered the conqueror', a phrase that was repeated through the salons of the city until it reached Harriet's ears.

'Well, this is Rome after all,' she said wryly to Lucia. 'The perfect place for going into the lion's den.'

'Don't worry,' Lucia told her. 'Marco knows all about the lions. He won't let you face them alone.'

Two days before the party Marco appeared at the villa and the three of them had a cheerful supper. Over coffee Lucia said, 'The family will start to arrive tomorrow. Are you ready to meet them?'

'A bit nervous,' Harriet admitted.

Lucia sighed. 'I'm a little nervous myself. Francesco is bringing Liza—I can hardly bring myself to call her his fiancée. It's an absurd name for a woman in her sixties.'

'It's not his fault they've left it so long,' Marco pointed out. 'He's been begging her to marry him for years, but since she was his housekeeper she had the strange idea that their marriage was inappropriate.'

Lucia sniffed. 'She was correct.'

Marco added, 'Harriet has already met Dulcie, Mamma.'

'It wouldn't surprise me to learn that Dulcie came into Harriet's shop to sell the family silver,' Lucia observed with some asperity.

'It was a marble horse head actually,' Harriet murmured without thinking. To cover this gaffe she added quickly, 'I really look forward to seeing her again. We got on very well. After we'd done business we'd have lunch together. She's great fun.'

Lucia blenched. 'Fun? Is that her only qualification for being the future Contessa Calvani?'

'Well I—'

'Don't try to answer that,' Marco told her quietly. 'Mamma, you're not being fair to Harriet.'

'No, of course I'm not. It isn't your fault, my dear.' She patted Harriet's hand and the moment mercifully passed.

'Leo, of course, won't arrive until the last moment,'

Lucia continued. 'He's uncomfortable in society, or anywhere civilised.'

'True,' Marco said with a grin. 'In fact he probably wouldn't come at all if he wasn't going on to America, and Rome Airport will give him a more direct flight to Texas.'

'Texas!' Lucia sniffed again. 'Anyone would think he was a cowboy.'

'Since he's going to a rodeo I suppose that's what he is,' Marco said mildly.

'A rodeo?' Harriet echoed.

'Leo breeds horses in Tuscany,' Marco explained. 'They're fine animals and much in demand. He'll be riding in this rodeo and making some sales, I dare say.'

'A cowboy!' Lucia sighed in despair. 'And he should be Francesco's heir!'

Next morning she and Lucia were waiting at the station for the Venice train, from which Count Francesco Calvani appeared, on his arm a thin elderly woman. This was Liza, his promised bride, and the sight of them together made Harriet smile. Their secret love had lasted all these years, and now that it could flower openly their pride and joy in each other was touching. How many young couples would still feel that way after years, she wondered? Certainly not herself and Marco, who didn't even start with love.

Of course, he might well be right, and a sensible arrangement was the best thing. But there was a lump in her throat as she regarded the elderly lovers.

Marco's cousin Guido was a good-looking charmer with a wicked glint in his eyes. But mostly those eyes rested on Dulcie, who would become his bride in a few weeks. If ever a man was in love—! Harriet thought, liking him for it.

Dulcie greeted her with a whoop and an embrace. 'I

can't believe it's really you. Just fancy, we're going to be related. That'll be great.'

'Yes,' Harriet agreed, wondering if that day would really come. The glittering ring on her finger was real enough but everything else had an air of unreality. For the moment the only thing to do was plunge into the festivities wholeheartedly, and she was eager to enjoy them, despite her many confusions.

She might disapprove of the count's marriage but Lucia's behaviour to Liza was charming. Behind her pride her heart was kind, and Liza was soon relaxing in her company.

She was also relaxed with Marco, Harriet noticed, evidently feeling that his kindness too could be relied on. He kissed her cheek, addressed her as Aunt, and gave her his arm into the house.

Over supper Guido entertained them with the story of the many misunderstandings that had attended his first meeting with Dulcie, in Venice, when she'd thought he was a gondolier, and he hadn't known that she was hiding a secret of her own. They were all laughing when Harriet looked up and saw a tall, massively built young man standing in the doorway. With his shaggy hair and rough-hewn appearance he was immediately identifiable as the 'country bumpkin'.

There was a general cry of *'Leo!'*, and Guido and Marco rose to shake his hand and thump him on the back. The young giant grinned and thumped them back, then kissed Lucia and Dulcie. Harriet got to her feet to meet him, and he gave her the appraising glance she was growing used to. He was as handsome as the other two, but the impression he made was more powerfully physical. The Calvani men, Harriet decided, were simply too much.

She instinctively liked Leo, who shook her hand and

kissed her cheek with the simplicity of a man who found actions easier than thought. Keeping her hand between his, he then looked her up and down with an appreciative grin that went on getting broader. Playing up to him, she gazed back, until Marco coughed significantly.

'Who are you?' she asked, giving him a dazed stare.

Everyone roared with laughter, including, she was glad to notice, Marco. He wasn't a man who would normally accept such teasing, but the family's appreciation of her quick wit had delighted him.

'Go away, Leo, while I remind my fiancée who I am,' Marco said with a grin. 'And leave her alone in future.'

Leo winked at her and hissed, 'The terrace at midnight,' in a stage whisper, but Harriet was prevented from answering by Marco's arm, firmly about her waist, drawing her away.

'We were just fooling,' she protested, still chuckling.

'I know, but you want to watch Leo. He "fools" with a lot of girls. He's a "love 'em and leave 'em" man.'

'Strange, I heard the same about you.'

His brows contracted. 'I wonder where you heard that.'

'Everywhere.' Her eyes challenged him and he backed down first.

'Let's finish supper,' he said.

Since the meal was half over Leo had a lot of catching up to do, and tucked in with gusto while the talk swirled around him. When he spoke it was usually to ask Harriet about herself, not pretending to be amorous now, but with every appearance of cousinly interest. It might have been simply good manners, but it warmed her heart. She began to feel as though a dream had come true against all the odds. This was the culmination of something that had been happening ever since Lucia had welcomed her at the station. She was accepted. The whole dashing, colourful

Calvani family had opened its collective arms to her. To someone who'd felt rejected most of her life it was overwhelming.

It was hard to believe that the Calvani men came from the same family, their looks were so different, although they were all, as Lucia had observed to Harriet, 'handsome as devils'.

At seventy-two the count bore the marks of a lifetime's self-indulgence, but not enough to obliterate the remains of brilliant good looks. Leo and Guido were half-brothers, Leo radiating the vigour and energy of a man of the earth: lusty, uncomplicated, great-hearted. Guido's build was slighter than his brother's, his boyish looks balanced by a shrewd intelligence, and he had a nervous energy that kept him restless, except when Dulcie was nearby.

To Harriet's eyes Marco was by far the most impressive, elegant, controlled, unrevealing, his own man in everything. In the heart of his family he was a changed man, relaxed, readier to laugh. But it was still hard to imagine him behaving with Leo's cheerful indifference, or regarding a woman with the blatant adoration that shone from Guido's eyes.

She wondered about the woman he'd nearly married, and whose name was never mentioned in this house. Had he truly loved her, or had she fled him in despair at being unable to penetrate his protective shell? That was more likely, she thought.

And yet he had a surprise for her as the party broke up to go to bed, taking her hand and leading her out onto the terrace.

'You have a midnight appointment out here,' he reminded her.

'But not with you,' she said provocatively.

'It had better be with me,' he said with a smile that provoked her even more.

And she wanted nothing better, she thought as his lips touched hers. There was a sweetness in this kiss that melted her and made her lean in to him, wanting more. But he drew back a little, and she saw him regarding her with an odd little half-smile. She raised her eyebrows in a query, but he only shook his head, and she felt the brief interlude had posed more questions than it answered.

On the night of the party Harriet was just finishing dressing when Dulcie, a dream in dark blue silk and diamonds, swept into her room.

'Wow!' she exclaimed. 'You look fantastic. No wonder you melted the Iceman's heart.'

'The Iceman?'

'I shouldn't have said that,' Dulcie was conscience stricken. 'But Guido says it's what the family have always called him. Not to his face, naturally. You know how grim he can be. But of course you see a side of him that nobody else does.' She gave a delighted chuckle. 'Now I've made you blush.'

'I'm not,' Harriet said, although conscious that she was going pink. There was something in the implication that she and Marco were lovers that discomposed her. To hide her face she turned away and patted down her dress.

The beautician had come out from the salon to take charge of her appearance, and Harriet's face was made-up with subtle flattery, so that her expressive green eyes dominated her face. Her hair was swept up on top of her head, with just a few curving wisps gently drifting down about her cheeks and neck.

She wore a clinging dress of golden brown crushed

velvet. She knew she looked good and the knowledge gave her confidence.

There was a knock at the door and Dulcie opened it to reveal Guido and Marco, both in bow-ties and dinner jackets, both incredibly handsome.

Marco surveyed Harriet with satisfaction. '*Bene!* Just as I hoped. This will look splendid on you.'

He opened a black box, revealing a heavy gold chain. Dulcie stared at it, wide-eyed, before seizing Guido's hand and whisking him away.

'Spoilsport,' her beloved chided her when they were out in the corridor. 'It would have been fun to see the Iceman playing the lover.'

'You wouldn't have seen it,' Dulcie told him. 'Marco wouldn't open up with us there. But now that we're gone I'll bet they're locked in a passionate embrace.'

Guido inched hopefully back towards the door. 'Can't we just—?'

'Behave yourself! Besides, I have other plans for you.'

His eyes gleamed. 'Ah, that's different.' He allowed himself to be led away in the opposite direction.

They would both have been disappointed had they seen Marco's calm demeanour as he raised the elaborate chain and draped it around Harriet's neck.

'I've always known that gold would suit you,' he said, fastening the clasp at the back. 'I was right.'

Awed, Harriet gazed at the woman in the mirror and didn't know her. This wasn't herself, but a magnificent creature, with a timeless splendour. She might have been Cleopatra, or some ancient pagan goddess. Marco had judged perfectly.

'Thank you,' she said. 'I never dreamed I could look like that.'

'I know. You have discerning eyes for everyone but

yourself. I have known this about you from the first moment.'

A special note in his voice made her conscious that his fingers were still resting against her neck. Glancing in the mirror she met his eyes and saw in them a glow that he'd never shown her face to face. Then he seemed to become self-conscious, and the shutters came down again.

'Are you ready?' Lucia asked from the door. 'People are beginning to arrive.'

The other five were waiting in the corridor. Even Leo had managed to shrug himself into a dinner jacket. Lucia, splendid in rubies, surveyed them all with satisfaction.

'The Calvanis are a handsome family,' she said. 'And they attract handsome women. Now let's all go down and *knock 'em dead.*'

CHAPTER SIX

STANDING in the receiving line Harriet thought the guests would go on forever. There were a number of banking 'big names' and some of Marco's most important clients, but there were also a lot of titles, Countess this, Princess that, Duke, Baron. This was society with a capital S.

Where it wasn't titled, it was wealthy. Harriet guessed that half the bank vaults in Rome must have disgorged their contents of family jewels. Tiaras, *rivières*, bracelets, earrings, diamonds, rubies, emeralds and pearls, each one signifying that its wearer would compete in riches with any other woman there.

As she could herself, she realised. The glowing gold that Marco had fastened around her neck was, in itself, a declaration. And so was the ring. She shuddered at the thought of wearing a ring worth a 'mere' ten thousand in this company. The one now weighing down her hand informed the world that Marco Calvani's chosen bride was a woman who commanded his respect, and therefore must command theirs.

The women seemed young or middle-aged, most of them older than they looked because they had time and money to spend fighting the years. They were dressed in the height of luxurious fashion, not merely to look good but to make a statement. Not a fashion statement. Something else.

Beware!

That was it.

There was a frisson in the air, a sense of danger, and

suddenly she could hear Olympia's voice saying, 'Marco's known as a lady-killer, with the emphasis on killer.'

They were watching her with hungry, glittering eyes. Curiosity, jealousy, cynicism? All these and more. Lust, envy, memories, anticipation. Some of these bold-eyed creatures had been his lovers, and wanted her to know that. And they were frankly calculating how long she could keep him faithful. Not long, some of them were doubtless thinking. They wanted her to know that, too.

She was in the lion's den.

A spurt of anger inspired her to raise her head and straighten her shoulders.

No matter that this engagement might soon be over. Tonight, at least, he was officially hers, and she would defend her right to him.

'Are you all right?' Marco asked, glancing at her.

'Fine. Never better,' she assured him.

'I believe you. This is a jungle, but you're strong.'

'I'm not scared, but perhaps they should be.'

'Yes,' he said, giving her one of his rare, brilliant smiles. 'Come,' he led her onto the floor as the music started. 'Let's tell them what they want to know.'

And they told those hot-eyed, resentful women exactly what they wanted to know, dancing close, head to head, body to body, hips moving together, seemingly lost in each other.

It was false, Harriet thought; all put on for the crowd. But the pleasure that came from just being near him was there again, infusing her limbs as they moved against his. The low-cut dress was revealing, but instead of being embarrassed, as last time, now she felt pride. She had come to believe that she was worth looking at, and she wanted this man to think so, too.

He did, if the look in his eyes was anything to go by. He seemed transfixed by her creamy bosom, her long neck, her bold eyes.

'You're beautiful,' he said softly. 'I don't want you to dance with anyone else.'

'Then I won't,' she said, smiling.

'Unfortunately you must, and so must I.'

'Yes, or all those women are going to be so disappointed.'

'Forget them.'

She laughed, so close to his face that her breath warmed him, and she felt him tremble. 'They don't want to be forgotten.'

'Forget them,' he said again. 'That's an order.'

'You give orders very easily, but it's unwise of you to tell me what to think.'

His eyes narrowed. 'Why is it "unwise"?'

'Because you should never give an order you can't enforce. How will you ever know if I'm doing what you want?'

His brow lightened. 'I shall just take it for granted that you're not. Then I can't go wrong.'

'You understand me almost as well as I understand you,' she teased.

'And what am I?'

'A tyrant.'

'And you're a witch.'

The music was coming to an end. He had just time to give her a wry look before they passed on to other partners.

The dances slid by, Count Calvani, Guido, Leo, then the local dignitaries, until finally she came to Baron Orazio Manelli.

She'd met him briefly at the start of the evening. He

was younger than she had expected, middle-aged rather than elderly, strongly built with a fleshy face and a haughty expression. She'd written to him so often that she wondered if he would react to her name. He gave her an appraising look but it was hard to be sure what it meant.

Now he approached her and asked her to dance, with a look in his eye that told her he'd remembered.

'I wondered why your name was familiar,' he said genially as they took the floor. 'You've been writing to me.'

'For two years now. Everyone knows your art and sculpture collection is fabulous but you hide it away.'

'My father and my grandfather were collectors. Me, I like to spend my time among the living, not the dead. Why should a beautiful young woman like you want to bury herself in the past?'

'I love it. It's my life.'

'Not your whole life surely? Your husband will want your attention.'

'And he'll have it,' she said demurely. 'Within reason.'

He laughed so loud that heads turned. 'Marco won't let you get away with that.'

'Who says I'll ask him? I shan't stop being an antiquarian just because I'm a wife.'

He gave a throaty laugh. 'I'm beginning to like you. Perhaps we should talk some more.'

'About your collection? And me coming to see it?'

'How can I refuse you?' Somebody jostled him from behind. 'Can we go to a place that's less crowded?'

It couldn't do any harm to slip away just for a moment, she reasoned. They would go into the next room, where the party was also taking place, but where there were fewer people. But next door somebody was singing a song, so they went on further, until they reached the garden and found a bench under a tree from which hung coloured lights.

Manelli began to talk of gold, vases, jewellery, spreading a carpet of wonders before her so that her inward eyes were dazzled. The outside world slipped away. Harriet forgot where she was and what she should be doing. Time passed unnoticed as new worlds opened before her.

'But you shouldn't hide all this away,' she said fervently at last. 'With treasures like yours you should let the whole world in to see them.'

He took her hand between his two. 'One day soon you must come to my house, and it will be my pleasure to show you everything.'

'That would be wonderful,' she breathed, closing her eyes in a happy dream.

But the dream was shattered by a cold voice. 'You are neglecting our guests *cara*.'

It was Marco, standing before them, his mouth stretched in a smile that didn't reach his eyes. His gaze was fixed on her hand, tenderly enfolded between those of the Baron.

'Forgive us,' Orazio said smoothly, rising but not releasing her. 'In my wonder at discovering a lady so full of wisdom and learning, as well as so beautiful, I forgot my manners and monopolised her. May I say, Marco, how profoundly fortunate you are to have secured the affections of this delightful—'

Harriet's lips twitched. It was an outrageous performance, but an amusing one. Then she stole another look at Marco's face. He didn't find any of this funny.

'You have already conveyed your congratulations, for which I thank you,' Marco said in a wintry voice.

His stony gaze was fixed on Harriet's hand, which she

quickly disentangled from Orazio, who managed to kiss it before letting go.

'I live in anticipation of your visit,' he said, 'and the time we will spend together.'

Marco's lips tightened. Harriet wanted to say, 'Don't let him tease a rise out of you. Can't you see he's doing it on purpose?' Instead she slipped her hand in the crook of his arm and walked back to the house with him.

'Don't be angry,' she said in a coaxing voice.

'Not angry?' he demanded harshly. 'Do you realise that it's nearly midnight?'

'Oh, goodness, I'm sorry. I shouldn't have been gone so long.'

'Perhaps we can discuss that later,' he said in a tight voice.

It astonished her to realise that he was taking this seriously. He knew she cared only for the treasures in Orazio's home. He was sophisticated. He should have been able to shrug it aside. But his cold fury left no doubt that this had flicked him on the raw.

They had begun to climb the steps that led up to the broad terrace that ran along the side of the house.

'Marco—'

'Let's not talk about it now. Our guests must see us in perfect accord.'

'Not if you're glowering at me.'

'I'm not. This is much simpler.'

The party had spilled out into the garden, from where the guests had a grandstand view of the terrace, and of Marco suddenly sweeping his bride into his arms and covering her face with kisses.

'I don't think—' she managed.

'Shut up,' he said savagely. 'Shut up and make it look good.'

Cheers rose from the garden as he tightened his arms in a rough simulation of desire and Harriet gave herself up to his embrace. She wouldn't have chosen it like this but she had a guilty feeling that she'd treated him badly and should help him save face.

If only he wouldn't hold her so tightly, kissing her again and again with a fierceness that looked like passion to the watchers, but which only she could sense was anger.

'Marco, don't—' she murmured. 'Enough.'

'Yes,' he said in a voice that shook. 'That's enough to convince them for the moment. Now we play the loving couple until the end of the evening.'

He loosened his grip and she swayed for a moment. Her head was spinning and she had to cling onto him. The guests, who'd crowded up onto the terrace, surrounded them, laughing and cheering at what they thought had happened. Some of the younger ones, their tongues loosened by wine, said what the rest were thinking.

'Marco, you've made the poor girl faint—'

'That's the way to kiss the woman you love—so that she really knows—'

'Now he wants to get rid of us quickly—' Roars of laughter.

'That's enough of that,' Lucia said, quelling the riot.

'We were just congratulating him,' one lad said, irrepressibly. 'Now, if Harriet were mine—'

'But she isn't,' Marco checked him. 'She's mine, and you'd be wise to remember it.' His voice was light, almost friendly. Only a few of his listeners heard the undertow of steel, and one of them was the woman standing in the circle of his arms, who could still feel that he was trembling, as she was herself. As he spoke his arm instinctively tightened about her, and she knew the message was as much for herself as for them. It was a warning.

'Bring some more champagne,' Marco called. 'Champagne for everyone.'

Servants hurried forward bearing foaming bottles, passing among the crowd until every glass was filled. Marco raised his hand for silence.

'I am the luckiest man on earth,' he said. 'The most wonderful woman in the world has promised to be my wife. There can be no greater happiness than this.'

How could he say that? she thought, when he'd all but accused her of playing him false. How could she ever know what this man was truly thinking?

'Raise your glasses, with me, to my bride!'

They all toasted her. Over the rim of Marco's glass she saw his eyes, but couldn't discern anything behind their smile.

Then the guests toasted the two of them and the evening ended in a riot of good fellowship. It took another hour for the long, shiny cars to come, one by one, to the front door, and carry the guests away, with the family standing on the steps to bid them farewell.

When the last car had gone Harriet closed her eyes, worn out but exhilarated. Now she must make things right between herself and Marco. But when she opened her eyes again there was no sign of him.

'Don't worry,' Lucia said, seeing her look around. 'He's probably taken his cousins to his study for a whisky. Don't wait up for him.'

Harriet agreed. It might be better to let his anger cool first. She kissed Lucia goodnight and went up to her room.

She meant to shower and go to bed, but she couldn't. Something about tonight hadn't ended yet. She reached behind her neck, trying to undo the clasp of the heavy gold necklace, while one level of her mind recited the usual commentary: French seventeenth century, genuine in gold, wrought in the style of—*oh, who cares?*

Who cared about anything except the look she'd seen in Marco's eyes when he'd found her with the Baron? What did anything matter except what that look had meant?

And then she saw it again. She hadn't heard him come into the room and the first she knew, he was there behind her, brushing her fingers aside so that he could undo the clasp. His face was so dark that she almost expected him to snatch the jewellery from her, but he removed the necklace quietly, although his fingers weren't quite steady.

'You're not still angry,' she coaxed. 'It was such a wonderful evening.'

'I'm glad you enjoyed it,' he said, tight-lipped. 'And yes, I'm still angry. You made a fool of me.'

'Just because I got into conversation with—'

'You disappeared from our engagement party with another man, and stayed away for nearly an hour,' he grated. 'Is that reason enough for you?'

'Was it really that long? I lost track of the time and forgot about—'

It was the wrong thing to say. *'You forgot!'* he snapped. 'Thank you, that was all I needed.'

'I'm sorry.'

Rage turned his voice to pure steel. 'I appreciate that your ideas of behaviour are unconventional, but did nobody ever explain to you that a woman is supposed to prefer her fiancé's company to that of any other man? If she can't manage that she's supposed to pretend. It's polite. It's the accepted thing. It stops him looking a complete fool in front of the whole world. Do you understand *that?*'

'Of course I do. Oh, look, I'm sorry Marco, I really am. I didn't mean to insult you, I just got carried away—' she saw his face. 'I'm making it worse, aren't I?'

'What you're doing is proving how English you are,' he said bitingly. 'You think having an Italian name makes you one of us, but I tell you that the name is nothing. What matters is the Italian heart and you have no idea of that.'

Harriet stared, astounded that the cool, composed man she thought she knew could have said something so cruel. 'How dare you say I'm not one of you!' she flashed. 'It's my heritage as much as yours.'

'Yes, you were born with warm Mediterranean blood in you, but it no longer speaks. Otherwise you'd know by instinct that it's vital to a man how his woman treats him.'

I am not your woman.

'You are—' he checked himself, then went on. 'You are as far as people here are concerned. They think of us as a couple, but you think that means being "jolly good friends" as though a man and a woman were a pair of neuters. And only the English think like that.'

His face was like that of a stranger, watching her. 'What is it? Can't you bear the truth?'

'It isn't the truth,' she cried.

'It is the truth and you know it. You take refuge in a dead world because the living are too much for you. Your heart is fixed on the past where nothing matters and nothing can hurt. What do you know of pride, or love or passion? They're just words to you.'

'It was just carelessness,' she cried. 'It had nothing to do with love or passion—'

'But everything to do with pride,' he said bitingly. 'My pride, that you humiliated in front of everyone. What were you talking about all that time?'

'What do I ever talk about? Antiques. And you knew I was going to make a beeline for him, because I told you. You even said you'd help me get past his front door.'

'You can forget that. You're not setting foot in that man's house.'

'Are you giving me more orders?'

'Let's say I'm pointing out certain realities. He makes trouble between us. Knowing that, it's inconceivable that you should seek his company.'

'It's not his company I want. It's his art treasures.'

'You won't understand, will you? Then let me put it plainly. I forbid you to go to his house.'

'You *forbid*—? You lay down the law from on high and I'm supposed to say, "Yes sir, no sir." Boy, did you pick the wrong person! All right, I was away too long, and I'm sorry. It was inconsiderate of me. But everyone there tonight knows that this engagement was arranged. We've put on a good pretence, but there are no secrets in Rome, you told me that yourself. And if you're going to talk about pride, what about mine? There was hardly a woman there tonight who didn't—how can I put this delicately?—know you better than I do.'

'Are you saying that was a kind of revenge?' Marco asked, his eyes kindling dangerously.

'No, of course not. But nobody thinks we really mean anything to each other—'

'Mean anything to each other?' he mocked. 'What trouble you have with the word "love".'

'Love has nothing to do with this,' she said angrily. 'You can't just change the terms when it suits you.'

'The terms always included making things look convincing, and you broke them tonight. I want your promise that you won't see him again whether I'm there or not.'

'I'll see him if I want to,' she cried. 'And the only promise I'll make is that there'll be no promises.'

'I'm warning you—'

'Don't warn me. I'm not impressed.'

'You won't see him again, Harriet, I mean it.'

'Or else what?'

'You'll find yourself on the first plane back to England.'

'In your dreams. You may be able to throw me out of this house, but would you like to bet against my moving into an hotel and visiting Manelli every day?'

His eyes narrowed. 'Don't do that. It would be an unwise move, I promise you.'

'Threats now!'

'It's not a threat, it's a promise. Do I make myself clear.'

'Perfectly, and now let me make myself clear.' She pulled off the ring and held it out to him. 'Is that clear enough?'

'Be damned to you!' With a swift movement he snatched the ring from her and hurled it away, not looking to see where it fell.

Stunned, she stared at him, realising how close he was to losing all control.

'Marco, I want you to leave now.'

She turned away but his hands were on her shoulders, forcing her back to face him. *'I haven't finished.'* She tried to wrench herself free but he kept his hands in place until she gave up.

'Let me go this minute,' she said.

'Perhaps you should take some of your own advice. Don't give an order you can't enforce. Unless you think you're strong enough to fight me.'

She didn't answer, just glared up at him from glittering,

fury-filled eyes. Her struggles had caused some of her hair to fall and her cheeks were flushed. He looked her over slowly, and her wild appearance seemed to strike him, for he drew in a breath and began to pull her towards him, moving as in a trance.

'Don't you dare,' she breathed. 'Our engagement is over.'

'No,' he said, lowering his mouth. 'It isn't.'

She tried to resist but he slipped his hands down her arms, imprisoning them, giving her no choice but to accept his kiss. She'd teased him about insisting on his own way, but he was insisting now, and it was no laughing matter. This was dangerous because he had the power, which no other man had possessed, to excite her body until it turned against her, sapping her will, making her anger irrelevant.

He kissed her like a man whose knowledge of her was already so intimate that he could do as he liked. The devil himself might have kissed like that, his tongue driving into her mouth without warning, shocking, thrilling.

He knew how to use his tongue to tease and excite her, flickering it skilfully against the tender inside of her mouth, sending shivers of delight through her, then slowing, leashing himself back and her too, to her frustration.

'How dare you!' she said in a shaking voice. She was furiously angry with him for forcing this on her, and even angrier that he had stopped when her pleasure was building.

He didn't reply. She wasn't sure he'd even heard her. His face was dark, troubled, his eyes fixed on her as though asking some question that she didn't understand. One hand moved slowly up her arm to her shoulder, her neck, the fingers entwining into her hair before he dropped his head to renew the assault.

Now her arms were free, and she could push him away, except that she lacked the will. His mouth drifted over her face, bestowing teasing kisses everywhere until he reached the tender place just beneath her ear, almost as though he knew that she was unbearably sensitive just there. She took a shuddering breath at the sweet, whispering sensation that trailed down her neck to her throat, then further to the swell of her breasts.

There was no chance to pretend now. He would sense the mad beating of her heart beneath his lips. He'd challenged her to fight him but she couldn't fight the need of her own flesh that made her raise her hands, not to fend him off, but to clasp them about his head, drawing it closer. She was afire, craving more sensations that she'd never felt before with such totality. For perhaps the first time in her life she was living brilliantly, urgently in the present, and it was electrifying. A moan broke from her and she arched against him.

She felt him stiffen and become totally still. He raised his head, shaking it a little, as though wondering what was happening, then fixed his gaze on her face. She almost cried out at his expression. There was no triumph, as she'd expected, only a kind of torment.

'Marco—'

'If I ever catch you doing this with any other man,' he said hoarsely, 'I'll—I'll—'

She waited for him to finish, hearing his urgent, rasping breath and the thunder of her own heart. This was a new and bewildering Marco, tortured by some violent emotion that was close to destroying him.

'You'll do what?' she whispered at last.

A shudder went through him. 'No matter.' His grip slackened and the blazing look went out of his eyes, leaving them strangely dead.

She clung to the furniture, feeling the world still rocking beneath her. 'Perhaps it does matter,' she suggested.

'It does *not*,' he said harshly, 'because this is now closed. I apologise for alarming you.'

'Marco—'

'You have my word that it won't happen again.'

'Marco!'

She was looking at a closed door.

CHAPTER SEVEN

IN THE early morning light Harriet awoke suddenly and sat up, listening to the silence. Slipping out of bed she went to the tall window and pushed it open, looking out onto the quiet countryside, dotted with pine trees.

The memory of last night still seemed to live in every part of her, mind, heart and body. She'd seen a side of Marco she'd never dreamed of. She'd known that he was full of contradictory qualities, that he could be charming, seductive, calculating and ruthlessly determined. But she hadn't known that he could be dangerous. She knew now. For the few moments that he'd held her in his arms, forcing bruising, desperate kisses onto her, the air had crackled with danger, and she had felt alive as never before. It was shocking, but it was true.

She tried to call common sense to her aid. Whatever tumult of feeling she'd thought she detected, the truth was that Marco had been trying to prove a point. She'd made a fool of him and he wouldn't stand for it. He'd reclaimed her in front of their guests, but pride had driven him to give her a demonstration of power when they were alone. He'd wanted to show her that he could fire her with such passion that she was his, whether she liked it or not.

And he'd succeeded. She knew now what his touch could do to her. The lightest caress could melt her so that she could think only of more caresses, and more…

But his own thoughts were different, she guessed, summoning his face to her mind and trying to read his eyes. He wanted to show her that, while he wouldn't allow himself to become hers, she had no choice but to be his. In the cold light of day there was no more to it than that.

But the light of day wasn't cold. As she raised her eyes to Rome's distant hills she could see the golden glow of the rising sun.

It was nearly six in the morning. Marco, the early-rising banker, would be up by now and she needed to hear his voice. But his phone was switched off and when she called his apartment she was answered by a machine. She didn't leave a message. How could she when she didn't know what she wanted to say?

She needed to be outdoors. Hastily throwing on jeans and a sweater she slipped down the stairs and into the grounds. For a while the trees pressed close together and she was able to get away from the house, moving down winding paths that led in several directions.

That was her life now, moving along winding paths to a destination she no longer knew. A voice inside warned her to go home, but there was a bittersweet ache in her heart that said stay. She was a mass of confused feelings, and she couldn't have said where she wanted her path to lead.

She came to a small lake and began to stroll along the edge of the water, relishing the beauty of the day. The morning mist had vanished, the light was fresh, and the sound of birdsong rose in the clear air.

Where was he?

Then she saw something that made her stop and catch her breath. A man was sitting on the ground against a tree, one arm flung across his bent knee, still in the clothes he'd worn last night, but for his jacket which had been tossed aside. His shirt was open halfway down, and the way his head was flung back against the tree showed the strong, brown column of his neck, and the thick curly hair that covered his chest.

Dropping down quietly beside him Harriet saw that his eyes were closed and he breathed heavily as though sleeping. For once all tension was drained away from his features, the mouth softened, gentle, as though it had never said a harsh or bitter word. She knelt there awhile, watching his unshaven face, the hair falling over his forehead and the dark shadows beneath his eyes, feeling a tenderness he'd never inspired in her before. She knew he would hate the idea of being studied like this, while he was vulnerable and unaware, but she lingered one more moment—just one more—

He opened his eyes.

Instead of being angry he surprised her again, simply sitting motionless, gazing at her so long that she wondered if he actually saw her. At last the dazed look faded from his eyes, replaced by a helpless pain.

'You still speaking to me?' he said at last.

She nodded. There was a lump in her throat.

He sighed and dropped his head onto the arm across his knee. 'That's more than I deserve,' he said in a muffled voice. He raised his head. 'I guess I had too much to drink.'

'I didn't see you drinking very much.'

'You weren't there to see—' he checked himself with a shrug. 'Forget it.'

'Have you been out here all night?'

'Since I left you, yes.'

'I thought you were going home.'

'I had to get away from you, but I couldn't leave you, if that makes any sense.'

It made perfect sense. Since he'd stormed out last night she'd felt a persistent tug in her heart, as though it was connected to his by an invisible thread. Now she knew that he had felt it, too.

She sat down properly beside him, took one of his cold hands and began to rub it. He let her, seemingly too drained to react, but his eyes were on her hand, minus the ring.

'I haven't looked for it yet,' she explained. 'It could be anywhere in that big room. Suppose we never find it?'

His answer was the faintest possible shrug. After a moment his fingers moved to grasp hers. 'Are you all right?' he asked quietly.

'Yes, I'm fine.'

'Did I—hurt you?'

It was there again; the force of his mouth against hers, bruising, crushing, driving her wild with its ruthless persistence: the feelings still lived in her flesh, excitement, alarm, the joy of risk-taking, never known before.

'No, you didn't hurt me,' she said.

'Are you sure? I have a hellish temper, I'm afraid.'

'You weren't trying to hurt me.'

'No,' he said huskily. 'No, I was trying to make you aware of me.' His mouth quirked faintly at the corner. 'When I was a child I used to cope with frustration by roaring at the top of my voice. Then people listened.'

'Yes, I think I would have guessed something like that,' she said gently.

'Time I grew out of it, huh?'

'People don't stop being the way they are. You don't frighten me.'

'Thank God! Because that's the last thing I'd ever want. Please Harriet, forget everything about last night.'

'Everything? You mean—?'

'Every last damned thing,' he said emphatically. 'Go to Manelli's house whenever you like. There'll be no more trouble, I promise. What's past is past. It was a kind of madness, no more.'

'But Marco, what got into you? It wasn't drink, I know that.'

'I can't explain, but there are some things I'm not—rational about. Let's just say that I get jealous easily. And possessive. It's not nice. I apologise.'

'You have nothing to be jealous about.'

'I know. But there are things I can't forget.'

'About the other woman, the one you were going to marry?'

He stirred. 'What do you know about her?'

'Not much. You were engaged, then you both changed your mind.'

A long silence, then he said as though the words were dredged up from some fearful depths. 'It was a little more complicated than that.'

'Break ups aren't usually completely equal,' she suggested tentatively.

He nodded. 'Something of the kind. Whatever! It makes me act unreasonably, and I'm sorry.'

She gave his hand a reassuring squeeze, thinking that she'd never in her life seen a man so unhappy.

'When you find the ring,' he said wearily, 'will you wear it again?'

She hesitated. 'I don't know.'

'If you leave now—so soon after last night—' he gave a bark of laughter. 'That'll give the gossips something to talk about. And also—' he grew quiet again '—it would hurt my mother badly.'

'I won't leave—for the moment.'

'Thank you.'

Suddenly he leaned forward, resting his head against her in an attitude of despondency, almost of despair, she thought. Her arms went about him and she held him close, longing to comfort him, but knowing that there was a part of him she still couldn't reach. She dropped her own head, resting her cheek against his dishevelled hair, and tried to tell him, through the strength of her embrace, that she was there for him. She thought she felt his arms tighten about her, as though he'd found something he needed to cling to.

They sat motionless while the warmth stole through her. Not the warmth of passion: something quite different and far more alarming. While they fought she could hold out against him, even in the face of her own desire. But his sudden vulnerability shook desire into a fierce longing to protect him that was suspiciously like love.

Disaster! She hadn't meant to love him, wasn't sure she wanted to. It was a trap and she'd fallen into it before she knew it was there.

Why couldn't you have gone on driving me nuts? she thought. It was easier then. This isn't fair.

He stirred and she released him. He pushed back his hair, which immediately fell over his forehead again. 'I suppose I look like a tramp?'

'A bit,' she said tenderly.

He started to get up and winced. 'I'm stiff!'

'If you've been here all night I'm not surprised. Let me help.'

He slipped an arm about her neck and got painfully to his feet, scooping up his leaf-stained jacket.

'The ground's damp,' she said. 'You could catch pneumonia like this.'

'I used to sleep out a lot when I was a kid. Just over there in the woods, there's a place where I'd make a camp and pretend I was an outlaw.'

'Show me.' She wanted to prolong this gentle time with him.

'All right.'

Still with his arm around her shoulders he guided her through the trees and up a steep slope to a clearing. 'This is where I used to sleep out under the stars,' he said.

'It's a wonderful view.'

'Yes, "the enemy" couldn't approach you unaware.'

'Unless they came from above,' she pointed out. 'But I expect you posted sentries. How many of you were there?'

'Just me. I used to envy Leo and Guido who were brothers and had each other. Actually they were separated when Guido was ten, and Uncle Francesco took him to live in Venice, leaving Leo in Tuscany. But I always thought of them as having each other.'

'It's a pity you didn't have any brothers and sisters.'

'My father died early, and Mamma never wanted to marry again.'

'But surely you had some friends?'

He shrugged. 'At school.'

But none for his fantasy life, she thought, pitying the lonely little boy. She thought of how much easier he was when surrounded by the rest of the boisterous Calvani family, like a man who would gladly be one of them, but always felt slightly apart.

'You can see almost as far as Rome from this spot,' he said. 'At night I used to sit under this tree and watch the lights. Just here.' He put his jacket on the ground and indicated for her to sit on it beside him.

'You too,' she said, making room for him.

They sat quietly together as the light expanded and the sound of birdsong grew louder. His hand had found its way into hers.

'This is a wonderful place,' she said. 'I can understand you wanting to come here often.'

There was no answer, and she became aware of a weight on her shoulder. Turning, she found his head lying against her, his eyes closed again.

Now she saw something else in his face. He was weary in a way that had nothing to do with missed sleep. Strain and tension had fallen away, but they left behind a bone-deep exhaustion that looked as if it had been there a long time, perhaps years.

She'd never thought to pity Marco, but she pitied him now in a way that she didn't entirely understand. But there would be time to learn about him, and reach out to the trouble deep within him. Gently she brushed the hair back from his forehead.

He stirred and opened his eyes, looking straight into her smiling ones.

'You fell asleep again,' she said tenderly.

'Yes—' he sounded unsure of himself. 'How long?'

'Just a few minutes.'

Then she saw the look that she'd dreaded, as though shutters had come down. Light faded from his eyes, leaving a deliberate emptiness as he withdrew back into the comfortless place within himself. He pulled away from her and got to his feet, not letting her assist him this time, but offering his own hand to help her up. She took it, rising so quickly that she almost lost her balance. He steadied her with his other hand on her arm, but didn't draw her close, as he could so easily have done.

With dismay she realised that it was all gone, the warmth and communication that had been there before. Now his eyes were watchful. Perhaps he was even more wary of her because he'd allowed her to draw near.

'What time is it?' he asked, consulting his watch. 'Past

seven. I've got to be going. I'm sorry for putting all this onto you.'

'I'm glad we talked,' she said, seeking a way back to him. 'I understand you better now.'

He shrugged. 'What is there to understand? I behaved badly, for which I'm sorry. You've been very patient, but there's no reason for you to put up with my moods. I won't inflict them on you again.'

She nearly said, 'Not even when we're married?' but the words wouldn't come. Everything that had seemed certain a moment ago had vanished into illusion. She no longer knew him.

She made one last try. 'Moods aren't the worst thing in the world. Maybe people shouldn't be polite all the time. I wasn't very polite to you last night and you—'

'Overreacted I'm afraid. But it won't happen again. Now, can we leave it?'

He rubbed his stubbled jaw. 'I'd better get inside and put myself right. I don't want my mother to see me like this. I'd prefer that you didn't tell her.'

'Of course not.'

They walked back in silence. Within sight of the house he said, 'Take a look first, and signal me if it's clear. No, wait!'

He grasped her arm and pulled her back into the trees as Lucia appeared at the rear door. Her voice reached them.

'Who left this door unlocked? Surely it hasn't been like this all night?'

'It's all right,' Harriet said, advancing so that Lucia could see her. 'I opened it. I've been out for an early-morning walk.'

She ran up the steps, kissed Lucia and drew her inside, chattering, apparently aimlessly, but actually manoeuvring her deep into the house. She resisted the temptation to look back, but she thought she heard the faint sound of footsteps going up the stairs.

Half an hour later Marco joined them for breakfast, showered, impeccably dressed and apparently his normal self. He thanked his mother charmingly for the successful party and complimented Harriet on her successful debut in society. He made no mention of anything else.

A few days later an invitation arrived to a party at the Palazzo Manelli.

'We've never been invited there before,' Lucia observed in surprise.

'It's Harriet he really wants, Mamma,' Marco said. 'She's after his collection.' He gave Harriet a brief smile. 'This will make your name. Nobody's ever been so privileged before. Of course we must accept.'

Nobody could have faulted his manner, which was charming, but impenetrable.

Life at the villa had settled into a contented routine. Lucia, whose days were filled with committees, was happy for her guest to spend her time in museums and art galleries. They would meet in the evening for a meal sometimes at home, sometimes at a restaurant before going to the opera. On these occasions Marco would usually join them after the meal, and Harriet realised that he loved opera. Comedies didn't interest him, but he was drawn to the emotional melodramas, and would sit through the music in a kind of brooding trance, emerging reluctantly.

She'd found the ring and slipped it back onto her finger for public occasions, explaining to Lucia that at other times she was afraid of losing it. She wore it when Marco invited her to lunch again at the bank. He was delightful, even amusing, but she felt he was sending her a silent message that there was no way back to the brief closeness they'd known.

'You're afraid I'll make trouble at Manelli's party, but I've already promised not to,' he said smoothly. 'And nobody will think anything of it if such a noted antiquarian as yourself goes off to explore. No, don't look so sceptical. I'm learning about your international reputation. Several of my colleagues here recognised your name and have asked to meet you.' He raised his glass. 'I'm very proud of my fiancée.'

Of his fiancée, she noted, not of herself. There was no way past such implacable charm.

The Palazzo Manelli was in the heart of Rome's old quarter, near St Peter's. The lights were already blazing forth from wide windows and doors as their car glided up. The Baron was there to greet them.

Harriet enjoyed herself from the first moment. She knew she was looking at her best in a dress of deep gold silk, with Marco's gift of rubies about her neck, and she was already acquainted with many of the people here.

Marco squired her conscientiously at first, introducing her to the few strangers, making clear his pride and admiration. Then, true to his promise, he faded away and turned his attention to other guests. These were his old friends and could keep him happily occupied all evening. All his fiancée required was the occasional glance to see if she needed his help. Which she never did.

As Harriet's confidence grew her wit flowered. Manelli's guests included several nationalities, and her ability to riposte quickly in each of their languages was making heads turn. This, plus her physical transformation, had made her into a 'figure', a slightly exotic personality.

She wasn't pretty, but she was magnificent, and every man in the place seemed increasingly aware of it.

'Marco, what are you doing neglecting poor Harriet?' Lucia chided him.

'"Poor" Harriet is doing very well without me.' Marco said calmly. 'Does she look neglected?'

'She looks submerged in men,' Lucia retorted tartly. 'One of them is positively drooling over her hand, and the other keeps trying to see down her dress.'

'Mamma, the man trying to see down her dress owns an original Michelangelo piece of sculpture,' Marco said, as if that explained everything. 'I can't compete with that. And it's all perfectly innocent.'

'Hmph! Manelli isn't innocent. He's one of the worst lechers in Rome.'

'But Harriet is innocent, which is what counts.' Then he drew a sharp breath.

'What is it? My dear boy, why do you look like that?'

'Nothing,' he said, pulling himself together. 'Please don't trouble yourself about this, Mamma. It's the modern way. Engaged couples don't live in each other's pockets. Will you excuse me for a moment?'

He moved away quickly, feeling that if he couldn't be alone soon he would suffocate. In the garden he managed to evade the lights and laughter and find solitude under the dark trees. His forehead was damp with the strain of what had just happened to him.

He'd said, 'Harriet is innocent,' and the word 'innocent' had been like a bullet, shattering the glass wall he kept between himself and the past.

She's innocent—innocent. That was what he'd said when they had tried to warn him about the woman to whom he'd given his heart once and for all time, with nothing held back. No defences. No suspicions, even when he heard the rumours. Just blind love. Blind and stupid. A mistake, never to be repeated. For she hadn't been innocent, and he'd found out in a way so brutal that it had almost destroyed him. Memory returned to him now, leaving him shaking like a man in the grip of fever.

But Harriet was different, not merely innocent but guileless and blinkered, as only the truly honest were. And there lay his safety, he reasoned. In the long run it was more reliable than trusting to her, or any woman's, heart.

After a while he pulled himself together. When he was sure he could appear his normal self he returned to the party, smiling broadly, not letting his eyes search for her.

Harriet was relishing her success. After squiring her around at first Marco had turned away with a smile, leaving her to her own devices, and thereafter he entertained himself with all the most beautiful women. Which suited her fine, she thought. Just fine.

And then she saw someone who drove all other thoughts out of her mind.

'Olympia!'

Her sister had just arrived, now she came sweeping across the floor, arms open to envelope Harriet, pretty face full of glee.

'I've been hearing so much about you,' she cried, managing to whisper under cover of their embrace. 'Are you really engaged to Marco?'

'I'm not sure,' Harriet said wryly.

Olympia stood back and regarded her. 'There's my cautious Harriet. If only I could learn from you!'

'Then you wouldn't be Olympia,' Harriet laughed. 'Where have you been all this time?'

'In America, with Mamma and Poppa. They're still there, but I came home today, and rushed here because I heard ''Marco and his bride'' were going to be at the party. Oh, you clever, clever sister. You got your own terms, then?'

'Well—'

'But of course you did. My dear, *that ring!* It must have cost—'

'Don't be vulgar,' Harriet chuckled.

'You're right. Play it cool. Keep him guessing. That's the way with Marco. And the others as well. They say you've got Manelli eating out of your hand.'

'He's going to show me around.'

Manelli appeared at that very moment and swept both women off for a tour of his mansion. He talked well and informatively, and Olympia's eyes were soon glazing with boredom. She made a desperate excuse and escaped, barely noticed by either of them.

Returning to the party, she was immediately claimed by admirers, and worked her way through them until she found Marco. He hadn't seen her since the day he'd made his proposition and she'd rejected him in five seconds. They greeted each other amiably.

'I didn't know what I was starting when I suggested Harriet, did I?' she teased. 'Did I do you a bad turn?'

'Not at all. Harriet is an excellent choice, barring her habit of vanishing with other men at parties.'

'Oh, Manelli's just showing her his pictures. No need to be jealous.'

'Don't be ridiculous. Of course I'm not jealous.'

'All right, don't snap at me. Harriet's a very unexpected person, as I dare say you know by now. I must admit I only suggested her to tease a rise out of you.'

'The sort of prank I'd have expected from you,' he said coldly. 'You haven't grown up since you were a child and I used to rescue you from trees when you'd climbed too

far. I can take care of myself, but did you ever think you
were being unfair to Harriet?'

'You mean she might have fallen for you?' Olympia
asked with a trill of laughter. 'Nonsense, *caro*. I wouldn't
have done it if I thought she might get hurt. I know you're
incapable of falling in love, but so is she. Haven't you
found that out yet?'

She passed on, saving him the necessity of replying.

CHAPTER EIGHT

MARCO had said Harriet had an international reputation and she was discovering how true it was. The news that she had broken 'the Manelli barrier' was soon all over Rome, and her services began to be much in demand.

'I'm here as an emissary,' Marco said to her one evening. 'Two of my colleagues at work want to consult you and they say you're putting them off. I've promised to use my influence. They seem to think I have some,' he added drily.

'I was being tactful,' Harriet said. 'Precisely because they're your colleagues it seemed better for me to stay clear. Suppose I give them wrong advice?'

'Is that possible?' he murmured slyly.

'Tell them about the necklace,' she challenged him.

'The less said about that necklace the better,' he said, almost teasing. 'May I inform my associates that my influence has been successful?'

'I'll bet you've already done so.'

He grinned and didn't deny it.

On this level they were easy with each other, but Harriet had learned that any attempt to draw closer to him was fruitless. After that one time in the garden he'd retreated into his shell, perhaps further back than before, wary, mistrustful of her and himself. Above all, mistrustful of what might happen between them.

It was lucky that she hadn't fallen in love with him, as she'd briefly feared. The moment when she'd sensed approaching disaster had been a warning which 'sensible

Harriet', now in the ascendant again, had heeded. Soon the time would come for them to go their separate ways, him to find a suitable bride elsewhere, and herself into an apartment in the city.

For she'd decided to stay here. With Marco's help she'd reclaimed her Italian heritage, and she would always be grateful to him for that. But as more people sought her expertise she realised that she was laying the groundwork for a life here that didn't include him.

So when he asked her to accompany him on a trip to visit a client, who lived in Corzena, about two hundred miles to the north of Rome, she had no trouble in claiming that her time was occupied.

'You can surely spare a couple of days for me,' he said impatiently.

'I'm busy.'

'Doing what?'

'I beg your pardon!'

'It can't be that important.'

'That's for me to say,' she insisted, riled by his tone. *'Give me that!'*

He'd snatched up the pad on which she'd scribbled notes on her current work.

'The Vatican Museum,' he read.

'Signor Carelli has asked me to check some references for him.' This should have been the killer fact, since Carelli was one of the banking colleagues for whom Marco had interceded. But he wasn't impressed.

'He won't mind waiting,' he said.

She knew it was true. She was finding excuses, and she wasn't sure exactly why, except that she felt herself subtly moving away from him, and perhaps it was best to keep it that way.

'I'm not going to ask him to wait,' she said firmly. 'I've made my plans and I'd prefer to stick to them.'

'Fine,' he said, tight-lipped. 'I won't ask again. Please tell my mother I called, and that I'll be away for the rest of the week.'

And when he'd gone it all seemed so stupid. Why had she taken such a stubborn line? Why refuse to spend a couple of days in his company?

Because the prospect was far too agreeable, that was the answer. It was a relief that he'd left, making it too late to change her mind. Not that she wanted to change her mind.

Lucia slept late next day and Harriet breakfasted alone. She was just finishing her coffee when Marco walked in. Her heart's flicker of delight was too intense to be ignored, but she concealed it.

'I thought you'd be on your way by now,' she exclaimed. 'Weren't you leaving early?'

He'd left in the dawn and driven for twenty miles before stopping the car and getting out to stand looking over the countryside. He'd stayed there for half an hour before getting back into the car and turning it around.

'I've come back because I want you to be honest with me,' he said quietly. 'I want the real reason you won't come to Corzena.'

'I've already told you—'

'Yes, you have, and it's bull. You know it and I know it. I want the other reason—' he faced her '—the one you can't bring yourself to tell me.'

Alarm and pleasure seized her equally. Had he really guessed that she'd turned coward, backing off because she feared the growing strength of her own feelings for a man who was incapable of returning them? Or did he return them, and this was his way of creating the mood for a declaration?

'Marco—'

'Harriet,' he said desperately, 'I know. Did you really think I wouldn't guess?'

'You've guessed—?' she whispered, not daring to hope.

'When I started to think hard it became obvious—especially after what happened the night of the party—Harriet, I may not be the most sensitive man in the world, but I think I'm sensitive enough to see this. We've been honest with each other from the start, why didn't you just tell me—? No, that's stupid, isn't it? How could you speak bluntly about such a delicate matter?'

'Marco, are you saying—?'

'I'll make it easy for you by saying it myself.' He took a deep breath, evidently having difficulty, and she waited, her heart beating eagerly. At last he said, 'You don't want to be alone with me. You're afraid of what I'll do.'

'Wh-what?'

'That's it, isn't it? You don't trust me, to behave decently. But you can, I swear it.'

She was coming out of her happy daze to a chilly reality. 'I see,' she managed to say, hoping desperately that her face didn't show her cruel disappointment.

'This is business,' he went on, 'and my client is an important one. The bank tends to indulge his wishes, and his present wish is to meet you.'

'That's blackmail!'

'Yes, I suppose it is, and that's just why you can trust me. Having more or less coerced you into this trip the last thing I'd do would be put you in an awkward situation.' He regarded her steadily. 'I hope you understand me.'

She wanted to laugh, perhaps hysterically. 'I think I do. You're promising to be the perfect gentleman, no midnight taps on my door—'

'I doubt our rooms will even be on the same floor. Our host is very old-fashioned. Nothing will happen, Harriet, you have my word of honour.'

She wanted to throw something at him and scream, I don't want your word of honour. I don't want you to be the perfect gentleman. I want you to kiss me as you did that night, and this time I don't want you to stop. Oh, you idiot!

But instead she said coolly, 'I suppose, that makes everything all right.'

'I hoped it would. This is really important, he's a very big client—'

'Then we must keep him happy,' she said brightly. 'Business comes first, after all.'

He smiled at her. 'You say that to the manner born.'

'You think I might be a credit to you?'

He put his hands on her shoulders, smiling into her eyes in a way that made her hold her breath. If only—

'You already are a credit to me,' he said warmly. 'I'm proud of you and I want to show you off. Get some clothes together quickly, while I go and see if my mother's awake.'

As she packed she heard murmurs coming from Lucia's room, and went in to bid her goodbye. 'I'm sorry to rush off without notice—'

'Nonsense. Go on and have a wonderful time, *cara*.'

It was a lovely day and their drive lay through beautiful countryside. Gradually her mood improved from the sheer pleasure of being with him. Marco drove fast but easily and with confidence, as he did everything.

'Tell me about this man,' she said.

'Elvino Lucci is one of the richest men in Italy. He started with nothing and he's built up to where he is through sheer hard work and brilliance. He's been my mentor for years.'

'I can't picture you with a mentor, somehow. I don't think you'd let him get a word in edgeways.'

'Everyone needs a mentor,' he said seriously. 'Not just at the start but maybe for always, to give you a sense of perspective. I learned a lot from him when I was just starting, and he still has things to teach me.'

'A great financial brain, then?'

'The greatest. He believed in keeping his attention focused and never taking his eye off the ball.'

'You mean there's been nothing in his life but financial wheeling and dealing?'

'He married and has a family, but he's been a widower for ten years.'

'I'll bet he married an heiress.'

'No, his own secretary.'

'Oh, well, nothing like securing cheap labour.'

Marco laughed. 'You may find him a little stiff and puritanical, but you'll like him when you get to know each other.'

'But why does he want to meet me?' she asked lightly. 'Am I being tested for suitability? If he gives me the thumbs down, am I out?'

'Don't be absurd. I think he's just lonely.'

'Lonely? With all that money?'

'Harriet please don't say that kind of thing in front him? I know it's a joke, but he wouldn't understand.'

'Hey, you recognised a joke. Better not let him suspect that, or you might not be his white-headed boy any more.'

Diplomatically he didn't answer this.

When they stopped for lunch Marco called Elvino

Lucci to apologise for being late. Harriet could just make out the man's voice.

'You, late? That must be a first! Only something special would make Marco Calvani break the habits of a lifetime!'

'It was,' Marco said.

'Well, I'm longing to meet her. I'm storing up a little surprise myself.'

They reached Corzena in the late afternoon. It was an old town built on a hill at the edge of a lake, with the villa on the lower part, near the shore. Huge wrought-iron gates swung open at their approach, and soon the house was in sight. There on the steps, waiting to greet them, was a tall man with white hair and a distinguished face. Beside him stood a very young woman who bore a strong resemblance to a sugar-coated doll. She had a mass of blonde hair, dressed high and wide, and sprayed into a confection like candyfloss. Her eyes were large and ingenuous.

'Good grief!' Marco murmured. 'What—'

Lucci advanced to greet them with outstretched arms. After kissing Harriet on both cheeks, he sprang his surprise.

'Meet Ginetta, my wife,' he said. 'We married on impulse, and you're the first to know.'

Marco maintained his composure, greeting the new Signora Lucci with perfect courtesy, but Harriet could imagine his thoughts. Elvino was at least thirty years older than his bride, and clearly took pleasure in buying her jewels. She was loaded down with them.

There was another shock awaiting. Marco had described Lucci as a man of old-fashioned values, but now Ginetta gave the orders, and her idea of how to accommodate an engaged couple was modern. While not going so far as to put them in the same room she'd given them adjoining rooms with a connecting door.

'We'll be waiting downstairs when you've freshened up,' she cooed, tripping daintily away.

When she'd gone Marco knocked on Harriet's door before entering.

'I hope you realise that I had no idea of this,' he said. 'I never meant to break my word to you.'

'I know that. You're not responsible for them putting us together.'

'Whatever is Lucci thinking of?'

'He's in love with her, that's obvious.'

'To think of him springing it on me! This visit is going to be an ordeal.'

At first Harriet thought the same, but it wasn't long before she began to like Ginetta, who seemed genuinely fond of her elderly husband, if not as besotted by him as he was by her. She also had a habit of making apparently naïve remarks that turned out, on examination, to be shrewd and witty. Several times over dinner Harriet found herself laughing.

After the meal Ginetta insisted on showing her over the villa, innocently proud of its luxury and her own good fortune in securing a husband who could lavish gifts on her. Even so, her happiness had a cloud.

'I'm really glad you came,' she confided. 'I made Vinni absolutely promise to get you here. Lots of wives don't want to know me.'

'I can't think why,' Harriet said warmly. 'I think you're great fun. But I'm not Marco's wife, you know.'

'But you soon will be. He's nuts about you, anyone can see that.'

Harriet gave a little laugh that sounded odd to herself.

'It's not Marco's way to be "nuts". And if he was he'd die rather than admit it.'

'It's just there in the way he looks at you, when you're not looking back. He does it all the time. He can't stop himself.'

'Nonsense,' Harriet said, colouring.

'It's true. And you do it, too.'

'I—'

'Yes, you do. You two fancy each other like crazy. It's a good thing I gave you connecting rooms.'

It was fortunate that she tripped away, calling back, 'Come on, let's find the men,' because Harriet wouldn't have known how to answer.

The men were sitting on the broad terrace that overlooked the lake, drinking brandy and deep in discussion. Harriet could see that Marco was displeased, although controlling it beneath a courteous front. Both men rose to greet them. Elvino ordered more champagne and they all strolled along the terrace, watching the moonlight on the water.

This joyful man bore no relation at all to the severe, practical 'brain' Marco had described, and which he clearly admired. He was triumphant in his happiness, wanting everyone to share it, laughing and kissing Ginetta repeatedly.

'This is truly a house of love,' he declared exuberantly, 'since it houses two pairs of lovers. I drink to your coming wedding, I drink to your wedding night, I drink to all the pleasure you will take in each other—'

'Caro,' Ginetta giggled.

'Oh, they don't mind. They're lovers, as we are.' He was becoming jollier with every glass, and there was no stopping him now. 'Come Marco, drink with me to the woman you love.'

Harriet could hardly look at Marco, guessing how he would regard such a boisterous display. But he said quietly, 'You are right, my friend. Let us drink.'

He raised his glass in Harriet's direction, she raised hers, and they clinked.

'Don't just drink to the girl,' Elvino bawled. 'Kiss her, and then kiss her again. And let your kisses be a pledge of the passion to come.'

To demonstrate his point he tightened the arm that was about Ginetta's shoulders, and gave her a smacking kiss. Marco responded by drawing Harriet close and laying his lips on hers. For a moment she raised her hands against him. She didn't want to kiss him like this, knowing he'd been forced by politeness, and when he'd been at such pains to assure her that he would keep his distance.

His lips lay lightly on hers, but that was somehow more unnerving than the night she'd sensed his fierce desire. He took her hand, still raised in an instinctive gesture of resistance.

'Kiss me back,' he murmured against her lips. 'Make it look good.'

Make it look good for the client, she thought angrily. But her hand was already reaching up to touch his face, while the other arm wound its way around him. His own arms tightened, drawing her very close. His lips moved across hers, subtly enticing, almost the ghost of a kiss, but a ghost that was enfolding her in a mysterious spell. She let herself slip into that spell easily, for now it was all right to caress his face and press against him, putting her whole heart and soul into what she was doing. He need never know. She was merely helping him keep a client happy.

Marco too played his part with conviction, slipping an arm beneath her neck and kissing her with a kind of dreamy absorption that she thought must delude anybody. Except her. The slow movement of his lips over hers was sweet, blissful, and the temptation to believe in it was overpowering. She opened her eyes to find his face hovering close, his eyes fixed on her with a kind of astonishment. He was breathing unevenly.

From Elvino came another burst of delight. 'That's the spirit,' he bawled. 'And now there's only one thing to do—carry the lady upstairs.'

On the word he lifted Ginetta and began to walk along the terrace, calling, 'Time for lovers to go to bed,' over his shoulder.

Marco didn't hesitate, and the next moment Harriet found herself lifted against his chest. She clung to him dizzily, confused as to how to get her bearings, but not really wanting to.

Elvino reached the top of the stairs first and stopped to wait for them.

'This is the way to live,' he said blissfully. 'Oh, I know that's not what I used to say, but I'm wiser now. So are you, eh, my boy?'

'You were always a wise man, Lucci,' Marco murmured diplomatically.

'Goodnight, goodnight—' His voice drifted away along the corridor.

But at the last minute he turned, just as Marco reached Harriet's bedroom door. The old man's eyes glinted with fun as Harriet turned the handle and Marco carried her in. She could feel him trembling, as she was herself.

Once inside he set her down and closed the door.

'You'd better lock it,' she said in a shaking voice that was half-laughter and half-excitement. 'I wouldn't put it past him to bounce in to see if we're living up to his expectations.'

'Harriet, please—let me apologise for—everything. I never meant to embarrass you like this—'

'I'm not embarrassed. I like him. Don't you?'

'I don't know any more. I used to respect him. There wasn't a shrewder brain anywhere—now I can't think what's gotten into him.'

'No,' she said wryly. 'I don't suppose you can.'

'He's always been so sane and level-headed.'

'Well, maybe he thinks being sane and level-headed is overrated. Marco, he's happy. Don't you realise that?'

She smiled, willing him to lighten up.

'Happy!' Marco said scathingly.

'It's generally considered a good thing to be.'

He began to stride about the room. 'And what happens when she betrays him?'

'Maybe she never will. Yes, I'm sure she married for security, but I think she's got a kind heart. She's nice to him.'

'She leads him by the nose, makes him her slave—'

'No, he makes himself her slave, because he loves her.'

'That's one way of putting it.'

'You don't think much of love, do you, Marco?'

'You're unjust to me,' he said after a moment. 'I think love has its place, but I don't like the kind of infatuation that makes a man behave like an imbecile.'

'Or woman?'

'Oh, no! Women are always one jump ahead, as *Signora Lucci* more than proves.'

'That's the most disgusting prejudice I ever heard. Women do make idiots of themselves over men—'

'You never felt it necessary. It's one of the things I've always admired about you. Your level head. Even that tomfool performance we had to put on out there didn't faze you.'

'Shut up!' she breathed. 'Shut up, *shut up!*' If she had to hear any more of this she would go mad.

'I apologise if I was being rude—'

'*And stop apologising!*' She took a long breath and pulled herself together. 'We're getting off the subject. There's nothing wrong with acting like an imbecile for the right person. If people really love, they don't care about that—'

'God help them then!' he said violently. 'And God help Lucci for acting like a fool!'

'But he's a happy fool.'

Marco stopped pacing and gave her a strange look. 'That's just sentimental talk, Harriet. It sounds good but it means nothing. No fool is really happy, because sooner or later he sees his folly and is ashamed of it. Then he wishes he'd never met her.'

'You're wrong about Elvino,' Harriet said fervently. 'He'll never be sorry he met Ginetta because even if he loses his happiness he'll still have had it. If he was wise, like you think he should be, he'd end up with nothing at all.'

His face was bleak. 'Better to have nothing than shame and bitterness.'

She sighed. 'Well, how do you choose between them? The man who believes in someone he loves, even if it makes him a little absurd, or the man who won't let himself believe in anyone? Who's the real fool, I wonder?'

He gave a hard little laugh. 'You mean me, don't you? Stop trying to analyse me, Harriet, you don't know enough.'

'Then tell me the rest,' she pleaded.

'It's not important,' he said impatiently. 'I am as I am. I can't change now.'

'That's the sad part. You have just so much to give, and no more.'

He went a little pale. 'I give all I can.'

'I know. But it isn't very much, is it?'

He was silent for a long moment, turning away to the window. When he turned back he said, 'You think badly of me because I don't fall over myself to endorse Lucci's idiocy. Well, consider this. He brought me here to help him hand over half his fortune to that little gold-digger.'

'She's his wife and she's making him happy,' Harriet said desperately. She felt as if she was banging her head against stone. Like his heart.

'He has four children who are going to lose half of their inheritance, only they don't know it yet. The lawyer's coming tomorrow, and he and I between us are supposed to connive at this disgrace. Plus I've broken a professional confidence by telling you.'

'You can trust me.'

'I never doubted that for a moment.'

It was lucky he'd turned back to the window or he might have seen the painful look that crossed her face. Her fiancé trusted her with his professional secrets. From a man with such a strong code of ethics it was high praise, but not the kind she longed for.

'It's late,' she said sadly. 'And I'm tired.'

'Then I won't keep you up any longer.' He opened the connecting door. 'Don't forget to lock this behind me,' he said with an attempt at lightness.

She matched his tone. 'Do I need to?'

'I wouldn't put it past Lucci to send an army in here to make sure I "do my duty". Goodnight, Harriet.'

She undressed and lay in the darkness, every inch of her aware and aching with longing. Elvino's romantic insistence on love at all costs had left her fired up, ready for something to happen.

Tonight she and Marco had talked of one thing while seeming to talk about another and the end of it was that she was no closer to him in any way that mattered. Just in one way.

You two fancy each other like crazy.

It was almost funny that Ginetta had spotted the strong physical attraction that she felt for him and that he, she was sure, felt for her. He couldn't love her but he wanted her. If he had his free choice now he would come to her bed.

But he had no free choice. He'd blocked it off with promises. He was a man of his word, and would resist what he saw as a weakness.

How badly did he want her?

She could hear him walking back and forth on the other side of the door.

Badly enough to break his word?

His footsteps stopped, then resumed again.

Badly enough to risk looking weak in his own eyes?

Silence. The footsteps had stopped right next to the door.

Holding her breath, Harriet kept her eyes fixed on the handle, which she could just see in the moonlight.

Very slowly it moved. There was the faintest noise as the door was opened a fraction, perhaps half an inch. Then it stopped.

She waited for it to move again, to open. She couldn't breathe. She could almost feel the air vibrating with the tormented indecision of the man on the other side. But he would come to her because she willed it so fiercely.

But then the incredible happened. Instead of opening further the door moved back, closing the tiny gap, and the handle was softly returned into place.

After that there was silence.

CHAPTER NINE

IT WAS a relief to spend a few days in the Vatican museum. Absorbed in the world that had always sustained her, Harriet thought she would soon be able to forget Corzena.

But the talisman failed this time. Halfway through a fourteenth-century parchment she would find herself thinking of the door that had so nearly opened, and then closed.

Closed against her. That was the thing that hurt. Marco had tested the door just far enough to discover that she'd left it open for him. Then he had rejected her. What message could be clearer?

From their manner to each other on the drive home nobody could have discerned anything in the air. For him, there probably hadn't been, she thought bitterly.

She returned home on the third evening to find Lucia eagerly looking for her.

'Your father called,' she said. 'They're back, and so anxious to see you. We're all three invited to dine tomorrow night. I tried to call you and Marco but you both had your phones switched off. So I said yes for us all. Did I do right?'

'Of course. My father! How did he sound?'

'Thrilled by your engagement. He's longing to see you. I found him almost likeable. I'm sorry, *cara*, I know he's your father, but there it is. But if he's good to you, I forgive him everything.'

Marco arrived for supper and heard the whole story.

'It makes a tight schedule now we're so busy getting ready to go to Venice for the weddings,' Lucia observed. 'But when I suggested putting it off until we returned he was most insistent that it must be tomorrow. Still, it's natural that he should be eager to see you.'

'It's a tighter schedule than you know,' Marco said. 'After tonight I was planning to sleep at my office to get through everything that needs doing before we leave for Venice.'

'I suppose you could always ask your uncle and Guido to delay their weddings?' Harriet suggested in the satirical tone she often used to him.

'True,' Marco said, appearing to consider this seriously. 'But they're so unreasonable that they'd probably put their weddings before my clients.'

He smiled at her to show that he was sharing the joke. Harriet wondered if she really had been joking. This was the first time she'd seen him since Corzena, and he'd just told her that after tomorrow she wouldn't see him again for days. To her dismay she discovered that it was a relief.

To cheer herself up she concentrated on the thought of her father.

'Tell me everything he said,' she begged Lucia.

'Again? All right, *cara*, I understand. He asked after you many times, were you well, were you happy in your engagement, could he give you to Marco with an easy mind? All the questions a loving father asks.'

'And which he's waited a very long time to ask,' Marco said drily. 'I wonder what lies behind this.'

'Does my father's interest need an explanation?' Harriet flashed.

'His *sudden* interest does.'

'I'm engaged. Isn't that enough?'

'Yes, I suppose so. Now, it's late and I must be going.'

She treated herself to a new gown for the following evening, elegant, figure-hugging black silk that made a perfect setting for Marco's gift of a diamond tiara. The hairdresser settled it into her upswept hair.

She touched the diamonds, feeling how cold they were: as cold as his attempt to spoil the evening in advance by his sceptical remarks about her father. But why should he have done so? she wondered. He could be hard, unfeeling, but this had felt like a deliberate attempt to hurt her.

She and Lucia were to travel together in the chauffeur-driven car, while Marco drove straight there from work. The d'Estinos lived in Rome's most fashionable quarter, near St Peter's, in a street where most of the other buildings were embassies. As they arrived they could see Marco getting out of his own car. He glanced at Harriet's magnificence and nodded.

'I knew that tiara was right for you,' he said. 'Not every woman could wear it.'

As they approached the wide front doors, standing open, flooding the gardens with light, her father appeared, flinging wide his arms and bearing down on her. 'Harriet, my dearest daughter. After so long.'

He embraced her in a bear hug, the first for years. He was wearing an overpowering cologne, and she had to fight not to flinch. He looked older than his years, and had put on too much weight, giving a strong impression of self-indulgence, and her acute instincts told her that there was something false and theatrical about this display.

But he was her father and she'd longed for this moment, so she smiled and told herself how wonderful it was.

He was all smiles to Lucia, and greeted Marco like a long-lost brother. Marco was, as always, courteous, but his manner lacked warmth. The older man's obsequiousness disgusted him, and Harriet sensed it, even if her father didn't.

Also unaware was his wife. Harriet saw that the wicked step-mother had vanished. In her place was a thin, brittle little woman, suddenly anxious to proclaim her connection to a step-daughter she'd previously despised.

Only Olympia behaved normally, cheeking Marco like a younger sister, embracing Lucia and Harriet, teasing everyone out of their unease.

As more guests arrived and Guiseppe d'Estino's attention was taken up with greeting them, Harriet took her sister aside, resisting Olympia's efforts to escape.

'Darling I'm joint hostess, I really have a lot to do—'

'You can do it when you've spent some time with me, little sister. Why does our father act as though he's only just found out about my engagement?'

'Because he has. That phone message you left for him when you arrived never reached him. Mamma made sure of that.'

'But you knew at Manelli's party,' Harriet said. 'Didn't you—?'

'No, I didn't tell him, because I didn't want him madder at me than he was already. He was furious when I turned Marco down. The title, you see.'

'But it's not Marco's title.'

'Darling, he's a count's nephew. Pappa's a snob, and Mamma's even worse. I really must be going, someone's calling me—'

She danced away, leaving Harriet to digest what she'd read between the lines. Guiseppe wanted Marco in the family as the husband of his favourite daughter, but Olympia wouldn't oblige. Then he'd remembered that Harriet was also his child, so she would have to do instead. She'd even been promoted to favourite offspring, now that she could be useful.

The party was in full swing. Her father made much of her, but even more of Marco, sometimes asking the same question several times when he ran out of inspiration. After her first severity of disappointment Harriet found herself feeling sorry for him. She was also growing more and more embarrassed to be introduced to people as, 'My daughter Harriet, engaged to *Count* Calvani's nephew.'

Just when she thought things couldn't get any worse, they did. Guiseppe launched into a speech about what a wonderful time 'my dear child' would have at the two weddings in Venice the following week. He would be thinking of her, he said repeatedly, and she must remember him to Count Calvani, 'an old and dear friend'. Harriet grew cold with shame as it dawned on her that her father was hinting for an invitation to the weddings. So that was why this meeting couldn't have waited.

She hardly dared look at Marco, but when she did his face was frozen into a mask of courtesy. At the first possible moment he excused himself and moved away. She wished the earth would open and swallow her up. Luckily Signor Carnelli was there, and he claimed her attention.

At the back of the house was a large, well-stocked conservatory, where several of the older guests had settled to talk. Seeing his mother, Marco drifted to the entrance where, from the other side of a bank of ferns, he heard a female voice, lofty, imperious.

'An extraordinary young woman, and more English than Italian, despite her name. Frankly, Lucia, I wonder at you promoting such a match for your son. Harriet lacks finish, and she'll never really be one of us.'

A hush fell as Marco appeared and stood there, taking the measure of the woman. She was the Baroness d'Alari, thin-faced, cold-eyed, a woman who made up in pride and spite what she lacked in almost everything else. The discovery that Marco had heard her made her fall silent, but from chagrin, not shame.

'I suppose it didn't occur to you, Baroness,' he said, 'that my fiancée isn't trying to be one of anything? She is unique, a brave, original woman, with a style—and a mind—of her own. In short, she is exactly what I wish her to be.'

It was years since anyone had snubbed the Baroness, and she had no resources to cope.

'I suppose it's natural that you should defend her,' she snapped, 'but beware defending her too rudely, young man. I believe my husband is one of your more important clients.'

'All my clients are important, and you must forgive me if I decline to discuss that matter with anyone but your husband,' Marco said, anger glinting in his dark eyes. 'If he wishes to take his business elsewhere, doubtless he will inform me. There are several other establishments where he will be gladly received. Excuse me.'

As he moved away Lucia rose and came after him, tucking her hand into his arm. 'Well done, my dear boy! I never could stand that woman,' she said happily. 'The perfect end to a perfect evening.'

'You're not leaving already?'

'Yes, I'm a little tired. The chauffeur will take me home, and you can bring Harriet on later.'

'I think she'll need to talk to you. I'm sure she's seen the truth about tonight.'

'Certain to. She blinded herself because she wanted to feel she still had a father, but she's too intelligent to blind herself for long. Awful, snobbish little man! How Etta produced him I'll never know. But the person she'll need to talk to is you.'

'Mamma—what can I say to her—?'

'My son, if you don't know how to comfort her when she's unhappy, I can only say that it's time you found out.'

'I'll do my best.'

'Marco,' she said anxiously, 'how are things between you and Harriet?'

He shrugged. 'What can I tell you? She blows hot and cold. Sometimes I think she disapproves of me.'

'Nonsense, how could she?'

He grinned, briefly boyish and delightful. 'There speaks my mother.' He kissed her cheek. 'Goodnight Mamma.'

The evening seemed to stretch endlessly ahead of Harriet. When Lucia said goodbye she wished she could have gone with her, but it was too soon. Lucia had the excuse of age, but her own early departure would be insulting.

Then Marco appeared beside her, carrying a much needed cup of coffee. 'Bear up. I promise I'll get you away soon.'

'Was I that obvious?' she said, accepting the cup gratefully.

'You were looking as if you'd had enough.'

'Oh, dear, I hope I haven't offended any of your important business contacts.'

'No, I did that. But it was worth it. I'll tell you another time.'

'Marco, my dear boy!' It was her father, clapping him on the shoulder. 'I've just said goodbye to your excellent mother. I understand, of course, that she needs to save her energy for the journey to Venice next week. Weddings can be so tiring, especially large weddings. Why I'll bet

they can't even keep track of all the people they've invited—'

Unable to stand any more, Harriet slipped away, leaving Marco in her father's clutches. She felt bad about that but she was ready to scream.

After an hour she found Marco beside her again. 'That wasn't very kind, but I don't blame you,' he said. 'Come on, we're leaving. Unless you'd prefer to stay.'

'Get me out of here,' she said with feeling.

It took nearly another hour to make their farewells, and Guiseppe walked with them to the car, talking non-stop. But at last they were on their way.

Harriet slumped silently in her seat as the car swung out of Rome headed for the Appian Way. Finally she roused herself.

'You knew, didn't you?' she said. 'You knew as soon as you heard about the invitation. That's what you were trying to warn me last night.'

'I guessed there was a reason why he'd suddenly decided to remember that he was your father. I'm sorry. That was a sad business for you.'

The words were kind but he didn't take her hand and his eyes were fixed on the road.

When they stopped outside the villa he said, 'I won't come in. I have to be getting back to my paperwork. Goodnight.'

'Goodnight,' she said huskily, and ran into the house and up the stairs. She wanted to be alone, and at the same time she wanted someone to be there. But there was no comfort to be found in Marco, and the sooner she finished with him the better.

In her room she tossed her bag aside and put her tiara back in its box. She stood at the window in the moonlight, feeling lonely and bleak. Tonight something had been taken from her that she knew she would never get back. It might have been a pointless hope, but she'd clung to it, and now it was over. Gradually she lost track of time and had no idea how long she'd been standing there when she heard the knock at her door. Outside she found Marco. He'd discarded his jacket and bow-tie, and was holding a vacuum jug and a mug.

'I brought you something you need,' he said, easing his way past her. 'English tea.'

He set the mug down and poured out the tea, already milked. It was exactly as she liked it.

'This was a wonderful idea. Thank you.'

She sat down on the bed, and he sat beside her. She met his eyes and found them very dark and kind.

'I thought you'd gone,' she said.

'I changed my mind. I came into the house and waited for you to come back downstairs. I thought you might need to talk. When you didn't return I—well, maybe I'm starting to understand you by now. I still reckoned you might need someone to listen. I'm quite good at that.'

'Thank you for coming,' she said softly. 'But there's nothing to say, is there? I've had something confirmed that I suppose I always knew. I should have faced it years ago. I thought I had. More fool me.'

'You're not going to make the mistake of minding what he says or does, are you?' Marco chided her gently.

'No, of course not. After all, he was saying all the right things, making a fuss of me, just as I always dreamed. Only—it wasn't me he was making a fuss of. It was you. He's just a petty snob. As he sees it I've snared myself a count's nephew, so suddenly I'm his daughter again.'

'Harriet, stop this,' he urged. 'You're a fine woman, beautiful, brainy and strong. You've built an independent life on your own talents. You don't need him. You never did.'

'I know, I know. It's silly isn't it?' Suddenly tears were pouring down her cheeks and she set the mug down hurriedly as her control deserted her. 'Why should it matter after all this time? I'm not a child any more.'

She finished on a husky sob and at once his arms were about her, holding her firmly in the comforting embrace her father had never given her.

'In a way you are,' he murmured against her hair. 'Your childhood is never really over. Its ghosts haunt you all your life.'

She clung to him, unable to stop crying now she'd started. The grief of years poured out and she could do nothing but yield to it.

'He never loved me,' she choked, 'not really.'

'He did at the start. Remember what you told me, how you two adored each other?'

'Not even then. If he'd really loved me he couldn't just have discarded me like that, could he?'

'I don't know,' he sighed. 'Some people love that way. Real enough at the time, but shallow. Others—do it differently.' He laid his cheek against her hair and held her again, saying, 'I'm here, I'm here,' as another paroxysm shook her.

She tried to speak but she couldn't get the words out coherently.

'What is it?' he asked gently, cupping her face and turning it up so that he could see her better. 'Tell me.'

'Nothing,' she choked, 'I'm all right now.'

'I don't think you are.' He took out a clean handkerchief and dabbed her wet cheeks. Her hair was coming down over his hands.

'What do I look like?' she asked shakily.

'Like a little girl who's just found out her father doesn't love her. But you won't give in to despair. You know the world still has much for you.'

'I don't know what the world holds for me,' she said huskily. 'Right now I'm not really sure that I care.'

'Never speak like that again,' he said sternly. 'I forbid it. Only weaklings say it doesn't matter what happens, and you are strong, *cara*. You're the kind of person who wrests life to your will.'

He looked down into her face for a moment, then he lowered his head and laid his lips on hers, keeping them still for a moment, then moving them very slowly. It was the lightest of touches, but it was enough to bring her to instant, eager life. Her own mouth began to move in helpless response, urging and encouraging him.

He had a moment of doubt, enough to make him raise his head and give her a troubled look. He'd come to her bedroom offering comfort, but not of this kind. Harriet saw the 'man of honour' in his eyes, threatening to restrain him.

She dealt with that man swiftly, slipping her hand behind Marco's head and drawing him back down to where her warm, persuasive lips could tell him, without words, what she wanted. Now she was ready for him, her lips already parted, welcoming the entry of his questing tongue. The signal she'd given him had taken the brakes off his control and his fevered movements were telling her that now he felt free to do whatever he liked.

Good!

His tongue teased her own before starting a lazy exploration of her mouth. Her response was electric. No other kiss had ever been so thrilling, and it wasn't enough. Now she had to have him in every possible way.

His mouth drifted down her neck and across her chest,

and she drew in a long, shaking breath. It felt shatteringly good to have his lips there, where she'd so often longed to feel them, tracing the swell of one breast while his fingers outlined the other. Her neckline was low, but not low enough for him, for he made a sound of impatience at the resistance of the material. The next moment she heard the sound of tearing, felt the shock of cool air, and her breasts were free. Instantly she sensed all constraint fell away from her, as though her spirit too had flown free. This was the man she wanted. She wanted his love, and she wanted his passion, and she vowed to herself that if she couldn't have one she was going to have the other.

He dropped his head between her breasts, rejoicing in their silkiness with his tongue, while his hand celebrated their shape with joy. Wherever he touched her the result was electric, sending shivers of sensation everywhere, along her arms, her legs, between her thighs.

The dress was torn to just below her breasts. As his fingers curled around the edge he met her glowing eyes. Reading consent in them, he tightened his hand and wrenched hard, ripping the dress open to the hem, revealing the whole length of her body. Half dazed she reached up for him, pulling at his black bow-tie, then the buttons of his shirt. He finished the job himself, tossing aside his clothes and pulling her against him while the remainder of her ruined dress slipped to the floor.

She wished the light was better, so that she could see him, but there was only the sensation of his nakedness pressed against hers, his hands exploring her intimately with slow, sensual movements that made her vibrantly aware in every inch of her own body.

She began her own exploration of him, discovering that his shoulders really were as broad as they seemed in an elegant dinner jacket, his spine as long and supple, his hips as narrow. Through her wild, whirling thoughts she promised herself that soon they would do this again, and she would know him better, know the caresses he liked and that provoked him. Meantime, she was learning and it was wonderful.

His fingers were on the soft insides of her thighs, making teasing promises that drove her half out of her mind. A long, soft moan broke from her and he moved slightly so that he could look into her wild face on the pillow, her magnificent hair spread out.

She thought she whispered his name, she wasn't sure, but the next moment he was between her thighs, skilfully urging her to greater and greater passion until she was ready for the moment he entered her. And then everything was right, and perfect. Everything was as it was always meant to be, and she was a part of it for ever.

He moved strongly inside her, and while she felt the pleasure mounting she was aware that his hands were touching her face softly. She would hardly have believed he could be so tender but each caress was unbelievably gentle, so unlike the Marco who dominated his world, but hinting at the man she was sure lived deep inside him. And she could coax that man out, she was sure of it, just as he was reaching out to her now...

Then all thought was shut off as the pleasure took her over, shook her until she seemed to dissolve. The world flew apart into a million pieces, that flamed in the universe before drifting back together and reforming into a world that was no longer the same, would never be the same again.

She tried to speak but Marco's fingertips were across her lips, his arms about her, his lips against her hair, murmuring reassurances. A heavy languor seemed to weigh her down until she fell into a deep sleep with his arms still about her.

As she dozed in the early morning she felt a slight disturbance in the bed next to her. Opening her eyes a crack she saw Marco rise and stand a moment in the grey light. Last night she'd felt his body but seen little of it. Now she saw him fully, the long legs, lean but with muscular thighs, the narrow hips with their unmistakable power. She remembered that power, how he'd used it to drive her to an ecstasy whose memory melted her again now. If he had reached for her, she would be his again.

Instead he dressed quickly, while she lay listening to the rustling movements, waiting for the moment when he would awaken her to say goodbye. Or perhaps he would simply kiss her, and she could put her arms about him. But then the movements stopped, and there was a long silence. She opened her eyes to see him standing in the window, his head sunk on his chest, the picture of a deeply troubled man. He seemed to be staring at the inner distance and seeing something there that disturbed him.

At last he straightened his shoulders and seemed to give himself a little shake, as though discarding thoughts that were no use to him. Then he walked out of the door.

CHAPTER TEN

THREE days later they all flew to Venice, Harriet and Lucia departing from the villa, and Marco going from his apartment and meeting them at Rome airport.

'Are you sure you're not sickening for something?' Lucia asked Harriet anxiously as they drove to the airport. 'You're very pale, and you've been quiet the last couple of days.'

'I just don't enjoy flying,' Harriet put her off.

It was true that she'd been quiet ever since the moment she'd seen her lover leave in the dawn, and lain there, aching with desolation.

She acquitted him of deliberate unkindness. She would never forget that he'd returned to the house to comfort her, how gently he'd spoken, and how much understanding he'd shown. He'd felt with her, as only a truly sensitive man could have done, and she would always love him for it.

In the moments of passion, too, he'd treated her with great tenderness. But then he'd left her alone in a way that felt nothing less than brutal.

The next day Lucia had told her excitedly of Marco's encounter with the Baroness d'Alari, and the way he'd risked losing valuable business to defend her. That too warmed her heart, but it cooled again when she realised that he wasn't going to tell her himself.

She could sympathise with the wariness that made him shrink from too much human contact. She could even pity him for it. But she increasingly felt that she couldn't live with it.

A resolution had formed in her, to leave as soon as possible after the wedding. It would break her heart, but the misery would be short-lived, unlike the misery of being married to a man who would allow himself to get close to her only to withdraw as though she'd turned into an enemy.

With the decision taken she pushed it aside until after the coming weddings, determined not to spoil them for anyone else. At Rome airport she greeted Marco with cool composure, and a smile that gave away no more than did his own. This was her first trip to Venice, and she was going to enjoy it. She could be wretched later.

The Calvani family began to gather in Venice two days before the first wedding. The Rome party arrived to find Guido and Dulcie waiting for them with two motor boats to take them across the lagoon, one driven by Guido himself.

'You're lucky he's not trying to take you in a gondola,' Dulcie chuckled, referring to their early courtship when she'd thought he was a gondolier, and he'd let her go on believing it, thinking that he was luring her into his net, while actually he was the one being lured.

The Palazzo Calvani was a treasure trove of masterpieces and Harriet soon settled to explore it in the company of the count's archivist, who had been put at her disposal.

Leo turned up next day, looking less cheerful than Harriet remembered. She and Dulcie were both fond of him, and it took them no time to divine his trouble. Settling on the big sofa, one each side of him, they went onto the attack.

'You've found her at last,' Harriet said.

He played dumb. 'Her?'

She thumped his shoulder. 'You know what I mean. *Her!* The one.' Remembering that he was at heart a cowboy she added, 'She's got you roped and tied.'

'What's her name?' Dulcie demanded.

'Selena. I met her in Texas. We stayed at the same ranch after she had an accident with her horse trailer.'

He fell silent.

'And?' they asked, in an agony of impatience.

'We practised for the rodeo together.'

'*And?*'

'She fell off. So did I. Mind you, she only fell off in the practise ring, and I did it in front of a crowd of thousands. But we both fell off.'

'So you started with something in common,' Dulcie said wisely.

'A marriage of true minds,' Harriet agreed.

'I shouldn't think minds had much to do with it,' Dulcie observed, recalling certain tales Guido had told her about Leo.

'Nothing at all,' Leo sighed like a man remembering bliss. 'It was wonderful.'

Harriet's lips twitched as she met Dulcie's eyes, equally full of mirth.

'You should have brought her here to meet us,' she said.

'That's just the trouble, I don't know where to find her.'

'But didn't you exchange names and addresses?' Dulcie asked.

'Yes, but—' He plunged into a long account of the troubles that had separated him from his true love, finishing gloomily, 'I might never see her again.'

A cry of, 'Hey, Leo!' made him drift off to join the

other men. Dulcie and Harriet refused to meet each other's eyes, but at last they couldn't stand it, and burst out laughing.

'Oh, we mustn't,' Harriet said, conscience stricken. 'We're terrible to laugh.'

'I know,' Dulcie choked. 'But I can't help it. Did you ever hear such a crazy story?'

Harriet shook her head. 'Poor Leo. It could only happen to him.'

The next day they all gathered in the small side chapel of St Mark's Basilica, for the wedding of Count Calvani to his beloved Liza. The count's three nephews were groomsmen, and Liza was attended by the three ladies.

The reception was a strange affair. Despite her new status Liza was first and foremost a housewife who'd spent the last three months organising Dulcie and Guido's wedding, set for next day. This was a big society occasion, with enough guests to fill the glorious St Mark's Basilica, followed by a huge reception at the Palazzo Calvani which she insisted on overseeing in every detail.

She lingered at her own reception long enough for her devoted groom to toast her, then hurried off to the kitchens, for 'a quick look.' At last Count Francesco yielded to the inevitable and followed her.

'I don't think she appreciates her good fortune at all,' Lucia said in bafflement. 'She treats him really badly.'

'That may be the secret,' Guido said with a grin. 'After all the women who put themselves out to catch his eye, the one he loves is the one who makes him fight for her attention.'

After that the party broke up into couples. Guido and Dulcie wandered away, arms about each other. Leo and Lucia settled down for a long comfortable talk in the moonlit garden, and Marco said abruptly to Harriet, 'Shall we take a walk?'

Venice at night, a city of dark alleys leading to mystery, half-lights, ancient stones, shadows. The faint sound of music reached them, intermingled with the haunting cries of gondoliers echoing back and forth through the tiny canals. They strolled in silence for a while, walking apart.

'I thought we should talk,' he said.

'It's time,' she agreed.

'Watching that wedding service today made me do a lot of thinking. You, too, I expect.'

'Oh, yes,' she mused. 'A lot.'

'They say one wedding begets another. Don't you realise how people are looking at us, expecting us to name the day?'

'I had noticed the odd significant look.'

'Tomorrow might be a good time.'

'A time for—?' she asked cautiously.

'To announce a wedding date. We've had enough time to make a decision. My own decision is made. I did a wise thing when I came to London to find you. And you're a natural Roman, anyone can see that. You're even building up a clientele. When you move your business here you'll have the basics already. We make a perfect team.'

'Looked at like that, I suppose we do,' she mused.

'So can I tell my mother that it's settled?' he asked briskly.

This was it? This was a proposal of marriage in the softly lit alleys of Venice, with the stars glowing up above, and the atmosphere of romance all around? She didn't know whether to laugh or cry.

'I don't think we should rush a decision,' she said at last. 'You say I'm suitable because I'm a natural Roman and because I've already started to build up a clientele. That's a pretty narrow list of qualifications for a wife. Also, there's something that's never been mentioned between us, and perhaps it should be.'

'I was waiting for you to speak about it,' he said. 'That night we spent together—came as quite a surprise.'

'You mean because you were the first man I'd slept with? Does it matter?'

'It took me completely by surprise. You're twenty-seven, and these days—'

'I know. But most men have always bored me after a short time, even the ones I briefly thought I fancied. When it came to the point, there was always something more interesting to do, and they never seemed to stick around to try to persuade me.'

'Can you blame them for losing heart once they realised they were competing with the Emperor Augustus?'

'I suppose not.'

They walked on and found themselves at the edge of St Mark's Square, which was emptying fast. At the outdoor cafés the chairs were being put on tables and the orchestras had fallen silent, all but one solitary violinist still playing for a couple dancing in the piazza, lost in each other.

'I thought we were reasonably good together,' he said. 'Didn't you?'

The warmth of his breath on her face, his body entwined with hers, urging, compelling, imploring, the hot, dark madness of him inside her. Reasonably good together.

'Oh, yes,' she said wryly, 'the experiment was a success in every way. Optimum results.'

Take me in your arms and dance with me under the stars, to a lone violin.

'I think things have gone well since the day you arrived. The best day is the first Saturday in September.'

The violin stopped.

'You've fixed the date without consulting me?'

'Not fixed, but I've been thinking of suitable dates. I've got some big deals going down.'

'All your deals are big,' she mused, playing for time.

'But these are different. They'll make me. It'll be a partnership.'

'And that's what you really want, more than anything in the world?'

He gave a little embarrassed laugh. 'Not just that. I'd be the youngest partner the bank's ever had. Maybe it's a kind of vanity, but it would please me. This will take all my attention for the next few weeks. By the time I can raise my head it will be September, and the summer will be over unless we make our plans now.'

'No, Marco stop it. I won't be rushed.'

'But it's common sense—'

'Listen,' she said desperately. 'Do you remember what you said to me in the *Bella Figura*? You said, "Control is the answer. If you're not in control, somebody else is. So you must always be the one in control." I didn't know then how true it was. Even with me.'

'You're reading more into that than it'll take. One of us has to plan ahead.'

'You're planning too far ahead for me. I'm sorry, but I'm just not sure about marriage.'

'But you just said—'

'Sometimes optimum results aren't enough.'

'Well, what *will* be enough?'

'I don't know, but the jury's still out. I don't know what my future plans are.'

'You don't mean—' he was peering at her in the semi darkness '—that you're actually thinking of leaving?'

'Not leaving Rome, just your home. There are some nice apartments on the Via del—'

He drew a sharp breath. 'You've been looking at apartments?'

'Only in the newspapers.'

'You've got it all worked out, haven't you?' he said coldly. 'May I ask when you were going to tell me?'

'Not until after we'd left here. And I still haven't quite decided.'

'So until you do I'm supposed to bide my time and be a suppliant, waiting on your pleasure? Perhaps I don't like that?'

'And perhaps I don't like your assumption that since *you've* made your decision *I* have to jump to it. There are two decisions to be made here, Marco. Not just yours.'

He turned away, striding up and down on the flag-stones. Harriet could sense his irritation at having his plans frustrated.

'Maybe people who fight as much as we do shouldn't think of marriage,' she suggested. 'Let's leave it there for tonight, or we'll really quarrel.'

'All right. Let's leave it there.'

They walked back through the little streets, where the ghosts of a thousand lovers lingered, whispering to those who had ears to hear. But these two passed on without a backward glance. When they came to the side entrance to the Palazzo Calvani they slipped indoors, bid each other a courteous goodnight, and went their separate ways.

One by one, the lights were going out along the Grand Canal. In the garden Leo rose and helped Lucia to her feet.

'Thank you for listening to my ramblings,' he said. 'I'm afraid Dulcie and Harriet thought me a bit of a clown.'

'Well, your life has been rather full of entanglements,' Lucia said, patting his hand. 'But if Selena is the right woman, you'll find her again. Although I think she's quite mad if *she* doesn't come to find *you*.'

'Maybe she doesn't want to find me,' Leo said gloomily.

'Enough of that kind of talk,' Lucia said severely. 'If your love is fated to be, it will be. Now, tomorrow's a wedding. We're all going to enjoy ourselves.'

Dulcie and Guido said goodnight outside her bedroom.

'Can't I come in, just for a moment?' he whispered.

'Not the night before the wedding. It isn't proper.'

'Proper? Hang it Dulcie, after what we've been doing whenever we got the chance—? No, don't laugh like that. It does things to me. I may lose all control.'

She kissed him tenderly. 'Go to bed and dream of me.'

'I always dream of you. Do you love me?'

'More than life. More than all the world.'

'There are no words to say how much I love you,' he whispered. 'Goodnight heart of my heart, until tomorrow, when I shall make you mine.'

'Now leave the work,' Francesco commanded his new countess as she took a last look around the great kitchens. 'It's time my bride stopped neglecting me and kissed me instead.'

'Your bride,' she whispered. 'After so long.'

'After too long, beloved.'

He took both her hands and gazed into her face, seeing not the lines, but the beautiful candour with which she'd first looked at him, forty-five years ago.

Liza smiled back. For her too the signs of age were invisible, and he was the young lion she'd first worshipped in those long-ago days when she'd been a kitchen maid and any thought of marriage had seemed hopeless. But through long years he'd loved her steadfastly, perhaps not always faithfully, but, she would have argued, who could blame him for that when she kept turning him down?

She rested her head against him. 'I'm sorry *caro*, but how could I neglect the preparation for tomorrow? It's the big wedding.'

'Oh, no,' he said, drawing her firmly away from the kitchen. 'Today was the big wedding. Come, my adored one…'

Dulcie was a traditional bride, glowing in white satin and lace, wearing the Calvani pearls for the first time. She looked serenely happy, while Guido looked as if he was taking something seriously for the first time in his life, according to Marco.

Marco and Leo were the groomsmen, Marco impeccably dressed and stylish, Leo occasionally running a finger around the inside of his formal collar.

Last night's reception had been confined to the family, at Liza's wish. This one was a glittering affair, spreading through most of the great *palazzo*. Light poured out of every door and window and gleamed from the jewellery of several hundred woman. The cream of Italian society was here.

Despite what she'd said the night before Harriet was wearing her engagement ring, not wanting to attract attention today. Dancing in Marco's arms, she played her role of the happy fiancée, and gradually realised that it was as he'd said. People were smiling at them significantly.

She'd dressed more sedately than had been her habit in company recently. This was the bride's day, so her gown was a demure olive-green silk, cut with extreme elegance and simplicity.

'Did I tell you that you look wonderful?' Marco said. 'I'm proud of you.'

The music seemed to be flowing through her veins, making her dip and sway as though there were no problems in the world. Thankfully his annoyance of last night hadn't carried over to today. He'd performed his wedding duties charmingly, and smiled through the first few dances before holding out his hand to Harriet in a silent invitation.

Dulcie, watching them, signalled to the band who promptly broke into a popular song called 'See How He Loves You'. The crowd cheered, thinking of the bride and groom who were dancing together, holding each other close, but Dulcie mischievously pointed a finger at Marco and Harriet.

Despite her resolution to be sensible she found herself responding to Marco's nearness, his arms about her, the closeness of his face to hers. Their last embrace had been in her bed, naked, limbs entwined, exchanging pleasure. The dance was like a teasing echo of that time, a reminder, a promise…

At this moment it was easy to believe that nothing else mattered. Warmth seemed to enfold her, his warmth, her own, welling up from deep inside her in response to him. The handsome face near hers was the face she loved, the dark eyes gentle, glowing, silently telling her that he too was thinking…

That was how they communicated best, she realised, in

silence. And surely they could find a way forward to a future together?

As the dance ended people crowded around them, laughing expectantly.

'Come on, tell us…'

'Time you set the date…'

Marco's arm was still about her waist. Harriet felt it tighten suddenly.

'We've set the date,' he said. 'The first Saturday in September.'

Her gasp of shock was drowned in the cheers. The Calvani men pressed forward, shaking Marco's hands, Lucia beamed, Dulcie threw her arms around Harriet, squealing, 'I'm so glad, I'm so glad.'

'That's great!' Guido yelled. 'I can't wait to see this. I suppose we are invited?' he clowned.

To everyone's astonishment Marco clowned back. 'Dulcie is, you're not.'

A roar of laughter went up at this very moderate joke which sounded like a major witticism coming from such an unexpected source.

'Kiss her,' somebody yelled. 'Kiss the bride!'

Harriet felt as though the ground had shattered beneath her. One moment she'd been dazed to the point of granting Marco anything, the next he'd given her a grandstand display of everything about him that antagonised her. It was as though the temperature had dropped to freezing in a split second and she was in a new world, bleak, unforgiving. As unforgiving as her own heart.

She let him kiss her. There was no choice in this gathering. What she had to say must wait.

But waiting meant enduring the count's delighted insistence that the wedding must take place in Venice, at the family home. It meant watching Lucia put her head together with Liza, making plans. She didn't know how she got through the next hour.

Lucia's joy was the hardest to bear. She made it clear that she loved Harriet, and nothing would make her happier than to see her married to her son. Harriet tried to give her a hint.

'He shouldn't have done it like that,' she said desperately. 'Announcing it to the world before telling you, but you see we're not—'

'Oh, my dear, I understand. You can't blame Marco if his feelings ran away with him. Besides, he told me last night.'

'He did what?'

'Just before you went out together, he said he'd been thinking of that Saturday, and he would finalise it with you.'

'And what did he say when he returned?' Harriet asked, her eyes kindling.

'I was asleep by then, and of course today has been so hectic I haven't even had the chance to tell you how pleased I am.' She kissed her cheek. 'Now we're all going to be so happy.'

She fluttered away, unaware that she'd filled Harriet's heart with anger and dismay.

The cake had been eaten, the bride and groom had slipped away, the band played its last number.

'My uncle asks that you join the rest of the family in saying goodbye to our guests,' Marco told her. 'He considers you one of us.'

She turned smouldering eyes on him. 'I wouldn't hurt your uncle for the world,' she said. 'But you and I have to talk.'

'There'll be time for that later. I know how it looks, but just be patient.'

His hand on her arm urged her away. The count made her stand beside him, his wife on the other side. It was a place of honour, but it also showed her how fast the net was closing about her.

When the last guest had gone she took firm hold of Marco.

'*Now!*' she said.

He let her draw him into the next room. 'Let me talk first,' he said.

'You've talked enough. Now you'll listen. How dare you do that! I told you last night that I wasn't ready for this. Didn't you hear me?'

'Yes, I heard you, but you didn't make any sense. Harriet, you know as well as I do that you're going to say yes eventually. We've both known that ever since—well, for some time. Why drag it out? All right, we fight sometimes, but we also go well together.'

'We don't go well together, because I could never "go well" with a man who rolls over me like a juggernaut.'

'All right, I'm sorry for the way I did it, but can't we put that behind us—?'

'And then do what? Go on where? To a wedding? Marco, I'm further from marrying you now than I've ever been. Please think about that before you make any more plans without consulting me.'

She walked away from him and up the stairs to her room. She had never been so angry in her life.

CHAPTER ELEVEN

MARCO'S secretary looked in alarm at the determined young woman who stood before her.

'Does Signor Calvani have anyone with him just now?'

'I don't see what—?'

'Does he?' Harriet repeated.

'No, but he has a board meeting in five—'

'Don't worry, I won't be that long,' she tossed over her shoulder as she opened the door to Marco's office.

He was engrossed in a computer screen and looked up in alarm.

'What's wrong? Has something happened to my mother?'

'No, I came to see you because this is the one place you can't run from me. You've been avoiding me since we returned from Venice.'

'Two days. You know I have work to do—'

'And you know what I want to say. I'll say it quickly so that you're not late for your meeting.'

His lips tightened. 'This isn't the time—'

'How much time does it take to say goodbye?'

'Can we talk about this later?'

'No, I fell for that one before. Not again. Besides, there's nothing to talk about. Goodbye! Finito. *Basta!* End of story. I can't marry you. This so-called engagement is over.'

'Don't be absurd,' he said impatiently. 'The invitations have started to go out.'

'And I'm upsetting the organisation, the ultimate crime,

157

I know. I'm sorry, but some things are more important than getting the books straight.'

Marco came out from behind his desk. He was pale but he spoke calmly. 'Look, you've been in a strange mood recently, and maybe I haven't been very sympathetic. And I shouldn't have announced our engagement like that, but it just seemed the right thing to do. I'm sorry. I'll do better in future.'

'Listen to yourself,' she cried. 'You talk like a man punching keys on a computer. This one for "sorry", this one for "do better", and out comes the right answer. Life doesn't work like that.'

He made a sound of impatience. 'Do these trivial details matter?'

'They're not trivial. They're the way you are. Everything labelled and in its little box. I've just told you that our engagement is off, and you're angry because I've stepped out of my box into one you don't know how to label.'

'I'm angry because I don't understand a word of this. Nothing you say is reasonable.'

'Is it unreasonable of me to want to marry a man who cares about me, the way you don't?'

He took a quick breath and seemed about to say something, but checked himself. When the words did come out they were calm. 'I thought we'd—managed to grow closer—'

'Not close enough. You're possessive, and you try to organise every step I take, but that isn't love.' She sighed. 'Well, maybe you're right and I have been unreasonable. I should have worried about love much sooner, shouldn't I? Like, the day we met. I'm sorry. I didn't know myself very well then. I do now, and different things matter. Love matters.'

'Love?' he echoed.

'Oh, Marco, you sound as though you'd never heard the word. There's no love between us, is there?'

He was very still now. She had his whole attention. 'It would seem not,' he said quietly. 'How stupid of me not to have understood.'

'It's my fault. I misled you, made you think I could live without it, like you.'

He regarded her sardonically. 'And when did this suddenly become so important?'

'Only recently. Do you remember the night of my father's party?'

'Do *you?*' he flashed unexpectedly.

'Vividly. But it's no good is it? You can't create what isn't there. I've tried to play it your way, but I can't do it, and it would only break us apart in the end.'

'Maybe you give up too easily.'

'I thought you prided yourself on being a realist. You're not being realistic now. It's not going to get any better, Marco. We're both what we are. It's too late to change.'

She watched his face, longing to see in it some softening, some hint that even now he could search his heart and discover that he didn't want to lose her. Behind her brave front she knew that a loving word from him would have sent her joyfully into his arms. But no word came.

Instead, into her mind slid the memory of something he'd said in one of their discussions about business, 'It's like playing poker. When the deal collapses you keep a blank face.'

The deal was collapsing and his face was as blank as death. His complexion was even a little grey, and there was a strange, withered look in his eyes, as though the life was draining out of him.

'Yes,' he said at last in a voice of stone. 'It's too late

for change. I thought—well, I was wrong. You can't change just because you want to.'

In the silence that followed she had the strange feeling that he was at a loss, something she'd never known in him before.

'What happens now?' he asked at last.

'I'll leave as soon as I've spoken to your mother. When I get back to London—'

'London? You were talking about staying in Rome.'

She surveyed him ironically. 'You actually remember that conversation? I thought you pressed the "Delete" button the way you do when something doesn't suit you. I did mean to stay in Rome, but I see now that I can't. I have to get right away from you. When I'm home I'll arrange to repay the money I owe you.'

'There's no rush. I promised you easy terms—'

'No, I want to pay it all at once.'

'You can't afford a lump sum, we both know that.'

'I'll manage it somehow. It's better if I'm not in your debt.'

Suddenly his face wasn't impassive any more, but twisted with bitterness. 'You can't wait to be rid of me, can you?'

The injustice was like a knife in her heart, making her reply with equal bitterness to cover her pain.

'I thought you'd be glad to see me gone, now that you know the proposed merger isn't coming off. Cut your losses and don't waste time over a dead deal. Your own principles, but useful for me, too.'

She heard the quick intake of breath before he said, 'I seem to have taught you more than I knew. I can recall a time when you were too generous to say something so cruel.'

'Marco—'

'You're quite right of course. Whatever made me think it worthy of discussion?'

'Nothing is worth discussing any more. It's over. There's no more to be said. You'd better hurry, you have a meeting.'

She almost ran out of his office, not knowing whether to cry or hurl something at him. How dare he confuse her with that air of suppressed pain! She knew him too well to be fooled. It was no more than his trick of putting her in the wrong. But right now she couldn't cope with it.

Telling Lucia was the hardest part, although the older woman was understanding.

'I always knew there was something wrong,' she sighed. 'Even in Venice I sensed it. But I suppose I saw only what I wanted to see. I'm afraid Marco gets that from me.' She squeezed Harriet's hand. 'What happened?'

'It's very simple. Marco and I made a business deal, but I found I couldn't stick to the terms. My feelings got all tangled up, the very thing we agreed wouldn't happen.'

'But he wants you so much—'

'Yes, he wants me, as he'd want anything that he'd decided suited him. But it's not enough.'

'Are you saying that you love him?'

'It's not as simple as that,' she said, on her guard, remembering that Lucia would probably report all this to her son. 'How can you love a man who doesn't need to be loved?'

'Every man needs to be loved, and Marco perhaps more than the others, because he fights it so hard.'

'Yes, he fights it, and I can't get past that. I don't want to spend my life fighting.'

'Can't I say anything to persuade you?'

Harriet shook her head. 'The hardest thing will be leaving you. You've been wonderful to me.'

'We mustn't lose that,' Lucia said eagerly. 'Now that we've found each other you must promise to stay in touch.'

Harriet promised, and the older woman put her arms around her. There were tears in her eyes. 'When will you leave?' she asked sadly.

'There's a plane at noon tomorrow.'

'I'll go to the airport with you.'

Harriet was half inclined to leave behind her new clothes. It didn't seem right somehow to take from a woman she was disappointing so badly. But Lucia insisted that every last gown was packed.

'*Cara Etta,*' she said earnestly, 'Forgive me for saying this, but I couldn't bear for you to go back to looking as you did before.'

Over supper they tried to cheer each other up, and not admit that they were both waiting for Marco. Lucia glanced at the clock several times until Harriet said, 'He isn't coming, you know.'

'Of course he's coming. He won't let you go without saying goodbye.'

'He doesn't need to say goodbye. He's already "signed me off".'

'Don't start to talk like him, my dear. That way of seeing the world hasn't made him happy.'

'I don't know what would make him happy,' Harriet sighed. 'I just don't think it's me.'

'And you?' Lucia asked. 'Could you have been happy with him?'

'Can one be happy without the other being happy?' was the only answer Harriet could make.

A heavy ache was pervading her, as though her chest

housed a stone where her heart should be. As the hands of the clock ticked on she faced the fact that Marco was going to let her go without another word, and despite her defiant words about ''signing off'', that hurt badly.

In a fine temper, Lucia called Marco's home and then, receiving no reply, his mobile phone.

'Don't try any more,' Harriet begged. 'It's better as it is.'

Yet she still lay awake most of the night, listening for the sound of his car. When it didn't come she repeated to herself that this was the best way, for she knew she was weakening. She was in too much danger of throwing herself into his arms and promising anything if only she could stay with him. And that would be fatal. There could be no self-respect in living with a man who knew that you would abandon pride to be with him.

She managed to sleep for a couple of hours, waking with an aching head. Neither she nor Lucia had more than black coffee for breakfast. The hands of the clock were creeping to the moment when she must leave the villa for ever. Leave Marco for ever. No, she had already left him.

There was the sound from the gravel outside.

'The chauffeur must have brought the car around,' Lucia said. 'Oh, Etta dear, remember you promised to keep in touch.'

'I promise,' Harriet said huskily, and was enveloped in Lucia's embrace. Then she felt her hostess stiffen in her arms, and Lucia let out a glad cry.

'*Marco!*'

He was standing in the doorway, very pale but composed. Harriet held her breath.

'You came!' Lucia was overjoyed.

'Naturally. Did you think me so lacking in manners that

I would allow our guest to depart without seeing her off? I'll drive Harriet to the airport myself.'

Her heart was beating strongly from the moment of blazing hope, but she forced herself to be calm. This was Marco's good manners. No more.

He waited in the car while she made her farewells to Lucia. She was still fighting back tears when she got in beside him. Marco studied her face, his own revealing little. Then his gaze dropped to her left hand, bare now.

'I didn't know you were coming,' Harriet said, so I've given me ring to your mother.'

He swung the car out on to the Appian Way. 'This has hurt my mother very much.'

'I know, but we had a long talk and I think she understands.'

'That's more than I do.'

'And I've promised to stay in touch with her.'

'Good. Then I may hope to hear some news of you.'

'What was that?' A heavy truck had passed, drowning out his words.

'I said *I may hope to hear some news of you,*' he repeated in a harsh, desperate voice.

'Yes, well—I'll be in touch about the money.'

'I've told you there's no rush for that. We can arrange instalments—'

'No, it's better to sort it all out now.'

He swore violently under his breath. 'You're a hard and stubborn woman.'

Stubborn, yes, she thought. But hard? Perhaps she was just growing a defensive shell against the pain of leaving him. It would work out for the best in the end, she told herself, especially as he was showing her his least amiable side. It really would stop hurting. One day.

At the airport he stayed with her until check-in, and

politely made sure that she had her ticket, passport, boarding pass.

'I'll go straight through,' she said. 'No need to hold you up. Thank you for bringing me.'

'It was no trouble.'

'Good luck with the partnership.'

'What—? Oh, yes. Thank you. Well, I mustn't waste time. Goodbye, and the best of luck for the future.'

He shook hands with her and strode away without looking back. He found his car, got in and switched on the engine. Then he switched it off again, dropped his head on his arms on the steering wheel, and stayed like that until somebody knocked on the window to see if he was all right.

'Why did you make me seek you out here, my son?' Lucia looked around at Marco's apartment which seemed even more austere and dismaying than ever. 'It's been two days now. Why didn't you come home and talk to me?'

His smiled was strained. 'You know how busy I am just now, Mamma. This partnership—'

'You made that excuse to her, and much good it did you.'

He was silent.

Lucia went into the kitchen and made some coffee. When she returned Marco was sitting with his fingers entwined between his knees, staring at the floor. He gave a faint smile of thanks accepting the cup, and one look at his face was enough to send her back to the kitchen, returning at last with a large plate of pasta.

'When did you last eat?' she demanded, setting it before him.

He shrugged. 'Some time. Thanks Mamma.' He ate a few mouthfuls. 'This is good.'

She regarded him pityingly. 'You've been very foolish.'

'Me?' He was stung. 'I was the one who wanted our marriage to go ahead.'

'Yes, and you went about it with all the subtlety of a bludgeon. What's the result? I've lost a daughter-in-law, one I was particularly fond of. It won't do.'

'What do you expect me to do? I can't force her to marry me.'

'So you've learned that, have you?'

'Mamma it's easy to talk, but you can't talk sense to Harriet. She lives in a dream world.' He gave a grunt of sardonic laughter. 'She calls herself a businesswoman but the man in the moon has more idea of commerce. She thinks running a business is a matter of loving the pieces and finding them "kind homes".'

'Oh, how like Harriet that sounds!' Lucia sighed.

'Yes it does. It also sounds like the way she ran the shop into the ground. Now she talks about repaying me the money I loaned her, in a lump sum. How does she think she can do that? She's not the expert that she thinks she is.'

'Really Marco, what do you know about the subject?'

He jumped up and went to a concealed safe. A few clicks on the combination lock and he opened the door, taking out an ornate gold necklace.

'You see this? I took it to London and showed it to Harriet on the first day. Do you remember how proud Poppa was of this, how he used to show it off and tell stories of the dig where it was discovered? Harriet told me that was a fake.'

'But, my dear boy, it *is* a fake.'

'What do you mean? It's genuine Etruscan.'

'No, the original was genuine Etruscan. But years ago

your father had financial problems, so he sold it. That's a copy made by a professional forger. He was the best in the business, so good that in all these years nobody has ever spotted it. Until Harriet. She, of course, could spot a phoney at fifty paces.'

He stared at her.

For the second time Harriet lifted the pen, then put it down.

'It just seems so final,' she said sadly.

Mr. Pendry, her lawyer, nodded. 'A sale *is* final,' he said. 'But you'd be very unwise to refuse Allum & Jonsey's offer.'

'But who is this firm?'

'Does it matter? A&J has met your full asking price without any argument, and as you know, I always thought it a little optimistic. Plus they want you to stay and run the place. In a sense you'll lose nothing.'

'Except that it won't be mine any more.'

'Well, if you really don't want to sell you could ask Signor Calvani if you could pay him by instalments. Shall I—?'

'No, thank you,' Harriet said firmly. He'd hit on the one argument that could sway her. She'd vowed to break all ties between herself and Marco. It was the only way to put him out of her life, if not her heart. Hell would freeze over before she asked him for a favour now. Swiftly she signed her name and pushed the paper over the desk.

'Now this one,' Mr. Pendry said. 'It's your contract, as manageress, for six months.'

Harriet paused again. 'I don't know. Isn't a clean break the best thing?'

There's no such thing as a clean break. Haven't you discovered that in the lonely days and aching nights?

'Do you have anything else lined up?' Mr. Pendry asked.

'No, I guess I don't,' she said, picking up the pen. 'So what happens now?'

'You just keep on running the shop. I dare say they'll send someone to see you sooner or later.'

She lay awake all night, knowing that she'd signed because she was a coward. She couldn't face another break so soon after the last one. She would see out her contract and separate herself from her beloved shop inch by inch.

Yet again, as she'd done so many times since returning to London, she asked herself why she'd taken such a stubborn stand against the man she couldn't stop loving? Truth to tell, she'd always considered herself a touch on the wimpish side. So how had she found the weapons in her hands?

Because Marco had shown them to her.

He'd told her that she was strong and brave and independent, and it was true. The neglect and loneliness that had marked her life had taught her how to be alone, but she hadn't known it until Marco revealed her strengths to her. He'd proved that she could do without the father she'd yearned for, and the next step was the knowledge that she could do without anyone.

Now she could do without Marco, because he'd taught her how.

Next day she overslept. It was Mrs Gilchrist's day off so she couldn't have picked a worse moment to be late. As she hastened to the shop, she crossed her fingers and prayed to whichever deity protected disorganised antique dealers not to let A&J send their representative today.

She knew her prayers weren't being answered when she arrived to find the front door standing open. She'd been beaten to it. She was late. Just like that other time. She could just imagine what Marco would say to this.

And that was exactly what he said as he emerged from her cubicle at the back of the shop to stand regarding her sardonically.

'Dammit Harriet, not again! Are you never on time?'

CHAPTER TWELVE

'I DON'T believe this,' Harriet said, setting down her things to confront him. 'What are you doing here?'

'Haven't you worked it out yet?'

'Allum & Jonsey—?'

'A tiny firm who were glad to let me take them over.'

'And if they hadn't been glad, you'd have taken over anyway.'

'No, I'd have found another firm. I needed a front. You wouldn't have sold if you'd known it was me.'

'In other words, this is another of your exercises in control. Sorry Marco, it's not going to work. I'm through.'

He held up the contract she'd signed only the previous day, committing her to run the shop for six months. 'What about this?'

'Sue me!'

'I will if you make me, but you won't. You're a woman of your word. This place needs you. Nobody else can run it. Between us we'll make it as profitable as it ought to be.'

Harriet gave an incredulous laugh. 'You want *me*? A woman who can't tell a fake from an original? Surely not.'

She had the satisfaction of seeing him redden. 'What do you want me to say? That I was wrong about that? All right, I'll say it. That necklace was a fake. My father sold the original years ago. My mother says you're the only person ever to notice.'

Harriet's face lightened. 'How is she?'

'I have strict instructions to send her news of you. I'll

do that later. For the moment we have to do some serious talking.'

'Well, I won't try to defend my accounts to you—'

'No, they're beyond defence.'

'Because you already knew the worst in advance. You're crazy, you know that?'

His eyes gleamed. 'I never do anything without a good reason.'

'You can't have a good reason for being here.'

'That's for me to say,' he said briskly. 'We had a deal. The loan was to be repaid in easy stages, instead you choose to deprive yourself of everything you love, to do it in one go. That gives me a certain responsibility.'

'You haven't—'

'Will you just be quiet while I'm speaking? When I want to hear what you have to say, I'll ask. I have a responsibility to you and I'm going to deal with it. I'll teach you to be a shrewd businesswoman if it turns us both grey-haired. In time you'll make enough to buy this place back from me, and then I won't have to reproach myself with having harmed you.'

'Can I speak now?' she snapped.

'If it's important.'

'All that is very conscientious of you—'

'Conscientiousness is the corner of good business. Now, I suggest you make some tea and we'll discuss your stock buying. Some of the web sites you visit look interesting.'

'You accessed my account? How?'

'I hacked in, of course.'

'Of course,' she murmured.

'If you'd been here on time, it would have been easier,' he said crisply, and something in his tone made her realise that this man was now her employer.

From then on she had no chance to forget it. Marco settled in as though he'd come for a long stay, taking a room at the Ritz Hotel, hiring a car, arriving at the shop early, leaving late. If Harriet suspected that he had come for her he made it hard for her to believe it. He gave her a crash course in financial management, with no concessions to whatever might have been between them. When he'd finished tearing her business practices to shreds he demolished the reputation of her accountant.

'He's been so much in awe of your academic knowledge that he's let you get away with accounting murder.'

'He's a dear old boy—'

'So I would have guessed. You don't need a dear old boy, you need someone who can keep you on a tight rein. What's this?' He was pointing at some squiggles in one of the ledgers.

'That's my code.'

'Translate,' he snapped.

Seething, she did so.

'Fine,' he said. 'That's lucid enough, but I'm not clairvoyant. How do I know what it means unless you explain?'

'I always write up the details later.'

'Do it now.'

'Why do you have to be a slave-driver over every detail?'

'Because, while you may be all kinds of an antiquarian genius, when it comes to the simplest commercial transaction *you are a bird-brained idiot*.'

'*I know that!*'

Silence. He was breathing hard.

'Fine!' he snapped. 'Then at last we're agreed on something. It makes a good starting point.'

'Why do we have to agree on anything? We never did

before. Why don't you just install the new accountant to keep an eye on me when you've gone home?'

'I'm not going home until I've taught you how not to bankrupt yourself.'

'You mean, bankrupt you?'

For once he was shaken. 'Yes—yes, that's what I meant.'

'But you can't stay here. You should be in Rome this minute, fighting for that partnership.'

He shrugged. 'I clinched that before I left.'

'So you've got it?'

'Yes, I've got it.' He was writing something.

'The youngest partner, just as you wanted. Congratulations!'

'Thank you!' he said shortly.

Of course he'd got exactly what he wanted. Everything neat and orderly. He'd sorted out his career, now he would deal with the little matter of his conscience, then he would go home and put her behind him.

But that was what she wanted him to do.

So she had no complaints. If there was one thing she was sure of, it was that.

'How do you buy stock?' he asked her one day. 'You can't always use the internet.'

'I use it rarely. Travelling the country is better.'

'When do we go?'

Next day they set off for a country house south of London. The owner had fallen on hard times, had sold the house to the local council, and was raising what he could from the contents.

'He won't get much for these, I'm afraid,' Harriet said regretfully as she examined the rather dull collection of items. 'And he's such a sweet little man.' She looked sympathetically across at the owner, a plump, white-haired man with a sad face.

'Anything of interest to us?' Marco asked.

'Well, this vase looks—' she stopped, examining an ornate glass vase. Marco saw her flicker of interest, quickly suppressed, like the professional she was.

'What?' he said.

'Genuine Venetian twelfth century,' she said quietly. 'Worth about fifty grand.'

'But the reserve price is only two grand.'

'I know. The owner can't have any idea what it's worth.'

'So you've spotted a real bargain. I'm impressed.'

The auctioneer banged his gavel. 'Take your places please, ladies and gentlemen.'

Marco bagged two seats in the front and looked around for Harriet. After a moment he saw her talking earnestly to the owner while the auctioneer stood listening, wide-eyed.

I don't believe this, he thought. *I simply don't believe it, not even of her.*

The auctioneer banged his gavel again.

'Ladies and gentlemen, I have to announce that Lot 43 now has a reserve price of fifty thousand...'

From the groan that went up behind him Marco judged that other dealers had spotted the same thing, and had kept quiet.

But they weren't Harriet, Marco thought with a private smile.

She was hailing him from the door, indicating that they should leave.

'We're not interested in anything else here,' she said as he joined her outside.

'Aren't *we*?'

'No, *we're* not.'

'I gather you told him?'

'I had to. That dear little old man, he was almost crying. He said it'll make all the difference to his retirement. Hey, what are you doing?' she protested as he grabbed her arm and began to hustle her.

'Getting you to safety before one of the other dealers murders you.'

'Or doing it yourself?'

He didn't answer this, except with a look.

When they were out in the sun she faced him, half-sheepish, half-defiant.

'I couldn't do anything else, don't you see? He's such an innocent, I couldn't just take the money when he needs it so much—'

'But Harriet, dear crazy Harriet, that's not how you do business.'

'It's how *I* do business. So you'd better fire me.'

'No, I'm glad you told him,' he said with a strange smile. 'If you'd done anything else, you wouldn't have been Harriet.'

It was early evening as they drove back to London.

'Now we need something to eat,' Marco said. 'I suppose I can't suggest that you invite me to your home for beans on toast. Since I'm your employer that might be "sexual harassment".'

'I'll risk it. After one taste of my cooking you won't be up to anything.'

'Witty lady!' he said admiringly. 'Come on, give me directions.'

Her home was a tiny one-bedroomed apartment an hour away, in a cheaper part of town. Harriet wondered how it appeared to Marco who'd grown up in the luxury of the

Villa Calvani. She saw him looking about the cramped rooms, but he said nothing.

She spared him beans on toast and made spaghetti, letting him create the sauce. Conversation was spasmodic and about nothing in particular. It had been a good day, and now neither of them knew how to end it.

He'd been very unfair to her, she thought. She'd meant to be strong, but that was when she'd thought he would be far away. How was she supposed to be strong when she was seeing him day after day, close to him, hearing his voice? And when she looked up to find him watching her, only to see him turn away without words, leaving the memory of the look in his eyes and a torturing feeling of delight—there had to be a way to defend herself against that, if only she could find it.

It wasn't fair that her love for him should flower more strongly than ever before. But love wasn't fair. If he went away now and left her to struggle with her misery that wouldn't be fair either. But it could happen.

She was on edge, wondering what he would do and how she would react. Why was he really here?

In the end he did something totally unexpected. As she was putting dishes into the sink he came up behind her and laid his hands on her shoulders. She waited, half hoping, half-unsure. After staying like that a moment, not moving, he slid one arm across her chest, drawing her back against him, and dropping his head to lay it gently against the side of her neck. She could feel his lips, lightly touching her skin, but he didn't kiss her. It was neither a passionate nor even a very romantic movement. He simply looked weary and disheartened, and she suddenly remembered when she'd found him sleeping rough in the garden, and he'd put his arms around her and rested his head, as though in her he found a refuge.

Slowly she put up her hand to touch his and they stayed like that for a long moment. Then he released her and went away. When she went to find him he was kneeling before her bookcase, reading the titles.

After that she made them both coffee, he exclaimed about the time, and went home.

Marco didn't come into the shop every day, and she supposed he was using the time to keep up with his work in Rome. One morning when she was alone she went into her cubby-hole to make some tea. Above the clatter of china she didn't hear the shop door open and someone come in, and emerged to find a young woman standing there. She was expensively dressed, about thirty, dark-haired, dark-eyed, pretty in a lush way, and about six months pregnant. She had the smile of someone who was deeply content with her life.

'You are *la Signorina d'Estino*?' She had a strong Italian accent and spoke carefully, like someone feeling her way in the language.

'Yes, I'm Harriet d'Estino. Can I show you something?'

'Oh, no, I do not come to buy, but to talk. About Marco.'

'I don't understand.'

'My name is Alessandra,' the young woman said simply. 'And I come to tell you how important it is that you marry him.'

Harriet stared, and the only words that came into her head were, 'Let's have a cup of tea.'

When they were seated Harriet said, 'Would you mind repeating that?'

'I say you must marry Marco. You think I'm *pazza*, no?'

'No, I don't think you're crazy, but I do wonder why Marco's marriage matters to you.'

'Why should I worry about a man in my past? And yet I do. Perhaps I feel a little guilty. Since we parted life has gone well for me, not for him. My friends who know him say that it was as if he shrivelled up inside, and began to keep the world at a distance. For that, I am, perhaps, to blame.'

'It's not your fault if you changed your mind,' Harriet ventured.

'No, but I should have had the courage to break our engagement honestly. You see, Marco feels too much. He *minds* too much, everything is too important. He acts otherwise. To the world he is a man who feels nothing, but the world doesn't know him.' She looked shrewdly at Harriet. 'But I think you know.'

'Yes,' Harriet said. 'Quite soon after I went to Italy I began to sense what he was hiding. He even hides it from himself.'

'Ah, that's bad. That too is my fault. Once he hid nothing. He overwhelmed me, and gradually I began to feel that it was more than I wanted. He was jealous, my whole life must belong to him. I became bored, and my love died. I fell in love with another man, but I didn't tell Marco. I worried about what he would do and besides, the man was married. His wife had money, he didn't want to leave her—'

Alessandra shrugged. Harriet maintained a diplomatic silence. She was on the verge of learning the key to Marco and she wasn't going to risk losing her chance through showing her opinion of this self-centred woman.

'Then I discovered that I was pregnant,' Alessandra continued. 'Marco saw me have a dizzy spell, and guessed. He assumed the baby was his—'

'Could it have been?'

'You mean was I sleeping with them both? Yes. The timing made Harvey more likely, but Marco didn't know about him so he just took it for granted that the child was his, and immediately began to plan our wedding. I argued for a delay but—you know how he can be.'

Harriet nodded.

'He was overjoyed—I tried to tell him the truth—but I confess I was scared of him. He can be a very frightening man. There is much love in him, and much hate when his anger is roused. He feels everything too much. That's why he struggles to hide it. If people knew they would think him weak and use it against him.'

'So what happened?' Harriet asked.

'One day Marco returned early from a business trip and came to my apartment without warning. He let himself in with his own key. Harvey was with me. We were making love.'

Harriet winced and closed her eyes.

'Of course it came out, about the child,' Alessandra said.

'What did he say?'

'Nothing. Not a word. He just stood there looking a man who was dying. Then he walked out. That was the last time I saw him. He sent me a note saying that he'd told people the wedding was off by mutual consent. Both of us had realised that we'd made a mistake. Of course I agreed to that.

'By that time Harvey's wife had found out about us and her brothers were on the warpath. He's English, so we ran away to England, and our son was born here. He really is Harvey's child. We did a test to make sure. But nobody in Rome knew the exact date of his birth, so they couldn't count back and realise that I must have betrayed

Marco during our engagement. In Rome they still believe it was ''mutual consent'' and I'm glad for Marco's sake. It would have killed him if the truth was known. People would have laughed.

'There were rumours, you see. People had warned him that I had a roving eye, and he'd refused to listen. He is a loyal and faithful man, and that is how he loves.'

'Not any more. I think all that died, and now he doesn't know how to love.'

'No,' Alessandra said urgently. 'No man with his capacity for love really loses it. He hides it, he tries to deny it, but it's always there. One day he was bound to fall in love again. I'm glad it was with you. I think you'll be good for him.'

'You're wrong. Marco isn't in love with me.'

'Nonsense, of course he is. What do you think he's been doing here for weeks when he should have been in Rome fighting for that partnership?'

'But he got the partnership before he left—' Harriet protested. Alessandra's raised eyebrows gave her a strange feeling. *'Didn't he?'*

'Not according to my cousin who works there. It's gone to somebody else. It's already been announced.'

Harriet had been pacing but now she sat down abruptly. 'Why did you come here?' she asked.

'To clear my conscience and try to put right the harm I did him. I owe him that. Don't give up on him Harriet. He couldn't endure it a second time.'

Two days passed with no sign of him. In that time she ran the whole gamut of emotions from joy, hope, disbelief, despair. After what Alessandra had told her she urgently needed to see Marco, to look into his eyes and discover if it was true that he loved her.

At last she heard a foot on the step that was unmistakably his, and looked up smiling, but the smile faded. This was Marco at his most formal, dressed for departure in an overcoat. He looked as though he hadn't slept.

'Are you taking a trip?' she asked.

'I'm going back to Rome.'

'For a few days?'

'For good. I shan't be coming back.'

The thud over her heart was like a punch. 'I see.'

'But before I leave I must give you this.' He took an envelope from his briefcase and handed it to her.

Moving mechanically she pulled out a paper and tried to read it, but the words danced before her eyes. Only one thought possessed her. He was going away, and in a few moments her life would be over. Somehow there must be a way to prevent him but her brain had become a terrible blank. The thudding of her heart seemed to fill the world.

'Read it,' he said quietly.

She tried to concentrate on the paper, and this time she made out figures, the amount of her debt to him. It was a receipt.

'This paper says I own the shop—but how can I?'

There was a look of intolerable sadness in his eyes. 'I could say that you repaid me what you owed, if it didn't offend me to speak of your gifts to me in terms of money. You've given me so much more than you'll ever know, so much more than I deserve.'

He looked around him. 'When I think how I came here that first day, so sure of myself, so confident that everything could be arranged to suit me, I want to shudder at the man I was then. He's gone now, thanks to you. This is so little in return.' He indicated the paper. 'I'd hoped to give it to you—well—under happier circumstances.

Now I think that's not going to happen. I want you to have it anyway.'

'But—' she stammered, frantically trying to find the words '—you can't just leave the shop with me. I'll make a mess of it again.'

'Not after all I've taught you,' he said with a faint smile. He brushed a stray wisp of hair back from her forehead.

'I wasn't a very good pupil.'

'You were the best kind of pupil. One who taught her teacher far more than he taught her. I shall carry your lessons all my life.'

'I shan't carry yours,' she said wildly. 'I'll forget them and go bankrupt. Besides, what became of the sharp-eyed businessman? You can't just give me all this money. Think of the shocking tax.'

'Tax?' he echoed, trying to keep up with her.

'Never forget the tax angle. You taught me that.'

He didn't answer for a moment. He'd understood now that she was following some new track of her own, and he was trying to keep up.

'What—are you saying?' he asked quietly at last.

'You talked about "happier circumstances". I don't know why you're so sure they're not going to happen. Maybe you've jumped to conclusions about that. But I think—as a wedding present, it would be treated much more favourably.'

He looked at her for a long moment before saying slowly, 'But the lady I love won't marry me. She told me so, and I've come to see that she might be right. I have no right to even try to persuade her.'

Harriet could hardly breathe. 'She might change her mind—just to secure a tax break.'

Slowly he shook his head. 'That's no good. It's not the right reason.'

'I was only joking.'

'I know, but there are some things you shouldn't joke about. They matter too much.'

'Business?'

'Love. I love you Harriet, and if you can't say the same just let me go quickly—'

'I can say it a million times over,' she said, touching his cheek. He immediately seized her hand and turned his head to kiss it. There was a desperate eagerness in his eyes.

'Tell me that you love me,' he pleaded. 'I need to hear you say it.'

She raised her other hand so that his face was held between them. 'I love you with all my heart and soul. I always will.'

She was in his arms before the words were quite out, having the breath kissed out of her in an embrace as crushing as he'd ever given her.

'I thought I'd lost you,' he said huskily. 'All the time you were in Rome I knew I was losing you and I didn't know how to stop it happening. I loved you but I couldn't tell you. I had the words ready a thousand times but lost my nerve. I didn't have the courage. I'm a coward, that's the truth and you may as well know it.'

'Marco, darling, please—'

'No, don't stop me. I want the truth there between us. Once before I—'

'I know.' She touched his lips gently. 'Alessandra. She came to see me.'

'She was here? In this shop? When?'

'A few days ago. She told me about the partnership you lost. You said you had it in the bag.'

'I had to. If I'd told you I was giving up the chance to be with you it would have been like blackmailing you.'

'But the partnership—it means everything to you—'

'No, you mean everything to me. There'll be other partnerships, but I knew this was my last chance with you. If I failed to win your love there'd never be another chance, and I couldn't face that.' He hesitated before saying awkwardly, 'What else did Alessandra tell you?'

'Everything. Do you mind?'

He shook his head. 'Now you know. I'm glad. I was a coward there too. I wasn't going to give anyone the chance to get to me again. I told myself that was a kind of strength, not seeing it for the weakness it really was.

'But you made everything different. I was so happy whenever I was with you. I tried to rationalise the happiness away, but it possessed me. I wanted to tell you but I couldn't. Then I tried to let you know without words, but I never seemed to get it right. And that night we were together, was so wonderful—so wonderful—I knew I was lost, as I'd sworn never to be again.

'I was so arrogant it shames me. I knew I couldn't let you go, but I thought I could have you on my own terms, without a surrender. And that evening in Venice, when we were walking, every word you said seemed designed to warn me off. You were planning to go away, so I tried to back you into a corner, force you to marry me, and I lost you completely.

'I didn't know how to get you back. This was the best I could think of, but you were so wary of me, I thought I had no hope. I was going to leave and set you free of me. That was the only way left to prove a love I thought you didn't want.'

'I'll always want your love. Never leave me, my darling.'

'You don't know what you're doing,' he said as he rained kisses over her face. 'You'll regret it—'

'Never!'

'I can't do things by half,' he murmured. 'I'll always be possessive. I'll want all of you—'

'All,' she whispered joyfully.

'You'll have to fight me—promise me that you will. Otherwise you might start to hate me and I couldn't endure that.'

'I'll fight you,' she promised.

'And I shall learn from you,' he said seriously. 'You've taught me so much. Go on teaching me. Be my mentor, keep me safe.' He dropped his head so that his mouth lay against her palm.

'Safe in my heart,' she whispered. 'Safe in my heart my beloved—for always.'

THE TUSCAN
TYCOON'S WIFE

by

Lucy Gordon

This book is dedicated to Janet Stover,
2001 World Champion Barrel Racer and
Olympic Medallist, who told me all about
barrel racing and rodeos.

CHAPTER ONE

'SELENA, you need either a miracle or a millionaire.'

Ben eased himself out from under the battered vehicle, monkey wrench in hand. He was lean, elderly, and had spent thirty years as a garage mechanic. Now those thirty years were telling him that Selena Gates wanted him to revive a corpse.

'This thing's had it,' he said gloomily surveying the van, which was actually a Mini Motor Home, with the accent on Mini.

'But you can make it go again?' Selena begged. 'I know you can, Ben. You're such a genius.'

'You stop that,' he said with an unconvincing attempt at severity. 'It doesn't work on me.'

'Always has so far,' she said, with perfect truth. 'You can make it go, can't you, Ben?'

'For a bit.'

'As far as Stephenville?'

'Three hundred miles? You don't want much! All right, it'll probably just about make it. But what then?'

'Then I'll win some money in the rodeo.'

'Riding that washed up brute?'

'Elliot is not washed up,' she flared. 'He's in his prime.'

Ben grunted. 'Been in his prime a few years, if you ask me.'

Any mention of her beloved Elliot touched a nerve, and Selena was about to defend him fiercely when she

5

remembered that Ben, good friend that he was, was fixing her van on the cheap, and calmed down.

'Elliot and I will win something,' she said stubbornly.

'Enough for a new van?'

'Enough to get this one fixed as good as new.'

'Selena, there ain't enough money in the world to get this ramshackle old bus fixed as good as new. It was falling to bits when you bought it, and that was way back. You'd do better sweet-talking a millionaire into buying you a new van.'

'No point in me chasing a millionaire,' Selena sighed. 'Haven't got the figure for it.'

'Sez who?' Ben demanded loyally.

'Sez me!'

He regarded her tall, ultra-slim figure. 'Maybe you're a little flat-chested,' he admitted.

'Ben, under these old jeans I'm flat everything.' She grinned with rueful self-mockery. 'It's no use. Millionaires like their women—' with both hands she traced the outline of a voluptuous figure. 'And that's something I never was. Haven't got the hair for it either. You need long, wavy tresses not—' she pointed to her boyish crop.

It was a startling red that blazed out like a beacon, telling the world, 'I'm here!' There was no way to overlook Selena. Smart, cheeky, independent, and optimistic to the point of craziness, she was her own woman. Anyone who challenged that soon learned the other lesson of that red hair. *Beware!*

'Besides,' Selena said, coming to her clincher argument, 'I don't *like* millionaires. They're not real people.'

Ben scratched his head. 'They aren't?'

'No way,' Selena said, like someone articulating an article of faith. 'They have too much money.'

'Too much money is what you could do with right now. Or a miracle.'

'A miracle would be easier,' she said. 'And I'll find one. No—it'll find me.'

'Darn it, Selena, will you try to be a bit realistic?'

'What for? What good did being realistic ever do me? Life's more fun if you expect the best.'

'And when the best don't happen?'

'Then think of another best and expect that. Ben, I promise you, somewhere, somehow, a genuine twenty-four-carat miracle is heading my way.'

Leo Calvani stretched his legs as far as he could, which wasn't far. The flight from Rome to Atlanta took twelve hours, and he travelled first class because if you were six foot three, and forty-two inches of that was leg, you needed all the help you could get.

Normally he didn't consider himself a 'first class' kind of man. Wealthy, yes. Afford the best, no problem. But frills and fuss made him nervous. So did cities, and fine clothes. That's why he travelled in his oldest jeans and denim jacket, complete with scuffed shoes. It was his way of saying that 'first class' wasn't going to get him.

An elegant stewardess hovered over him as solicitously as if he didn't look like a hobo. 'Champagne, sir?'

He took a moment to relish her large blue eyes and seductively curved figure. It was an instinctive reaction, a tribute paid to every woman under fifty, and since he was a warm-hearted man he usually found something to enjoy.

'Sir?'

'I'm sorry?'

'Would you like some champagne?'

'Whisky would be better.'

'Of course, sir. We have—' she rattled off a list of expensive brands until Leo's eyes glazed.

'Just whisky,' he said, with a touch of desperation.

As he sipped the drink he yawned and wished the journey away. Eleven hours gone and the last was the worst because he'd run out of distractions. He'd watched the film, enjoyed two excellent meals and flirted with the lady sitting beside him.

She'd responded cheerfully, attracted by his handsome, blunt-featured face framed by dark-brown hair with a touch of curl, and the lusty gleam in his blue eyes. They'd enjoyed a pleasant hour or two until she fell asleep. After that he flirted with the air hostesses.

But for the moment he was alone, with only his thoughts of the coming visit to occupy him. A couple of weeks on the Four-Ten, Barton Hanworth's ranch near Stephenville, Texas, enjoying wide-open spaces, the outdoor life, riding, attending the nearby rodeo, was his idea of heaven.

At last the great jet was descending to Atlanta. Soon he'd be able to stretch his legs, even if only for a couple of hours before squeezing his protesting frame onto the connecting flight to Dallas.

Ben pared the bill to the bone because he was fond of Selena, and he knew her next few dollars would go on Elliot's welfare. Any cents left over would buy food for herself, and if there were none, she'd go without. He helped her hitch the horse trailer onto the back of the van, kissed her cheek for luck and watched as she eased her way carefully out of his yard. As she vanished he sent up a prayer to whichever deity watched over crazy young women who had nothing in the world but a horse, a clapped-out van, the heart of a lion and a bellyful of stubbornness.

By the time Leo boarded the connecting flight at Atlanta jet lag was catching up with him and he managed to doze until they touched down. As he unfolded his long body he vowed never to get on another aeroplane as long as he lived. He did that after every flight.

As he came out of Customs he heard a booming voice. *'Leo, you young rascal!'*

Leo's face lit up at the sight of his friend advancing on him with open arms.

'Barton, you *old* rascal!'

The next moment the two men were pummelling each other joyfully.

Barton Hanworth was in his fifties, a large amiable man with grizzled hair and the start of a paunch that his height still disguised. His voice and his laugh were enormous. So were his car, his ranch and his heart.

Leo made sure to study the car. In the six weeks since this trip was planned he'd spoken to Barton several times on the telephone, and never once had his friend missed the chance to talk about his 'new baby'. It was the latest, the loveliest, the fastest. He didn't mention price, but Leo had checked it online, and it was the costliest.

So now he knew his duty, and lavished praise on the big, silver beauty, and was rewarded by Barton's beaming smile.

Since Leo travelled light it took barely a moment to load his few bags, and they were away on the two-hour journey to the ranch near Stephenville.

'How come you flew from Rome?' Barton said, his eyes on the road. 'I thought Pisa was closer for you.'

'I was in Rome for my cousin Marco's engagement party,' Leo said. 'Do you know him? I forget.'

Barton grunted. 'He was at your farm when I came to Italy two years back, and bought those horses of yours. What's she like?'

'Harriet?' A big grin broke over Leo's handsome face. 'I tell you, Barton, if she weren't my cousin's fiancée—well, she is, more's the pity.'

'So Marco drew the prize and he's hog-tied at last?'

'Yes, I think he is,' Leo said thoughtfully. 'But I'm not sure if he knows it yet. If you believe him, he's making a ''suitable'' marriage to the granddaughter of his mother's old friend, but there was something very odd about that party. I don't know what happened exactly, but afterward Marco spent the night outside, sleeping on the ground. I went out for a breather at dawn, and saw him. He didn't see me, so I vanished.'

'No explanations?'

'He never said a word. You know, Marco's last engagement got broken off in a way nobody ever talks about.'

'And you think this one'll be the same?'

'Could be. It depends on how soon he realises he's crazy about Harriet.'

'What about your brother? Isn't he going the same way?'

'Oh, Guido's got enough sense to know when he's crazy. He's all right. Dulcie's perfect for him.'

'So that just leaves you on the loose?' Barton said with a fat chuckle.

'On the loose and happy to stay that way. They won't catch me.'

'That's what they all say, but look around. Good men are going down like ninepins.'

'Barton, have you any idea how many women there are in the world?' Leo demanded. 'And how few of them I've managed to meet so far? A man should be broad-minded, expand his horizons.'

'You'll find "the one", in the end,' Barton said.

'But I do, time and again. Then the next day I find another one who is also "the one". That's how I get short-changed.'

'You? Short-changed?' Barton guffawed.

'True, I swear it. Look at me, all alone. No loving wife, no kids.' He sighed sorrowfully. 'You don't know what a tragedy it is for a man to realise that nature has made him fickle.'

'Yeah, sure!'

This time they both laughed. Leo had a delightful laugh, full of sun and wine, lusty with life. He was a man of the earth, who instinctively sought the open air and the pleasures of the senses. It was all there in his eyes, and in his big, relaxed body. But above all it was there in his laugh.

On the last lap to Stephenville Barton began to yawn.

'It's enough to make a man cross-eyed to be staring at a horse's ass for so long,' he said.

Just ahead of them was an ancient, shabby horse trailer, displaying a large equine rump. It had been there for some time.

'Plus I had to get up at some ungodly hour to be at the airport on time,' Barton added.

'Hey, I'm sorry. You should have told me.'

'Well, it wasn't just that. We were up late last night, celebrating your visit.'

'But I wasn't there.'

'Don't fret. We'll celebrate again tonight,' Barton said, adding, by way of explanation, 'this is Texas.'

'So I see,' Leo said, grinning. 'I'm already beginning to wonder if I can take the pace. I'd offer to drive, but after that flight I'm in a worse state than you.'

'Well, it's not much further,' Barton grunted. 'Which is lucky because whoever's driving that horse trailer can't be doing more than fifty. Let's step on it.'

'Better not,' Leo advised quickly. 'If you're tired—'

'The sooner we're there the better. Here we go.'

He pulled out behind the horse trailer and speeded up to pass it. Glancing out of his window Leo saw the trailer slide back past them, then the van in front. He had a glimpse of the driver, a young woman with short, bristly red hair. She glanced up briefly and saw him looking at her.

What happened next became a bone of contention between them. She always said he winked at her. He swore she'd winked at him first. She said no way! It was a trick of the light and he had windmills in his head. They never did settle it.

Then Barton put his foot down, and they left her behind.

'Did you see that?' Leo asked. 'She winked at me. Barton? *Barton*!'

'OK, OK, I was just resting my eyes for a moment. But maybe you'd better talk to me—you know, just—sort of—'

'Just sort of keep you awake. Well, I'm not sure that overtaking has left us any better off.' Leo said, observing the pick-up truck that was now just ahead of them, and which was being driven erratically, swerving from lane to lane. Barton swung right, meaning to overtake again, but the truck swung at the same moment, blocking him so that he had to fall back. He tried once more and the truck swung out a second time, and then slowed abruptly.

'Barton!' Leo said urgently, for his friend hadn't reacted.

At last Barton's reflexes seemed to kick in. It was too late to slow down. Only a halt would avoid a collision now and he slammed on the brakes, stopping just in time.

The van behind them wasn't so lucky. From out of sight came a squeal of brakes, then a thump, a shudder that went right through the car, and finally a howl of rage and anguish.

The truck that had caused the trouble sped on its way, the driver oblivious. The two men leapt out and ran behind to inspect the damage. The sight that met their eyes appalled them.

There was an ugly dent in the back of Barton's pride and joy, which exactly mirrored one in the front of the van. At the rear of the van things were even worse. The sudden braking had caused the horse trailer to slew sideways and crash against the vehicle with a force that had dented them both. The trailer had half overturned and was leaning drunkenly against the van, while inside, the terrified animal was lashing out, completing the demolition. Leo could see flying hooves appearing through the widening holes, then retreating for more kicks.

The young woman with red hair was struggling to get the trailer upright, an impossible task, but she went at it with frantic strength.

'Don't do that,' Leo yelled. 'You'll get hurt.'

She turned on him. *'Stay out of it!'* Her forehead was bleeding.

'You're hurt,' he said. 'Let me help—'

'I said stay out of it. Haven't you done enough?'

'Hey, I wasn't driving, and anyway it wasn't our—'

'What do I care which of you was driving? You're all the same. You rush around in your flash cars as though you owned the road, and you could have killed Elliot.'

'Elliot?'

Another crash from inside the trailer answered his question. The next moment the door had given way and the horse, hooves flailing, leapt out and into the road. Leo and the young woman raced for his head, but he evaded them both and galloped away, straight across the highway. Without a second's hesitation she tore after him, dodging the oncoming traffic.

'Crazy woman!' Leo said violently, and took off after her.

More squeals, braking, curses, frustrated drivers bawling graphic descriptions of how they would like to alter Leo's personal attributes. He ignored them and sprinted madly after her.

Barton scratched his head, muttered, 'Crazy as each other,' and got out his mobile phone.

Luckily for his two pursuers Elliot was slightly hurt and unable to go fast. Unluckily for them he was determined not to be caught. What he couldn't manage in speed he made up for in cunning, turning this way and that until he vanished into a clump of trees.

'You go that way,' Leo roared, 'I'll go this way, and between us we'll head him off.'

But their best efforts were unable to persuade the horse. Selena nearly succeeded, calling his name so that he paused and looked back. But then he was off again, managing to dart between them and heading back the way he'd come.

'Oh, no!' Leo breathed. 'Not the highway.'

In a frighteningly short space of time the traffic was

in sight again. Appalled at what he could imagine happening, Leo put on a burst of speed, commanding his long legs to do their stuff. They obliged and he just made it, seizing the bridle with two yards to spare.

Elliot eyed him warily, but with Leo's first soothing words something seemed to come over him. He'd never heard the words before, for they were Italian, but Leo had the voice of a man who loved horses, speaking a universal language of affection. Elliot's shivering abated and he stood still, nervous and confused, but willing to trust.

Selena noticed all this subconsciously while she covered the last few yards, and the easy conquering of her beloved Elliot did nothing to improve her temper. Nor did the expert way this man was examining the animal's fetlocks, running gentle hands over them and finally saying, 'I don't think it's more serious than a slight strain, but a vet will confirm it.'

A vet's bill, when she was already scraping the bottom of her financial barrel. Lest he suspect that she was verging on despair she turned away, brushing a hand fiercely across her eyes. When she turned back anger and accusation were in place like a visor.

'More than a slight strain,' she echoed bitterly. 'There needn't have been any strain if you hadn't braked so suddenly.'

'Excuse me, I didn't do anything because I wasn't driving,' Leo said, breathing hard after his exertions. 'That was my friend, and it wasn't his fault either. Try blaming the guy who slowed in front of *us*. Not that you can do that because he's long gone, but if there's any fairness in the world—hell, what would you know about fairness?'

'I know about my injured horse and my damaged van.

I know they got that way because I had to slam on my brakes at the last minute—'

'Ah, yes, your brakes. I'd be very interested to see your brakes. I'll bet they'd really prove interesting.'

'So now you're trying to put the blame on me!'

'I'm just—'

'That's the oldest scam in the book and you should be ashamed to try it.'

'I—'

'I know your sort. You think "woman alone", must be helpless. Let's try it on, see if she scares easy.'

'It never crossed my mind that you scared easy,' Leo retorted with perfect truth. 'As for helpless, I've seen man-eating tigers who were more helpless.'

Barton had crossed the road and caught up with them.

'Hold on a minute, Leo—'

Leo was normally the most easygoing of men, but he had a Latin temper that could flare impressively when it got going. It was going now.

'We're here aren't we? So blame us. We're just convenient scapegoats and—and—' As always when his English failed him he fell back on his native language and for the next minute words poured out of him in an unstoppable stream.

'Darn it, Leo!' Barton roared at last. 'Will you stop being so excitable and—and *Italian*?'

'I just wanted to say what I feel,' Leo said.

'Well, you did that. So why don't we all calm down and get acquainted?'

He turned to the young woman and introduced himself in his easygoing way.

'Barton Hanworth, Four-Ten Ranch, just outside Stephenville, about five miles ahead.'

'Selena Gates. On my way to Stephenville.'

'Fine. We can get your—er—vehicle seen to when we're there, and a vet for your horse.'

Selena tore her hair. 'But how are we going to get there? Fly?'

'Nope. I just made a call and help is on its way now. While we're waiting for things to get sorted out you'll stay with us a day or so.'

'I will?'

'Where else?' he asked genially. 'If I landed you in this fix, it's for me to get you out.'

Selena shot a suspicious look at Leo. 'But *he* says it wasn't your fault.'

'Well, I may have reacted just a little too late,' Barton conceded, unable to meet Leo's eye. 'Fact is, if I'd slowed sooner—well anyway, you don't want to take any notice of what my friend here says.' He leaned towards her conspiratorially. 'He's a foreigner—talks funny.'

'Thanks Barton,' Leo grinned.

He was still giving most of his attention to Elliot, stroking the horse's nose and murmuring in a way that the animal seemed to find calming. Selena watched him, saying nothing, seeing everything.

Whatever orders Barton had given must have been to the point, because in a short time things started happening. A truck appeared, drawing a slant-load gooseneck trailer, bearing the logo of the Four-Ten Ranch, and large enough for three horses.

Gently Selena led Elliot up the ramp. He was clearly limping now.

'There'll be a vet and a doctor waiting when we get home,' Barton said. 'Now, you get in the car with us, and we'll be off.'

'Thanks but I'll stay with Elliot,' she said.

Barton frowned. 'It's against the law for you to do that. Oh, what the hell?' he retreated, seeing her stubborn expression. 'It's only five miles.'

'I have to stay with Elliot,' Selena explained. 'He'll be nervous in a new place without me. What about my van?'

'Don't you worry, that's being attached now,' Barton assured her.

'Elliot doesn't like going too fast,' she said quickly.

'I'll make sure the driver knows that. Leo, you coming?'

'No, I think I'll stay here,' he said.

'I don't need any help with Elliot,' Selena said quickly.

'It's not Elliot I'm thinking of. You took a nasty bump on the head, and you shouldn't be on your own.'

'I'm all right.'

Leo climbed into the trailer and stood, arms folded, looking stubborn.

'We can start the journey and get Elliot to a vet, or we can stand here talking until you give in. It's up to you.'

He pulled the door closed as he spoke. Selena glared but didn't argue further. She even allowed him to help her settle Elliot in one of the stalls.

She was angry with him, without being quite sure why. She knew he hadn't been driving, and Barton Hanworth, who had been driving, was making handsome amends. But her nerves were jangled, she'd had the fright of her life, and all her agitation seemed to be homing in on this man who had the nerve to order her about, and was now talking to her in much the same soothing voice he'd used to calm Elliot. Crime of crimes!

'We'll be there soon,' he said. 'You can get some proper treatment.'

'I don't need mollycoddling,' she said through gritted teeth.

'Well, I would if I'd had a crash like you did.'

'I guess some of us are just tougher than others,' she said grumpily.

He left it there. She looked ill and he reckoned she was entitled to her bad temper. When she turned away to Elliot he watched, observing with wonder how she'd switched from bawling him out to being gentle and tender with the animal.

He was a quarter horse, not beautiful but solid and showing signs of a hard life. From the way she rested her cheek against his nose it was clear that he was perfect in her eyes.

At first glance she too wasn't beautiful, except for her eyes which were large and green. Her skin had the peachy glow of health and outdoor living, and her face looked as though it might be engagingly mischievous at a better time. Also Leo's observant eyes had noticed her movements with pleasure. She was as slim as a lathe, not elegant but tough and wiry, yet she moved with the instinctive grace of a dancer.

He tried to see her marvellous eyes again, without being obvious about it. With eyes like that a woman didn't need anything else. They did it all for her.

'My name's Leo Calvani,' he said, offering his hand.

She took it, and he immediately sensed the strength he'd guessed was there. He tightened his fingers a little, seeking to know more, but she withdrew her hand at once, having left it in his for no more than the minimum that courtesy demanded.

They started to move, slowly as Selena had insisted.

After a few minutes he realised that she was studying him with curiosity. Not erotic curiosity, as he was used to. Or romantic fascination, which also came his way satisfyingly often.

Just curiosity. As though maybe he wasn't as bad as she'd first thought, and she was prepared to make allowances.

But no more than that.

CHAPTER TWO

THE Four-Ten Ranch was ten thousand acres of prime land, populated by five thousand head of cattle, two hundred horses, fifty employees and a family of six.

Selena knew she was in the presence of very serious money when she climbed stiffly out of the horse trailer and saw the stables where Barton kept his prize horseflesh. She knew humans who lived worse.

Everything moved like clockwork. As she walked in, leading Elliot, a man was pulling open the door of a large, comfortable stall. A vet was already there. So was a doctor, who would have drawn her aside, but Leo Calvani forestalled him with the quiet words, 'Let her attend the horse first. She won't settle down until she's seen him OK.'

She gave him a brief look of gratitude for his understanding, and watched jealously as the vet passed expert hands over Elliot and gave a diagnosis that was roughly the same as Leo's, with a little elaboration to justify his fee. An anti-inflammatory injection, some bandaging, and it was over.

'Will he be fit for the rodeo next week?' Selena asked anxiously.

'We'll see. He's not a young horse any more.'

'How about letting the doctor look at you now?' Leo asked her.

She nodded and sat while the doctor examined her head. Beneath her apparent calm she was fighting de-

21

spair. Her head was aching, her heart was aching and she was aching all over.

'How are those animals I sold you two years back?' Leo asked Barton. 'Shaping up?'

'Come and see for yourself.'

Together the two men walked along the stalls, and long, intelligent faces turned to watch them go by.

The five horses Barton had bought from Leo were in beautiful condition. They were large beasts with powerful hocks, and they'd been worked hard but treated like royalty.

'I'll swear they remember you,' Barton said as they nuzzled Leo.

'They don't forget a sucker.' Leo grinned.

While admiring the horses he contrived to glance at Selena, who was having a dressing fixed to her forehead.

'Take it easy for a day or two,' the doctor was saying. 'Plenty of rest.'

'It was just a little bump,' she insisted.

'Just a little bump on your head.'

'I'll make sure she rests,' Barton said. 'My wife's getting a room ready right now.'

'That's nice of her,' Selena said awkwardly, 'but I'd rather stay here with Elliot.'

She indicated the piles of hay as though wondering why anyone could want more.

'Well, you've gotta come in to eat,' Barton exclaimed. 'We're just having a snack because we'll be starting the barbecue in a couple of hours.'

'You're very kind but I can't come in the house,' Selena said, horribly conscious of her shabby, dishevelled appearance.

Barton scratched his head. 'Mrs Hanworth will be offended if you don't.'

'Then I'll come in and say thank you.'

She wouldn't need to stay long, she reckoned: just enough to be polite.

Reluctantly she followed them across to the house, which was a huge white mansion, the very sight of which made her feel awkward. She wondered how Leo would cope. In his shabby jeans and scuffed trainers he looked as out of place as she felt, although it didn't seem to bother him.

The sound of eager shrieks made Leo look up, and the next moment he was engulfed by the Hanworth family.

Delia, Barton's wife, was colourful, exuberant, and looked ten years younger than her true age. She and Barton had three children, two daughters, Carrie and Billie, younger versions of their mother, plus Jack, a studious son who seemed to live in a dream world, semi-detached from the rest of the family.

The household was completed by Paul, or Paulie as Delia insisted on calling him. He was her son by an earlier marriage, and the apple of her eye. She spoiled him absurdly, to the groaning exasperation of everyone else.

Paulie greeted Leo as a kindred spirit, slapping him on the back and predicting 'great times' together, which made Leo feel like groaning too. Paulie was in his late twenties, good-looking in a fleshy, superficial way, but self-indulgence was already blurring his features. He was a businessman in his own estimation, but his 'business' consisted of an internet company, his fifth, which was rapidly failing, as the other four had failed.

Barton had bailed him out, time and again, always swearing that this time was the last, and always yielding to Delia's entreaties for 'just one more'.

But just now the atmosphere was genial. Paulie, on his best behaviour, had recognised Selena.

'I've seen you riding in the rodeo at—' he rattled off a list of names. 'Seen you win, too.'

Selena relaxed, managing a smile.

'I don't win much,' she admitted. 'But enough to keep going.'

'You're a star,' Paulie said, taking her hand and pumping it up and down between his two. 'It surely is an honour to meet you.'

If Selena felt the same she disguised it successfully. There was something about Paulie that laid a disagreeable sheen even over his attempts to flatter. She thanked him and withdrew her hand, fighting the temptation to rub it on her jeans. Paulie had a clammy palm.

'Your room is ready now,' Delia said kindly. 'The girls will show you upstairs.'

Carrie and Billie immediately took charge of Selena, drawing her up the huge staircase before she had time to protest. Paulie followed, impossible to shake off, and by the time they reached the best guest bedroom he'd contrived to get in front and throw open the door.

'Only the best for our famous guest,' he carolled facetiously.

Since Selena wasn't famous, and knew it, this only made her look at him askance. Already she could see a neon sign over Paulie's head, reading 'Trouble'. She was glad when Carrie eased her brother out of the room.

She looked around her, made even more uneasy by the magnificence. The large room had been decorated in pink, mauve and white, Delia's favourite colours. The carpet was a delicate pink that made Selena check her boots for mud. The curtains were pink and mauve brocade and the huge four-poster bed was hung with fine white net curtains. It could have slept four, she thought, testing the mattress gingerly. It was so soft and springy that she took a step back. How did anyone sleep on that without bouncing off?

She took a tour of the room, wondering if they'd put her in the wrong place. Perhaps the Queen of England would step out of the wardrobe and say this was really her room.

The bathroom was equally alarming, being frilly and feminine, with a tub shaped like a huge seashell. If there was one thing Selena knew she wasn't, it was frilly and feminine. She would have preferred a shower, but the cap wasn't quite big enough to protect the dressing on her forehead, so she ran a bath.

When it was just right she climbed in gingerly, relishing the comfort of sinking into the hot water and feeling it soothe her bruises. She sorted her way through the profusion of soaps until she found the least heavily perfumed and began to lather herself with it. Gradually the turmoil of the day slipped away from her. Maybe there was something to be said for soft living after all. Not much, but something.

A row of glass jars stood along a shelf just above the bath, each filled with crystals of a different colour. Curious, she took one down, unscrewed the top and gagged at the aroma, which was even more overpowering than the soap. Gasping, she hastened to replace the top, but her fingers were too slippery to grip properly and the jar slipped straight through them, down into the water and crashed against the bath with an ominous splintering sound. The shock, coming on top of everything else, surprised a yell from her.

Leo, settling into his own room across the hall, was undressing for a shower and had just stripped off his shirt when he heard the yell and paused. Stepping out into the corridor, he stopped again, listening. Silence. Then, from behind Selena's door came a despairing voice.

'Oh no! What am I going to do?'

He knocked on her door. 'Hello? Are you all right?'

Her voice reached him faintly. 'Not really.'

He pushed open the door, but could see nobody inside. 'Hello?'

'In here.' Now he could tell that she was in the bathroom, and he approached the open door gingerly, trying not to gasp from the sweet, powerful aroma that surged out and surrounded his head like a cloud.

'Is it all right for me to come in?' he asked.

'I'm stuck here forever if you don't.'

Moving cautiously he looked around the door to the great pink shell. Selena was in the middle of it, her arms crossed over her chest, glaring at him with frantic eyes.

'I smashed a jar of crystals,' she said desperately.

He looked around. 'Where?'

'In the bath. There's broken glass everywhere under the water, but I can't see where it is. I daren't move.'

'OK, don't panic.' He found a white towel and handed it to her, averting his eyes as she reached for it.

When she'd covered her top she said, 'You can look. I'm decent—ish.'

'Can you reach the plug?'

'Not without stretching.'

'Then I'll do it. Don't move. Just tell me where it is.'

'Between my feet.'

Gingerly he slid his fingers down the inner surface of the bath, trying to find the plug without touching her, an almost impossible task. At last he found it and managed to ease it open so that the bath could start draining.

'When the water's gone right down I can start to re-move the glass,' he said.

At last it came into view, ugly, sharp pieces, danger-ously close to her body. He began to pick them out one by one. It was a long process because the jar had smashed into dozens of fragments, and the movement of the water meant that as he cleared one place of tiny, threatening shards, it filled up again with others. Gradually the level dropped, and more of her came into view, which gave him another problem...

'I'm trying not to look, but I really do need to see what I'm doing,' he said desperately.

'Do what you have to,' she agreed.

He took a deep breath. The towel could only cover so much of her, and the water was vanishing fast.

'I've shifted all I can,' Leo said at last. 'You've got to get out by only moving upward, not sideways.'

'But how can I? I shall have to shift around to get my balance, and hold onto something.'

'You hold onto me.' He leaned down. 'Put your arms around my neck.'

She did so, and the towel immediately slithered away.

'Forget it,' Leo said. 'I'm trying to be a gentleman, but would you rather be safe or modest?'

'Safe,' she said at once. 'Let's go.'

She gripped her hands behind his neck and felt his hands on her waist. They were big hands, and they al-most encompassed her tiny span. Slowly he straightened up, drawing her with him. She was pressed right against him now, trying not to be too conscious of her bare breasts against his chest, and the way the light covering of hair tickled her.

A bit more, a bit more. Inch by inch they were man-aging it. The last of the water vanished, revealing a very nasty piece of glass that he'd missed. Selena looked down, horrified, then tried to kick it away.

It was a fatal error. The next moment her foot had slithered from under her and she was falling. But Leo tightened one arm about her, and with the other he reached down, grabbed her behind, and stepped away so fast that he was caught off balance. He staggered back out of the bathroom and for several wild steps he fought to stay upright. But it was no good. The next moment he was on his back on the plush pink carpet, with Selena sprawled naked on top of him.

'Oh God!' she shivered, clinging onto him and forgetting about modesty, about everything except that wicked looking spike.

He held on to her, breathing hard, trying to regain his equilibrium which was whirling away into space, among the stars and planets, wild, glorious, dizzying. The feel of her on top of him was both scary and wonderful, and he knew he had to put a stop to it, fast.

Then his blood froze at an ominous sound.

A female giggle. Two female giggles. Right outside the door.

'Selena,' came Carrie's voice. 'Can we come in?'

'No!' Selena's voice rose to a yelp and she jumped up. She just made it to the door in time, reaching out to turn the key.

There wasn't one. The door didn't lock.

Disaster!

'Don't come in, I'm not decent,' she called, putting her back against the door and pushing. 'I'll be down in a minute. Please tell your mom thank you, for me.'

To their relief the voices faded away.

Leo pulled himself together, wondering how much more he could stand. If holding her against him on the floor hadn't destroyed his nervous system, watching her streak across the room like a gazelle had nearly finished him off.

But it had been useful in ascertaining one thing.

His rescue had been successful. There wasn't a scratch on her anywhere.

She dashed into the bathroom and returned in a towelling robe, which mercifully enveloped her.

'Thanks,' she said. 'You saved me from something very nasty.'

He'd gotten to his feet. 'I'd better go before both our reputations are ruined.'

'What am I going to say to Mrs Hanworth?'

'Leave that to me. I don't think you should go downstairs at all. Go to bed. That's an order.'

He checked the corridor and was relieved to find it empty. But no sooner had he stepped out than Carrie and Billie appeared, almost as though they'd been hiding around the corner.

'Hi Leo! Everything OK?'

'Not quite,' he said, horribly conscious that he was only half dressed, and trying not to go red. 'Selena dropped one of the glass jars into the bath, while she was in it, and it smashed.'

'Poor Selena! Is she still trapped in there?'

'No, I got her out, and she's safe,' he said, wishing the earth would swallow him up. 'I promised her I'd tell your mom about the jar. I'll do that—er—just as soon as I've put on a shirt.'

He got into his room as fast as he could, trying not to hear two teenage girls snickering significantly. It was a sound calculated to freeze a man's blood.

*   *   *

Delia reacted just as Leo had known she would, with sympathy and kindness.

'What's a jar?' she said. 'I'll go and make sure she's all right.'

She was back in a few minutes, sweeping into the kitchen to order food to be taken upstairs to Selena. She seemed to have spoken to her daughters in the meantime, for her attitude to Leo had developed a tinge of roguishness.

'I gather you played knight in shining armour. And who could blame you? She's a very nice-looking girl.'

'Delia, I swear I never met her before today.'

Fatal mistake. Delia smiled knowingly. 'You Italians are so dashing and romantic, never missing a chance with the ladies.'

'What are those wonderful smells coming from the kitchen?' he asked desperately, 'because you are looking at a starving man.'

Mercifully food was allowed to drive out all other topics of conversation, and the only other person who raised the matter was Paulie, who nudged Leo aside and said much the same as his mother, except that he made it sound vulgar and offensive. When Leo had smilingly explained to Paulie all the unpleasant things he would do to his person if he ever mentioned it again, the matter was allowed to drop.

While he dressed for the barbecue Leo tried to get his own reactions in perspective. Despite her prickly defensiveness, for which he reckoned nobody could blame her, Selena was oddly appealing. But there wasn't, at first glance, anything special about her. Even holding her naked body shouldn't have been a big deal, since she lacked the buxomness he preferred in women.

Yet, mysteriously, something about her had got to

him. He still couldn't figure out what, but the sight of Paulie smacking his fat lips over what he thought had gone on in her room had filled him with rage. Leo, the most amiable of men, had only been restrained from violence by recalling that this was his hostess's son.

Guests were starting to arrive, heading for the field where the big party was taking place, the same field where last night's big party had taken place, and where there would be another one just as soon as someone could think of an excuse. Leo watched it from his window, grinning, anticipating the evening.

'Ready for a great time?' Barton hollered as Leo came down the stairs.

'I'm always ready for that,' Leo said, truthfully. 'But can we call in at the stables first?'

'Sure, if you want. But Leo, you don't have to worry. She's going to be all right.'

'Elliot's a he.'

'It wasn't Elliot I was meaning,' Barton said, seeming to speak to nobody in particular.

The anti-inflammatory drug was evidently taking effect, and Elliot seemed contented. The way to the barbecue field led past Barton's garage, and through the open door Leo could see Selena's van, and the remains of the horse trailer.

'That's had its day,' Barton mused. 'The wonder is, how it lasted so long.'

Leo climbed into the van. What he saw there made him grow very still.

He thought of himself as a man who could cope with tough living, but the inside of her home shocked him. Everything was the barest and meanest possible. There was a couch just long enough for her to sleep, a tiny stove, a minute washing area. The best that could be said for the place was that it was spotlessly clean.

His own experiences of living rough, he realised, had been those of a rich man, playing with a kind of toy. However harsh the conditions, he could always return to a comfortable life when he got bored with playing. But for her there was no escape. This was her reality.

What could have made her choose the life of a wanderer, which seemed to offer her so little?

One thing was becoming horribly clear. The accident had robbed her of almost everything she had.

After that he had no chance to think gloomy thoughts. Texas hospitality opened its arms to him, and he rushed into them, enjoying every moment, and telling himself he'd have time to be exhausted later. What with plentiful food and drink, music and pretty girls to dance with, several hours slipped happily away.

When he could pause for breath he wondered how Selena was fixed? Had she eaten the supper Delia sent up, and was she hungry again?

He piled a plate high with steak and potatoes, tucked some cans of beer under his arm and headed for the house. But some instinct made him check the stables— just in case. As he'd half expected, Selena was there, leaning on the door of Elliot's stall, just watching him contentedly.

'How is he?' Leo asked, looking in.

She jumped up. 'He's better. He's calmed down a lot.'

She was better too, he could see that. Her cheeks had colour and her eyes were bright. He raised the plate to show her and she eyed the steak hungrily.

'That for me?'

'Well, it sure as hell isn't for Elliot. Come on out.'

He found a solid bale of hay and they sat down together. He handed her a beer and she tipped her head back to take most of it in one go.

'Oh, that was good!' she sighed.

'Well, there's plenty more out there,' he said, indicating the door with his head. 'In fact there's plenty of steaks too. Why not come out and join the party?'

'Thanks, but I won't.'

'Still not feeling up to partying?'

'No, I'm better. I slept well. It's just—all those people, looking at me and thinking my voice isn't right, and—everything isn't right.'

'Who says you're not right?'

'I do. This house—everything—it gives me the heebie-jeebies.'

'You've never been in a house like that before?'

'Oh, sure, plenty of times. Just not through the front door. I've worked in places like this, mopping floors, cleaning up in the kitchen, anything that was going. Mind you, I preferred a job in the stable.'

'When was this? You talk like you were ancient, but you can't be more than forty.'

'More than—?' She saw the wicked gleam in his eyes, and laughed. 'I'd thump you if you weren't sitting between me and the beer.'

'That's what I like,' he said, handing her another can. 'A woman with a sense of priorities. So, not forty then?'

'I'm twenty-six.'

'And when was all this ancient history?'

'I've been looking after myself since I was fourteen.'

'Shouldn't you have been at school?'

Another shrug. 'I suppose.'

'What happened to your parents?'

After a few moment's silence she said, 'I was raised in a home, several actually.'

'You mean you're an orphan?'

'Probably not. Nobody knew who my father was. Not sure even my mom knew that. All I really knew about her was that she was just a kid herself when she had me, couldn't cope, put me in a home. I expect she meant to come back for me, but things got too much for her.' Selena took another swig.

'And what then?' Leo asked, in the grip of an appalled fascination.

'Foster homes.'

'Homes? Plural?'

'The first one was OK. That's where I found out about horses. After that I knew whatever I did it had to be with horses. But the old man died and the stock got sold off and I was sent somewhere else. That was bad. The food was rotten and I was cheap labour, kept off from school because they were too mean to pay an extra hand. I told them where they could stick it and they sent me packing. Said I was "out of control". Which was true. In a pig's ear I was going to let them control me.'

'But aren't there laws to protect kids in this situation?'

She looked at him as if he was crazy.

'Of course there are laws,' she said patiently. 'And inspectors to see that the laws are followed.'

'So?'

'So bad things happen anyway. Some of the inspectors are decent people, but they get swamped. There's just too much to do. And some of them just see what they want to see because that way they finish work early.'

She spoke lightly, without bitterness, like someone describing life on another planet. Leo was aghast. His own existence in Italy, a country where family ties were still stronger than almost anywhere else, seemed like paradise in comparison.

'What happened after that?' he asked, in a daze.

She shrugged again and he realised how eloquent her shrugs were, each one seeming to contain a whole speech.

'A new foster home, no different. I ran away, got caught and sent back to the institution, and after a while there was another foster home. That lasted three weeks.'

'What then?' he asked, for she'd fallen silent again.

'This time I made sure they didn't catch me. I was fourteen and could pass for sixteen. I don't suppose they looked for me long. You know, this steak is really good.'

He accepted her change of subject without protest. Why should she want to discuss her life if it had been like that?

CHAPTER THREE

Now that her fear for Elliot had been eased Selena was growing more relaxed, exuding an air of taking life as it came that Leo guessed was more normal with her.

'Have you and Elliot been together long?' he asked.

'Five years. I got some work doing odd jobs about the rodeos, and bought him cheap from a guy who owed me money. He reckoned Elliot's career was over, but I thought he still had good things in him if he was treated right. And I do treat him right.'

'I guess he appreciates that,' Leo said as she rose and went to fondle Elliot's nose. The horse pressed forward to her.

He rose too and began to stroll along the stalls, looking in at the animals, who gazed back, peaceful, beautiful, almost seeming to glow in the dim light.

'You know about horses,' Selena asked, joining him. 'I could tell.'

'I breed a few, back home.'

'Where's home?'

'Italy.'

'Then you really are a foreigner.'

He grinned. 'Couldn't you tell by my ''funny accent''?'

She gave a sudden blazing grin. 'It's not as funny as some I've heard.'

It was as though the sun had come up with her smile. Wanting to make her laugh, Leo went into a clowning

36

version of Italian. Seizing her hand he kissed the back
and crooned theatrically,

'*Bella signorina*, letta me tell you abouta my country.
In Eeetaly we know 'ow to appreciate a beautiful lai-ee-
dy.'

She stared, more flabbergasted than impressed.

'You *talk* like that in Italy?'

'No, of course not,' he said, reverting to his normal
voice. 'But when we're abroad it's how we're expected
to talk.'

'Only by folk who need their heads examined.'

'Well, I meet a lot of them. Most people's ideas about
Italians come straight out of cliché. We're not all bottom
pinchers.'

'No, you just wink at women on the highway.'

'Who does?'

'You do. Did. When Mr Hanworth's car passed me, I
saw you looking at me, and you winked.'

'Only because you winked first.'

'I did not,' she said, up in arms.

'You did.'

'I did not.'

'I saw you.'

'It was a trick of the light. I do not wink at strange
men.'

'And I don't wink at strange women—unless they
wink at me first.'

Suddenly she began to laugh, just as he'd wanted her
to, and the sun came out again. He took her hand and
led her back to the bale where they'd been sitting, and
they clinked beer cans.

'Tell me about your home,' she said. 'Where in Italy?'

'Tuscany, the northern part, near the coast. I have a

farm, breed some horses, grow some grapes. Ride in the rodeo.'

'Rodeo? In Italy? You're kidding me.'

'No way! We have a little town called Grosseto, which has a rodeo every year, complete with a parade through the town. There's a building there with walls covered with photos of the local ''cowboys''. Until I was six I thought all cowboys were Italian. When my cousin Marco told me they came from the States I called him a liar. We had to be separated by our parents.'

He paused, for she was choking with laughter.

'In the end,' he said, 'I had to come and see the real thing.'

'Got any family, apart from your cousin?'

'Some. Not a wife. I live alone except for Gina.'

'She's a live-in girlfriend?'

'No, she's over fifty. She cooks and cleans and makes dire predictions about how I'll never find a wife because no younger woman will put up with that draughty building.'

'Are the draughts really bad?'

'They are in winter. Thick stone walls and flagstones to walk on.'

'Sounds really primitive.'

'I guess it is. It was built eight hundred years ago and as soon as I finish one repair it seems I have to start another. But in summer it's beautiful. That's when you appreciate the stone keeping you cool. And when you go out in the early morning and look down the valley, there's a soft light that you see at no other time. But you have to be there at exactly the right moment, because it only lasts a few minutes. Then the light changes, becomes harsher, and if you want to see the magic again you have to go back next morning.'

He stopped, slightly surprised at himself for using so many words, and for the almost poetic strain of feeling that had come through them. He realised that she was looking at him with gentle interest.

'Tell me more,' she said. 'I like listening to people talk about what they love.'

'Yes, I suppose I do love it,' he said thoughtfully. 'I love the whole life, even though it's demanding, and sometimes rough and uncomfortable. At harvest you get up at dawn and go to bed when you're in a state of collapse, but I wouldn't have it any other way.'

'You got brothers, sisters?'

'I've got a younger brother—' Leo grinned '—although technically Guido is the elder. In fact, legally I barely exist because it turned out my parents weren't married, only nobody knew at the time.'

She made a quick, alert movement. 'You mean you're a bastard too?'

'Yes, I guess I am.'

'Do you care?'

'Not in the slightest.'

'Me neither,' she said contentedly. 'It sort of leaves you free. You can go where you want and do what you want, be who you want. Do you find it's like that?'

Receiving no answer she turned to look at Leo and found him leaned right back, his eyes closed, his body stretched out in an attitude of abandon. Jet lag wouldn't be fought off any longer.

Selena reached out to nudge him awake, but stopped with her hand an inch away, and watched him. The day's turbulent events had left her no chance to consider him at leisure. He'd been the rescuer who'd caught up with Elliot, when she herself might not have done so in time, and whose gentle hands and voice had calmed the animal. If her beloved Elliot accepted him then she must too.

In the bathroom he'd saved her from nasty injury. Beyond that she hadn't allowed herself to think. But she could think about it now, how it had felt to be held tightly against him, the soft scratching of the hairs on his chest against her bare breasts. She could remember, too, the bold way he'd grasped her behind with his big hand, hauling her to safety and removing his hand at once.

A gentleman, she thought. Even at that moment.

Everything about him pleased her, starting with the broad sweep of his forehead, half hidden now by a lock of hair that had fallen over it, and the heavy brows, and the dark-brown eyes beneath them. She liked the straight nose and the slightly heavy curved mouth that could smile in a way that hinted at delight to come for a woman with a brave spirit.

She wondered just how brave her own spirit was. In the ring she would take any risk, dare any fall, chance any unfamiliar horse, and laugh. But folk were different, harder to understand than horses. They were awkward and they could hurt you more than any tumble.

And yet she wanted to see Leo's smile again, and follow the tempting hints to their conclusion.

She liked his foreignness, his faint Italian accent, his way of pronouncing certain words in a way that was strange to her, but delightful. She wanted to know him better, to discover more about the big, generously proportioned body, and to realise the promise implicit in those broad shoulders and lean, hard torso. As if drawn by a magnet her eyes fell on his hands, and memories sprang alive in her flesh. Those long fingers, touching her nakedness as he lifted her out of the bath. They seemed to be touching her now, this minute. She could feel them....

Hell, who did she think she was kidding? Everyone knew that Italians liked curvy females, with hour-glass figures.

And I don't have any in-and-out, she reminded herself sorrowfully. Just 'in.' And he's seen me now, so there's no way to fool him.

Life was very hard!

Elliot whinnied softly, and the sound was enough to awaken Leo. He opened his eyes while her face was still close to his, and smiled.

'I've died and gone to heaven,' he said. 'And you're an angel.'

'I don't think they'll be sending me to heaven. Not unless someone's changed the rules.'

They both laughed, and she went to Elliot, who had whinnied again.

'He's just jealous because you're giving me so much attention,' Leo said.

'He's got nothing to be jealous about, and he knows it,' Selena said. 'He's my family.'

'Where do you live?'

'Wherever Elliot and I happen to be.'

'But you must have some sort of home base, where you stay when you're not travelling?'

'Nope.'

'You mean, you're travelling all the time?'

'Yup.'

'With no home to go to?' he asked, aghast.

'I've got a place where I'm registered for paying taxes. But I don't live there. I live with Elliot. He's my home as well as my family. And he always will be.'

'It can't be "always",' he pointed out. 'I don't know how old he is, but—'

'He's not old,' Selena said quickly. 'He looks older than he is because he's a bit battered, but that's all.'

'Yes, I'm sure,' Leo said gently. 'But just how old is he?'

She sighed. 'I'm not sure. But he's not finished yet.' She laid her cheek against Elliot's nose. 'They don't know you like I do,' she whispered, and turned her head away so that he couldn't see the anguish that swamped her.

But he did see it, and his heart ached for her. That raw-boned animal, past his best, was all she had in the world to love.

Suddenly her strength seemed to drain away. Leo quickly took hold of her.

'That's it, you're going to bed. Don't argue because I won't take no for an answer.'

He kept his arm firmly fixed about her waist in case she had any other ideas, but she was too weary to argue, and let him lead her away to the house and up the stairs to her room.

'Goodnight,' he said at her door. 'Sleep well.'

'Leo, you don't understand,' she confided in a low voice. 'I can't sleep in that bed. It's too soft. Every time I move it bounces.'

His lips twitched. 'They're supposed to. Still, I know what you mean. If it's not what you're used to it can be worse than stones. You'll just have to try to put up with all this comfort. You'll get used to it.'

'Not me,' she said with conviction, and slipped into her room.

He stood looking at the closed door, a prey to unfamiliar feelings that confused him. He wanted to follow her into her bedroom, not to have his evil way, but to ask her to lay her problems on him, and promise to make everything right for her.

Having his evil way could come later. When he'd earned the right.

It was almost dawn when the last guest drove away, waving an arm out of the window and yodelling, 'See ya!' Bleary eyed and cheerful, the household drifted off to bed.

Leo sat down on his bed with a feeling of pleasant vagueness. The evening had contained much bourbon and rye, especially the last part, after he'd said goodnight to Selena and returned to the festivities. Now he was at peace with the world.

But he didn't miss the sound of footsteps that stopped outside Selena's bedroom door. A pause, then a soft creak as the door was opened. That was enough to make Leo's tipsy haze pass, and send him out into the corridor in time to catch Paulie halfway through Selena's door.

'Why, isn't this nice?' he said in a voice that made Paulie jump. 'Both of us so concerned about Selena that we couldn't sleep until we knew she was fine.'

Paulie gave him a glassy smile. 'Can't neglect a guest.'

'Paulie, you're an example to us all.'

Leo was moving into the room as he spoke, switching on the light. Then both men stopped, taken aback by the sight of the empty bed.

'That tomfool female has gone back to the stables,' Leo muttered.

'No I haven't,' came from a heap on the floor.

Leo switched on the bedside light and saw the heap separate itself into its various parts, which included a blanket, a pillow, and one tomfool female whose red hair stood up on her head in a shock.

'What is it?' she asked, sitting up. 'Has something happened?'

'No, Paulie and I were concerned for you, so we came to see how you were.'

'That's very kind,' she said, guessing the truth at once. 'I'm fine.'

'She's fine, Paulie. You can go to bed now, and sleep tight.' Leo sat down on the floor beside Selena with the air of a man taking root.

'Er—well, I just—'

'Goodnight, Paulie.' They spoke as one.

Forced to accept defeat, Paulie backed himself out of the door. The last thing they saw was his scowl.

'I could have coped, you know,' Selena said.

'When you're well, I'm sure you could,' Leo said tactfully. 'But let's wait until then. Underneath Paulie's flabby exterior there's a very ugly customer waiting to get out.'

'I reckoned that. But that's three times in one day you've come galloping to my rescue. I just don't want you to think I'm a wimp.'

'After the day you've had, aren't you entitled to be just a bit of a wimp?'

'Nobody is entitled to be a wimp.'

'Sorry!'

'No, I'm sorry,' she said contritely. 'I didn't mean to be rude. I know you were trying to be kind, but all this rescuing is getting to be a bad habit.'

'I promise not to do it again. Next time I'll abandon you to your fate, I swear.'

'Do that.'

'Are you all right on the floor?'

'I put up with the bed as long as I could,' she complained, 'but it's insane. Every time I turned over I went six feet in the air. This is much better.'

'I'd better leave before I fall asleep.' Suddenly he found himself vague. 'Where am I? Is the party over?'

'Must be.' She smiled, fully understanding. 'Was the whisky very good?'

'Barton's whisky is always good. And I should know. I had plenty of it.'

'Shall I help you back to your room?'

'I think I can make it. Lock your door when I'm gone. I wouldn't put it past Delia's little boy to try again.'

But then he remembered that the door it didn't lock. He sighed. There was only one thing for it.

'What are you doing?' she asked as he returned to the bed and scooped up a blanket and pillow.

'What does it look as if I'm doing?' he said, dropping to the floor and stretching out across the door. 'If he can open this door now he's a better man than I take him for.'

'You promised to leave me to my fate next time,' she reminded him indignantly.

'I know, but you can't trust a word I say.'

Blessed sleep was overtaking him. His last coherent thought was that he'd be made to suffer for this in the morning.

But at least she would be safe.

He awoke feeling better than he had any right to after what he recalled of the barbecue. Already he could sense the house stirring about him, and reckoned it was safe to leave her.

It was better to be gone before she awoke. He wouldn't have known what to say to her. Inside him he was jeering at himself for going into what he ironically called 'chivalrous mode'.

That was something he'd never done before in his life. The women whose company he sought were cut from the same cloth as himself, and after much the same things. Fun, laughter, uncomplicated pleasure, a good time had by all, and no hearts broken. It had always worked beautifully.

Until now.

Now, suddenly, he found himself acting like a knight in shining armour, and it worried him.

Chivalry or no, he dropped gently down beside her sleeping form, and studied her face. Her colour had improved since last night and he could see that she slept, as he always did himself, dead to the world, like a contented animal.

She'd removed her dressing, so that the cut and bruise on her forehead showed up starkly against her pallor. She had a funny little face, he thought, right now looking as vulnerable as child's, with the caution and worldly wisdom smoothed from it by sleep.

He reflected on the story she'd told him the night before, and guessed that she'd learned too much of the world in one way, and not enough in another.

He had an almost overmastering desire to lean down and kiss her, but the next moment he was glad he hadn't, because she opened her eyes. They were wonderful eyes, large and sea deep, and they made the child vanish.

'Hi,' he said. 'I'm off now. When I've showered I'll go downstairs, trying to look like a man who slept in his own room. Perhaps you should try to look as if you slept in this bed, for Delia's sake.'

'You think she'd be offended?'

'No, I think she'd be afraid the bed wasn't soft

enough, and heaven knows what you'd find on it to-night.'

They laughed, and he helped her up. She was wearing a man's shirt that came down almost to her knees.

'How are you feeling this morning?' he asked.

'Great. I just had the most comfortable night of my life.'

'On the floor?'

'This carpet is inches thick. Perfect.'

'Cross your fingers that I don't get seen leaving here.'

'I'll check the corridor for you.'

She looked and gave him the thumbs up. It took just a brief moment to dash back to his own room, and safety. True, he thought he heard the girls giggling again, but that was probably just paranoia.

He showered and dressed in a mood that was unusually thoughtful, for him, because he was uneasily aware that he didn't have a completely clear conscience. Without actually saying anything untrue he'd left Selena with the impression that he was almost as poor as herself. She'd seen him in worn clothing, heard him talk about living rough, and taken on board the fact that he was illegitimate.

But he'd neglected to mention that his uncle was Count Calvani, with a palace in Venice, and his family were millionaires. What he had casually referred to as his farm was a rich-man's estate, and if he helped out with the rough work it was because he preferred it that way.

He hadn't made these things clear because of a deep, instinctive conviction that they would have made her think badly of him.

He remembered her words, just after the accident.

'You're all the same. You rush around in your flash cars as though you owned the road.'

His car back home was a heavy duty, four-wheel drive, suitable for the hills of Tuscany. A working man's car, but a rich working man, who'd bought the best because he never bought anything else. In that he was a true Calvani, and now his sense of self-preservation was telling him that this would be fatal in Selena's eyes.

And why risk a falling out when he would only be here a couple of weeks, and then they would never see each other again?

In the end he did the only thing a sensible man could possibly do.

Pushed it to the back of his mind and hoped for the best.

He spent the day with Barton, riding his friend's acres. Barton reared cattle for money and horses for love; he bred and trained them for the rodeo.

Leo's eye was taken by a chestnut. He was a quarter horse, short, muscular, bred for speed over a quarter mile, the perfect barrel racer.

'Beautiful, isn't he?' Barton said as they looked him over. 'He came from here originally, bought by the wife of a friend of mine. I bought him back when she gave up the rodeo to have kids.'

'Can we take him back with us, and put him in the stable?' Leo asked thoughtfully.

Barton nodded, but as they rode home he mused, 'My friend, you are getting in over your head.'

'C'mon Barton, you know what the insurance guys are going to say. They'll take one look at Elliot and one at the van, and when they've stopped laughing they'll offer her ten cents.'

'And what's it to you? None of it was your fault.'

'She's going to lose everything.'

'Yes, but what's it to you?'

Leo ground his teeth. 'Can we just get home?'

Barton grinned.

They arrived to find a mood of gloom. Selena was sitting on the step of her van, staring at the ground while the two girls tried to comfort her, and Paulie hovered, clucking.

'The vet says Elliot won't be well enough for her to ride next week,' Carrie said. 'If she tries, it could really injure him.'

'Of course I won't do that,' Selena said at once. 'But now I'll have no chance to win anything, and I must owe you so much—'

'Now, now, none of that,' Barton said. 'The insurance—'

'The insurance will just about buy me a wheelbarrow and a donkey,' Selena said with a wry smile. She pointed to her forehead. 'I'm over this now. I can face the truth.'

'We won't know the truth until you've ridden a couple of races,' Barton declared.

'On what?' With a faint attempt at comedy she added, 'I don't have the donkey yet.'

'No, but you can do me a favour.' Barton indicated the quarter horse. 'His name's Jeepers. I've got a buyer interested, and if he wins a barrel race or two I can up the price. So you ride him, show him off, and that'll more than repay me.'

'He's beautiful,' Selena breathed, running her hands lovingly over the animal. 'Not as beautiful as Elliot of course,' she added quickly.

'Of course not,' Leo said gently.

'He's well trained,' Barton told her. He explained the story of the previous owner and Selena was scandalised.

'She gave up the rodeo to stay in one place and have babies?'

'Some women are funny like that,' Leo observed, grinning.

Selena's look showed him what she thought of such an idea. 'Can I put my saddle on him now?'

'Good idea.'

While Selena got to work Leo drew Barton aside.

'So tell me about this mysterious buyer,' he said.

Barton looked him full in the eye.

'You know who's gonna buy that horse, as well as I do,' he said.

The whole family turned out to watch Selena try out Jeepers in Barton's testing ring. The three barrels were set up in a triangle, with one side of ninety feet, and the other two sides one hundred and five feet each. Selena and Jeepers came flying across the starting line, into the triangle, turned sharply right around the first barrel, back into the triangle, around the second barrel, turned left and headed up the centre for the last barrel.

Each turn was a tight forty-five degrees, testing a horse's balance and agility as well as speed. Jeepers was swift yet steady as a rock, and Selena controlled him with light, strong hands. Even Leo, no expert in barrel racing, could see that they were a match made in heaven.

After the final turn they headed back down the centre of the triangle, and out, to the cheers of the family and the hands.

'Eighteen seconds,' Barton called.

Selena's eyes were shining. 'We took it slow the first time. Wait till we get going. It'll be fourteen in no time.'

She let out a joyous *'Yahoooo!'* up to the sky and everyone joined her.

Leo, watching her face, thought he'd never seen any human being look so totally happy.

CHAPTER FOUR

Selena had said there was no excuse for being a wimp, and over the next few days she lived up to her belief. She brushed off her injury with the airiness of someone who'd had worse and ignored it, and she rode hell-for-leather on Jeepers until she'd gotten his time down to fourteen seconds, just as she'd vowed.

Barton insisted that she stay at the Four-Ten until after the rodeo. This made sense as Elliot's recovery was slow, and she had no money to go anywhere else, but privately he gave Leo a wink, proving there was more to his offer than kindness.

'It's all in your head,' Leo growled when they were alone. 'Sure I like the girl, sure I want to help her. Dammit, nobody ever did until us! But that doesn't mean—'

'Of course not,' Barton said, and went on his way whistling.

Leo had a horrible suspicion that the events of the first night had somehow become known throughout the house, which meant that Billie and Carrie's giggling meant something after all. Paulie clearly thought so, because his manner towards Leo became cool.

Leo dropped in at the stables each evening, knowing he'd find Selena there, saying goodnight to Elliot. She always did this at length, and Leo was privately convinced that she was trying to make sure that he knew he still came first with her, despite Jeepers. Sometimes she stayed all night.

52

But tonight something was different. Instead of her softly murmuring voice he could hear the sounds of a scuffle as he pushed open the stable door. Somewhere deep in the shadows a fight was going on.

After a moment he saw the two combatants. There was Selena, fending off advances from Paulie, who wouldn't take no for an answer.

'C'mon, stop fooling. I've seen the looks you've been giving me. I know when a woman wants it.'

He made a lunge. Leo swore under his breath and gathered himself to spring on Paulie, a knight coming to the rescue of a damsel in distress.

But this damsel needed no such help. There was a yell from Paulie, who went reeling back, clutching his nose, while Selena blew on her knuckles.

'Nice,' Leo mused. 'I'll make a note not to get on your wrong side. Not that I planned to anyway, but now I've had my warning.'

'He asked for it,' Selena said, still blowing.

'Not a doubt.'

Abruptly her manner changed. 'But I shouldn't have done it,' she said. 'Oh, lord, I wish I hadn't.'

'What for?' Leo demanded. 'Why stop when you're having fun? And I should think socking him must have been great fun. I'm green with envy.'

'But they'll throw me out,' she said frantically. 'And Elliot's not ready to go. Do you think if I apologised—?'

He stared at her. Talk of an apology was the last thing he'd expected from her.

'Apologise? You?'

'I can't move Elliot yet. Let me talk to that creature.'

'No, let me,' he said, taking firm hold of her and keeping her where she was.

He strolled over to where Paulie had just staggered

upright, glaring over a hand that was clutched to his nose.

'How y'doing, Paulie?' Leo asked affably.

Paulie carefully lowered his hand, revealing a red, enlarged nose and streaming eyes.

'Did you see what she did?' he snarled.

'Yes, and I saw what you did. I'd say you'd gotten off lightly.'

'That bitch—'

'Well, you can always have your revenge,' Leo observed, studying the injured proboscis with interest. 'Just go back and tell Mommy that you got slugged in the kisser by a woman. I'll be your witness. In fact I'll make sure the story's known all over Texas. It'll probably get into the newspapers. Of course they'll want a picture of you looking just as you do now.'

There was a deadly silence while Paulie digested the implications of this. His piggy eyes, full of spite, went from one to the other.

'What do you take me for?' he snapped at last.

'If I told you what I took you for we'd be here all night,' Leo said.

Paulie wisely decided to overlook this.

'She's a guest here. Naturally I shall—' he almost choked over the last words '—say nothing.'

'I felt sure you'd see it that way. A gentleman to the end. And if anyone asks how you got that shiner you can say you tripped on a pitchfork. Or tell them I did it, I don't mind.'

'But I do,' Selena protested. 'In a pig's ear you're getting the credit. If I can't take it myself, he'll have to say it was a pitchfork.'

Leo grinned, delighted with her. 'Atta girl,' he said softly.

'You're crazy, the pair of you,' Paulie howled.

Giving them a wide berth he sidled his way out of the stable, breaking into a run as soon as he was out of the door.

'Thank you,' Selena said fervently. 'That was terrific.'

'Glad to be of some help. I should have knocked him down for you, but you didn't seem to need me.'

'Oh, I can do that bit for myself,' she said blithely. 'It's the words that confuse me. You knew just what to say to keep him quiet. I never know what to say. The more I try, the more it comes out wrong.'

'Better with your fists, huh?'

'I've had plenty of practise.'

He appeared to consider the matter seriously. 'I'd have guessed you to be more of a knee in the groin girl, myself.'

She regarded him steadily. 'I use whatever weapons are needed.'

'I suppose this kind of thing happens to you a lot?'

'Some guys think a woman travelling alone is fair game. I just show them that they're wrong.'

She spoke lightly, with another of her eloquent shrugs. In some mysterious way that shrug hurt him, with its implied acceptance of all the risks. He thought of her lonely life, always on the move, with only a horse to love. Yet he knew that if she guessed that he was concerned for her she would be incredulous. She would probably accuse him of being sentimental.

Then it occurred to him that she didn't even realise that she was lonely. She'd known nothing else. And that hurt him more than anything.

Selena watched him, trying to read his thoughts. It irked her not to be able to. Men were usually so easy to read.

She shook her hand, flexing the fingers, and he took it between his, massaging it between his strong, warm palms. She stood there, feeling peace and contentment flood her, almost for the first time in her life. It was a blissful feeling.

'Are you all right?' he asked.

'Everything's fine,' she assured him.

'Until the next time.'

'Hey, you didn't save me. I saved myself,' she said at once.

'Will you stop being so prickly? Am I the enemy?'

She shook her head, softened, smiling at him. Moved by an impulse too strong for him, Leo enfolded her in his arms, where she almost vanished. He cradled her carefully, longing to hold her there for ever, desperate to kiss her, but knowing that he mustn't do it while she was so vulnerable.

Selena could hear his heart beating and the sound comforted her. It would have been so easy to lean on this big, generous man, and let him shoulder her problems.

If she had been that kind of female. Which she wasn't. If she knew anything about herself, she knew that.

She looked up and saw the sudden trouble in his face.

'What is it?' she whispered.

He leaned down so that his forehead rested on hers. From here, a kiss was only an inch away, and she waited, wanting it to happen.

'Nothing,' he said. 'I was just wishing—no, nothing's the matter.'

'Leo—' she reached up, but he raised his head quickly.

'You've got to stop sleeping out here,' he said, releasing her and stepping back. 'It's too easy for him to get at you.'

She took a moment to still the pang of disappointment at his rejection.

'He can do that in the house,' she said. 'Unless you sleep across my door again.'

'No, that's not a good idea,' he said desperately. He'd shared her room once without trying to get into her bed, but he knew he couldn't trust himself to do it again.

'Let's go,' he said, leading the way out, keeping his distance from her.

All the way across the yard she lectured herself silently about staying level-headed. So she didn't attract him? Well, she'd known that! And the pain in her heart could have been saved if she hadn't indulged in silly fantasies.

She kept this up until they reached the house and she could assume a sensible manner, and listen to Delia telling how poor Paulie had stepped on a pitchfork and bruised his nose.

Leo made a point of getting Selena alone next morning.

'Let's ride,' he said. 'I want to try out one of Barton's horses over a distance.'

He had an ulterior motive, since he'd connived with Barton to get her away while the insurance assessors came to look things over. He had a fair idea what would happen then, and he needed time to sort out his thoughts.

He'd seen her racing around barrels and been impressed. Now he could watch her at ease, riding for the pleasure of it, and thought how natural and elegant she looked. Even on an unfamiliar horse she rode as though they were one. He thought of a fiery mare of his own back home, and wished he could introduce them.

They raced. He was riding the more powerful animal but he only just beat her. She had the trick of getting the best out of her horse, and Jeepers was at ease with her.

They found a shaded stream and stretched out under the trees with the beer and hot dogs they'd brought with them. Selena took a deep breath and leaned back, thinking how good it felt to be here like this, with the sun, the sparkling water, the invigorated feeling of having ridden for miles.

Get real, she told herself. What you really mean is, to be here with him. You've got windmills in your head. He's not for you. Be strong. You can cope as long as he doesn't talk in that gentle voice that knocks you sideways.

Forewarned should have been forearmed, but she still felt shaken when he asked quietly, 'Are you all right now?'

She meant to pass it off lightly with some remark about how many people were looking after her these days, but his eyes were kind and warm, and suddenly she couldn't joke.

'Yes, I'm feeling really good,' she said. 'It's funny, all the things I ought to be worrying about—I can't make myself think of them. They're still there, but—sort of vague, and in the background.'

'Well, you can't do anything about them at this moment,' he said, 'so why not let yourself float? You may cope better for it.'

'I know but—' she gave an awkward little laugh '—it's not like me. Normally I worry at things like a dog with a bone. Does no good, but I still do it.'

He nodded. 'Worrying's a waste of time.'

'You're not a worrying sort of person, are you?'

He grinned and shook his head ruefully. 'If it happens, it happens. If it doesn't happen, maybe that was for the best.'

'I envy you. Everything matters so much to me. It's like—' She fell silent, wondering at herself. Analysing also wasn't like her. Her thoughts and feelings were her own private property, and she guarded them behind barriers. But something about Leo drew her out from behind those barriers. Into the open. Into places she'd never ventured before. That's why he was a dangerous man, for all his quiet ways.

'Like what?' he asked, watching her with a little smile.

'Nothing.' She was retreating fast.

But he cut off her retreat, taking her hand gently in his, silently telling her she was safe with him.

'Tell me,' he said.

'No, I—I've forgotten what I was going to say.' She laughed awkwardly.

He didn't reply in words, but his raised eyebrows called her a coward.

Take the chance. Trust him.

'It's like all my life I was walking on a tightrope over a chasm,' she blurted out. 'I keep thinking I'll reach the other side but—' She waved her hands. Words came hard to her.

'What's waiting on the other side?' Leo asked, still holding her hand in his.

She met his eyes, shaking her head. 'I'm not sure there is one. Or if there is, I'll never find it.'

'You're wrong about that Selena. There's always another side, but you have to know what you want to find there. You just haven't decided yet. When you've made up your mind, you'll see the far ledge. And you'll get there.'

'Unless I fall off first. I keep feeling myself get wobbly.'

'I can't imagine you getting wobbly.'

'That's because I shout a lot, to hide it. Sometimes, the louder I yell, the more I'm like jelly inside.'

'I don't believe it. You're too gutsy.'

'Thanks but you don't know me.'

'Funny, but I feel as though I do. When we met up on that highway and you bawled me out, it felt like you'd been bawling me out all my life.'

She gave a shaky laugh. 'Yes, I'm good at bawling people out.'

'My back's broad.' He released her hand and leaned back against a tree, looking deeply content, like a man who already had everything life had to offer.

'Leo, doesn't anything faze you?'

'Bad harvests. Bad weather. Big cities. Meanness, dishonesty, unkindness.'

She nodded vigorously. 'Oh, yes.'

He asked suddenly, 'What do you want to do with your life, Selena?'

'I'm doing it.'

'But in the end?'

'You tell me when the end's going to come,' she parried, 'and I'll tell you what I'll be doing.'

'I meant you can't do this forever. One day it'll be too much for you and you'll have to settle down.'

She made a face. 'You mean pipe and slippers?'

He laughed. 'Well, not the pipe if you don't want to.'

'Domesticity. Home and hearth. No thanks! Not me! Four walls make me crazy. Staying in one place makes me even crazier.'

'And the loneliness?'

She gave an incredulous laugh. 'I'm not lonely. I'm free. No, no, don't say it.'

'Don't say what?'

'Something about loneliness and freedom being the same thing. Where does one shade into the other? Will I know the difference before it's too late? Et cetera, et cetera, et cetera.'

'You've heard that line before, huh?'

'A dozen times. It's such a cliché.'

'Well, most clichés are true. That's how they become clichés.'

'But I'm talking about freedom. Nobody telling me what to do. Nobody expects anything of me, except Elliot, and I love him so that's OK.'

'But you might get to love a person,' Leo suggested cautiously, 'maybe almost as much as you love Elliot.'

'Nah, people are tricky. You've got to watch your back all the time. Elliot's better. He keeps it simple.'

'I think you're teasing a rise out of me.' Leo was watching her carefully, like a man trying to decide which way a cat would jump.

'No way. Give me a horse any day. Take the other night in the stable, did you see Elliot trying to paw me about, breathing whisky fumes all over me? Did you hear him neighing, "Go on Selena, you know you want it really."?'

'Yes, I heard Paulie's line in charm,' Leo said in disgust. 'You should have socked him with both fists.'

'No need. He got the message after one. I don't like unnecessary violence. It's wasteful and it hurts your hands.' She added mischievously, 'Never use two fists where one will do. I learned that early.'

'I guess you've learned a lot of things most women never need to.'

She nodded.

'You still haven't answered my question,' Leo said. 'What will you do when you have to give up rodeo?'

'Get myself a farm. Breed horses.'

'Won't that mean living in one place all the time?'

'I can camp out sometimes.'

'Are you all alone on this farm?'

'No, there's the horses.'

'You know what I mean, stop dodging the issue.'

'You mean have I tied myself down to a husband? No way. What for? Having some guy drive me nuts. Knowing I was driving him nuts.'

'That's not always how it works out,' Leo said, choosing his words carefully, because he'd often said the same, and it alarmed him to find himself defending the other side. 'People can actually get on well, for a long time. Sometimes they even love each other. No, really, they can.'

'Sure they do. At the start. Then she has a baby and her waistline goes, he gets bored and hits the bottle, she nags, he gets mad, she nags some more.'

'That's life in the foster homes speaking, is it?'

'One after another. Wherever it was—always the same. And you can keep it.'

'You don't believe people can ever love each other for life?'

Her face lit up with hilarity. 'Leo, you're a sentimentalist. You believe in that stuff.'

'I'm Italian,' he said evasively. 'We're supposed to believe in "that stuff".'

'No kidding! I'll bet you think moon rhymes with

June, and love is for ever and a day. Oh, boy, you're priceless. Well, it's a better line than Paulie's.'

He didn't answer, and after a moment she was alerted by a new quality in the silence. Looking up, she saw Leo's eyes dark with anger. He met her puzzled gaze with one of fire.

'What did I say?' she asked.

'If you don't know the answer I can't tell you. But I'll try. You reckon I'm no better than Paulie, that I'm handing you a line prior to pawing you about in the stable. *Thanks*!'

'I didn't mean—'

'I think you did. Every man is the same in your eyes because you won't take the trouble to look up.'

He jumped to his feet and strode away from the stream to where the land rose sharply. At the top of the steep incline was a rock, and he scrabbled up there until he could sit on the top, staring angrily into space.

Selena glared at him in her dismay, furious with him, herself, the world. It hadn't occurred to her that she could hurt him. Her rough and tumble life had taught her directness but not subtlety. If you wanted something, you went for it, because nobody was going to give it to you. She had the tough skills of survival but not the gentle ones of beguilement, and for the first time it occurred to her that there was something missing in her armoury.

She scrambled up the incline until she was just below him, and was relieved to see that the anger had faded from his face. She didn't fear his anger, but it was his gentleness that was beginning to weave spells about her heart.

He reached down a hand to haul her up, so that she could sit down beside him.

'You're not really mad at me, are you?'

'Grrr!' he said, like a bear.

She chuckled, wrapping both arms around one of his and leaning her head against his shoulder.

'I'm sorry, Leo. I'm always like this. I open my big mouth first and think later.'

'You? Think?'

'I manage it sometimes.'

'You must send me a ticket. I'll bet it's quite an event.'

She freed a hand long enough to thump him, then put it back, and they sat contentedly together for a while.

He turned his head so that he could see as much of her face as was visible, and placed one of his big hands over her narrow one.

'I really didn't mean to lump you with Paulie,' she said. 'I should have known you're not like him, groping around, trying to sneak a kiss.'

Leo spoke quietly. 'I did not say I didn't want to kiss you.'

'What was that?' she asked quickly.

'Nothing.' This conversation was getting dangerous. He was too close to admitting what he really wanted, and shattering the delicate web of trust that was building up between them. And when he thought of what he would probably discover when they returned home he knew that web had to be protected at all costs.

'Perhaps it's time we went back,' he said.

They took the journey home easily as the sun slid down the sky. As they cantered back into the yard Leo exchanged a silent glance with Barton, and knew that their worst fears had been realised.

'She said it herself,' Barton told him, when Selena was out of earshot in the stable. 'They took one look at her van and roared with laughter. Oh, they'll pay for the damage, but only as a write-off. It won't buy her any replacements.'

'That settles it,' Leo said. 'It has to be Plan B.'

'I didn't know we even had a Plan A,' Barton said, startled.

'Plan A is the one that's just collapsed. Now, this is Plan B…'

He took Barton's arm and drew him well out of the way, so that all Selena heard from inside the stable, was Barton's roar of, *'Are you out of your mind?'*

CHAPTER FIVE

LEO not only meant to attend the rodeo in Stephenville, he was going to be a part of it. With what Barton called 'more nerve than common sense' he was determined to ride a bull.

'Just one bull,' he argued with Barton. 'What harm can it do?'

'Break your neck. That enough?'

They were at breakfast with the family, and since they were at opposite ends of the table the others began looking back and forth like spectators at a tennis match. Jack, who studied even at the table, took his nose out of his book long enough to begin scoring them.

'Barton I know what I'm doing,' Leo insisted.

'Fifteen love,' Jack intoned. 'Leo serving.'

'In a pig's ear you know what you're doing,' Barton retorted.

'Fifteen all.'

'It just takes practise.'

'Been doing that in Italy have you? First I knew they had bucking bulls out there. Does it say *Mama Mia!* as it throws you off?' Barton roared at his own joke.

'Fifteen thirty!'

'I just need to practise with your bucking machine.'

'And make it my fault? No way!'

'OK,' Leo sighed. 'I'll just have to enter without getting any practise, so when I break my neck, it *will* be your fault.'

'That's hitting below the belt,' Barton roared.

66

'Let him do it, Dad,' Carrie begged.

'You *want* him to get hurt? Thought you'd taken a shine to him.'

'Dad!' she hissed in an agony of embarrassment.

Selena had been enjoying the scene until then, but she pitied the girl, having her teenage crush exposed, and her misery compounded by a deep blush. Leo, she was sure, would pretend nothing had happened.

To her astonishment he did just the opposite.

'You see, I have a supporter,' he announced, pointing at Carrie. 'Carrie, you think I can do it, don't you?'

'Yes,' she said defiantly.

'And you don't think I'll break my neck?'

'I think you'll be great.'

'There you are, Barton. Listen to my friend over there. She knows what she's talking about.'

It was beautifully done, Selena had to admit that, watching Carrie's blush fade and her smile return. In a few seconds Leo had 'repackaged' her crush on him into a friendship he openly valued. It was clever, and it was kind.

Warmth and happiness pervaded her. She didn't know why Leo's kindness to someone else should give her that feeling. Yet it was like receiving a personal gift. The nicer he was than other men, the happier it made her.

Grumbling, Barton gave in, and after breakfast they all went out to his mechanical bull, an electrically driven machine, designed to be ridden, that bucked and tossed to give the rider some practise in hanging on for dear life. It had a range of speeds, starting with 'gentle' for beginners, and Barton, to Leo's disgust, insisted on setting it as low as possible.

With the whole family and Selena watching avidly

Leo sailed through the first test. Encouraged, he raised the stakes, and still managed to hang on.

'Isn't he wonderful?' Carrie whispered to Selena. 'You'd never know he hadn't done it before.'

'Yes, you would,' Selena said with a grin.

'Well, you know what I mean.'

'Yes, I know,' Selena murmured so quietly that Carrie didn't hear her.

Jack had joined them, another book in his hand.

'Wanna know Leo's chance of getting killed the first time he—?'

'*No!*' they both said firmly.

A scream from Billie made them turn their heads sharply in time to see Leo flying through the air, to land with a crash, and lie still.

Carrie buried her face in her hands. 'I can't look. Is he all right?'

'I don't know,' Selena said in a voice that didn't sound like her own. 'He isn't moving.'

She had the horrible feeling that time had stopped as she began to run to where Leo lay. As she reached him he let out a hideous whooping sound. Again and again he made the dreadful noise and she felt time begin again as she recognised the symptoms of a man who'd had the breath knocked out of his body.

She dropped down beside him just as he managed to half raise himself. Still unable to speak, he clutched hold of her while the hoots and gasps came from him without end. Selena held onto him, knowing there was nothing to do until he'd struggled back to some sort of normality.

When the fit had passed he seemed exhausted, leaning against her and heaving. But then he looked up at the others who'd crowded around him, and gave his irrepressible grin.

'I told you I could do it,' he said.

*   *   *

From then on they were in countdown to the rodeo. The town was filling up, Barton entertained a constant stream of buyers who looked over his excellent horses, nodded and reached for their wallets. Delia, a great entertainer, was in her element, giving parties and overseeing the stock of cowboy clothes and memorabilia for the stall she would set up.

There was a strict dress code. Riders must wear a western hat, long-sleeved shirt and cowboy boots. Leo, who had none of these things, went to town among Delia's stock, kitting himself out both for now and for Grosseto when he returned home.

'They're going to think you're so fine,' Carrie said, regarding him admiringly in his new stetson and decorated boots.

'Nothing like a new hat to make an impression,' Leo said cheerfully. 'Let's see one on you.'

He settled a stetson on Carrie's head, then one on Billie's and finally on Selena's, nodded with satisfaction and took out his credit card.

'Delia, I'll have those three as well.'

In this way he contrived to buy Selena a present without offending her. He'd spent a lot of time working out how to do that.

Sometimes they practised together. If he did nothing else in his life he was determined to ride that bull.

On the face of it, it was simple. To stay eight seconds on the back of a heaving, thrashing mountain of furious bull. And live. That was the target.

'Think you'll do it?' she asked him one evening as they limped stiffly home.

'Do *you* think I will?'

'Nope.'

'Me neither. I don't care. I'm just doing it for fun. I'm no threat to anyone trying to earn a living.'

She grinned. 'That's true.'

'OK, OK, no need to rub it in.'

Leo had graduated from the bucking machine to Old Jim, a real live bull. The problem was that Jim had mellowed with age. He liked people, and he took an immediate shine to Leo, which was pleasant in its way but made him useless for practical purposes. Leo could manage eight seconds on Old Jim's back, but so could Selena. So, for that matter, could Delia, Billie and Carrie. And Jack.

Selena practised fiercely, racing around the barrels on Jeepers, aiming to keep their time down to fourteen seconds, or even under.

'Is that the ''gold standard''?' Leo asked her.

'It is for here,' she said, indicating the barrels that Barton had set up. 'They're not the same in every rodeo. Sometimes they're further apart and that can be a seventeen-second circuit. But barrels at this distance should be fourteen seconds. Jeepers can do it. We're just not quite used to each other yet. I still make mistakes on him.'

As if to prove it she tried to take a corner too tightly and landed in the dust.

Leo, watching from a fence rail, started to race towards her, but she was up at once, leaping back into the saddle to try again, more carefully this time. Leo retreated.

'I thought you might have hurt yourself,' he said when she dismounted.

'Me?' she asked hilariously. 'With that little fall? I've

had worse. I've probably got worse to come in the future. It's no big deal.'

He sighed. 'Couldn't you be frail and vulnerable sometimes, like other women?'

She hooted with laughter. 'Leo, what planet have you been living on? Women aren't frail and vulnerable these days.' She slapped him on the shoulder and every bone in his bruised body seemed to clang.

What could you do with a woman like this? he wondered. You couldn't say consoling things like 'Let me make it better,' because she'd think you were nuts and probably step on your toe, by way of bringing you to your senses.

You could only wait and hope, certain that the sweet kernel was in there, however well hidden by the prickly skin, knowing that what happened would be in her own good time, or not at all.

'Let's go and rub ourselves down with liniment,' she said.

'I'll do you if you'll do me,' he said hopefully.

She chuckled and thumped him again.

Barton was in his study that evening, watching for their return, and at his signal Leo halted Selena with the words, 'Come back outside, there's something I want you to see.'

In the yard stood a Mini Motor Home, functional rather than luxurious, but a palace compared to what Selena had originally driven. Attached to it was a horse trailer, plain but of good design.

'They're yours,' Barton said. 'To replace the ones you lost.'

'The insurers came through?' she breathed.

'The fact is,' Barton said with a hint of awkwardness, 'I don't really want to go to my insurers about this. I haven't had a claim in years, and if I make one now—well it would be cheaper if I just replace what I wrecked.'

'But—I don't get that,' Selena said. 'The damage to your car—it can't be cheaper than—'

'You just leave that to me,' Barton interrupted. 'It's cheaper because—that's how it works out.'

'But Barton—'

'Women don't understand these things,' Barton said desperately.

'I understand—'

'No, you don't, you don't understand anything. I've gone into it and—I don't want any more argument. You take Jeepers, you take the vehicles, and we call it quits.'

'You're—giving me these?' Selena asked, dazed. 'But I can't accept. My things weren't nearly as good—'

'But they got you from place to place OK,' Barton said. 'Well, this will get you from place to place as well.'

'I—'

'It's no more than your right,' Barton finished with a hunted look. He was running out of inspiration.

'But Jeepers—'

'He likes you. He works well for you. And the trailer will take two horses, so when Elliot's recovered you can take them both.'

'That won't be long now,' Selena said firmly.

'Sure it won't. But until then, Jeepers will keep you going.'

Leo watched them in silence. One thing they all knew, although she wasn't ready to admit it. Elliot's rodeo days were over.

He left Selena looking over her new home, and pounced on Barton halfway to the house.

'I thought you were going to blow everything,' he muttered.

'Not my fault. She was bound to be suspicious. I had to improvise.'

'"Women don't understand these things,"' Leo scoffed. 'No man dares say that these days, not if he wants to live.'

Barton turned on him.

'All right, you do better. Try telling her the truth. Tell her you're paying for everything, and see how she takes it.'

'Sssshh!' Leo said frantically. 'She mustn't know that. She'd skin me alive.'

'Great! Then we know where we are. Now are you gonna stand here yakking all night, or are you coming in the house for a whisky?'

'I'm coming in the house for a whisky.'

Everyone was up early on the first day of the rodeo. Delia and her daughters loaded piles of new stock into the truck. Barton checked off a list of contacts he was planning to do business with in a convivial atmosphere. Jeepers was groomed until he shone, and led out into the horse trailer.

Instinct sent Leo into the stables in search of Selena. He found her, as he'd expected, in Elliot's stall, caressing the horse's nose, murmuring tenderly.

'This isn't for good, you've got to understand that. Jeepers is a fine horse, but he's not you. It'll never be with him like it was with you and me. We're going to be together again. That's a promise.'

She rested her cheek against his nose. 'I love you, you ramshackle old brute. More than anyone in the world. Do you hear that?'

Leo tried to back out quietly, but he didn't quite manage it, and Selena looked up.

'Now who's being sentimental?' he asked kindly.

'I am not. I'm just thinking of his feelings. Have you thought what it must be like for him to see another horse being groomed and led out for me to ride, in his place? Do you think he doesn't know?'

'I guess he knows everything you're thinking.'

'And I know everything he's thinking.'

'Well, what are you going to tell him if you win?'

She whirled on him, an almost painful intensity in her face. 'Leo, do you think I might win?'

'Does it really mean that much?' he asked, studying her face as though hoping to find something there.

'It means everything. I have to make some money to keep going onto the next rodeo, and the next. It's my whole life, *everything*.'

'Well, if you don't I could always—' he stopped because her fingertips were over his mouth.

'Don't say it. I don't take charity and I won't take money from you.'

He maintained a diplomatic silence. This was no time to tell her how much he'd already given her.

'After all, why should you take financial risks for me?' she went on. 'Suppose I couldn't pay it back? Where would you be?'

'Selena, I'm not at my last gasp, like you. What's wrong with letting a friend help you? There's no law that says you have to be independent all the time.'

'Yes there is. I passed one. It's my law, the one I live by, and I can't change. I do it myself or no deal.'

'Selena, it's not weakness to accept help.'

'No, but it's weakness to rely on it. You become weak

by believing that someone'll always be there for you. Because sooner or later, they won't.'

He frowned. 'If you really believe that, heaven help you!'

'Leo, why are we quarrelling? It's a wonderful day. We're going to have a great time, and I'm going to win. I can't lose.'

He regarded her with his head on one side. 'Why can't you lose?'

'Because I got my miracle. You know when we met on the highway?'

'Met isn't quite the word I'd have used, but go on.'

'Before that I'd been with Ben, he's an old friend and he was fixing my van. He said I needed a miracle or a millionaire, but I said forget millionaires. They're not good for anything.'

'So you settled for a miracle?' Leo asked, feeling the beginnings of a smile somewhere inside him.

'Right. I said I just knew my miracle was on its way to me.'

The smile grew bigger. 'And it was?'

'You know it was. All the time Barton was on the highway, and we were fated to meet.'

The smile faded. 'Barton?'

'Well, wasn't it a miracle that he turned out to be a good man with a conscience, who didn't duck his obligations, as a lot of them would have?'

'But a millionaire, don't forget,' Leo quibbled.

'Ah, well, there must be one or two good ones. The point is, he was nice about it, which just proves what a decent man he is.'

'Right,' Leo said in a hollow voice.

'So I got my miracle. And now I'm going to win.'

'So am I. All right, stop laughing.' Selena had doubled

up. 'I can do eight seconds on Old Jim, you saw me yesterday.'

'Sure, and I've also seen him accepting tidbits from your hand. Old Jim is a pussy cat. You won't be riding him in the ring.' She got out of range and added wickedly, 'You won't be riding anything for very long.'

'Now there's a thing. I thought we were friends, and you hurt my feelings like that.'

At once she came back into range, putting her hands on either side of his head, full of contrition.

'Leo, I'm so sorry. I didn't mean to hurt you after you've been good to me. It was just a joke—'

'Hell, I knew that.'

'Are you sure? I can be a bitch sometimes. I don't mean to be, but that doesn't stop me.'

Leo, who knew a thing or two about doing things he hadn't meant to do ten seconds earlier, nodded in perfect understanding.

'Say you're not really hurt,' she pleaded. 'You're my best friend and if you get mad at me, I'd really hate it.'

Leo let his arms slip around her waist. His feelings weren't hurt at all, but he managed to regard her sadly, while silencing his conscience. He couldn't be blamed for making the most of this, could he?

'I'm not mad,' he said bravely.

'You're not hurt either, are you?' she demanded, reading him without trouble. But she didn't move her hands, except to slide them behind his neck. Nor did she resist when he drew her closer.

'Stricken to the heart, I promise,' he said.

She didn't answer, but stood there gazing into his face, while mischief danced over her face, her eyes, her smiling lips.

'Selena,' he said unsteadily, 'you are putting me under a lot of strain here.'

'You think I ought to do something about that?'

'Yes, I really do.'

She tilted her head in a way that made his heart do somersaults.

'Well, I got tired of waiting for you to do something about it,' she said as she laid her lips on his.

They were just as he'd imagined them, sweet and enticing, yet with a hint of something underneath that wasn't sweet at all: spicy, challenging, hot as a pepper. Not an *ingénue*, but a woman of determination, ready to take him on.

Selena's head was whirling. She hadn't meant to do this, but there was something she needed to know, and suddenly her impatience had become too much to bear. Laying her mouth against his was an act of exploration and defiance in equal measure.

She knew at once that she would have done better to wait. No woman, with a busy day ahead, could afford this kind of distraction. And she had only herself to blame because she'd always known that this man would take all of a woman's attention. Some pleasures weren't to be skimped.

He seemed to feel the same because he slid his arms about her with a gentleness that didn't disguise their power. She wanted to know all about that power. She could feel it in his lips, testing hers cautiously to divine her true meaning, then seeming to think he understood and coming on strongly in a way that excited her.

She mustn't do this, she thought dizzily. Her timing was dreadful.

'Leo—'

'Yes—'

From outside came Barton's bellow. 'Anyone in there? We're ready to go.'

Leo released her, groaning. 'I like Barton, but—'

Selena came back to earth and the realisation that she'd nearly thrown everything away for this man. With a great effort she pulled herself together, saying urgently, 'No, he's right. We have to stop this.'

'We do?'

'It—it wastes vital energy.' She could feel her vital energy being sapped just by being this close to him.

'I didn't think it was a waste.'

'There'll be time later. For now we've got to psych ourselves up for the big day. Shoulders back, head up. Believe in yourself.'

'I find it easier to believe in you. You're going to win. You've got Jeepers down to fourteen seconds, which I never thought you'd do.'

She danced with excitement. 'I knew he could do it, he is such a fantastic horse, so fast and strong—'

'Careful! You said that in front of Elliot! You could give him a complex.'

'Oh—*you*!'

She thumped him, he put his arm about her shoulders and they went out, laughing, together.

CHAPTER SIX

REACHING the rodeo site was like entering a village. There was the arena where the events took place, the area where the horses were delivered and kept until ready, and the shopping mall where Delia and dozens of others set out their stalls.

Leo had driven to the arena with Selena and together they delivered Jeepers to his stall. When he was settled they headed for Delia's stall and Leo promptly embarked on another spending spree.

'Who are they for?' Selena asked as he paid for a pair of extremely glamorous and impractical spurs.

'My cousin Marco.' Leo grinned. 'Never sat on a horse in his life. They'll really annoy him.'

'You're wicked in your own way, y'know that?'

'Proud of it. Now this—' he held up a figure of a cowboy on horseback made of painted stone. It was exquisite, full of life. 'This is for my brother Guido,' he said. 'He sells souvenirs in Venice. This'll show him how it's done.'

'What kind of souvenirs?'

'Venetian masks mostly. And gondola lamps. They go on top of television sets. Some of them play ''O sole mio'' when you switch them on.'

'You're kidding me!'

'Nope.'

'Well, you shouldn't be hard on a man trying to earn a living.'

'He—certainly—does very well out of souvenirs,' Leo

79

said cautiously. 'Perhaps it's time we were going. They'll be starting soon.'

Leo had arranged to do his bull riding on the first day, in order to 'get the disaster over fast,' Selena had cheekily observed.

As he'd expected, there was a great deal of difference between Old Jim and the huge, furious animal he encountered now. Nothing in the previous few days with the machine had prepared him for it. It felt as though the bull had personally decided to smash him to fragments as a punishment for his impertinence in even trying.

And he must try to endure this for eight seconds, he thought fuzzily as his brain was bounced around in his skull.

But it was a considerate bull.

It had him off him in three.

He landed hard but he survived. By that time he was getting good at falling off, having had so much practise.

As he limped out of the ring he heard the kindly applause of the crowd, a tribute to his guts at doing something he was so hopelessly bad at, and saw the Hanworths clapping for him with the warmth of friends. All except Paulie whose sneer of pleasure was unmistakable.

But Selena wasn't sneering. Her eyes were bright with pleasure that he'd made the attempt, and her smile was a promise and a reminder. Leo grinned back at her, happy and content. Paulie could go stuff himself up a drainpipe!

Behind her smile Selena felt wrung out. When Leo had gone flying over the bull's head she'd ground her nails into her palm until he picked himself up. He hadn't broken his neck. He was alive. The world could start again.

She chided herself for making a fuss about nothing. How many men had she seen thrown? But none of them had been Leo.

She slipped away to get ready. Jeepers was there, calmly waiting for her. They'd done well together in the practise ring, but this was different. This was opening night. She adjusted her stetson, making sure it was firmly fixed on. Losing a hat could cost valuable points. Not as many as knocking over a barrel, but enough to do damage.

There were five riders going before her, and they all did well.

'All right,' she told Jeepers. 'The trick is not to let them scare you. You're—*we're* as good as they are. C'mon boy! Let's show 'em.'

As the bell rang she went flying over the starting line heading for the first barrel inside the triangle, a sharp turn, but not too sharp, allowing Jeepers space to move. They were around, then on to the next, neat turn, on to the last, then over the finishing line to cheers as the clock showed her in the lead.

Leo was waiting for her just out of the ring and together they watched the next rider.

'She's not a patch on you,' he said loyally. 'None of them are.'

'The next one's good though. Jan Dennem. I've raced against her a lot and she's always been just ahead of me.'

'This time you'll beat her,' he said confidently.

They held their breaths while fourteen interminable seconds ticked away and Jan swept across the line one-tenth of a second outside Selena's time.

'*Yeeee-eeess!*' they roared from the sanctuary of each other's arms.

Next competitor. Very fast. A real threat. Ahead of Selena by half a second as she approached the final barrel, but then—

A roar went up from the crowd as the barrel was knocked over.

The next two were slower. No question. Selena was still ahead.

'One more,' she said. 'I can't bear it. Leo?'

When he didn't answer she looked and found him standing with the fingers of both hands crossed, his eyes closed, his lips moving.

'Just praying,' he said when he'd opened his eyes. 'You never know.'

She gave a shaky laugh. 'Does God follow the rodeo?'

'Never misses.'

There was a cheer as the last competitor came flying out into the ring.

'I can't look,' Selena said, and buried her face against Leo's chest. At once he put his arms about her. 'What's happening?'

'First barrel, she's fast but you're all right, second barrel—now the third—'

The crowd's cheers became deafening. Leo groaned as he tightened his arms and rested his head on hers.

'Oh, no!' she cried. 'No, no, no!'

'By a tenth of a second,' Leo said. 'I'm sorry *carissima*.'

She raised her head. 'What did you call me?'

'*Carissima*. It's Italian.'

'Yes, but what does it mean?'

'Well—'

But while he wondered whether to risk telling her that

the word meant 'Darling' they heard a bellow from Barton, congratulating and commiserating with her both together.

The moment passed, and Leo was left reflecting that he who hesitated was lost. Or if not actually lost, then forced to wait for another chance.

It was a cheerful party that drove home that night. Delia had done excellent business, Selena had picked up some prize money for coming second, and Leo had stayed on the bull for a whole three seconds. That was cause for rejoicing, so they did, far into the night.

Despite her defeat Selena was happy. The money for second had been better than usual. Leo found her sitting on the porch, contemplating it blissfully.

'I'm rich, I'm rich!'

'A hundred dollars is rich?' he asked quizzically.

'It's a king's ransom. Well, OK, maybe a very minor king. Who wants to ransom a king anyway? Do away with the lot!'

She was drunk with her little bit of success, laughing as she talked, going wildly, joyfully over the top.

'So much for royalty,' Leo observed. 'Obviously you don't believe in them.'

'Who needs 'em? Or guys with handles.'

'You mean titles?' he asked, sensing the conversation taking a dangerous turn. 'Down with the wicked aristocrats? Ouch!' He rubbed his shoulder.

'What's the matter?' she asked quickly. 'You got a neck pain, shoulder pain?'

'More of a whole body pain,' he said ruefully. 'But perhaps the neck more than the rest.'

'Here, let me have a go,' she said, getting behind him and rubbing his neck. 'This is no good. Your collar's in the way. Take your shirt off.'

She helped him off with it, then got to work on his neck, his shoulders, his spine, with deft, skilful fingers.

'Thanks,' he said gratefully. 'Hey, you're good at this.'

'I do it a lot.'

'You do this for all the guys? Aren't there medical people whose job it is?'

'Sure, but if you can't afford them you do it for each other.'

He considered this, not liking the implications. But her fingers were spreading welcome warmth and ease, and he settled for counting his blessings.

'You've got them in Italy, haven't you?' she asked.

'What?'

'Aristocrats. Careful, don't jump like that or I might hurt you.'

'Did I? Didn't mean to.' The word aristocrats had caught him by surprise.

'Italy is a republic—but we've still got one or two of them,' he said cautiously.

'Ever actually met them, I mean talked to them, face to face?'

'They're not a species of reptile, Selena.'

'That's just what they are. They should be in a cage in a zoo.'

'But you know nothing about them.'

'Well, do you?'

'I know that some of them aren't so bad.'

'Why are you defending them? You should be on my side—down the aristos, up the workers.'

'So you'd like to send them all to the guillotine?'

She shook her head. 'No, I'd make them get their hands dirty in the fields, with the workers, like us.'

'You don't know I'm a worker,' he said. 'Who knows what I do when I'm back in Italy?'

She left what she was doing and took one of his hands in hers. It was large and roughened.

'Of course I know,' she said. 'This is a worker's hand. It's been battered and hurt a few times. It's got scars.'

It was all true, but the fields were his own and they brought him a fortune larger than Barton's. His innocent deception lay heavy on him, and suddenly he couldn't bear it.

'Selena—'

She didn't seem to hear him. She was turning his hand over, holding it gently. Then she looked up and her gaze shocked him with its innocent candour. There was a glow in her eyes that seemed to dazzle him, and he looked quickly away.

'What is it?' she asked quietly, laying down his hand.

'Nothing, I—' He gave her a bright, forced smile, and spoke hurriedly. 'I'm just aching all over. Tomorrow I'll see a bone-setter. Well, now, I reckon it's time to turn in. You too. You've had a long, hard day.'

'Yes, I have,' she murmured bleakly. 'Very hard.'

The last night of the rodeo was to be marked by one of the barbecues that Barton gave at the drop of a hat. There was no hospitality like that to be found at the Four-Ten, and as they drove back they were followed by a procession of vehicles.

Leo knew a curious sense of dissatisfaction. He would be leaving next day, but he wasn't ready for that. Something had started here but not finished, and he couldn't make things happen because he didn't know enough about his own feelings.

Selena tugged at his heart as no other woman had ever

done, but there were chasms between them, chasms of lifestyle, country, language. They didn't even believe in the same kind of future. Only the most overwhelming love could overcome such problems. And how could he hope for such love from a woman who seemed not to believe in it?

The thought of saying goodbye hurt badly. He'd hoped she minded as much, but she made it impossible to tell. And perhaps that was his answer.

They'd seen little of each other since the night she'd rubbed his back and he'd nearly been overwhelmed by his longing for her, and his conscience-stricken awareness that he was treading a fine line.

The next day he'd been to a chiropractor, who pulled and pushed him, told him not to be such a darned fool another time, and left him a hundred dollars poorer. He'd still ached afterward, although whether it was from the fall or the treatment he couldn't say, but he felt a good deal better now.

He dressed quickly for the evening. From down below came the sounds of music and laughter and he looked out on the pleasant scene. Sweet-smelling smoke came from the barbecue, lights were strung between the trees and the music seemed to beckon him.

Selena was already there. He could see her in the centre of a small crowd, and guessed she'd done herself some good with her fizzing performances. Her future would be brighter now, and the help he'd given her would bear fruit, even if she didn't know it; even if she forgot about him completely and never gave him another thought for the rest of her days.

On that gloomy reflection he went down to join the party.

There was plenty to distract him, great food, fine

whisky, smiling ladies. But suddenly his appetite had gone and he didn't want to drink. He followed her jealously with his eyes, dancing when he had to, but always trying to keep her in view.

Barton, good host that he was, made much of his guests, calling for toasts and rounds of applause. Leo joined in the applause for Selena and raised his glass to her. She raised hers back.

As everyone broke into another boisterous dance he made his way through the crowd to her and saw that her eyes were shining.

'I feel so good,' she said happily. 'Oh, Leo, if you only knew how good I feel!'

'That's great,' he said tenderly. 'That's how I always want you to feel.'

'I've just been interviewed by the local paper about my "successes"—both of them.'

After being narrowly beaten in the first barrel race, she'd won on the following day, and achieved another second on the day after. On the final day there had been a big event for the best ten competitors from the previous races. And she'd stormed to victory.

'Do you know how much money I've got now?' she asked in wonder.

'Yes, I do. You told me. And take care of it.'

'It's more than I've ever had before at one time.'

'What are you going to do with it?'

'Enter more events. This could see me through my next six months.'

'And then?'

'By then I should have enough for the next year. I'm on my way.'

Which didn't sound much as if she was planning to pine for him.

He chinked glasses with her, then walked away to sweep Carrie into the mêlée. They danced until they were both breathless and laughing, then went into the waltz together.

'Did you manage it?' Carrie asked.

'It?'

'Selena. Is she as nuts about you as you are about her?' Since the day Leo had appealed to her in the discussion about bull riding she'd settled into the role of the understanding sister.

'She sure isn't nuts about me.'

'But you are about her.'

'Carrie, please!'

'OK. Only I think I saw her looking for you, and I was planning to melt tactfully away, but if—'

'You're a darling.'

He kissed her cheek and turned to find Selena eyeing him with a curious little smile on her lips.

'You haven't danced with me yet,' she said.

Carrie melted, as promised, only taking a quick look back to see Leo and Selena go into each other's arms like two halves of a whole.

They danced in silence for a while, each thinking that by this time tomorrow they would have gone their separate ways.

Selena was full of confusion. She'd said goodbyes before, but never like this. She tried to be practical. All she had to do was hold out until he'd gone, and then forget him. It should be easy forgetting a man half a world away. But her heart was telling her that he would never be far away from her again, because she would carry him with her every moment, for the rest of her life.

The music changed. Suddenly a lone violin was playing a melancholy strain of longing and farewell. She would never see him again. She held him close and her heart ached.

With her eyes closed, she didn't see where he was taking her. She only knew that they were dancing, circling, circling, while the sounds faded. She danced on in a dream where there was only herself and him, circling around and around.

'Selena…'

His voice whispering her name made her open her eyes to find his face close to hers.

'Selena,' he said again, his breath brushing her face, and her murmured, 'Yes,' was so swift that their breath intermingled.

Then his mouth was on hers, and he was kissing her with a fierceness born out of desperation. She was slipping through his fingers, and holding her was like trying to hold onto quicksilver.

She answered him with the same fierceness. From the moment they'd met something had been bound to happen between them, and it had taken too long. Now she wouldn't let it go. She would have her hour, whatever it cost, and live in its glory all her days.

Her life had taught her little about love and tenderness. What she knew she'd discovered for herself. Something was happening inside her now that was totally new. She hadn't known before that just being in a man's arms could make her ache with joy and sadness together, so that she didn't know which one was the greater. Nor did it matter. She was alive to feelings and sensations that she would never regret, no matter how much pain they might cost her. And there would be pain. Life had taught her that much.

She'd kissed other men, but none like this. He was a man whom, she guessed, had lived a full life with women, yet his touch had a curious innocence about it, as though he too was experiencing something for the first time. Through the driving urgency she could still feel the tenderness, as though caring for her mattered more to him than any other satisfaction.

Yet he wanted her to the point where it was driving him crazy. She could sense that through the trembling of his great, powerful body, the rise and fall of his chest. It excited her to know that she affected him so much. She wanted him as much in thrall to her as she was to him, and she teased him with her lips, urging him on to the point where they would meet.

It was he who ended the kiss, seizing her shoulders and pushing her back a few inches, so that he could look into her face. His own was wild.

'We picked one heckuva time,' he gasped. 'Maybe we should—'

'Maybe we should what? Be sensible? Who wants to be sensible?'

'Well I sure don't, but you—Selena, tomorrow—' He stopped. The words of cool wisdom hung in the air and died unspoken.

'Yes,' she whispered. 'Yes—'

From somewhere in the background a sound was growing closer. Cheering, laughing, singing, cheerful guests in the last yell of enjoyment before the party began to break up. Leo looked desperately to where light and noise were streaming towards him, engulfing him.

'Hey, look who's hiding himself under the trees!'

'Who is she, Leo?'

He laughed loudly, trying to brush it off. Someone pressed a drink on him and he took it. Everyone was kissing everyone.

When he looked around for Selena she had gone.

* * *

It seemed an age before the goodnights were said, but at last the place was quiet and Leo could draw a long breath. Perhaps they could still have a moment alone together, and answer some of the questions that had been raised under the trees.

But there was no sign of Selena. So many promises in her kiss, and she'd just left him.

He made his way up to bed, frowning, trying to see a way through the confusion. Hell would freeze over before he would go knocking on her door. The next move had to be hers.

So he told himself. But he still went to her door and knocked softly. It was that or spend the rest of his life wondering. Getting no reply he knocked a little louder, and waited. Still no reply.

He went to his own room. At the window he looked out on the dark landscape, knowing it had been foolish to indulge in dreams when he was leaving tomorrow. Whatever happened now was too late. He stood there, telling himself it was best to be sensible, and trying to believe it.

He didn't know what made him aware that he wasn't alone in the room. It wasn't even as definite as the sound of breathing, but something changed in the atmosphere, and when he stretched out his hand to the lamp a voice in the darkness whispered, 'Don't put on the light.'

'Where are you?' he said.

She didn't answer, but the next moment two soft arms were around his neck, and a slim, naked body was pressed against his.

'You were here all the time?' he asked. 'I just got back from—'

'I know, I heard you.' Her chuckle delighted him.

He'd remembered her from the first day as a gazelle, a nymph, so delicately built was she. Now in the darkness his hands discovered what his eyes had known, and found the beauty he'd dreamed of since that moment.

Her fingers were working on his shirt, opening the buttons, finding his chest, the slight rise and fall of his muscles, sliding her palms over them.

'If you don't mean to follow through, you're doing something very dangerous,' Leo groaned.

'I never start what I don't mean to finish,' she murmured so that her breath fanned his face.

She was easing his shirt down his arms as she spoke, inch by inch until he couldn't stand it any more and wrenched it off. Then he could pull her against him, revelling in the feel of her soft skin against his own. He closed his eyes, wondering how anything could feel so good and still leave him standing.

He stripped off the rest of his clothes as fast as he could. This had been too long in coming to waste any time. Holding onto each other they made their way to the bed and collapsed on it so that he fell on his back with her on top of him.

'Remember when we were like this before?' she asked.

'The first day—I got you out of the bath—how can I forget?'

'We didn't end up like this though.'

'We would have done if I'd had anything to do with it,' he growled.

'Me too.'

'As soon as that?'

'As soon as that.'

She was laughing like a siren who'd finally enticed

her prey into her circle, and that was fine by him. He'd happily be the prey, or anything, as long it led to this.

His hands were all over her, enjoying her lithe strength, her fluid movements, and what she was doing to him.

'I thought you were stiff and bruised,' she teased.

'My energy's coming back by the minute.'

She began covering him with kisses. She seemed to know him already, understanding by instinct the little caresses that drove him wild. When Leo slowly sat up, holding her in his lap, her fingers immediately found the place on the back of his neck where the lightest touch could reduce him to shivers. From there it was just a matter of time before she discovered how vulnerable his spine was as well.

'Witch,' he growled.

'Hmm!'

Suddenly he could stand it no longer. With a deep laugh he rolled over, tossing her onto her back with him on top of her.

'I've been thinking about this until I nearly went crazy,' he groaned.

Her whisper went through him like electricity. 'Why did we waste so much time?'

'Who cares?' he said. 'As long as we don't waste any more.'

He kissed her everywhere, celebrating her breasts, her tiny waist, her long, slim legs. She was quickly ready for him, telling him wordlessly of her eagerness, and when he entered her she gave a sigh of fulfilment.

His loving was like himself, robust and full-hearted, short on subtlety but long on warmth and generosity, giving more than he took. His slow movements increased her pleasure, driving it forward, harder, more intense, beautiful, ecstatic. He had the control to hold back, giving her every last moment before letting himself go.

And then it was like nothing in the world had ever been or ever would be again. Just for a few moments. Not long enough. She wanted so much more, and she would never stop wanting him. She knew, even as she felt her heartbeat slow to contentment, that he could start it racing again with a word.

They shared a glance, eyes gleaming in the dark, and suddenly they clutched each other, not in passion this time but in joyous mirth. For it was the biggest and most exhilarating joke in the whole world. Arms about each other's necks, they roared with laughter, knowing the joke was on them.

And then it wasn't funny any more, but only beautiful and fulfilling, and they were no longer themselves, but something entirely different called 'us'.

And tomorrow they were saying goodbye.

She'd known that Leo was a dangerously lovable man, but she was never more sure of it than when sex was over and he turned towards her, enfolding her in his arms and resting his face against her warm flesh, as though he needed more from her than physical pleasure.

That was a real dirty trick, she thought. How was a girl supposed to keep her independence of spirit with a man who behaved like that?

But when she was quite sure he was asleep she put her own arms around him, as far as she could, and stroked his hair, and kissed him again and again in a passion of tenderness and farewell.

CHAPTER SEVEN

The worst thing about airports was having to arrive early, so that the goodbyes stretched out painfully. It was worse, Selena thought, if you were waiting for the other person to say something and you weren't sure what. And whatever it was, he didn't say it.

She drove him to Dallas Airport. They checked the time of the Atlanta flight, sent his luggage on its way, and found a coffee bar. But suddenly Leo jumped up and said, 'Come with me.'

'Where are we going?' she asked as he grasped her hand and hurried her away.

'I want to buy you a present before I go, and I've just realised what it should be.'

He led her to a shop that sold mobile phones. 'Anyone who moves around as much as you needs one of these,' he said.

'Couldn't afford it before.' She was briefly happy at this sign that he wanted to keep in touch. But no happiness could survive the reflection that he was going away, and she might never see him again.

They chose the phone together, and he bought the first thirty hours. She scribbled the number on a small piece of paper and watched as he tucked it away in his wallet.

'Time I was going through Passport Control.'

'Not just yet,' she said quickly. 'We've got time for another coffee.'

She had a terrifying feeling that everything was rushing to the edge of a precipice. She was the only one who could stop it, but she didn't know how. She couldn't manage the words, had never spoken them, barely knew them.

She'd done all she could to show him how she felt the night before. Now her heart was breaking, and she could only wonder that he seemed oblivious.

She spent the last few minutes drinking in the sight of him, trying to remember every line, every intonation of his voice.

He was going away. He would forget her.

She had never smiled so brightly.

'Will passengers—?'

'I guess that's it,' Leo said, getting to his feet.

She came with him almost to the gate. He stopped and touched her face gently.

'I wouldn't have missed this for the world,' he said.

'Oh, yeah?' she said lightly, and aimed a punch at his arm. 'You'll forget me as soon as the hostess flutters her eyelashes at you.'

But he didn't smile back. 'I'll never forget you, Selena.'

His face seemed to constrict and she thought for a moment that he would say something more. She waited, her heart beating with wild hope, but he only leaned down and kissed her cheek.

'Don't you forget me,' he said.

'Better call that number and make sure I don't.'

'I'll do that.'

He kissed her again before walking off. Try as she might she couldn't find in those kisses any echo of the night before when he'd kissed her in a very different way. Then he'd been a man thinking only of a woman, absorbed only in her, giving and receiving pleasure, and not only pleasure: tenderness and affection. Now he was a man who wanted to go home.

At the gate he turned and waved to her. She waved back, keeping a smile on her face by sheer force of will.

Then he was gone.

She didn't leave at once, as she'd meant to. Instead she waited by the window until the flight took off, and watched until the sky swallowed it up.

Then she walked back to the parking lot and got behind the wheel, talking to herself like a Dutch uncle.

What the heck! They were ships that passed in the night, and they'd passed. That was all. Ahead of her stretched a brighter future than she'd ever known. That was what she should be thinking of.

She slammed her hand down on the wheel. She'd never told herself pretty lies before.

But now she needed a comforting lie to get her over this moment.

'I should have said something,' she raged. 'Said anything, so he'd know. Then he might even have asked me to go with him. Oh, who am I fooling? He could have asked me to go, but he never thought of it. He won't call. That phone was a goodbye present. Stop being a fool Selena. You can't cry in a parking lot.'

The Atlanta/Pisa flight seemed to go on for ever, into not just another day, but another dimension, another world. Leo tried to sleep but couldn't. He left the aircraft, dazed with weariness and yawned his way through Passport Control and customs. It felt strange to be back in his own country.

He headed for the taxi rank, so absorbed in calculating how long it would take him to get home that he had no attention for the sounds of someone behind him. He didn't see what hit him, or how many of them there were, although witnesses later attested to four. He only knew that suddenly he was on the ground, being swarmed over by strangers.

Shouts, the sound of running. He sat up, feeling his head, wondering why there were so many policemen around. Hands helped him stagger to his feet.

'What happened?' he demanded.

'You were robbed, *signore*.'

He groaned and felt for the place where his wallet should have been. It was empty. His head was aching too much for him to think any further than this. Somebody called an ambulance and he was taken to the local hospital.

He awoke next morning to find a policeman by his bed, holding the missing wallet.

'We found it in an alley,' he said.

As expected, the wallet was empty. Money, credit cards were all gone. But what really appalled Leo was the fact that the slip of paper with Selena's number had also vanished.

Renzo, his overseer, collected him from the hospital and drove him the fifty miles home to Bella Podena. As soon as he found himself among the rolling hills of Tuscany Leo began to relax. Whatever the surface turmoil of his life, his instincts were telling him that what really mattered was to be home, where his vines grew and his fields of wheat lay under a benevolent sun.

He was popular with his employees because he paid them generously, trusted them and let them get on with their jobs. For the last lap of the journey they waved and yelled to him, glad to see him back.

The Calvani lands were extensive. For the last few

miles he was looking at his own fields, and even his own village. Morenza, a tiny community of medieval buildings, stood on Calvani land, at the foot of the incline that led up to Leo's house. Its high street curved around the church, and a small duck pond, before leading out of the village and up through vines planted on the slope to catch the sun.

There at the top was the farmhouse, also medieval, made of stone, with a magnificent view down the valley. He entered it with a sigh of satisfaction, dropping his bags onto the floor and looking around him at the familiar things he loved.

There was Gina, with his favourite dish, already prepared and ready to serve. His favourite wine was at exactly the right temperature. His favourite dogs swarmed around his feet.

He ate a huge meal, kissed Gina on the cheek in thanks, and went to the room he used as a study, and from which he ran his estate. A couple of hours with Enrico, the assistant who supervised the paperwork during his absence, showed him that Enrico could manage this side of things perfectly well without him. He asked no more. The next day he would go over the land with men as close to the earth as himself.

He spent the next couple of hours on the telephone to his family, catching up on the news. Finally he went out and stood with a glass of wine, gazing down to the village, where the lights were coming on. He stood for a long time, listening to the breeze in the trees and the sound of bells echoing across the valley, and thought that he had never known such peace and beauty. And yet…

It was the perfect homecoming to the perfect place.

But suddenly he felt alone as he had never done in his life before.

He went to bed and tried to sleep, but it was useless, and he got up and went downstairs to the study. In Texas it was early morning. It was Barton who answered.

'Selena isn't still there by any chance?' he asked hopefully.

'No, she left straight after you did. Just drove back here, collected Jeepers, and headed off. Didn't she do great? Jeepers was just the horse she needed. She's going to be a star with that animal.'

'Great. Great.' Leo tried to sound cheerful, but for a reason he didn't want to explore he wasn't pleased to hear of her success a world away. 'Has she called you at all?'

'Called yesterday to ask after Elliot. I told her he was doing fine.'

'Did she ask after me?' He'd promised himself not to ask that, but it came out anyway.

'No, she never mentioned you. But I'm sure if you called her—'

Why the devil should I call her if she doesn't care enough about me to ask? he thought.

'Barton, I can't call her. I got mugged and lost the paper with her mobile phone number. Can you let me have it?'

'I would if I had it myself. I wouldn't know how to contact her.'

'Next time she calls, will you explain and get her to call me?'

'Sure thing.'

'Did she tell you where she was going?'

'Reno—I think.'

'I'll leave a message for her there.'

He tried to concentrate on his coming visit to Venice, for the wedding of his younger half-brother, Guido, to his English fiancée, Dulcie. There would be another wedding the day before, when his uncle, Count Francesco Calvani, would marry Liza, his one-time housekeeper and the love of his life. That ceremony would be small and private.

He'd been looking forward to a cheerful family occasion, but now, suddenly, he didn't have the heart for weddings.

Where was she? Why didn't she contact him? Had she forgotten their night together so easily?

He sent emails to the rodeo web site at Reno, detailing his movements over the coming days, giving the phone number of his uncle's home in Venice and his own mobile. For good measure he reminded her of his home number.

To the last minute he clung to the hope that she would telephone him. But the phone remained silent, and at last he left for Venice.

Leo had never been a man to brood. It was rare for a woman to pass out of his life against his will, but if it happened he'd always been positive. The world was full of laughing ladies, as easygoing as himself, with whom he could pass the time. Suddenly, that thought brought him no cheer.

He took the train from Florence to Venice, where there was a family motor boat waiting to convey him to the Palazzo Calvani on the Grand Canal. He arrived to find the family at supper. He kissed Liza, then his uncle, then Dulcie, Harriet, and Lucia, Marco's mother. Guido was there too, and his cousin Marco. When he'd thumped them and been thumped back, the greetings were complete.

As he ate he tried to seem his normal self, and maybe he fooled his male relatives. But the women had sharper eyes, and when the meal was over Dulcie and Harriet corralled him onto the sofa like a pair of eager sheep dogs herding a lion, and settled one each side of him.

'You've found her at last,' Harriet said.

'Her?' he asked uneasily.

'You know what I mean. *Her*! The one. She's got you roped and tied.'

'What's her name?' Dulcie demanded.

He gave up stalling. He wasn't kidding them. 'She's called Selena,' he admitted. I met her in Texas. We were both in the rodeo.' He fell silent.

'And?' they asked eagerly. *'And?'*

'She fell off. So did I.'

'So you had something in common,' Dulcie said, nodding.

'A marriage of true minds,' Harriet agreed.

'I shouldn't think minds had much to do with it,' Dulcie suggested.

'Nothing at all,' Leo said, remembering Selena's sweetness, the tensile strength in her slim body, like spun steel, yet feeling so delicate in his hands. For a moment her hot breath seemed to whisper against his skin, inciting him to ever greater passion and tenderness.

'It was wonderful,' he said abruptly.

'You should have brought her here to meet us,' Harriet told him.

'That's just the trouble, I don't know where to find her.'

'But didn't you exchange names and addresses?' Dulcie asked.

'She doesn't have an address. She drives around the rodeos and lives wherever she is. I had her mobile phone number, but—well, if you must know someone stole my wallet, with the paper. I've tried to track her down over the internet, but for some reason I always seem to miss her. I might never see her again.'

The two young women made sympathetic noises, but Leo suspected they secretly found it rather funny. Perhaps it was. Leo Calvani, stallion and free spirit, off his feed because one young woman, with a prickly temper and no figure to speak of, had vanished. Hilarious.

After a while he joined the other men, but even their company couldn't soothe him. Two blissful bridegrooms and a fiancé weren't what he needed in his present disconsolate mood.

Gradually the party broke up. Guido and Dulcie disappeared together to enjoy the sweet nothings of a soon-to-be married couple. Marco and Harriet went off to stroll the streets of Venice. Leo went out into the garden, where he found his Aunt Lucia sitting peacefully, gazing up at the stars.

'I suppose Marco and Harriet will be setting the date at any moment,' Leo said, sitting down with her.

'I do hope so,' Lucia said eagerly. 'I know they've gone off together now, so maybe they'll come back with it all settled.'

'You're very keen on this marriage, aren't you?' he asked curiously. 'Even though—well, it's not exactly a love match, is it?'

'You mean I arranged it? Yes, I did, I don't deny it.'

'Wouldn't it have been safer to let him pick his own bride?'

'I'm afraid I'd have waited for ever for that. Marco

must have somebody, or he'll end his days alone, and that would be terrible.'

'There are worse things than being alone, Aunt.'

'No, my dear boy, there aren't.'

He couldn't answer. For the first time in his life he felt it was true.

'I think you're just discovering that, aren't you?' she urged gently.

He shrugged. 'It's just a mood. I was away too long. Now I'm back there's a mountain of work to do....' His voice ran down.

'What is she like?'

He told his story again, this time taking longer to describe Selena. For once the words came easily to him and he managed to speak of the sweetness beneath the thorny shell, the way he'd discovered it slowly, and how it had captivated him.

'You love her very much, don't you?' Lucia said.

'No, I don't think I exactly—' he hastened to defend himself. 'It's just that I can't help worrying about her. She has nobody to look after her. She never has had anybody. Just people making use of her. The only family she has is Elliot. That's why it's breaking her heart knowing that his useful days are over. Apart from him, she's alone.'

'According to you she has quite a left hook.'

'Oh, she can take care of herself that way. But she's alone inside. I don't think I've ever met anyone as completely alone. She thinks she doesn't mind. She thinks she's happier that way.'

'Maybe she is. You've just said there are worse things.'

'I was wrong. When I think of her going on like that

for years—fooling herself that she's happy, just getting more isolated—'

'It probably won't happen. She'll meet some nice young man and marry him. In a few years you'll bump into her again and she'll have a couple of children and another on the way.'

Leo grinned. 'You're a clever woman, Aunt. You know I don't want that.'

'I wonder what you do really want.'

'Whatever it is, I don't think I'll get it.'

The lights were going out along the Grand Canal. Behind them the great palace was closing down for the night. Leo rose and helped Lucia to her feet.

'Thank you for listening,' he said. 'I'm afraid Dulcie and Harriet thought me a bit of a clown.'

'Well, your life has been rather full of brief entanglements,' Lucia said, patting his hand. 'But if Selena is the right woman, you'll find her again. Although I think she's quite mad if *she* doesn't come to find *you*.'

'Maybe she doesn't want to find me,' Leo said gloomily. 'And even if she did, what good would it do me? She doesn't care for an ordinary life, in one place with a husband and kids.'

'I didn't know your thoughts had got that far.'

'They haven't,' he said quickly. 'I was talking generally.'

'Oh, I see.'

'She likes the open road, moving from place to place, never knowing what tomorrow may bring. So I probably couldn't make her happy anyway.'

'Enough of that kind of talk. If your love is fated to be, it will be. Now, tomorrow's a wedding. We're all going to enjoy ourselves.'

It was late when Selena came to a halt in the yard of the Four-Ten. Barton was waiting for her.

'Heard you really did well in Reno.'

'I'll be a millionaire yet,' she said. 'Barton, is something wrong?'

'I've heard from Leo.'

'Oh, really?'

'Don't you pretend you don't care. My guess is you're in as big a state as he is.'

'Why should he be in a state?'

'Because he lost your phone number. He's been going crazy, calling here, leaving messages for you to call him back.'

'But I didn't know—'

'No, I had to be away for a while, so I left word that if you called you were to be told all about it. Unfortunately the person I left word with was Paulie. Now, I don't know if he's just plum forgetful, or if there's more to it—' he looked at her face. 'Would this have anything to do with that time Paulie "stepped on a pitchfork"?'

'Well, I didn't want to tell you, when you've been so good to me—'

'If it helps any I've often wanted to sock him myself.'

'He just got a bit fresh, and I—well—'

'It was you? Not Leo?'

'In a pig's ear it was Leo. He came in when the fighting was over. But maybe I went too far.'

'Shouldn't think you did,' Barton said with relish. 'But you were quite right not to tell his mother. She overreacts to that kind of thing. Well, well, so he got his revenge.'

'Maybe I should call Leo now,' but Selena sounded vague and abstracted.

'Don't you want to?'

'Course I want to, but he's so far away, and he'll be another person in his own country.'

'Then go and find him in his own country. Find out if it can be your country. Selena, when a man keeps calling and getting agitated like this one has, then he has things to say to a woman that he can't say over the phone.'

'You mean me—go to Italy?'

'It's not the other side of the moon. You know I'll look after Jeepers and Elliot for you while you're gone. You've got all that prize money. What's stopping you?'

When she still didn't answer Barton began to cluck like a chicken.

'I am *not a chicken*.'

'Not when you're in the ring, sure. Never seen anyone braver. But that's the easy part. The world's a much scarier place. Maybe you should think about that.'

By the time he was on his way back home Leo had half talked himself into thinking things were for the best. This was fate's way of telling him that he and Selena weren't meant to be together.

The wedding had been a strain. The sight of his brother so blissfully happy as he'd become Dulcie's husband had made him suddenly discontented with his own lot.

Not that he was thinking of marriage for himself. The mere thought of Selena in the glimmering white satin and lace creation that Dulcie had worn put the whole matter into perspective. Selena would probably marry in a stetson and cowboy boots.

By the time he reached his own house he'd settled the matter in his mind. They'd had a great time together, but it was over, and that was as it should be. He wouldn't think of her any more.

Gina had just finished making up his bed. She greeted him and went to collect a duster that she'd left by the window.

'Renzo wanted to see you this afternoon,' she started to say, 'so that he can—I wonder who that is.'

'Who?' He went to stand beside her at the window that looked down on the path that led up from Morenza.

A tall slender figure, in jeans and shirt, and weighed down by a couple of bags, was walking towards the house, sometimes stopping to stare upward, her hand shading her eyes. She was too far away for Leo to see her face, but he recognised everything else, from her swaying walk to the angle of her head as she tilted it back.

'She must be a stranger in these parts,' Gina was saying, 'Because—*signore*?'

Her employer was no longer with her. She heard his feet thundering down the stairs and the next moment he appeared below, running so fast that Gina thought he would topple headlong into the valley.

The young woman dropped her bags and began to run too, and the next moment they were locked in each other's arms, oblivious to the rest of the world.

'Celia,' Gina yelled to one of the maids, 'We've got a guest. Stop what you're doing and prepare a room for her.

'Not,' she added, her eyes on the entwined figures, 'that I think she'll spend much time sleeping in it.'

CHAPTER EIGHT

'TELL me I'm not dreaming. You're really here!'

'I'm here, I'm here! Feel me.' Selena was laughing and crying together.

He did his best, crushing her in a fierce grip and kissing every part of her face.

'I've imagined you walking up that road so often but it was always a trick of the light.'

'Not this time. Oh, Leo, are you really glad to see me?'

Suddenly the words failed him. Was he glad to see her? All he knew was that the lump in his throat made it hard to speak.

'You're crying,' she said in wonder.

'Of course I'm not. Only wimps cry,' he teased her with the reminder of her own words. But his eyes were wet and he didn't dry them. He was a Latin, raised not to be ashamed of his emotions, and he had no wish to hide them with this woman.

He took her face between his hands, looking at her tenderly before laying his lips on hers in a long kiss. She answered, putting her heart into it, knowing this was why she'd come such a great distance, and nothing could have kept her away.

Something butted her from behind, then from the side, and she looked down to find herself surrounded by goats. They were coming down the hill, milling around the two of them, while a grinning goatherd made a gesture that was half greeting, half salute.

' '*Notte* Franco,' Leo said, grinning back.

It would be all over the valley now, he thought. So let them talk!

He tucked one of Selena's bags under his arm, took the other in his hand, disentangled himself and her from curious goats, and put his free arm around her. Then, together they went up the hill to home.

'Are your family visiting you?' Selena asked, seeing all the faces at the windows.

'No, they're—' he stopped himself from saying '—the servants.' 'Two of the girls are Gina's nieces,' he said. It was true. When he needed to employ somebody new he just told Gina and she produced some of her own vast family.

The faces vanished, and when they reached the door there was only Gina, smiling a welcome and explaining that the *signorina's* room was being prepared, and in the meantime refreshments were on their way from the kitchen.

Gina departed, and Leo took Selena back into his arms, not kissing her this time but pulling her against him and resting his head against her hair.

'How come she's already preparing a room for me?' Selena asked.

'She saw you come up the hill, and when I—when we—well, I guess everyone knows all about us by now.'

It was on the tip of her tongue to ask what he thought 'all about us' might be, but she let it go. She didn't know the answer herself. It was what she was here to find out. For the moment nothing mattered next to the joyous glow that enveloped her at being with him. In this country where everything looked strange and she didn't know the language she felt that she'd come home. Because he was here.

'Why didn't you take a cab all the way to the door?' Leo asked.

'I didn't know how to tell him your address. I found a bus which had 'Morenza' written on the front, only I didn't know you had to buy the tickets in a sweet shop first, and by the time I'd done that the bus had gone. Yes, all right, make fun of me.'

He was chuckling at her droll manner, but he controlled himself. 'I'm sorry, *carissima*, I can't help it. It was the way you said it. We are a little mad in Italy. We buy bus tickets in sweet shops.'

'What happens if the sweet shops are closed?'

'We walk.'

She gave a choke of laughter. He dropped his head so that his forehead rested against hers, and grinned with sheer delight at having her here.

'So I waited for the next bus,' she said, 'and then I recognised your house from what you'd told me.'

'But why didn't you call me to collect you?'

'Well—you know—'

All the way over she'd been tormented by the thought that he didn't really want her at all. She would call and hear the awkwardness in his voice. Perhaps he'd only called her in Texas to tell her not to call him because it had all been a big mistake. Only the fact that she was high above the Atlantic at the time stopped her getting out of the aircraft there and then.

She'd promised herself that when she landed she'd go straight back. Or call him. Or do anything rather than seek him out. Then she would hear again the sound of Barton clucking, and make herself go on, telling herself that no member of the Gates family had ever been a quitter. She had no idea if this were true, but it helped.

The bus had deposited her by the duck pond in

Morenza, from where she could see the house at the top of the incline. There was an ancient cab waiting, and she could have simply pointed out the house to the driver, but she couldn't bring herself to do it—not if she might be coming back that way soon, a reject.

So she'd walked the last mile, dropping with weariness until a familiar and inexpressibly dear figure had come flying down to meet her, weeping with joy as he enfolded her against his heart. Then she'd known all she needed to know.

He showed her up to the room the maids had just finished, and on the way she looked at the house with its heavy stone walls. It was just as he'd told her, except for being much larger.

Her room, too, was large, with a polished wooden floor and the biggest bed she had ever seen, with a carved walnut head. The windows were guarded by heavy wooden shutters to keep out the heat, and when Gina pulled them open Selena could step out onto a tiny balcony to look down over the valley and the most beautiful countryside she had ever seen. The hills rolled away, greens and blues fading into misty distance, the lines broken by pine trees.

It was still warm enough to have supper outside, watching the sun set. Gina served them fish soup, a mixture of squid, prawns and mussels, garlic, onions and tomatoes. Selena felt that she'd died and gone to heaven.

'I got back to find Barton jumping up and down,' she said, sipping white wine. 'He'd left the message with Paulie who'd "forgotten" it.'

'But my irresistible attraction drew you anyway?' he ventured.

'I came to see the Grosseto rodeo,' she said firmly. 'That was all.'

'Nothing to do with me?'

'Nothing to do with you. Don't flatter yourself.'

'No, ma'am.'

'And you can stop grinning like that.'

'I wasn't grinning.'

'You were, like the cat that swallowed the cream. Just because I came halfway around the world looking for you, it doesn't mean anything. Do you understand that?'

'Sure. And just because I've spent the last few weeks going crazy looking through websites trying to get one step ahead of you, that doesn't mean anything either.'

'Fine!'

'Fine!'

They sat in silence, contemplating each other with joy.

'You did it again,' she said. 'When I arrived you called me *carissima*, but you didn't tell me what it meant.'

'In Italian *cara* means dear,' he said. 'And when you add *issima* it's a kind of emphasis, the most extreme form of something that you can say.'

She was looking at him.

'And so you see,' he said, taking her hand, 'when a man calls a woman *carissima*—'

Suddenly it was hard. In the past he'd used the word casually, almost without meaning. Now everything was different and he was left only with the old debased currency.

'It means that she is more than dear to him,' he said. 'It means—'

He broke off as Gina returned for the plates.

'*Tagliatelle* with pumpkin, *signore*,' she said.

Smiling, Leo let it go. There would be time later to say everything he wanted to say.

They finished the meal with Tuscan honey and nut

cake. By then Selena's eyes were closing. At last Leo took her hand and led her upstairs, stopping at her door.

'Goodnight,' he said softly. *'Carissima.'*

'Goodnight.'

He kissed her cheek and left her.

He lay awake most of that night. The knowledge that she was sleeping next door made him feel like a man with hoarded treasure under his roof. The treasure was his and he would keep it, fighting off the world if need be.

He awoke in the early dawn and went to the window, opening the shutters and standing out on the small balcony. He was still filled with a sense of wonder at her coming, and he wanted to look again at the road that led down to the village, a road he'd so often gazed at, longing to see her, until one day she'd been there.

A shadow in the next window made him look. She was standing there, not looking at him but down into the valley, her face quiet and absorbed, as though in another world.

As he watched, she raised her head long enough to give him a brief smile, but then became absorbed once more in watching the valley.

Now he understood.

Throwing on a robe he slipped out of his own room and into hers, coming up behind her at the window and laying his hands gently on her shoulders. When she leaned back on him he slid his arms around her so that they crossed over her chest. She raised her hands to curve over his forearms, and he held her there against him, filled with a deep contentment that was unlike anything he'd ever known in his life before.

Down below them a soft glow was creeping over the

valley, faint at first, then growing in intensity. The light was magical, unearthly, for just a few blessed moments.

Then it changed, grew harsher, firmer, more prosaic, ready for the working day. Only the memory was left.

Selena gave a little sigh of satisfaction, so quiet that he sensed it through his flesh rather than heard it.

'That's what I wanted,' she said. 'Ever since you told me about that light, I've longed to see it.'

'What did you think?'

'It was just as beautiful as you promised. The most beautiful thing I ever saw.'

'It'll be there again tomorrow,' he said. 'But now—'

He drew her gently back into the room and took her to bed, where they found another kind of beauty.

In his mind Leo had often imagined the moment when he introduced Selena to Peri, the mare who had been ready for him to sell for months, but whose elegance and spirit had made him keep her back, waiting for the right person.

Selena was that person. He'd always suspected it and he knew for sure when he witnessed their love at first sight. By now he reckoned he knew a bit about love at first sight.

He thought perhaps he would give Peri to her as a wedding present. He no longer shied away from that kind of thought. A man should know how to accept when it was all up with him.

They spent their days riding his fields and vineyards, and their nights in each other's arms.

'Stay here,' he said one night when they had loved each other to exhaustion. 'Don't leave me again.'

She made the little restless movement that he always sensed at any mention of permanency, and he quickly added, 'Take charge of the horses. Take charge of me. Either or both, as you like.'

She raised herself on one elbow and looked down into his face. The shutters were open, flooding the room with moonlight, throwing shadows between her breasts, absorbing all his attention so that he didn't hear her question.

'What was that?' he murmured, tracing the swell with his finger.

'I said it was about time you finished telling me what *carissima* means.'

As she spoke she was easing herself over him, moving slowly and with purpose.

'If you are my *carissima*,' he said, 'you are dearer to me than all the world. You are my love, my beloved, the only one who exists for me.'

A week later they went to Maremma, an area in the south of Tuscany, near the coast. It was often known as 'the Wild West of Tuscany', since there cattle were raised in large numbers, and the traditional cowboy skills were still in everyday use.

Each year this was celebrated by a rodeo that consisted of a parade through the nearby town of Grosseto, and a show that lasted one afternoon. Leo took Selena to the town to meet the organisers, describing her achievements in glowing terms.

Then Selena produced a surprise of her own. All the way over she'd been clutching a large, flat object, refusing to let Leo see it. It turned out to be a photograph of him bull riding.

'I know this guy who takes photographs of everything,' she said, 'even the people who don't win. I looked him up, and he had this one of you. You look real good, don't you?'

He looked magnificent. One arm was high in the air, his head was up, his face full of a wide grin of delight and triumph.

'You'd never know that I was off the next second,' he said.

One of the organisers regarded the picture and coughed respectfully.

'Perhaps, *signore*, you could give us a demonstration of bull riding, at our rodeo.'

'I don't think so,' Leo said hastily. 'They have very special bulls in Texas. Bred for their ferocity.'

'I don't think we would disappoint you, *signore*. We have a bull here that has already gored two men to death—'

It took Leo ten minutes to talk his way out of that one, with Selena doubled up with laughter.

'I told him that you'd demonstrate barrel racing,' he told her as they made their escape.

'That's fine. But it won't be the same without you riding that bull.'

'Get lost!'

Leo's family had never made the trip before. This year, however, they were coming in force, for by now they knew what everyone knew—that Leo, the all-embracing lover of ladies with voluptuous forms, had fallen 'victim' to an angular young woman with a figure like a rail and a head like fire. Temper, ditto.

So the bulk of the Calvani family planned to head for the farm to stay the night before going on to Grosseto. Only Marco was missing. The Count and Countess Calvani, with Guido and Dulcie, would be travelling from Venice.

Knowing these plans were afoot, Leo knew that the day of reckoning couldn't be postponed much longer. Some time soon he must confess all to Selena—his reprehensible wealth or his shocking connection to a title. It was a moot point which one would horrify her the most.

While he was still trying to broach the subject he was overtaken by events. Selena, seeking him one morning, came to his study.

'Leo, are you in here?'

She pushed the door further open. There was no sign of Leo but she could hear his voice coming from the passage beyond, and went further into the room to wait for him.

Then something caught her eye.

Several photographs were spread out on the desk, and curiosity drew her over to look at them. What she saw made her first frown, then stare.

They were wedding pictures, reminding her that Leo had recently been to the marriage of his brother, Guido. There were the bride and groom, the bride gorgeous in white satin and lace, the groom with a wicked, appealing face. And there, next to him, was Leo, dressed as she'd never seen him before.

Dressed for best. In costly finery. With a top hat!

So what? Everyone dressed up at weddings.

But there was something in the background that wouldn't be dismissed. Chandeliers, old pictures, mirrors with gilt frames. The clothes fitted perfectly, which hired clothes never did. And the people had the awesome confidence that came with money and status.

A strange feeling, something like dismay, was starting to take over her stomach, prior to invading the rest of her.

'They just arrived.'

Leo was standing in the doorway, smiling in the way that could make her forget everything else.

'Let me introduce you to my family,' he said, coming forward and sorting the pictures. 'That's my brother Guido, and Dulcie. These two cheesy characters here are her father and brother, and if I never see them again it'll be too soon. This one here is my cousin Marco, and that's his fiancée Harriet. And this man is my uncle Francesco, and his wife, Liza.'

'What's that place behind all of you. Did you hire the town hall or something?'

'No,' he said casually, 'that's my uncle's home.'

'That? He lives there? It's like a palace.'

Leo's tone became even more casual. 'I suppose that's what it is, really.'

'What do you mean?'

'It's called the Palazzo Calvani. It's on the Grand Canal in Venice.'

'Your uncle lives in a palace? What is he, royalty?'

'No, no, nothing so grand. Just a count.'

'What was that? You mumbled that last word.'

'He's a count,' Leo said reluctantly.

She stared at him. 'You're related to a real count?'

'Yes, but on the wrong side of the blanket,' he assured her, like a man arguing mitigating circumstances to a crime.

'But they know you, don't they?' she accused him. 'You're part of the family.'

He sighed and admitted it.

'My father was Uncle Francesco's brother. If his marriage to my mother had been valid I'd be—well—the heir.'

She turned an appalled gaze on him.

'But it wasn't,' he placated her, 'so I'm not. That's Guido's problem, not mine. And boy is he mad at me about it. Like it was my fault. He doesn't want it any more than I do. All I ever wanted was this farm and the life I have here. You've got to believe me, Selena.'

'Give me one reason I should ever believe a word you say again.'

'Now, come on, I never lied to you.'

'You sure as heck never told me the truth either.'

'Well, did you give me your life story from day one?'

'*Yes.*'

She had him there.

'And you're not being logical,' he changed tack hastily. 'If I was that poor, how come I knew Barton, and went to visit him?'

'You sold him some horses, you told me. And you can get cheap air tickets these days. And there's other things. This place, the people, the land—the way you talked I thought you rented some dirt-poor little place at the back of beyond, but you own it don't you?'

'I've never pretended about that.'

'And how much do you own? You're the *padrone*, aren't you? Not just here but the village and halfway to Florence, for all I know.'

'Rather more than that, actually,' he confessed miserably.

'You could buy Barton out, couldn't you?'

He shrugged. 'I don't know. Probably.'

'I thought you were just a country boy—you let me think that. But you're really more like a—a tycoon.'

'I *am* a country boy.'

'You're a country tycoon, that's what you are.'

She was pale with shock.

'Leo, be honest with me for the first time since we've known each other. Just how rich are you?'

'Darn it, Selena, are you only going to marry me for my money?'

'I'm not going to marry you at all, you conceited—'

'I didn't mean it like that, you know I didn't.'

'All those things I said to you, about millionaires not being real people—'

'Well, now you know you were wrong.'

'The hell I do! I reckon you've proved me right about all the worst. I wouldn't have thought you could do a thing like this to me!'

'What have I done?' he implored the room. 'Will someone please tell me what I've done?'

'You've pretended to be one thing, while actually being another.'

'Well, of course I did,' he roared. 'I wasn't going to take the chance on losing you. Think I didn't know? Sure I knew. We hadn't met five minutes before I knew you were the most awkward, unreasonable female with no common sense. I didn't want to scare you off, so we played by your rules. I couldn't even tell you I'd—' He stopped with his feet at the edge of the precipice.

'Tell me you'd done what?'

'I forget.' But then, with her eyes on him he reckoned he might as well be hung for a sheep as a lamb. 'All right, the van and the horse trailer—they came from me.'

'You—bought the replacement van—and horse trailer?'

'And Jeepers. Selena, the insurers would have laughed at you. You knew that yourself. It was the only way to get you back on the road. I just hoped you wouldn't find out, or that you wouldn't be too mad at me if you did.' He studied her face, hardly daring to believe what he saw there. 'Why—are you laughing?'

'You mean—' she choked '—that you were the miracle after all? Not Barton?'

'Yes, me, not Barton.'

'No wonder you looked green around the gills when I said that.'

'I could have killed him,' Leo confessed. 'I wanted to tell you the truth but I couldn't, because I knew you wouldn't want to be beholden to me. But I've thought of a way around that. We get married and then it's your wedding present, and we're all straight.'

She stared. 'You're serious, aren't you?'

'Well, the way I see it, if you marry me, all that disgusting money will be yours too, and then you'll have to shut up about it.'

She considered this. 'OK, it's a deal.'

She didn't say she loved him then. She said it later that night, when he was breathing deeply beside her, the sleep of peace and satiety, as he always did when they'd released each other from passion by indulging it without limit. He slept heavily, so she could smooth his hair, kiss him without his knowing, and whisper the words she didn't know how to say when he heard her.

Another night he brought wine and peaches, and they sat feasting and talking.

'How do your family come to be out here?' she asked. 'If you're Venetian counts, what are you doing in Tuscany?'

'How can you ask? Everyone knows the evil aristos commandeer property wherever they can. That's how we keep our feet on the necks of the deserving poor.'

'Oh, very funny! I'll thump you in a minute. What are you doing here?'

'My grandfather, Count Angelo, fell in love with a

woman from Tuscany, called Maria Rinucci. This—' he indicated the valley '—was her dowry. Since he had the Venetian property to bequeath to his eldest son and heir—that's my uncle Francesco—this was used to provide an inheritance for Francesco's younger brothers, Bertrando and Silvio.

'Silvio took his share in cash and married a banker's daughter in Rome. Their son is Marco. You won't meet him next week because something's gone wrong between him and Harriet, his English fiancée. She's gone back to England and he's followed her, trying to talk her around. Let's hope he brings her back for our wedding.'

He stroked her face, trying to distract her with the thought of their wedding. She accepted his caress and kissed him enthusiastically, but she wouldn't be distracted.

'And?' she insisted.

'Bertrando liked living on the land, so he came out here and married a widow, Elissa, who became my mother.

'She died soon after I was born, and he married again, Donna, Guido's mother. But then it turned out that Elissa hadn't been a widow, as everyone had thought, but still married to her first husband. So I was illegitimate, and as she was dead it was too late to validate her marriage to my father, so that was that. Guido and I kind of swapped inheritances.

'I can't tell you how glad I am now that we did. Because otherwise, you and I—'

'Nix,' she said as he'd known she would say. 'I couldn't marry you if you had a title. It's against my principles, and besides—well anyway, it doesn't matter. But your family wouldn't fancy me as the countess.'

'You don't know anything about them. Forget those

stereotypes you're carrying in your head. We don't all eat off gold plate—'

'Shame, I was looking forward to that.'

'Will you hush, and let me finish? And don't look at me like that or I'll forget what I was going to stay.'

'Well, there are more interesting things to do—'

'When I've finished,' he said, seizing her wandering fingers. 'My family aren't the way you think. All they'll care about is that we love each other. Guido and Dulcie have just married for love, so did Uncle Francesco. He waited forty years for her to say yes, and refused to marry anyone else. She had some funny ideas too and he was a patient man, but I'm not. If you think I'm waiting forty years for you to see sense, you're nuts. Now, you were saying about doing more interesting things…'

CHAPTER NINE

SELENA had tried to keep it light, but she was more nervous about Leo's family than she would have let on. He'd said her head was full of stereotypes, and it was partly true. Her dread was concentrated on the thought of doing or saying something that would embarrass Leo by drawing down icy stares on herself. She would rather ride a bull than risk looking foolish.

With a few days to go the house was turned upside down. Leo and Selena changed rooms, retreating to smaller ones at the back of the house so that his uncle and aunt might have the best, with Guido and Dulcie in the next best.

It made Selena stare to see Gina preparing the house for a gala occasion, with the assistance of two maids, a cook and two extra girls in from the village. Being waited on by servants unnerved her.

'Well, you're the mistress of the house now,' Leo said. 'Dismiss the lot of them, and do it virtuously yourself.'

'Oh, yeah?' she demanded, checkmated. Leo's eyes were full of wicked fun.

'You could do all the cooking as well,' he suggested.

'Have you tasted my cooking?'

'Have I—? I had a sandwich you made the other day, and I'm still getting up in the night. Leave them to their job, *carissima*, and you get on with your job, which is the horses.'

She was virtually running that side of things now.

125

Things were simpler with horses. You knew what was expected of you. That made her think of Elliot, and she felt a pang of homesickness. Elliot was the faithful friend who'd seen her through the bad times, and whom she might never see again.

After the first bout of homesickness she found it could attack again without warning. The sheer grandeur of the house when Gina had finished transforming it had the same effect on her, making her think of a mini van, a battered horse trailer at the back, Elliot and herself chasing the far horizons with just enough money to reach the next stop, then relying on each other to win some for the next stage.

There were far horizons here, she thought, looking out on Tuscany's rolling hills, but they seemed somehow tame now that she knew they belonged to Leo, and by extension to herself. There was no mystery in a horizon that you owned. And no excitement either.

But she pushed those thoughts aside. She knew the coming visit was important to Leo. Whatever he might say to disparage his aristocratic background, these people were the family he loved, and she suspected that he shared their values more than he realised. The thought made him seem a little distant.

As the day grew nearer she became so demoralised that when Leo suggested that she buy a couple of dresses she made no protest. She chose items as unobtrusive as possible because she was no longer sure of herself, and she didn't want to be noticed.

Count Francesco Calvani had decided to travel the hundred and sixty miles from Venice in his own chauffeur-driven limousine, which he felt would be more comfortable for his beloved Liza, who disliked trains.

Guido and Dulcie travelled in their own jaunty sports

car. With a stop at Florence for lunch they made Bella Podena by late afternoon. They had driven ahead of the two, and arrived before them.

'We just couldn't wait to meet you,' Guido said, enveloping Selena in a hug.

She liked him at once. He bore very little physical resemblance to his brother, but their eyes had the same twinkle. In Leo perhaps it was warmer, and in Guido more mischievous, but it was the link between them.

Dulcie was almost as slender as Selena herself, but with a mass of wavy blonde hair that Selena secretly envied. She too hugged her, and said eagerly how glad she was that she would soon have a sister. Selena began to relax.

A few minutes later they gathered outside for the arrival of the Count and Countess Calvani. The shiny black car glided to a standstill, the chauffeur emerged and proceeded to open one of the passenger doors.

From it descended a tiny woman with a lean face and hooded eyes. Selena had a strange feeling that she was full of tension as she looked around her.

I'll bet she's looking down on us because this is a farm, she thought, angry for Leo's sake. Just because she's used to a palace…

She saw the count appear from his side of the car and smile at his wife, who smiled back and laid her hand on his arm. Together they entered the house, and the introductions were made.

Count Francesco Calvani had the family charm. He too embraced Selena like a long-lost daughter and spoke to her in excellent English. Liza smiled and shook her hand, then made a stilted little speech of welcome which had to be translated into English. Selena thanked her in terms equally stilted, which the count translated into Venetian.

The two women looked at each other across a chasm.

As mistress of the house Selena escorted Liza to her room, and gave thanks for Dulcie who came too, and translated them to each other. She finally escaped, thanking heaven for a merciful release, and had a horrible feeling that the countess was doing the same.

She had a feeling of being stranded in a desert. She'd spent the last few years doing something she did well, and because of it she had confidence in herself. But now her confidence seemed to have drained away through the soles of her feet. Everything she did felt wrong, even when Leo smiled encouragement and told her she was doing well.

Her dress felt dowdy beside the countess's quiet elegance and Dulcie's glowing beauty. When Gina drew her into the dining room to approve the elegant table settings she wanted to sink from the conviction that Gina knew that refined dining was a mystery to her, and despised her accordingly.

'That's great,' she said desperately. 'It looks lovely, Gina.'

'The food is ready to serve, *signorina*.'

'In that case—I suppose I should bring people in.'

She did this by conveying the message to Leo and letting him make the announcement. She knew she should have done it herself, but she would rather have ridden a bull than stand up in that company and invite them into 'her' dining room. She began to wonder when there was a flight back to Texas.

Things improved a little when she found herself talking to Dulcie. They swapped stories about 'life before

Calvani' as Dulcie teasingly put it. Dulcie was thrilled by Selena's background.

'I've always loved Westerns,' she said longingly. 'You mean you do real Wild West stuff? Roping and riding and such?'

'Riding. I don't actually do roping—although, I can. This guy showed me how. Said I was pretty good.'

'Are you going to do roping at Grosseto tomorrow?'

Selena shook her head. 'Women don't do that in rodeos. We just do barrel racing.'

Dulcie's eyes were mischievous. 'Do you think the Grosseto organisers know that?'

Selena grinned. 'You're wicked,' she said appreciatively, and Dulcie nodded.

From the other end of the table Guido and Leo watched their womenfolk with satisfaction.

'We always do it,' Guido observed.

'What's that?' his brother asked.

'Uncle Francesco has a saying that the Calvanis always choose the best, the best food, the best wine, the best women. We did well, brother. Both of us.'

The meal was superb. The count congratulated Leo's cook and the atmosphere became genial. This lasted until the subject of the wedding came up, and the count immediately declared that of course it must take place in St Mark's Basilica, in Venice.

'Selena and I thought the parish church in Morenza would suit us,' Leo said.

'The parish—?' The count seemed lost for words. 'A Calvani, marry in a village?'

'This is our home,' Leo said firmly. 'It's what Selena and I both wish.'

'But—'

'No, uncle,' Leo said firmly.

He would have said more but the countess laid her hand on his arm and said something Selena didn't understand, except that she caught her own name.

'All right, all right,' he said placatingly. 'I won't say any more.'

He patted his wife's hand and responded in the same language she'd used.

You didn't have to be a genius to know what they'd said, Selena reckoned. The countess couldn't think what the fuss was about. St Mark's was too good for Selena Gates. And the count had agreed with her.

Luckily everyone wanted an early night, to be ready for the pleasures of the following day. Normally Selena slept easily, but tonight she lay awake for hours, wondering what she was doing here.

They left early for Grosseto, the family to take up position in a hotel room Leo had booked for them, which overlooked the procession. Leo and Selena went straight to the meeting place from where the procession was to start.

Today they were both dressed to kill, in the finest available from Delia's stall, cowboy shirts, buttoned to the neck, colourful cowboy boots and belts with large silver buckles. When Leo had rammed a stetson squarely on his head, and Selena had settled hers on at a rakish angle they were ready for the parade.

It was quite a parade. The town band had turned out in force, well rehearsed, and if it sounded a little too Italian to be authentic nobody cared for that. The horsemen, or *butteri* as they were known locally, had the rough splendour of men who lived hard lives and performed the difficult feats of roping and riding not only in performance but in their everyday lives.

After the parade everyone moved to a nearby field for the contests that would take up the afternoon. First off was the bucking-bronco contest. Leo had elected to enter this, and did creditably without winning. Then the barrels were set up, a voice from a loudspeaker told the crowd all about Selena and predicted that she would do the circuit in no more than fourteen seconds.

This gave her a real challenge as the barrels were set just too far apart for that, and Peri lacked experience. The two of them gave it all they had, taking fourteen and a half, which didn't stop the announcer yelling, 'Fourteen seconds,' as she finished. And the cheerful crowd took his word for it.

If she thought the day was over she had a shock coming. Next came the calf roping, and some mischievous person had entered her in it. Guido always swore that it wasn't him.

Like Leo she managed well enough not to lose face, and the afternoon ended in a riot of good fellowship. The Calvanis cheered her to the echo, all except the countess, who applauded, but quietly, and left Selena wondering what she was really thinking. 'Brash and un-ladylike, I reckon,' she thought. 'Can't be helped.'

There were a dozen food stalls selling local specialities, and they all consumed freely, even the countess, who tucked in with gusto.

'She comes from these parts,' Leo explained. 'She doesn't often get the chance of good Tuscan eats.'

But by the time they reached home everyone was hungry again, and Selena's thoughts had flown back across the Atlantic.

'I could just do with a hot dog,' she sighed.

'We could make some,' Gina said. 'What do we need?'

'Sausages and rolls.'

'Rolls we have. Sausages I must send for.'

'But it's late, the shops are shut.'

'I will send Sara. The butcher is her uncle.'

In half an hour the little maid was back with her uncle's finest. Selena made hot dogs, Tuscan style, and everybody pronounced them excellent.

Even the countess ate two, Selena noticed. And she smiled at her, and said, *'Grazie, Selena.'*

Afterwards, as they drank coffee and sipped wine, Dulcie said to her, 'Do you know, you're just the way I expected.'

Selena was startled. 'You knew about me?'

'When Leo came back from Texas he couldn't talk about anything else but you, how he'd met you, and you were wonderful, and he didn't have your number any more. He was going crazy. If you hadn't come over here, I'm pretty sure he'd have taken off to find you.'

Selena looked up to find Leo's eyes on them. He was grinning, embarrassed, but too good-natured to mind being laughed at.

'So now you know,' he told Selena.

'Go on,' she ribbed him, 'I knew anyway. Always reckoned you couldn't resist me.'

He slipped a friendly arm about her.

'On the other hand,' he mused, 'It was you who came looking for me.'

'In a pig's eye I came looking for you. I came for the rodeo.'

'Sure you did.'

'Sure I did.'

'Well, it's over now,' he said, 'so you can go back.' But his arm tightened as he spoke.

The others were watching them, smiling.

'Then I'll go,' she said defiantly.

'Fine. Go.' The arm tightened.

'I'm going.'

'Good.'

'Good.'

'Oh, get on with it and kiss each other,' Guido said in exasperation. 'I need a drink. Ouch!' He rubbed his ribs which had collided with a wifely elbow.

After that everybody sat up much too late, unwilling to let a happy occasion end. Toast followed toast until they all trooped off to bed.

Next morning they parted with many promises to see each other soon, when Leo and Selena tied the knot. Even the countess smiled and kissed Selena's cheek, so that she began to feel she'd been worrying about nothing.

She and Leo stood, arms entwined, until the last car had vanished from sight. Then they hurried back to work.

Now they were in the season of harvests. Leo had grapes and olives to bring safely in, and there would be no time to marry until that was done. Selena became fascinated by this side of their lives, and spent long hours in the saddle, riding his acres with him.

They would return every evening, worn out but content, and satisfied with what they were bringing to fruition. Gradually her restlessness abated. There was nothing to worry about, and this happy life would go on forever.

The phone call came out of the blue one morning. Selena emerged from the shower to find Leo looking harassed.

'Uncle Francesco has been on the telephone. He wants

us to drop everything and go to Venice now, this minute.'

'Is he crazy. We're about to start bringing in the grapes.'

'That's what I told him. He just said it was urgent.'

'You don't think he wants to have another go at you about the wedding.'

'I hope it's not that. I've told him time and again we're going to marry in Morenza and that's final. If he's dragged us all the way to Venice to have the argument again, I'll—' he searched for something that his amiable temper could rise to '—I'll tell him he shouldn't have done it.'

'So you're going?'

'We're going. I must have a talk to Renzo and then I'll get the car out.' He groaned. 'Why couldn't he at least tell me what's happened? Ah well, the sooner we're there the sooner we'll know, and the sooner we can get home.'

As they neared the city Selena asked, 'If the streets of Venice are water, where do we park the car?'

'There's a causeway that stretches from the mainland, over the lagoon, to Venice. At the Venice end is a terminus called Piazzale Roma where we leave the car and take the boat the rest of the way.'

'A gondola?'

'No, they don't work like taxis. They just do round trips for tourists. Uncle will have sent his boat for us.'

But when they got there they were greeted by a surprise. It was Guido who greeted them, and the boat he'd brought with him was a gondola.

'I'd forgotten that you fancied yourself as a gondolier,' Leo said with a grin. To Selena he added, 'Guido has some gondolier friends, and he borrows their boat whenever the mood takes him. It's his idea of honest toil.'

'Ignore him,' Guido said, kissing Selena and assisting her into the gondola.

He put their bags in, then turned to usher Leo into the boat with a theatrical flourish. '*Signore!*'

'You're up to something, little brother,' Leo said with a grin.

'Who, me?'

'Don't give me that innocent look. You always looked innocent when you'd done something that made everyone groan. What do you know that I don't?'

'The things I know that you don't would fill a book,' Guido ribbed him. 'Don't blame me. It's life. Fate. Kismet.'

He cast off, and for a while Selena was distracted by her first gondola ride and her first visit to Venice. It seemed like no time before they had glided out of a side canal into the Grand Canal, the great highway through the centre of town.

'That's where Uncle lives,' Leo said, indicating a building on the right.

The Palazzo Calvani was a monumental building, whose front was decorated with stone decorations of a lacy appearance that almost disguised its size. Selena could understand why it was called a palace. It exuded confidence and beauty in equal measure. It had been the home of great lords for centuries, and its spirit bowed to no man.

She could appreciate the beauty and the confidence, while being profoundly glad that nobody was asking her to live in it.

The impression was heightened as they drew up to the landing stage and there were servants, reaching forward to help them. Then the big, glamorous house seemed to reach out too, enveloping them.

'I know,' Leo murmured in her ear. 'Sometimes I don't think I'm going to escape alive either.'

She chuckled and felt better. If they were together in this, it wasn't so bad.

Her eyes widened when she saw her room. Even the Four-Ten hadn't been as outrageous as this.

'It's as big as a tennis court,' she muttered to Leo. 'We'll get lost in it.'

'Not us, you,' he said. 'My room's at the other end of the corridor.'

'They haven't put us together? Why?'

'Because we're not married. We have to think of the proprieties.'

'But they know we're together.'

'I know we are, and they know we are. But we're not supposed to know that they know, and they're not supposed to know that we know they know. And none of us can admit what anyone knows. It's called doing things properly.'

'It's called sticking your head in the sand.'

'That too,' he agreed.

Then Selena saw something that made her jump.

'Leo, who's that, and what's she doing with my bag?'

'That Liza's maid,' Dulcie said, slipping in behind them 'She sent her to help you.'

'You mean she thinks I'm useless by myself?'

'Stop being so prickly,' Dulcie said. 'It's meant as a compliment, because you're an honoured guest.'

You could take it like that, Selena reckoned. Or you could take it as a subtle insult, a way of saying the countess just knew you wouldn't have a maid of your own.

That was the trouble with these folk. You didn't know which way to take them.

She'd counted on Leo for support, but she soon realised that he only half understood. Whatever he might say about not being at ease in this place, the fact remained that this was his family, and he loved them. They had shared history, and shared thoughts that needed no words. They called him 'the country bumpkin' in a tone of half-derisive affection, but he was one of them in a way Selena knew she never could be.

From then on she felt a double meaning in everything. When the countess came to her room and personally took her down to supper, was this a compliment, or a wordless way of saying she was too stupid to find the way? When the count rose to take her hand, murmur a compliment on her dress, and lead her to the table, wasn't he really noticing that the dress had been bought in the Morenza market?

Well, they weren't going to intimidate her.

She took a deep breath and accepted the seat of honour, at right angles to the count. After that she managed pretty well. Her fear was that she might mishandle one of the priceless crystal goblets, and smash it, but the light, skilful touch that had carried her through countless races came to her aid. It was like a horse, really. The trick was not to grab, but to caress.

The food was superb, and even her morbid sensitivity couldn't turn that into an insult. She was beginning to relax when there was a faint commotion from just outside the dining room. The next moment the Calvani family had risen *en masse* to welcome a man and a woman who had come into the room.

'Marco!' the count cried joyfully. 'Harriet!'

A tall, elegantly handsome man stood there with a statuesque young woman.

'I didn't dare to hope you could make it,' the count said, going forward eagerly to embrace the two of them.

'We just managed to get a flight,' Marco said. 'We weren't going to miss the big occasion if we could help it. Have you—?'

'No, no, not yet,' the count said hurriedly cutting him off. 'Come, both of you, and meet the newest member of our family.'

Selena's eyes met Leo's over the table, both equally puzzled. Big occasion?

So this was Marco, she thought, the cousin Leo had mentioned, the one who never showed his feelings but had gone chasing off to England, neglecting his banking job in Rome, in order to win back the woman he loved. Now his manner was cool and composed, as though such emotional behaviour was beyond him. Yet she noticed how his eyes constantly wandered to Harriet, as though he couldn't quite believe that she was there.

She'd taken an instant liking to Dulcie, and now she found herself liking Harriet who sat beside her and chattered between mouthfuls as she hurried to catch up with the meal.

'I'm so glad you and Leo managed to get it together,' she said. 'Dulcie and I hoped you would.'

'I've already told her how much he talked about her,' Dulcie said.

Harriet nodded. 'I remember that.'

'Actually the two of you thought me very funny,' Leo said, overhearing. He grinned at Harriet. 'But the laugh's on Marco now. You must really have gotten under his skin to make him follow you all the way to London, and stay there for weeks. When are you going to make an honest man of him?'

'Well, it'll have to be soon,' Harriet said, laughing. 'He's giving me the shop as a wedding present. I have an antique shop,' she said to Harriet. 'The trouble is I'm a terrible businesswoman, so Marco's been teaching me "financial common sense".'

'Antiques?' Selena said in a hollow voice. 'You mean—?' She looked at their surroundings, the crystal chandeliers, the priceless paintings. 'You mean—this kind of stuff?'

'Oh, yes,' Harriet said eagerly. 'This place makes my mouth water it's so full of history and beauty. You could sum up the story of Venice in this house, the people, the occasions—'

Selena didn't hear any more. A depression had settled over her heart. For one moment she'd hoped to find a kindred spirit in Harriet, someone who might also feel like a fish out of water in these surroundings. And now it turned out that she belonged here as much as any Calvani. She would fit seamlessly into the family, and underline the fact that Selena herself stuck out like a sore thumb.

Still, she thought, there was always Dulcie, the private detective, the working girl who'd known what it was to scrabble for a living.

She had to cling to that thought, because she was realising that there were thoughts she couldn't share with Leo. He simply didn't understand.

And that was the worst thing of all.

CHAPTER TEN

THE meal was drawing to a close. The plates had been cleared and there were coffee and liqueurs on the table. A hush fell on the conversation, as though everyone recognised that the time had come.

'Does everybody have a glass?' the count demanded. 'Splendid. Then I have an announcement to make.' His eyes fell on Leo and Selena.

Oh no! she thought. This is to tell us that he's arranged our marriage in St Marks, and we just have to fall into line.

'As you know,' Francesco went on, 'soon we will all be going to Tuscany for the marriage of our dear Leo and Selena. A joyful occasion, made even more joyful by what I have to tell you.'

A pause. He seemed uncertain how to go on. Selena relaxed. At least it wasn't the wedding.

'It's another wedding I wish to speak of tonight,' Francesco continued. 'One that we thought—that is, we have been in some confusion all these years—but now that things are clear—'

He looked at Guido. 'You tell them,' he said. 'This is your story.'

Guido took the floor and addressed Leo. 'Uncle Francesco's trying to tell you that it was a mistake about your mother's marriage all those years ago. She never was married before. So her marriage to our father was valid, and you're legitimate.'

In the thunderstruck silence Selena saw Leo turn pale. Then he managed some kind of laugh.

'Very funny, little brother. You were always good for a joke, and that's your best yet.'

'It's no joke,' Guido said. 'It's all been proved. That man who turned up alive, saying Elissa was his wife—Franco Vinelli. They were never married. Vinelli had been married before, in England. He was an actor, in a Commedia dell'Arte troop, and they toured all over.

'He married an Englishwoman in a register office. When his tour ended he just abandoned her. He seems to have thought an English civil ceremony wouldn't count when he got back to Italy.'

'He was right,' Leo said firmly. 'It wouldn't be recognised over here, not in those days.'

'But it was,' Guido said. 'There was an international convention, saying that if a marriage was valid in the country where it was contracted then it would be recognised in any other country that was a signatory. Both England and Italy were signatories, so the marriage counted here.

'He was a married man when he took Elissa to wife, which means that she was a free woman when she married our father. Their marriage was legitimate. And so are you.'

'What do you mean it's all been proved?' Leo demanded. 'What can be proved after all this time?'

'It can be done, with a little ferreting around.'

'Which I'll bet you did.'

'Sure. I never wanted all this, never pretended about it. It's all yours.'

Leo was looking around him with a trapped look.

'This is nonsense,' he said. 'You have to forget it.'

'It's the law,' the count roared. 'It cannot be forgotten.

You are my heir, and that is how it should be. You've always been the eldest son—'

'The illegitimate eldest son,' Leo said firmly.

'Not any more,' Marco reminded him.

'You keep out of this,' Leo ordered him, 'You—you *banker*!'

Marco poured himself a drink, unperturbed.

'It's too late to change anything,' Leo insisted. 'I don't believe in this so-called proof. It wouldn't stand up to scrutiny by a lawyer—'

'It already has,' Guido said. 'It's been gone over and over by lawyers, sworn statements, properly notarised, records from the English registers.'

'What does Vinelli say?' Leo challenged. 'Bring him here to face me.'

'Vinelli died last year. He had no family, and nobody near him knew about that English marriage.'

'There must be somebody.'

'There's only written records.'

'I'll bet you thought of every detail,' Leo fumed.

'You bet I did.'

'You're loving this, aren't you?' Leo flung at him.

'Every minute.'

'That's fine for you but what about—' Leo's eyes fell on Selena, pale and distraught, watching him beseechingly. 'What about us?' he finished quietly, taking her hand.

She rose and stood beside him. The sight of them side by side seemed to alert the others to the fact that something was really wrong. This wasn't the joyous announcement that Count Francesco had counted on.

The count began to huff and puff. 'Well, I must say, I expected better than this,' he said. 'It should be a great day.'

'Having your life overturned doesn't make for a great day,' Leo said firmly. 'Now, if you'll excuse us, Selena and I will go upstairs. We've got some talking to do.'

They walked from the room, hand in hand, and broke into a run as soon as they were out of sight. They didn't stop until they reached his room.

'Leo, they can't do this to us.'

'Don't you worry, I won't let them.'

But she heard the uncertainty in his voice and it made her shiver. She'd always known him light-hearted in the face of any challenge, as though nothing could ever be too much for him. Now she sensed that he didn't feel confident of overcoming this.

'You know,' she said huskily, 'some people would dream of this. They'd say we were being unreasonable. Suddenly you're an important man with a great inheritance. Why aren't we glad?'

'Because it's a nightmare,' he said. 'Me, a count. The country bumpkin, which is all I've ever wanted to be. Do you want to be a contessa?'

'Are you kidding? I'd rather be a cow-pat.'

They clung together, seeking reassurance from each other, but each knowing they were fighting something that could suffocate them.

There was a knock on the door, and Dulcie looked in.

'Your uncle wants you in his study,' she said to Leo. 'He's got papers to show you.'

'Hell!'

'Best get it over with,' she said sympathetically.

When he'd gone Selena said, 'How do you feel about this? You were going to be a contessa, and now you're not. How can you smile?'

Dulcie laughed and shrugged. 'I've had enough of titles to last me a lifetime. Being a countess never made my mother happy.'

'Your mother—is a countess?' Selena echoed.

'My father's an earl, that's a sort of English count.'

'And you live—like this?' Selena indicated their surroundings.

'Goodness no!' Dulcie laughed. 'We never had two pennies to rub together. My father gambled it all away. That's why I had to work as a private detective. I couldn't do anything else. Having a title doesn't qualify you for a proper job.' She looked at Selena, suddenly alert. 'Selena, what's the matter? Are you ill?'

'No, I'm not ill, but I've stepped into a crazy house.'

Another knock on the door. This time it was Harriet, and behind her a servant with a trolley bearing champagne. While Dulcie began to pour, Harriet stretched out on a sofa and kicked off her shoes.

'Bubble, bubble, toil and trouble,' she said. 'You— *would—not—believe* the commotion that's going on downstairs.'

'We would,' Dulcie chuckled, handing the other two a glass each. 'We're well out of it.'

'Leo and Guido were practically coming to blows,' Harriet said cheerfully. 'Leo says he's going to wring Guido's neck. Oh, by the way, Liza would have come with me, but she's a little tired, and she's gone to bed. Actually I think it's her English that's troubling her. She doesn't speak it very well and she's afraid you may be offended.' This last was to Selena.

So that was the countess's excuse, Selena thought glumly. That was how these people operated. No outright snub, nothing you could take offence at. Just a half-truth that left you clutching at shadows.

She downed the champagne, which she suddenly needed badly.

Leo waited until the house was quiet before he slipped out of his room. Propriety be blowed, tonight he needed to be with Selena.

But when he opened her door he found her bed empty and no sign of her. He switched on the light to be sure, then switched it off again and went to the window. The Grand Canal lay before him, silent, mysterious, melancholy in its beauty. Many a man would envy him, the inheritor of all this, but it was his wide, rolling acres that called to him.

And his instincts told him that there was another trouble coming, and that was the one he dreaded.

Something caught his eye and he looked to see where the palace made a right angle to itself. Through the large windows he could see a white shape wandering through the great rooms.

Like any self-respecting palace this one had its ghosts, but none like this. Leo left the room quickly and hurried down through the building, across the marble floors that echoed the lightest footsteps.

He found the ghost in the ballroom, walking forlornly along the huge windows that went from floor to ceiling. All around them shone decorations of gold leaf. Above them hung gigantic crystal chandeliers, silent in the gloom.

He spoke her name softly, and she turned to look at him. Even in this light he could see her face well enough to know that it was distraught. The next moment they'd thrown themselves into each other's arms.

'I can't do it,' she cried. 'I just can't do this.'

'Of course you can,' he soothed her, stroking her hair although his heart was full of fear. 'You can do anything you set your mind to. I know that, even if you don't.'

'Oh, sure, I can do anything that takes grit and bull-headedness, but this—it would crush me.'

That was what he'd been afraid of. But he wasn't ready to give up.

'We wouldn't be trapped here all the time—'

'We would in the end.' She pulled away from him and began to pace restlessly. 'Look at this room. Dulcie would be at home here because she was raised in a place like this. Harriet would be all right because it's full of antiques. But me? I just spend my whole time hoping I don't bump into things.'

'It would be different in time,' he pleaded. 'You'll change—'

'Maybe I don't want to change,' she flashed at him. 'Maybe I think there's nothing wrong with the way I am.'

'I didn't say—'

'No, and you never will. But the truth is the truth, whether anyone says it or not. Leo, we don't just come from different worlds. It's different planets, different universes. You know it yourself.'

'We've overcome that before.'

'Yes, because of the farm. Because of the land, and the animals, and all the things we both love. It didn't matter where we came from, because we were heading in the same direction. But now—' she looked around her in despair.

'We don't have to spend much time here—we'll still have the farm—'

'Will we? This was going to be Guido's inheritance, and now he's lost it to you. Aren't you going to have to give him yours in exchange?'

That thought had been nibbling uneasily at the edge of his consciousness.

'Guido's not interested in farming, I can repay him in money. And if I have to I'll sell some of the antiques in this place. Every single one if I have to.'

'And we live on the farm and let your ancestral palace stand empty? Even I know better than that.' She tore at her short hair. 'If it was anywhere else you could simply move into the palace and buy up some farming land around it, but what can you do in Venice?'

'*Carissima*, please—'

'Don't call me that,' she said quickly.

'Why, suddenly—now?'

'Because everything's changed—now.'

'So suddenly I can't tell you that I love you more than life? I can't say that I don't want this either, but it'll be bearable if I have you?'

'*Don't!*' She turned away, her hands over her ears.

'Why mustn't I say that your love is everything to me?' he asked in a voice that was suddenly hard. 'Because you can't say the same?'

In the long silence that followed Leo felt his heart almost stop.

'I don't know,' she whispered at last. 'Oh, Leo, forgive me, but I don't know. I—I do love you—'

'Do you?' he asked in a harder voice than she had ever heard him use.

'Yes, I do love you, I do, I do—' With every repetition she grew more frantic. 'Please try to understand—'

'I understand this—that you only love me on certain conditions. When things get tough, suddenly the love isn't enough.'

He gave a bitter laugh. 'It's ironical isn't it? If I lost every penny I could count on your love. If I was left to starve in the streets I know you'd starve with me and never complain.'

'Yes—yes—'

'If I had to sell the shirt off my back you'd sell the shirt off yours, and we'd fight the world together and be happy. But if I'm rich, that means trouble. You turn away from me and wonder if I'm worth loving.'

'It's not like that,' she cried.

'I'm the same man, rich or poor, but you can only love me if we have the life you want. But I want that life too. I don't want all this either.'

'Then leave it. Tell them you won't accept. Let's go back to the farm and be happy.'

'You don't understand. It can't be done like that. All this is now my responsibility, to my family, to the people who work for us and depend on us. I can't just turn my back on all that.'

He took her gently by the shoulders and looked into her face. 'My darling, it's still a fight, just a different one. Why can't you stand by me in this one, as you would have done the other?'

'Because we'd each be fighting a different enemy, and we'd end up fighting each other. In a sense we already are.'

'This is just a little argument—'

'But you fired the first shot in the war a moment ago, didn't you notice? You said, "You don't understand". You're right. And as we go on there'll be a million things I don't understand, but you will. And more and more you won't understand the things that are important to me, and in the end we'll be saying "You don't understand" to each other a dozen times a day.'

They were silent with fear, each seeing the cracks in

the ground beneath their feet that would soon become a chasm that love couldn't bridge.

But not yet. They couldn't face it just now.

'Don't let's talk any more tonight,' Leo said hurriedly. 'We're both in a state of shock. Let's leave it until we're calmer.'

'Yes, we'll do that. We'll talk when we get home.'

That put it at a safe distance. In the meantime they could hide from what was happening.

He took her back to her room and kissed her cheek at the door.

'Try to sleep well,' he said. 'We're going to need all our strength.'

As soon as she had closed the door he walked away. He hadn't tried to go in, and she hadn't said, 'Stay with me'.

Leo spent the next day closeted with his uncle, Guido and a brace of lawyers, while Dulcie and Harriet showed Selena Venice. For an hour she tried to make the right noises, but the truth was the narrow alleys and canals suffocated her.

They went into St Mark's where Dulcie and Guido had married recently, and where Harriet and Marco would marry soon.

It was like being an ant, Selena thought, looking up into the ancient, echoing building. It was magnificent, splendid, beautiful. But it turned you into an ant.

She thought of the little parish church at Morenza, and was glad that her own wedding would be there, and not in this place that crushed her.

Dulcie seemed to understand, for as they left she took a close look at Selena's face and said, 'Come with me,' and shepherded them both to the nearby landing stage, where there were *vaporetti*, the boats Venetians used as buses.

'Three to the Lido,' she told the man in the ticket booth. To Harriet and Selena she said, 'We're going to spend the rest of the day on the beach.'

Selena's spirits had perked up as the boat headed out for the forty-minute journey across the wide lagoon. After all those alleys she was in the open at last. And when they reached the Lido, the long thin island that bounded the lagoon and boasted one of the best beaches in the world, she caught her first ever glimpse of the sea, and it cheered her even more. Now that was some open space!

They bought bathing costumes and towels in the beach shops. When they'd changed they hired a huge umbrella and sat beneath it, rubbing each other with sun cream. Dulcie told of the day she'd come here with Guido.

'He rubbed me with sun cream and I still managed to get burned, so he took me to his little bachelor flat and I was poorly for days.' She smiled reminiscently. 'It was very romantic.'

'But if you were poorly—' Selena said.

'He looked after me wonderfully.'

'But you didn't—he didn't—?'

'No. We didn't. That's what made it so romantic.'

Later they ran down the beach to swim in the sea. Selena loved it. All work and no play had been the pattern of her life, and fooling around in the sun and the waves with no purpose but to enjoy herself was a novel experience. She began to think there might be something to be said for Venice after all.

But when the day was over and it was time to return, the great palace seemed to loom, waiting to swallow her up. It was actually very well lit, with huge windows that let in the light, but in her present mood the shades seemed to fall on her as soon as she entered.

She found Leo depressed but resigned.

'There's no way out,' he said. 'I've spent the day looking over my future with lawyers and accountants until my eyes have crossed. They're trying to work out a way for me to compensate Guido financially, without having to sell the farm.'

'Can it be done?'

'If I spread it over several years.'

'How is Guido about that?'

'Great. He just shrugged and said, "It's cool. Whatever." He doesn't care. He's so happy to have dumped it on me that he's like a kid out of school. And behind that juvenile charm he's a very astute business-man. What he really lives off is his souvenir business and it's making him a fortune. But of course I've got to do the right thing by him.'

'And you'll keep the farm?'

'Yes, but life's going to change for us.'

She nodded. 'For *us*. Maybe I should have been in there too instead of being sent off to play.'

'I don't think anyone was trying to exclude you, it's just that we were all talking Italian, and you wouldn't have understood.'

He could have bitten his tongue off as soon as he said the last words, but she only smiled and said, 'Sure.'

'I mean, neither the lawyer nor the accountant speak any English, so we'd have been translating—'

'It's all right. You were absolutely right. It doesn't really concern me, does it?'

'Everything that happens to me concerns you,' he said

emphatically. 'I'm sorry, darling, maybe you should have come in, despite the practical problems.'

She nodded, still smiling but still keeping her distance. But his face looked so desperate and weary that she couldn't stand it.

'I'm sorry,' she said huskily, throwing her arms around him. 'I'm a bitch to nag you when you're unhappy.'

'Just stay with me,' he said, holding her tight. 'Don't leave me to struggle through this alone.'

'I won't, I won't.'

He sighed. 'I've got a confession to make. Uncle started on again about our wedding. According to him it has to be St Mark's. I told him it was up to you.'

'Oh, great! Blame me!' She managed to smile. 'You'd better say yes. You can't start your new life by fighting with your family.'

'Thank you *carissima*.' He held her fiercely. 'We'll be out of here tomorrow.'

'It'll be all right when we're home,' she insisted.

But her words sounded hollow even to her own ears. She was full of dread, and she could sense that his own dread matched it.

She kept repeating to herself that everything would be all right when they were away from here. It was a mantra that kept her going as they packed their things next morning. Just a few more hours, a few more minutes— Even then she knew there was no real escape. They would have to return in a couple of weeks for Leo to sign papers.

'You come alone,' she told him.

'I want you with me. After all, you said yourself that it concerns you too.'

'But there's nothing for me to sign. I'll stay home and—'

'And be there when I get back?' he asked fiercely. 'Will you?'

'Of—of course I will.'

'I want you with me,' he repeated with a hint of mulishness around his mouth.

So he sensed it too, she thought.

It was like an ugly demon sitting on the floor between them, forcing them both to sidestep, but without ever admitting that it was there.

More than anyone it was the countess who unsettled her. Her English was so poor that they couldn't communicate except through an interpreter, and then Selena didn't know how to interpret her awkwardness. It might be shyness, unease, or downright disapproval. Selena reckoned she could guess which one.

In the last few minutes before they left the countess approached her. There was nobody else there, and in her hand she clutched a dictionary.

'I speak—with you,' she said in a voice that showed she was reciting prepared words.

'Yes?' Selena tried to look composed.

'Things are—different now—your marriage—we must speak—'

'But I know,' Selena said passionately. 'You don't have to tell me, I know. How can I marry him? You don't want me to, and you're right. I don't belong here. I don't belong in your world. *I know*.'

A tense, haughty look came over the countess's face. She took a sharp breath. The next moment there was the sound of footsteps on marble and she stepped back.

The rest of the family appeared, engulfing them. There

were goodbyes, attempts at cheer. The boat was at the landing stage, then they were drawing away, the strip of water growing wide, and the problems were just beginning.

CHAPTER ELEVEN

Now there was the relief of attending to the harvest. All over the valley the vineyards and the olive groves were humming with activity. Carts passed along the lines, gradually filling up with the best the earth had to offer. Selena was there, sometimes with Leo, sometimes alone. Even alone she could communicate with Leo's people for most of them had a smattering of English and she had mastered a few words of Tuscan, which she used badly enough to amuse everyone. In this way she forged her links with them.

And it might all be for nothing, she would think, looking out over the acres as the sun descended. For who knew how things would be this time next year? Who knew how much of the farm would still belong to him? And these new friends she was making, with whom she felt so much more at ease than her fine new family in their grandiose palace, how many of them would still think of her as a friend?

They too were worried, she sensed it. They would stop and ask her questions, because she was going to marry the *padrone*, and therefore she must know him best. How could she tell them that she didn't feel she knew him at all any more? The instinctive fellow-feeling that had united her with Leo increasingly seemed no more than a happy memory.

And besides, she saw him less because he was constantly being recalled to Venice to settle some point or other. He'd sworn it would make very little difference to them, but by now they both knew that it wasn't in his power to keep that promise. Inch by inch he was being forced onto a road where she couldn't follow.

These days she often slept in her own room to hide the fact that she sometimes awoke gasping for breath. She had a sense of floundering in a maze from which there was no way out, but only roads growing narrower until they vanished altogether, and herself with them.

She called the Four-Ten, and avidly drank in news about the Hanworth family. Paulie had gone to Dallas to start another internet firm—or so he said, but Barton confided that a jealous husband had been haunting the ranch for a while, uttering dire threats should Paulie ever reappear.

Billie was marrying her guy, Carrie was exercising Jeepers, and they'd had two offers for him. If Selena wasn't coming back—

'No,' Selena said quickly. 'If I'm not sending you enough money for him—'

'You're sending more than enough,' Barton boomed, offended. 'Think I grudge you a little horse feed?'

'I know you don't. You've all been such good friends to me, but I'm not going to take advantage of it—'

'What else are friends for? You don't want me to sell Jeepers? He's a good racer and he's going to waste right now.'

'I know but—just hang onto him a little longer, please Barton. How's Elliot?'

'He's fine. Carrie rides him, and she says he's a real sweet old feller.'

'Yes,' Selena said. 'I remember that.'

She hung up, and went into the kitchen to discuss the evening meal with Gina. Leo was due back from Venice and Gina was preparing sardine and potato bake for him.

After that Selena went into the office and worked hard on paperwork for the horse farm.

Then she dropped her head on her hands and wept.

It was dark when Leo drove up, for the nights were drawing in. He ate his meal with gusto but when Selena asked about his trip he had strangely little to say.

She knew what that meant. Bit by bit he was being drawn into their world, and he didn't know how to tell her.

After supper she headed back to the office, to 'finish some stuff.'

'Aren't you coming to bed?' he asked.

'Well, I just thought I'd—'

'No,' he said. 'Come to bed.'

Arms about each other they climbed the stairs. In his room he took her in his arms and kissed her deeply. The desire was always there, perhaps deeper now that it was almost the only way they could communicate. They undressed each other swiftly, eager for the union that was still perfect and in which there were no problems.

For a short, blissful time there was a hot urgency that swept everything before it. She called his name as if from a long distance, and tried to find comfort in his look of tender adoration. As passion faded into contentment she fell asleep with her head against him.

But as soon as she slept her surroundings changed. She was fighting her way through a thicket. She struggled but it was closing in on her, shutting out the air, suffocating her. She awoke, gasping for breath.

'*Carissima*—' Leo sat up and put on the bedside light. 'Wake up, wake up!'

She held him until the shaking stopped and he drew her close, stroking her hair.

'It's all right,' he murmured. 'I'm here. Hold on to me, it was only a dream.'

'I couldn't breathe,' she choked. 'Everything's closing in on me and I can't find a way through.'

'You've had that dream before, haven't you?' he said sadly. 'I've see you toss and turn and I know you're unhappy. And then the next night you've insisted on sleeping apart. But you never tell me. Why won't you let me share it?'

As though he didn't know the answer!

'It's nothing,' she said quickly. 'Just a dream. Hold me.'

They clung together until he asked quietly, 'Are you going to leave me?'

In the long silence he felt the darkness fall over his heart.

'No,' she said at last, 'I don't think so—but—I need to go back for a while. Just for a while—'

'Yes,' he said heavily, 'just for a while.'

He drove her to Pisa Airport next day. They were late arriving and the flight to Dallas had already been called.

'I'd better hurry then,' she said.

'Have you got everything?'

She gave an edgy little laugh. 'You keep asking me that. I guess I'll find I've left something important behind.'

He nodded. 'Yes.'

'Will passengers—?'

Suddenly he said, 'Selena, don't go.'

'I have to.'

'No, you don't. If you go, you won't come back. This is where we have to work it out. Don't go.'

'There's my flight.'

'*Don't go!* You know as well as I do what'll happen if you do.'

She faced him. 'I'm sorry—I'm sorry.' Tears were pouring down her face. 'I did try, but I just can't—Leo, I'm sorry—so sorry—'

He reached out but she slipped through his fingers. At the gate she turned back for a last look. She wasn't crying now, but the misery on her face reflected his own. For one moment he thought she would run back to him. But then she was gone.

Winter was a busy time in the souvenir business. Guido had decided on his lines for the following year and was busy showing his product to customers. In a couple of weeks he had a show so big that the only place for it was the Palazzo Calvani. The count had grumbled at the 'indignity' but given his consent.

But in the midst of his preparations Guido found the time to take off for Rome, with Dulcie, to share their great news.

After two days in Rome, celebrating with Marco and Harriet, now in countdown to their wedding, and Lucia, who was in seventh heaven, they headed for Bella Podena.

'So I'm going to be an uncle,' Leo said, toasting them.

It was the fifth time he'd done so. Everyone in the household had toasted them the first time, and the proud parents-to-be were sitting in a glow of happiness.

But Dulcie was a little uncomfortable with her own joy. She'd sensed something forced about Leo's celebrating. When they were taking plates out into the kitchen, Gina having gone to bed, she touched his arm and asked gently, 'Is there any news?'

He shook his head. There was a heaviness about him

that hurt her, because it was so unlike the cheerful, take-life-as-it-comes Leo that they all knew.

'She'll come back,' she said gently. 'It's not long—'

'One month, one week and three days,' he said simply.

'Do you know where she is?'

'Yes, I've started tracking her through the internet again. She's doing well.'

'You haven't spoken to her?'

'I called her once. She was very nice.' There was a heaviness in his voice that told Dulcie all she needed to know about that call.

'Call her again and tell her to come home,' Dulcie said firmly.

But Leo shook his head. 'It has to be how she wants. I can't take her freedom away from her.'

'But we all lose our freedom for the one we love. Some of it, anyway.'

'Yes, and that's fine, if it's given up gladly. But if it's coerced it can't work. If she doesn't come back to me of her own free will, she won't stay.'

'And if she doesn't come back because she doesn't know how badly you want her?'

Leo gave a painful smile. 'She knows that.'

'Oh, Leo!'

She put her arms around him, hugging tightly. He hugged her back, dropping his shaggy head to rest on her shoulder, where she stroked it tenderly.

Guido, coming into the kitchen with plates, stopped on the threshold.

'My wife in my brother's arms!' he announced. 'Should I be jealous, creep away, shoot myself?'

'Oh, stop your nonsense!' his wife ordered him.

'Yes, dear!'

Dulcie gave Leo a little shake. 'It's going to be all right.'

'Of course it is,' he replied.

'He didn't mean a word of it,' Dulcie told her husband as they prepared for bed. 'It's not all right for him at all. He's living in a half-world. Gina told me today that sometimes he stands at the window looking down the road where he first saw her. It's as though he expected her to appear again, as if by magic. Just like last time.'

'Drat the woman!' Guido said, getting into bed and curving his arm for her. 'What does she mean by doing this to him?'

'Don't let Leo hear you say a word against her,' Dulcie advised, snuggling up to her husband. 'He understands her. He says she must find her own way home. If she doesn't, it means it's not really her home.'

'That's very profound for Leo,' Guido said, much struck. 'His mind never used to rise above the very basic—horses, crops and willing ladies, not necessarily in that order.'

'But he's changed. Even I've seen that, and I didn't really know the old Leo. I'll tell you this, Leo reckons her feelings are more important than his own.'

'I wish *I* did.' Guido sighed. 'The truth is, I suppose I'm feeling guilty. If I'd left well alone—?'

'What else could you do? The records were there. They have to work their own salvation out.'

'And if they fail—? What's that noise?' He rose and went to the window, looking out at a high barn, from which came the sound of a voice, coaxing and pleading. A faint light shone from one of the windows.

'It sounds like Leo,' he said, pulling on a dressing gown. 'What's he playing at? He's supposed to be in bed.'

Dulcie paused long enough to put on her own dressing gown, then followed her husband down to the yard and across to the barn. The door stood open.

Inside, the hay was piled up to the high ceiling just below which there was a ledge. A ladder stood propped against one of the supports, with Leo climbing unsteadily to the top, which fell several feet short of the ledge.

'Leo, whatever's the matter up there?' Guido yelled.

'It's a barn owl. She's trapped. I think she's hurt her wing.'

'Isn't she safe up there?'

Leo's voice reached him faintly. 'She can't fly for food, and she has young. I'm trying to bring them all down to safety.'

'Careful,' Guido called his alarm. 'It's dangerous. Haven't you got a longer ladder?'

'It's being mended. I'm all right. Just a little further.'

Leo had reached the top now, so that he was on a level with the birds. Guido, watching below, could see a white owl face in the gloom.

'Is he all right?' Dulcie asked, coming to stand beside her husband.

'Well, he's got rocks in his head, but that's nothing new,' Guido said with a shrug that was pure Venetian in its mixture of humour, resignation, affection and wryness.

'He's risking a terrible fall,' Dulcie said worriedly. 'For an owl?'

'The way he sees it, it's his owl. Whatever's his he looks after.'

A low whisper of triumph overhead announced that Leo had succeeded, at least. He was holding the injured barn owl in one hand, and supporting himself with the

other, moving back very carefully, unable to see where
he was going.

'How near am I to the ladder?' he yelled.

'Another three feet,' Guido called. 'But you can't do
it with one hand full.'

Guido was level with the ladder now. Gently Leo laid
the owl down in the hay and began to lower himself, his
feet seeking the top rung. When he'd found it he reached
back for the owl, but the nervous creature suddenly took
fright and began to flutter awkwardly, moving just out
of reach.

'Don't be difficult, *cara*,' Leo pleaded. 'Just a few
minutes and we'll both be safe.'

'Leave it,' Dulcie pleaded from below. 'It's too dan—
Leo!'

The owl had edged back, causing Leo to lunge after
it. It all happened in a flash. He lost contact with the
ladder, tried frantically to regain his footing, and the next
moment was plunging to the ground.

After Dallas Selena's next move should have been to
Abilene, where she'd always done well. But by giving
Abilene a miss she was able to head back to
Stephenville, and the chance to see Elliot.

She'd formed a bond with Jeepers that went deeper
than she could have believed possible. But Elliot was
her family. He'd been with her through the times when
she didn't have two cents to rub together. The way she
saw it, he'd introduced her to Leo.

She didn't quite admit to herself that it was also a
chance to see the Hanworths, and talk about Leo. She
was working on being strong and sensible about that.
Since she'd made the decision to cut him out of her life
it was pure self-indulgence to revel in talking about him.

But if the subject happened to come up it would do a little to ease the ache in her heart that was with her, night and day. The temptation to stay with him had been overwhelming. She'd fought it as much for his sake as her own. To be with him year after year, failing him, never quite understanding the things that mattered in his world, and to see the disillusion appearing in his eyes— these things would have been unendurable.

He would have been kind, she had no doubt of that. As the dimensions of his mistake became clear to him he would have become increasingly gentle, determined not to blame her for the disaster he had urged on her. And it would have been his kindness that broke her heart.

Several times she started to dial his number, but she always managed to be strong in time, and hang up with the number incomplete.

It was nearly dark when she reached the Four-Ten, later than she'd intended because she'd stopped twice on the way, trying to decide if she was really going or not. There were lights on in the house, but at the sound of her engine a dozen more came on. The front door was thrown open and Barton came hurrying out to greet her.

'Get inside fast,' he said tensely. 'Leo's brother's here.'

'Barton, has something happened?'

'Guido will tell you. Hurry!'

She didn't know how she got inside. Guido was there. He rose to his feet as she appeared and her heart nearly failed her, for she had never seen a face so pale and distraught.

'Guido, what's happened?'

'Leo had a fall,' he said, and stopped as though he couldn't bear to go on.

'And?' she repeated in agony.

'He was up high in the barn, chasing after a hurt owl—you know what he's like—and he missed his footing and fell—best part of forty feet.'

'Oh, God! Please Guido, tell me he's alive.'

'Yes, he is, but we don't know when he'll walk again.'

Her hands flew to her mouth. Leo, the man who never sat when he could stand, never walked when he could run; Leo in a wheelchair, or worse. She turned away so that Guido couldn't see that she was fighting not to cry.

'I came to take you home,' Guido said. 'He needs you, Selena.'

'Of course. Oh, why didn't you just telephone me? I could have been on my way.'

'To be honest, I didn't think you'd be willing. I came here to take you by force if I had to.'

'Of course she'll come,' Barton said, entering from the hall. 'You leave everything here, Selena. Elliot and Jeepers will be just fine with us. Get going, girl.'

He drove them to the airport himself. Guido already had her air tickets.

'I told you I wasn't going to take no for an answer,' he said with a wan smile. 'I meant it.'

'You really thought I wouldn't come if Leo needs me?'

'I don't think you'd have believed a phone call. It's just words coming from a long way away.'

'But you came all this way for me,' she said, softened.

'I had to. I don't know how he's going to be, but I do know you've got to be there.'

He dozed most of the journey, and Selena didn't care to talk. Too many thoughts were confusing her all at once. She wouldn't know what she thought until she saw Leo again.

From Pisa Airport a car conveyed them to the hospital. Selena's nails ground into her palm. Now the moment had come she was terrified at what she would find. The last few yards to Leo's ward seemed endless.

His door was just in front of them. Guido opened it and stood back to let her go in.

Her eyes went swiftly to the bed, and then she stopped, frozen.

There was nobody there.

'Selena?'

The voice came from the window. She turned and saw a man standing there supported by crutches, one leg in plaster.

'Selena?' He made an unsteady, hobbling step towards her, and the next moment she was in his arms.

It was an awkward kind of kiss, holding each other up, not daring to clasp too tight, but it was the sweetest they had ever known.

'How do you come to be here?' he managed to say at last, when he could speak.

'That—brother of yours—'

Leo gave a shaky laugh. 'Has he been up to his tricks again?'

'*You!*' From the safety of Leo's arms Selena turned on Guido, watching them with immense satisfaction, from the doorway. 'You told me he couldn't walk.'

'Well, he can't walk,' Guido said innocently. 'That's why he's got crutches. He broke his ankle.'

'He broke—?'

'Any other man would have been killed by that fall,' Guido added. 'But the devil looks after his own, and Leo landed on a bale of hay.'

He vanished tactfully.

'You came back to me,' Leo said huskily. 'Hold me tightly.'

She did so and he immediately winced.

'It doesn't matter,' he said. 'All that matters is that you're back, and you're staying. Yes, you are—' he said it quickly before she could argue. 'You're not going to leave me again, I couldn't bear it.'

'I couldn't bear it either,' she said fervently. 'It was so dreadful without you. I kept trying to believe I'd done the right thing, then I'd weaken and decide to follow you, but then I'd be afraid of embarrassing you because you'd probably found somebody else—'

'You stupid, stupid woman,' he said lovingly.

He winced again at he spoke.

'Come on,' she said tenderly, 'you should be in bed.'

With his arm around her shoulders he hobbled the few steps to the bed, where she helped him off with his robe. Beneath it his chest was bare, except for some strapping, and she gasped at the multitude of bruises, blue, black, red, overlapping each other.

'It's all right, they're getting better,' he said.

Clinging to her he eased himself down onto the bed and lay back, exhausted.

'If you could pull the sheet up—Selena? Don't cry.'

'I'm not crying,' she wept, trying to brush back the tears that flowed down her cheeks.

'You're not?' he asked tenderly.

'No, I'm not. You know I never cry, and don't you dare try to suggest—oh, look at you! Oh, my darling, darling—'

He held her as close against him as he dared, kissing the top of her head.

'It looks worse than it is,' he reassured her. 'Just a

few bruises—well, OK, a cracked rib or two, but nothing to what it might have been.'

Guido slid out of the door, unnoticed by either of them.

'I never thought I'd see you again,' Leo said. 'It's like a dream come true. How could you leave me?'

'I don't know. But I never will again.'

He was home in a week, promising the doctor to go straight to bed, and spending the first day in the car while Selena drove him over his lands.

'Now you're going to bed, as you promised,' she said firmly when they got home.

'Only if you come with me.'

'You're not well enough.'

'I'm well enough to hold you against my heart,' he said. 'That's what I've missed the most. Don't you know that?'

He was still a very odd colour but he moved more easily, and when he'd settled into bed he was able to put his arms about her without wincing too much.

'Are you going to be all right for the journey next week?' she asked.

'Sure, Venice is no distance, and I wouldn't miss seeing Marco's wedding for anything. And don't worry, just because they're marrying in St Mark's, that doesn't mean that people will start nagging us to do the same. They understand that we'll be marrying here.'

He sighed. 'It can't be soon enough for me. We might go down to the church and talk about it tomorrow.'

Silence.

'*Carissima*? Is something the matter?'

'Don't let's rush anything, Leo.'

'Well, I can't rush anything, can I? Look at me. I need

to get fully fit because I want to enjoy our wedding day, but that won't take long—'

'No, that's not what I mean.' She sat up, evading his hand that would have drawn her back.

'Leo, I do love you, please believe that. And now that I've come back I won't go away again. It hurt too much. But in a sense, nothing has changed. The things that were wrong before are still wrong now.

'I won't leave you, I swear it, but—I can't marry you.'

CHAPTER TWELVE

FOR breakfast Gina had a wide choice of dishes, each one a favorite of Leo's, which she pressed on him until he begged for mercy.

'I'll clear away, Gina,' Selena said. 'I know you've got masses to do.'

'*Si, signorina.*' Gina nodded and went on her way.

'That's it,' Leo said when she'd gone. 'Gina's accepted you as her employer. As far as she's concerned it's a done deal.'

'Gina's flattering me. I wouldn't know how to run a house and she knows it even better than I do.'

'Of course. That's her job. Your job is to leave everything to her. But haven't you noticed that these days she asks you, not me?' He rested his fingertips on the back of her hand. 'Signora Calvani,' he murmured.

'Leo—I told you last night—'

'I was hoping that was a nightmare,' he groaned. 'You went away so soon afterwards—'

'You weren't saying anything.'

'I was trying to pretend it hadn't happened. Selena, please let's forget last night. After everything that's happened we weren't our normal selves.' When she shook her head he demanded, 'Are you trying to send me white haired?'

'I can't marry you. I couldn't be a countess if my life depended on it. Your uncle won't live for ever. What happens when you inherit? One day you'll want to do the whole "count thing" properly, Venice, the palace, society, the whole lot.'

'*Me?*' he demanded aghast. 'Selena, for pity's sake, I'm a country man. You can't rear horses in Venice. They'd drown.'

But the attempt at a joke fell on stony ground. Selena's face was as stubborn as he'd ever seen it, and he was filled with alarm.

'I don't believe this,' he said. 'I thought we'd settled that we loved each other and were going to be together for ever. Or did I miss something?'

'No, my darling, I do love you. Oh, Leo, if you knew how much I love you. I'll stay, but not like that.'

'Well that's too bad, because *like that* is how I am,' he snapped.

He spoke more harshly than she ever heard him before, but his nerves were taut. His head was aching, his foot was aching, and his normal resilience was at a low ebb.

'But it can't be how *I* am,' she said, setting her chin.

And suddenly the chasm was there again, as though they had never been reunited.

They papered over the cracks to drive to Venice for the wedding. There they smiled and played their roles perfectly. The palace had only just got back to normal after Guido's trade show, before it was snowed under with guests for the wedding.

Selena was glad to vanish into the crowd. She and Leo had agreed not to alert the family to their differences, and there were a few of the usual hints about setting the date. But they could cope with these more easily than the truth.

And she knew that Leo was hoping that if nothing was said, her resolution would simply wear out.

In the great basilica of St Mark's she watched the bride arrive, and knew that Harriet was at home in these grand surroundings. There was a magnificence about her as she gave her hand to the man she loved, and he looked at her out of eyes full of emotion. Their happiness seemed to fill the church and reach out to touch everyone there.

Selena turned and met Leo's eyes. She was sure she saw reproach in them, as though he was accusing her of denying him the same happiness. She looked away. Why couldn't he understand that she was doing what was best for both of them?

At the reception she drank champagne, toasted the bride and groom and cheered them when they left on honeymoon. As the evening wore on she looked around for Leo, but he'd vanished into the count's study with some of the other men. And he stayed there until she'd gone to bed.

Next day he was subdued during the farewells, and on the journey home he dozed while she drove. They left late and it was dark when they reached home. Selena had told Gina to go to bed, and they found supper waiting for them.

As they uncovered the dishes she said, 'You told them, didn't you?'

'I didn't need to. They could tell. They kept asking me about our wedding, and you can only put people off just so often before they guess the truth.'

'So now they know. Perhaps it's best.'

'Selena, didn't anything that happened back there mean anything to you? Didn't you see Marco and Harriet, the way they committed themselves to each other? That's why marriage is important. Without it there's no commitment. I thought we were committed, but now you're telling me that you're not. What kind of a future can we have?'

'We'll make our future in our own way—'

'In your way, you mean? I love you, I want you for my wife.'

'It's impossible,' she said despairingly.

'It's only impossible if you make it so.' He took a deep breath. 'What's impossible to me is to go on like this.'

'What are you saying?'

'I'm saying that I love you, and I'm proud of you. I want to walk out of church with you on my arm and tell the world this is the woman I've chosen, and she's chosen me. I hope you wanted the same, but if you don't—'

'Go on.'

He said, as though the words were torn out of him, 'If you don't, then we have nothing. You may as well go home again.'

'Are you throwing me out, Leo?'

Suddenly he slammed his hand on the table, and in this sweet-tempered man the gesture was more shocking than it would have been in anyone else.

'No, dammit!' he roared. 'I want you to stay here. I want you to love me, and marry me and have my children. I want to spend the rest of my life with you. But it has to be *married*. Does that sound like throwing you out?'

'It sounds like giving me an ultimatum.'

'All right then, I'm giving you one. If you love me one tenth as much as you've always said you do, then marry me. I can't compromise on this, it's too important to me.'

'And what about what's important to me?'

'I've heard about nothing except what's important to you, and I've tried to understand, although it put me through hell. Now it's my turn to tell you what I want.'

She stared at him, a man she'd thought she knew through and through. Leo had finally lost his temper, not in the half humorous way she'd seen when he roared with frustration, but in deep, genuine anger. His eyes were as gleaming and dangerous as any man's she'd ever seen. It was as though the last piece of him had slid into place.

That feeling persisted even when he immediately ran his hand through his hair and said, 'I'm sorry. I didn't mean to shout.'

'I don't mind shouting,' she said truthfully. 'I can always shout back. I'm good at that.'

'Yes, I know,' he said shakily. 'I don't mind the shouting either. It's the silent distances I can't stand.'

'There are too many of them now,' she agreed.

She took a step towards him. He moved in the same moment, and they were in each other's arms.

It was a long, fulfilling kiss and she felt her fears and tensions ease. While they had this—

'Don't ever frighten me like that again,' she said. 'I really thought you meant it.'

He released her. 'I did mean it.'

She stepped back. 'No, Leo, please—listen—'

'I've listened as much as I mean to,' he said firmly. 'I can't do it your way. In here—' he touched his heart '—you're already my wife. I can't live differently on the outside. I can't live a divided life.'

'And you'd really send me away?'

'My darling, if we tried to do it your way we'd pull apart sooner rather than later, and part miserably. We'd have nothing left but bitter memories. It would be better to part now, while there's still love to remember.'

'Oh, you—'

She turned away, waving her arms in angry, helpless gestures, then began to bang her head against the wall. He quickly took hold of her and pulled her away, pressing her against him.

'I feel like doing that too,' he said, 'but it just gives you a headache.'

'What are we going to do?' she wept.

'We're going to have something to eat, and we're going to talk like civilised people.'

But they couldn't talk. They had each stated their position, and each recognised that the other was immovable. What was there to say after that?

They were both glad to go to bed, in their separate rooms, but after a couple of hours of lying awake Selena got dressed and came downstairs.

She didn't put any lights on, but walked from room to room in silence, wondering if she would soon leave here. It would have been so easy to run back to Leo and promise to marry him, anything rather than leave him. But the conviction that they would both pay a heavy price for a brief happiness lay heavy on her. She could take the risk for herself, but not for him.

She wanted to bang her head against the wall again, but she didn't because she was too tired and her head was aching already. At last she settled on a sofa by the window, put her arms on the back, and dozed off uneasily.

She was awoken by a hand on her shoulder.

'Darling, wake up,' Leo said.

'What time is it?' she asked, moving stiffly.

'Seven in the morning. We've got visitors, look.'

They went out into the yard, where two cars that they recognised were coming up the slope.

'It's the family,' she said. 'But we saw them only yesterday. Why have they followed us here?'

The cars drew to a halt, and Guido and Dulcie got out of the first. Out of the second, to their astonishment, stepped the count and countess.

'We are here on a very important matter,' Count Calvani announced. 'My wife insists that she must speak to Selena. The rest of us merely travel as her entourage.'

'Come inside,' Leo said. 'It's too cold to stay out here.'

Inside Gina served them with hot coffee. Selena was still trying to sort out what was happening. Why did the old woman want to see her? Why were her eyes fixed on her so urgently?

'Will someone tell me what's happening?' she said.

'I come to you,' Liza said slowly, 'because there are things—' she hesitated, frowning '—things that only I can say.'

'We're here to help,' Dulcie said, 'in case Liza's English runs out. She's been working hard at learning it, for your sake, and as far as possible she wants to say this herself.'

'I tried before,' Liza said. 'But then—I do not have the words—and you do not listen.'

'When you were in Venice the first time,' Dulcie said. 'Liza tried to talk to you, but you ran away.'

'There was no need for her to tell me I was the wrong person for Leo,' Selena said. 'I knew that.'

'No, no, no!' Liza said firmly. She glared at Selena. 'You should talk less, listen more. *Si*?'

'*Si!*' Leo said at once.

Unexpectedly Selena also smiled. '*Si,*' she said.

'Good,' Liza spoke robustly. 'I come to say—you do a terrible thing—as I did. And you must not.'

'What am I doing that's terrible?' Selena asked cautiously.

'After what Leo told us we had a family conference last night,' Guido said, 'and we reckoned we all had to come out here and talk some sense into you. But Liza most of all.'

'Now, you come with me,' Liza said firmly. She set down her cup and headed for the door.

'Can I come?' Leo asked.

Liza regarded him. 'Can you keep quiet?'

'Yes, Aunt,' he said meekly.

'Then you can come.' She marched out.

'What is she doing?' Selena asked him.

'I think I know. You can trust her.'

He followed them out to the car, handing Liza in, while Dulcie got behind the wheel.

'Drive down through Morenza,' Liza said, 'and then—two miles further on—a farm.'

Dulcie followed instructions and they were soon out in the countryside, surrounded by fields, with the occasional low-roofed building. The others came behind them.

'There,' Liza said, indicating a farm house.

Dulcie turned in and drove the short distance to the cluster of buildings. A middle-aged man looked up and greeted Liza. Selena didn't hear the words they exchanged. Liza led the way past the house to a collection of outbuildings, and into a cow byre.

It was a large building, filled with animals, for they had arrived at milking time.

Liza turned and faced Selena.

'I was born here,' she said.

Selena frowned. 'You mean—in the house?'

'No, I mean here, in this room, where we stand now. My mother was a servant and she lived here, with the animals. In those days—it sometimes happened. Poor people lived like that. And we were very, very poor.'

'But—' Selena looked around helplessly.

'I was not born a fine lady. You didn't know?'

'Yes, I knew you weren't born with a title but—this—'

'Yes,' Liza nodded. 'This. In those days there was—big gap between rich and poor.' She demonstrated with her hands. 'And my mother was not married. She never told my father's name, and there was much disgrace for her. This was seventy years ago, you understand. Not like now.

'When I was a child—my mother died, and I was put to work in the house. Always I was told—I was lucky to have food and work. I was a bastard. I had no rights. I was taught nothing.

'It was Maria Rinucci who saved me. These lands—her dowry when she married Count Angelo Calvani. She was sorry for me—took me to Venice with her. That was how I met my Francesco.'

A glow came over her face as she turned to look at the count, watching her, smiling.

'If you could have seen him then,' she said, returning his smile, 'how young and handsome—he loved me, and of course I loved him. But—no use. He must marry—great lady. He ask me. I say no. How can he marry me? For forty years I say no. And then—I understand—I make big mistake. And now I come to tell you—don't make my mistake.'

'But Liza—' Selena stammered '—you don't know—'

'Don't be stupid,' Liza said flatly. 'Of course I know. I tell *you*. People think it must be—wonderful to be Cinderella. I say no. Sometimes—a burden.'

'Yes,' Selena said in relief at finding someone who understood. 'Yes.'

'But if it's your destiny,' Liza said fiercely, 'you must accept that burden—else you will break Prince Charming's heart.'

She took her husband's hand. He was looking at her with a world of love in his eyes.

'People see us and they think how romantic that our story had a happy ending,' Liza said, a little sadly. 'But what they do not see is in here—' she indicated her breast '—my bitter regret that our love was only fulfilled at the end. We could have been happy long ago, I could have had his children. But I wasted all those years because I made too much of things that didn't matter.'

Leo had come quietly forward until he was standing beside Selena. Liza saw it, and smiled.

She had one last thing to say to Selena, and now her words began to come easily, as though she had found the key.

'In all your life, nobody has valued you, and so you did not learn to value yourself. Then how can you understand Leo, who values you more than anything in the world? How can you accept his love, when you think you are not worthy of love?'

'Is that what I think?' Selena asked, dazed.

'Has anyone else ever loved you?'

Selena shook her head. 'No. Nobody. You're right. You grow up thinking that you're not entitled to much—' she saw Liza nod in a comprehension that included only the two of them '—and when Leo loved me

I kept thinking he'd made a mistake, and he'd wake up soon and realise that it was only me after all.'

'Only you,' Liza echoed. 'Only the woman he adores. Only the first woman he has ever asked to marry him. And, I think, the last. Don't harm him as I harmed my Francesco. But trust him. Trust his love for you. Trust your own love for him. Don't make my mistake, and throw away your happiness until it is almost too late.'

Selena turned to Leo and found him looking anxiously into her face. The enormity of what she'd nearly done to him shook her and she couldn't stop the tears coming.

'I love you,' she said huskily. 'I love you so much— and I never understood a thing.'

'You just didn't know about families,' he said tenderly. 'Now you do.'

She was wanted. The whole family was opening its hearts and its arms to her—she, who'd never had kin that she could recall—not who'd wanted her, anyway.

'Marry me,' he said at once. 'Let me hear you say it.'

She never did say it. She could only nod vigorously while he took her into his arms and held her. Leaning down so that his chin rested on her head. Recovered treasure.

'I'm never letting you go again,' he said.

They set the wedding for as soon as possible, before winter closed in. Count Francesco was so delighted to be welcoming Selena into the family at last that he yielded about St Mark's, and happily agreed that the village church in Morenza was the only suitable place.

The date was booked at the little church, and a flurry of cleaning got the house ready for guests.

For the groom there was the entire Calvani family, but now they were Selena's family too. Selena had invited Ben, the loyal friend who'd kept her on the road long enough to meet Leo, and his wife, Martha. She sent them the tickets, and on the day she and Leo drove to the airport to collect them.

This wedding wouldn't have been complete without the Hanworths, all except Paulie, who found something better to do. Leo went to meet them alone, leaving Selena with Ben and Martha, catching up on old times.

'I'd better give you this before I forget it,' Selena said casually, handing Ben an envelope.

'*How much?*' Ben yelped at the size of the cheque he pulled out.

'That's all the money I must owe you going back a few years. Do you think I didn't know how you pared the bills down? And you couldn't afford it.'

'Can *you* afford it? You must have won every race in sight.'

'It's not all winnings. I'm working for Leo now, with his horses.'

'He pays you?'

'You bet he pays me. I'm very good at my job. I don't come cheap.'

'Well, I guess you found your right place. You always did have a way with horses. Look what you managed to do with Elliot. Nobody else could have done as well with him.'

'Oh, Ben, don't. The one thing that isn't perfect was that I just abandoned Elliot.'

'I thought he was being cared for by that Hanworth fellow who's coming this afternoon.'

'He is. He'll have the best of everything, but I just know he's wondering why I don't come back. Talking of coming back, where is everyone? Leo should have brought them home by now.'

As the day wore on Selena had the feeling that everyone was in on a secret from which only she was excluded. Maids giggled in doorways and vanished at her approach. Once Gina asked if Leo had given her a wedding present yet.

'Not yet,' Selena said, bewildered.

'Perhaps you get it today,' Gina observed, and went away smiling.

Hours passed. She began to feel nervous. Surely they should have been home by now?

In the late afternoon Gina came to find her.

'*Signorina*, I think you should look out of the window. There is something there for you to see.'

Puzzled, Selena went to look down the road that led to the village. A little group of people were walking slowly up to her. She recognised Barton, Delia and the rest of the family. But she also recognised a figure that she hadn't dared hope to see again.

'*Elliot!*' she shrieked and flew out of the house.

Leo was leading the way up the road, holding Elliot's bridle, grinning as he saw her. All the others were smiling too as she arrived in a rush and threw her arms about the old horse's neck.

'You—' she whirled on the Hanworth family. 'You brought him over with you?'

'Sure did,' Barton said, beaming. 'Me and Leo stitched it all up, and he swore he wouldn't let you get wind of it.'

Selena had remembered her manners and embraced Delia, Barton, then the girls. She would have hugged Jack too but he warned her off with a boyish glare.

'Elliot, Elliot—' Tears poured down her face.

'That's why we've been so long,' Leo said. 'It took time to get him off the plane and clear him for entry.

Never seen so much paperwork, but in the end they passed him. By the way, that offer on Jeepers is still open.'

'Better take it,' Selena agreed. 'He's a racer, he needs to do his stuff. Elliot—' she kissed his nose again ''—just needs to rest and be loved.'

The Calvanis arrived next day, and they and the Hanworths immediately took to each other. In the rowdy party that followed Selena saw Liza looking a little overwhelmed and took her up to bed.

'Thank you. Thank you for everything.'

When they had hugged she said, 'You really think I can do it—be a *contessa*?'

'Not in the old way,' Liza said. 'That belonged to another age. You will do it your own way, and that is right. Things must change if they are to live.'

Selena considered this. 'A cowgirl *contessa*?'

'I like that,' Liza said at once. 'I admired you so much at the rodeo. It's such a shame that I'm too old to learn to ride.' They laughed, then she became serious again. 'Only one thing makes you a *contessa*, and that is the love of a count. Never forget that.'

Downstairs Selena found the brothers arguing about money. Guido didn't want to take any from Leo, know that the raising of it might damage the farm.

'And who wants to live in the palace once you've sold off everything?' he demanded.

'I don't want to live in it at all,' Leo retorted. 'Uncle, please arrange to live a very long time so that this will remain academic.'

'I'll do my best,' the count agreed imperturbably, 'but when I'm not there this problem *will* be there. Still. You should settle it now.'

'I don't want to live in the palace,' Leo said stubbornly.

'Then we needn't,' Selena said. 'Guido can stay there.'

Everyone turned to look at her.

'Guido, have I got this right?' Selena asked him. 'You don't want the title and all the stuff that goes with it. But you love Venice, and you love the palace.'

'Right.'

'And it's a great backdrop for your business.' She turned to Leo. 'So he stays there. We just have to turn up for special occasions. You work out the rent and discount it against the compensation. That way the palace isn't standing empty, and the money worries are sorted. Everyone's happy.'

In the silence the brothers looked at each other.

'She's a brilliant lady you're marrying,' Guido said with a grin.

'What did I tell you?' the count roared. 'I said the Calvanis always get the best wives,' he swung Selena around in a dance, '*and we've done it again.*'

The wedding was a true family occasion, with the family being the whole village. When Leo walked Selena out of the church and three times around the duck pond—because they always did that in Morenza—he started up the hill, followed by everyone in the village who could walk, and every tenant they had.

At the gate of the farmhouse the crowd gave them a rousing cheer before going back to the public hall where a spread was laid out for them. Leo would gladly have invited them all inside, but the house would have burst at the seams.

The sight of herself in bridal white with a flowing veil

had taken Selena's breath away. She didn't look like the person she knew at all, but perhaps that was the way to start a new life. She wasn't sure who this person was, but she belonged to Leo body, heart and soul, because he had given her the same, and given it first.

She wondered what would have happened if Guido hadn't brought her back to Italy by subterfuge. As the party quietened down, she felt moved to remind her husband, 'I guess we owe a lot to Guido. If he hadn't been able to cook up a good story, none of us would be here.'

Leo raised his glass to his brother. 'I guess that's true.'

'It's in the blood of the Venetians,' Guido said cheerfully. He'd had a little too much champagne, or he would never have said the next words. 'We all have those little skills, inventing, forgery—'

There was a sudden silence, in which his last words seemed to echo.

'Forgery?' Leo repeated. 'What do you mean—forgery?'

The silence had taken on a stunned quality as the implications sank in. Everyone was looking at Guido.

Guido, who had discovered the evidence that made Leo legitimate. Guido, who had sworn he would escape the title, no matter what he had to do.

Guido—the master of tricks and spells, the man of masks and illusions, the *Venetian*.

'Oh, no!' Leo groaned. 'You wouldn't do that to me! Tell me you wouldn't.'

Guido looked at him, bland and innocent. 'Who me?'

'Yes, you, *brother*! You sneaky, tricky, unscrupulous—'

He set down his glass and began to advance on Guido, who backed off cautiously.

'Now, Leo, don't do anything you'll regret—'

'I won't regret anything I do to you.'

But he was checked by the last sound anyone there had expected to hear. Selena burst into peals of laughter. The others relaxed and began to smile as her mirth echoed around the room.

'Selena, *carissima*—'

'Oh, my goodness!' she choked. 'This will be the death of me! I haven't heard anything as good as this in years.'

'Well, I'm glad you find it funny—'

'It's your face that's funny, my darling.' She put her hands on either side of his head and kissed him, still laughing.

Her mirth was infectious. He couldn't help himself laughing with her, even through his dismay.

'But don't you realise what Guido's done to us?' he demanded. 'He forged that evidence.'

'Has he? Are you sure of that? He hasn't admitted it.'

'And he'll never tell you, one way or the other,' Marco observed, eyeing Guido judicially. 'But I'm betting he's innocent, although it pains me to find him innocent of anything.'

Guido ran a finger around his collar.

'What I think happened is this,' Marco continued. 'He got wind of the Vinelli marriage in England, and he employed an army of private investigators to hunt it down. After all, we have a P.I. in the family.' His amused eyes rested on Dulcie. 'I dare say she put him in touch with a few?'

Guido seized his wife's hand and muttered, 'Say nothing.'

'Very wise,' Marco continued. 'Well, that's my theory for what it's worth.'

'You think it's real?' Leo asked him. 'Not a forgery.'

'I doubt he forged anything, although he'll let you think he did, just to tease a rise out of you.'

'I'll break every bone in his body,' Leo said.

Guido hopped nimbly out of range. 'No violence,' he said. 'Remember I'm an expectant father.'

Marco said in Leo's ear, 'And that's where you'll get your revenge.'

'What do you mean?' the brothers demanded with one voice.

'Children tend to take the opposite tack to their fathers. It would serve Guido right if his son wanted all the things he was so glad to give up. When that day comes, he may have some explaining to do.'

'But you just said—he didn't forge it,' Leo reminded him.

'Well, I don't think even Guido would go that far.'

'But how can we be sure?' Leo groaned.

'Easy,' Marco said, 'you check the English register offices. I think you'll find it there.'

'But let's not do that,' Selena said. 'Let's not know. Then it's not boring and predictable any more.'

'Will I ever understand you?' Leo asked tenderly.

'You do,' she said simply. 'You've always understood me, when I never understood myself.'

She touched his face.

'I had the prize,' she said softly, 'and I nearly let it go. But I'll never let it go again. All my life, for ever and ever.'

If you enjoyed
THE COUNTS OF CALVANI,
*you'll love Lucy Gordon's next book, which is
available in September 2006 from
Mills & Boon® Romance:*
MARRIED UNDER THE ITALIAN SUN.

For a sneak preview, turn the page...

Married Under the Italian Sun

by

Lucy Gordon

The journey began with a flight to Naples. It would have been easy to call the villa and ask for someone to collect her from the airport, but getting there under her own steam seemed a good way to start her new, low-profile life. Besides, Angel liked the idea of arriving unexpectedly and seeing the house as it was naturally.

It was an impulse she soon regretted. Being independent was fine if you had only a few bags. But if you were carrying all your worldly goods it was a pain in the neck to have to load them into a taxi at Naples airport, unload them again at the railway station, then onto the train to Sorrento, followed by a bus to Amalfi. By the time she was in the last taxi, to the villa, she was frazzled.

But she forgot the feeling as she gained her first glimpse of the dramatic Amalfi coast. She'd heard of it, and studied pictures, but nothing could have prepared her for the dazzling reality of the cliffs swooping down, down, down into the sea.

'They're so high,' she said in wonder. 'And those little villages clinging to the sides—how come they don't slide down into the water?'

'They are protected by a great hero,' the driver announced proudly. 'The legend says that Hercules loved a beautiful nymph, called Amalfi. When she died, he buried her here, and placed huge cliffs all around to safeguard her peace. But then the fishermen protested that they would starve because now they couldn't get to the sea, so he built them villages on his cliffs, and vowed that he would always keep them safe. And he always has.'

Looking down, Angel found the pretty tale easy to believe. What else could explain how the little towns clung on to the steep sides, rising almost vertically, white walls blazing in the sun?

'Is the Tazzini estate up there?' she asked.

'Right on top, although the lemon orchard stretches down the cliff face, in tiers, to catch as much sun as possible.'

'Are the lemons good?' she asked, trying to sound casual.

'The best. The makers of limoncello always compete to buy Tazzini lemons.'

'Whatever is limoncello?'

'It is a liqueur, made with lemons and vodka, straight out of heaven.'

So she had a ready market for her produce, she thought, with a surge of relief.

'There they are,' the driver said suddenly, pointing as they rounded a bend. 'Those are lemon flowers.'

Angel gasped and sat totally still, riveted by the sight that met her eyes. It was as though someone had tossed a basket of white blooms from the top of the cliff so that they cascaded down, shimmering, gleaming, dazzling in the sun, awesome in their beauty.

On the last stretch she took out a mirror and checked her appearance. She'd resolved that those days were behind her, and in future she would worry less about her appearance. But she simply couldn't let her first entrance be less than perfect, and so she checked her mascara and refreshed her lipstick. Now she was ready for the fray.

They were approaching a large pair of wrought-iron gates which were closed but not locked, so the driver was able to open them and go through. Another few minutes and she could see the villa.

As she'd told Nina, it wasn't a palace but a large country house, although built on impressive lines. Made of pale grey coloured stone, it reared up three floors, with a flight of stairs running up to the second floor from the outside, where a covered balcony ran the length of the building. Down below there was a riot of decorations. Little half-fountains appeared out of the walls, watched over by stone animals carved to incredible perfection. Angel found herself smiling.

Three broad steps led up to the double doors that formed the entrance, and which stood open. She went right in, followed by the driver, who was hauling her many bags. Looking around, she saw a hall that was spacious yet strangely domestic, even cosy. Warm red tiles stretched away across the floor, leading to archways that seemed to invite her in. Incredibly, she felt welcome.

She tried to be sensible. This feeling of having come home to the place where she belonged was the merest sentimentality, sugar coated with wishful thinking. Yet the sensation pervaded her, despite her efforts to resist it. It was almost like being happy.

She paid the driver, refusing his offer to carry the bags further. She wanted to be alone to enjoy her first minutes in this lovely place.

From the hall a flight of stone stairs with wrought-iron banisters streamed upwards, beckoning her. Angel began to climb it slowly, feeling as though she were moving in a dream. Halfway up she stopped to look out of a window, and realised that the house was close to the edge of the cliff, directly overlooking the sea. From here she could see the water stretching into the distance, incredibly blue, shining serenely under the clear sky. The window was open and she stood there a moment, breathing in the clear air, listening to the silence.

When had she last heard silence? When, in her rackety life, had there been such peace, such potential for tranquil joy? If she hadn't come here, how much longer would she have survived?

Soon she began to climb again. After the heat outside, the house was blessedly cool, protected by the thick stone walls. She emerged onto a large landing, leading to a corridor with several doors. One in particular attracted her attention, because it was the only double door. No doubt this would be the master bedroom, and the one she would take as her own.

Eager to see it, she pushed open both doors and walked in.

For a moment she could discern nothing, as the wooden shutters at the three windows were mostly closed. Then the gloom cleared slightly and she saw that one of them was open a few inches, and a man was standing there, looking out through the narrow gap.

At first Angel could make out little of him, except that he was tall and lean. Then, as her eyes grew accustomed to the gloom, she saw that he was dressed in old jeans and a frayed denim shirt, with scuffed shoes to complete the picture. Probably the gardener, she thought. But what was he doing here?

'Hello?' she said.

He turned quickly.

'Who are you?' they both said together, in Italian.

Angel gave a brief laugh, realising that her indignation was a tad illogical.

'I'm sorry, this is my fault,' she said, 'for not letting anyone know I was coming today.'

He pushed the shutters further open so that light streamed into the room, falling directly onto her like a spotlight as she moved towards him. She saw him grow suddenly tense, his face harden, but he didn't speak.

'I'm the new owner of the estate,' she said.

'The Signora Clannan.'

Angel had reverted to her maiden name, but she let it go for the moment.

'That's right. Obviously you've been expecting me.'

'Oh, yes, we've all known you were coming, although not exactly when. You kept that detail to yourself, so that you could catch us unawares. Very shrewd. Who knows what discoveries you might have made?'

She could see him better now, and thought she'd never come across any man who looked so hard and unyielding. There was a gaunt wariness about him, not just in his face, but in his tall, angular shape, the way he crossed his arms defensively over his chest, telling the world to keep its distance.

He might as well have warded her off with a sword, she thought.

'I wasn't trying to catch anyone out,' she said, trying to remain good-tempered. 'It was an impulse decision.'

'And you couldn't even have made a phone call from the airport to give Berta a chance to be ready for you? She's your housekeeper, and a more faithful, hard-working soul never lived. She deserves better.'

Angel had a faint sense of remorse, but it was quashed in the rush of indignation. What the hell did he think gave him the right to talk to her like this?

'Look,' she said, 'I presume you're one of my staff, so let me make it clear right now that you don't speak to me like that. Not if you want to go on working for me.'

'Is that so? Then how fortunate that I don't work for you, or I'd be shaking in my shoes now.'

'Don't be impertinent. If you're not one of my employees, what are you doing in this room, where you most decidedly have no right to be?'

She thought he grew a little paler, the twist to his mouth a little more sardonic.

'True,' he said. 'I have no right. Not any more.'

'What do you mean?'

'My name is Vittorio Tazzini, and I used to own this place.'

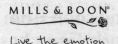

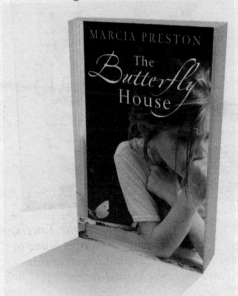

"People look at me and they see this happy face, but inside I'm screaming. It's just that no-one hears me."

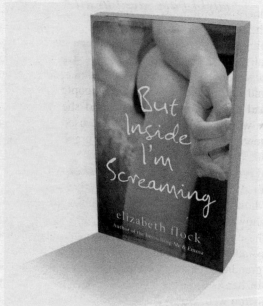

While breaking the news of Princess Diana's death to millions, reporter Isabel Murphy unravels on live television. *But Inside I'm Screaming* is the heart-rending tale of her struggle to regain the life that everyone thought she had.

21st July 2006